# SECRETS
## AND
# SURPRISES

## Short Stories by

## Ann Beattie

FAWCETT POPULAR LIBRARY • NEW YORK

Portions of this book have previously appeared in the following: *Canto, Fiction Magazine, Mississippi Review, The New England Review, The New York Times Magazine,* and *Viva*.

The following stories originally appeared in *The New Yorker*: "Colorado," "The Lawn Party," "Secrets and Surprises," "Weekend," "Tuesday Night," "Shifting," "Distant Music," and "A Vintage Thunderbird."

*Grateful acknowledgement is made to the following for permission to reprint previously published material:*
Belwin Mills Publishing Corp.: Lyrics from "In My Solitude." Copyright © 1934 by American Academy of Music, Inc. Copyright renewed. Used with permission. All rights reserved.
Trio Music, Inc.: Lyrics from "I'm a Woman" by Jerry Leiber and Mike Stoller. Copyright © 1961 by Yellow Dog Music, Inc. Used by permission. All rights reserved.
Warner Bros. Inc.: Lyrics from "As Time Goes By" by Herman Hupfeld. Copyright © 1931 by Warner Bros. Inc. Copyright renewed. All rights reserved. Used by permission.

SECRETS AND SURPRISES

Published by Fawcett Popular Library, a unit of CBS Publications, the Consumer Publishing Division of CBS Inc., by arrangement with Random House, Inc.

ISBN: 0-445-04534-5

Printed in the United States of America

First Fawcett Popular Library printing: March 1980

10   9   8   7   6   5   4   3

# TO ROGER ANGELL

# Contents

A VINTAGE THUNDERBIRD    11

DISTANT MUSIC    33

A REASONABLE MAN    49

SHIFTING    61

LA PETITE DANSEUSE DE
QUATORZE ANS    77

OCTASCOPE    105

WEEKEND    117

COLORADO    137

STARLEY    163

DEER SEASON    181

THE LAWN PARTY    197

FRIENDS    215

A CLEVER-KIDS STORY    273

TUESDAY NIGHT    293

SECRETS AND SURPRISES    309

# SECRETS
## AND
# SURPRISES

# A Vintage Thunderbird

Nick and Karen had driven from Virginia to New York in a little under six hours. They had made good time, keeping ahead of the rain all the way, and it was only now, while they were in the restaurant, that the rain began. It had been a nice summer weekend in the country with their friends Stephanie and Sammy, but all the time he was there Nick had worried that Karen had consented to go with him only out of pity; she had been dating another man, and when Nick suggested the weekend she had been reluctant. When she said she would go, he decided that she had given in for old time's sake.

The car they drove was hers—a white Thunderbird convertible. Every time he drove the car, he admired it more. She owned many things that he admired: a squirrel coat with a black taffeta lining, a pair of carved soapstone bookends that held some books of poetry on her night table, her collection of Louis Armstrong 78s. He loved to go to her apartment and look at her things. He was excited by them, the way he had been spellbound, as a child, exploring the playrooms of schoolmates.

He had met Karen several years before, soon after he came to New York. Her brother had lived in the same building he lived in then, and the three of them met on the volleyball courts adjacent to the building. Her brother moved across town within a few months, but by then Nick knew Karen's telephone number. At her suggestion, they had started running in Central Park on Sundays. It was something he looked forward to all week. When they left the park, his elation was always mixed with a little embarrassment over his panting and his being sweaty on the street, but she had no self-consciousness. She didn't care if her shirt stuck to her body, or if she looked unattractive with her wet, matted hair. Or perhaps she knew that she never looked really unattractive; men always looked at her. One time, on Forty-second Street, during a light rain, Nick stopped to read a movie marquee, and when he turned back to Karen she was laughing and protesting that she couldn't take the umbrella that a man was offering her. It was only when Nick came to her side that the man stopped insisting—a nicely dressed man who was only offering her his big black umbrella, and not trying to pick her up. Things like this were hard for Nick to accept, but Karen was not flirtatious, and he could see that it was not her fault that men looked at her and made gestures.

It became a routine that on Sundays they jogged or went to a basketball court. One time, when she got frustrated because she hadn't been able to do a simple hook shot—hadn't made a basket that way all morning—he lifted her to his shoulders and charged the backboard so fast that she almost missed the basket from there too. After playing basketball, they would go to her apartment and she would make dinner. He would collapse, but she was full of energy and she would poke fun at him while she studied a cookbook, staring at it until she knew enough of a recipe to begin preparing the food. His two cookbooks were dog-eared and sauce-stained, but Karen's were perfectly clean. She looked at recipes, but never followed them exactly. He admired this—her creativity, her energy. It took him a long while to accept that she thought he was special, and later, when she began to date other men, it took him a long while to realize that she did not mean to shut him out of her life. The first time she went away with a man for the weekend—about a year after he first met her—she stopped by his apartment on her way to Pennsylvania and gave him the keys to her Thunderbird. She left so quickly—the man was downstairs in his car, waiting—that as he watched her go he could feel the warmth of the keys from her hand.

Just recently Nick had met the man she was dating now: a gaunt psychology professor, with a black-and-white tweed cap and a thick mustache that made him look like a sad-mouthed clown. Nick had gone to her apartment not knowing for certain that the man would be there—actually, it was Friday night, the beginning of the weekend, and he had gone on the hunch that he finally would meet him—and had drunk a vodka Collins that the man mixed for him. He remembered that the man had complained tediously that Paul McCartney had stolen words from Thomas Dekker for a song on the "Abbey Road" album, and that the man said he got hives from eating shellfish.

In the restaurant now, Nick looked across the table at Karen and said, "That man you're dating is a real bore. What is he—a scholar?"

He fumbled for a cigarette and then remembered that he no longer smoked. He had given it up a year before, when he went to visit an old girlfriend in New

Haven. Things had gone badly, they had quarreled, and he had left her to go to a bar. Coming out, he was approached by a tall black round-faced teen-ager and told to hand over his wallet, and he had mutely reached inside his coat and pulled it out and given it to the boy. A couple of people came out of the bar, took in the situation and walked away quickly, pretending not to notice. The boy had a small penknife in his hand. "And your cigarettes," the boy said. Nick had reached inside his jacket pocket and handed over the cigarettes. The boy pocketed them. Then the boy smiled and cocked his head and held up the wallet, like a hypnotist dangling a pocket watch. Nick stared dumbly at his own wallet. Then, before he knew what was happening, the boy turned into a blur of motion: he grabbed his arm and yanked hard, like a judo wrestler, and threw him across the sidewalk. Nick fell against a car that was parked at the curb. He was so frightened that his legs buckled and he went down. The boy watched him fall. The he nodded and walked down the sidewalk past the bar. When the boy was out of sight, Nick got up and went into the bar to tell his story. He let the bartender give him a beer and call the police. He declined the bartender's offer of a cigarette, and had never smoked since.

His thoughts were drifting, and Karen still had not answered his question. He knew that he had already angered her once that day, and that it had been a mistake to speak of the man again. Just an hour or so earlier, when they got back to the city, he had been abrupt with her friend Kirby. She kept her car in Kirby's garage, and in exchange for the privilege she moved into his brownstone whenever he went out of town and took care of his six de-clawed chocolate-point cats. Actually, Kirby's psychiatrist, a Dr. Kellogg, lived in the same house, but the doctor had made it clear he did not live there to take care of cats.

From his seat Nick could see the sign of the restaurant hanging outside the front window. "Star Thrower

Café," it said, in lavender neon. He got depressed thinking that if she became more serious about the professor—he had lasted longer than any of the others—he would only be able to see her by pretending to run into her at places like the Star Thrower. He had also begun to think that he had driven the Thunderbird for the last time. She had almost refused to let him drive it again after the time, two weeks earlier, when he tapped a car in front of them on Sixth Avenue, making a dent above their left headlight. Long ago she had stopped letting him use her squirrel coat as a kind of blanket. He used to like to lie naked on the tiny balcony outside her apartment in the autumn, with the Sunday *Times* arranged under him for padding and the coat spread on top of him. Now he counted back and came up with the figure: he had known Karen for seven years.

"What are you thinking?" he said to her.

"That I'm glad I'm not thirty-eight years old, with a man putting pressure on me to have a baby." She was talking about Stephanie and Sammy.

Her hand was on the table. He cupped his hand over it just as the waiter came with the plates.

"What are *you* thinking?" she said, withdrawing her hand.

"At least Stephanie has the sense not to do it," he said. He picked up his fork and put it down. "Do you really love that man?"

"If I loved him, I suppose I'd be at my apartment, where he's been waiting for over an hour. If he waited."

When they finished she ordered espresso. He ordered it also. He had half expected her to say at some point that the trip with him was the end, and he still thought she might say that. Part of the problem was that she had money and he didn't. She had had money since she was twenty-one, when she got control of a fifty-thousand-dollar trust fund her grandfather had left her. He remembered the day she had bought the Thunderbird. It was the day after her birthday, five years ago. That night, laughing, they had driven the car through the

Lincoln Tunnel and then down the back roads in Jersey, with a stream of orange crepe paper blowing from the radio antenna, until the wind ripped it off.

"Am I still going to see you?" Nick said.

"I suppose," Karen said. "Although things have changed between us."

"I've known you for seven years. You're my oldest friend."

She did not react to what he said, but much later, around midnight, she called him at his apartment. "Was what you said at the Star Thrower calculated to make me feel bad?" she said. "When you said that I was your oldest friend?"

"No," he said. "You are my oldest friend."

"You must know somebody longer than you've known me."

"You're the only person I've seen regularly for seven years."

She sighed.

"Professor go home?" he said.

"No. He's here."

"You're saying all this in front of him?"

"I don't see why there has to be any secret about this."

"You could put an announcement in the paper," Nick said. "Run a little picture of me with it."

"Why are you so sarcastic?"

"It's embarrassing. It's embarrassing that you'd say this in front of that man."

He was sitting in the dark, in a chair by the phone. He had wanted to call her ever since he got back from the restaurant. The long day of driving had finally caught up with him, and his shoulders ached. He felt the black man's hands on his shoulders, felt his own body folding up, felt himself flying backward. He had lost sixty-five dollars that night. The day she bought the Thunderbird, he had driven it through the tunnel into New Jersey. He had driven, then she had driven, and then he had driven again. Once he had pulled into the parking lot of a shopping center and told her to wait, and had come back with the orange crepe paper. Years later he had looked for the road they had been on that night, but he could never find it.

The next time Nick heard from her was almost three weeks after the trip to Virginia. Since he didn't have the courage to call her, and since he expected not to hear from her at all, he was surprised to pick up the phone and hear her voice. Petra had been in his apartment—a woman at his office whom he had always wanted to date and who had just broken off an unhappy engagement. As he held the phone clamped between his ear and shoulder, he looked admiringly at Petra's profile.

"What's up?" he said to Karen, trying to sound very casual for Petra.

"Get ready," Karen said. "Stephanie called and said that she was going to have a baby."

"What do you mean? I thought she told you in Virginia that she thought Sammy was crazy to want a kid."

"It happened by accident. She missed her period just after we left."

Petra shifted on the couch and began leafing through *Newsweek*.

"Can I call you back?" he said.

"Throw whatever woman is there out of your apartment and talk to me now," Karen said. "I'm about to go out."

He looked at Petra, who was sipping her drink. "I can't do that," he said.

"Then call me when you can. But call back tonight."

When he hung up, he took Petra's glass but found that he had run out of Scotch. He suggested that they go to a bar on West Tenth Street.

When they got to the bar, he excused himself almost immediately. Karen had sounded depressed, and he could not enjoy his evening with Petra until he made sure everything was all right. Once he heard her voice, he knew he was going to come to her apartment when he had finished having a drink, and she said that he should come over immediately or not at all, because she was about to go to the professor's. She was so abrupt that he wondered if she could be jealous.

He went back to the bar and sat on the stool next to Petra and picked up his Scotch and water and took a big drink. It was so cold that it made his teeth ache. Petra had on blue slacks and a white blouse. He rubbed his hand up and down her back, just below the shoulders. She was not wearing a brassiere.

"I have to leave," he said.

"You have to leave? Are you coming back?"

He started to speak, but she put up her hand. "Never mind," she said. "I don't want you to come back." She sipped her Margarita. "Whoever the woman is you just called, I hope the two of you have a splendid evening."

Petra gave him a hard look, and he knew that she really wanted him to go. He stared at her—at the little crust of salt on her bottom lip—and then she turned away from him.

He hesitated for just a second before he left the bar. He went outside and walked about ten steps, and then he was jumped. They got him from behind, and in his shock and confusion he thought that he had been hit by a car. He lost sense of where he was, and although it was a dull blow, he thought that somehow a car had hit him. Looking up from the sidewalk, he saw them— two men, younger than he was, picking at him like vultures, pushing him, rummaging through his jacket and his pockets. The crazy thing was he was on West Tenth Street; there should have been other people on the street, but there were not. His clothes were tearing. His right hand was wet with blood. They had cut his arm, the shirt was bloodstained, he saw his own blood spreading out into a little puddle. He stared at it and was afraid to move his hand out of it. Then the men were gone and he was left half sitting, propped up against a building where they had dragged him. He was able to push himself up, but the man he began telling the story to, a passer-by, kept coming into focus and fading out again. The man had on a sombrero, and he was pulling him up but pulling too hard. His legs didn't have the power to support him—something had happened to his legs—so that when the man loosened his grip he went down on his knees. He kept blinking to stay conscious. He blacked out before he could stand again.

Back in his apartmemt, later that night, with his arm in a cast, he felt confused and ashamed—ashamed for the way he had treated Petra, and ashamed for having been mugged. He wanted to call Karen, but he was too embarrassed. He sat in the chair by the phone, willing her to call him. At midnight the phone rang, and he picked it up at once, sure that his telepathic message had worked. The phone call was from Stephanie, at La Guardia. She had been trying to reach Karen and couldn't. She wanted to know if she could come to his apartment.

"I'm not going through with it," Stephanie said, her voice wavering. "I'm thirty-eight years old, and this was a goddamn accident."

"Calm down," he said. "We can get you an abortion."

"I don't know if I could take a human life," she said, and she began to cry.

"Stephanie?" he said. "You okay? Are you going to get a cab?"

More crying, no answer.

"Because it would be silly for me to get a cab just to come get you. You can make it here okay, can't you, Steph?"

The cabdriver who took him to La Guardia was named Arthur Shales. A small pink baby shoe was glued to the dashboard of the cab. Arthur Shales chain-smoked Picayunes. "Woman I took to Bendel's today, I'm still trying to get over it," he said. "I picked her up at Madison and Seventy-fifth. Took her to Bendel's and pulled up in front and she said, 'Oh, screw Bendel's.' I took her back to Madison and Seventy-fifth."

Going across the bridge, Nick said to Arthur Shales that the woman he was going to pick up was going to be very upset.

"Upset? What do I care? Neither of you are gonna hold a gun to my head, I can take anything. You're my last fares of the night. Take you back where you came from, then I'm heading home myself."

When they were almost at the airport exit, Arthur Shales snorted and said, "Home is a room over an Italian grocery. Guy who runs it woke me up at six this morning, yelling so loud at his supplier. 'You call these tomatoes?' he was saying. 'I could take these out and bat them on the tennis court.' Guy is always griping about tomatoes being so unripe."

Stephanie was standing on the walkway, right where she had said she would be. She looked haggard, and Nick was not sure that he could cope with her. He raised his hand to his shirt pocket for cigarettes, forgetting once again that he had given up smoking. He also forgot that he couldn't grab anything with his right hand because it was in a cast.

"You know who I had in my cab the other day?" Arthur Shales said, coasting to a stop in front of the terminal. "You're not going to believe it. Al Pacino."

For more than a week, Nick and Stephanie tried to reach Karen. Stephanie began to think that Karen was dead. And although Nick chided her for calling Karen's number so often, he began to worry too. Once he went to her apartment on his lunch hour and listened at the door. He heard nothing, but he put his mouth close to the door and asked her to please open the door, if she was there, because there was trouble with Stephanie. As he left the building he had to laugh at what it would have looked like if someone had seen him—a nicely dressed man, with his hands on either side of his mouth, leaning into a door and talking to it. And one of the hands in a cast.

For a week he came straight home from work, to keep Stephanie company. Then he asked Petra if she would have dinner with him. She said no. As he was leaving the office, he passed by her desk without looking at her. She got up and followed him down the hall and said, "I'm having a drink with somebody after work, but I could meet you for a drink around seven o'clock."

He went home to see if Stephanie was all right. She said that she had been sick in the morning, but after the card came in the mail—she held out a postcard to him—she felt much better. The card was addressed to him; it was from Karen, in Bermuda. She said she had spent the afternoon in a sailboat. No explanation. He read the message several times. He felt very relieved. He asked Stephanie if she wanted to go out for a drink with him and Petra. She said no, as he had known she would.

At seven he sat alone at a table in the Blue Bar, with the postcard in his inside pocket. There was a folded newspaper on the little round table where he sat, and his broken right wrist rested on it. He sipped a beer. At seven-thirty he opened the paper and looked through the theater section. At quarter to eight he got up and left. He walked over to Fifth Avenue and began to walk downtown. In one of the store windows there was a poster for Bermuda tourism. A woman in a turquoise-blue bathing suit was rising out of blue waves, her mouth in an unnaturally wide smile. She seemed oblivious of the little boy next to her who was tossing a ball into the sky. Standing there, looking at the poster, Nick began a mental game that he had sometimes played in college. He invented a cartoon about Bermuda. It was a split-frame drawing. Half of it showed a beautiful girl, in the arms of her lover, on the pink sandy beach of Bermuda, with the caption: "It's glo-

rious to be here in Bermuda." The other half of the
frame showed a tall tired man looking into the window
of a travel agency at a picture of the lady and her lover.
He would have no lines, but in a balloon above his head
he would be wondering if, when he went home, it was
the right time to urge an abortion to the friend who
had moved into his apartment.

When he got home, Stephanie was not there. She
had said that if she felt better, she would go out to eat.
He sat down and took off his shoes and socks and hung
forward, with his head almost touching his knees, like
a droopy doll. Then he went into the bedroom, carrying
the shoes and socks, and took off his clothes and put
on jeans. The phone rang and he picked it up just as
he heard Stephanie's key in the door.

"I'm sorry," Petra said, "I've never stood anybody up
before in my life."

"Never mind," he said. "I'm not mad."

"I'm very sorry," she said.

"I drank a beer and read the paper. After what I
did to you the other night, I don't blame you."

"I like you," she said. "That was why I didn't come.
Because I knew I wouldn't say what I wanted to say.
I got as far as Forty-eighth Street and turned around."

"What did you want to say?"

"That I like you. That I like you and that it's a
mistake, because I'm always letting myself in for it,
agreeing to see men who treat me badly. I wasn't very
flattered the other night."

"I know. I apologize. Look, why don't you meet me
at that bar now and let me not walk out on you. Okay?"

"No," she said, her voice changing. "That wasn't why
I called. I called to say I was sorry, but I know I did
the right thing. I have to hang up now."

He put the phone back and continued to look at the
floor. He knew that Stephanie was not even pretending
not to have heard. He took a step forward and ripped
the phone out of the wall. It was not a very successful

dramatic gesture. The phone just popped out of the jack, and he stood there, holding it in his good hand.

"Would you think it was awful if I offered to go to bed with you?" Stephanie asked.

"No," he said. "I think it would be very nice."

Two days later he left work early in the afternoon and went to Kirby's. Dr. Kellogg opened the door and then pointed toward the back of the house and said, "The man you're looking for is reading." He was wearing baggy white pants and a Japanese kimono.

Nick almost had to push through the half-open door because the psychiatrist was so intent on holding the cats back with one foot. In the kitchen Kirby was indeed reading—he was looking at a Bermuda travel brochure and listening to Karen.

She looked sheepish when she saw him. Her face was tan, and her eyes, which were always beautiful, looked startlingly blue now that her face was so dark. She had lavender-tinted sunglasses pushed on top of her head. She and Kirby seemed happy and comfortable in the elegant, air-conditioned house.

"When did you get back?" Nick said.

"A couple of days ago," she said. "The night I last talked to you, I went over to the professor's apartment, and in the morning we went to Bermuda."

Nick had come to Kirby's to get the car keys and borrow the Thunderbird—to go for a ride and be by himself for a while—and for a moment now he thought of asking her for the keys anyway. He sat down at the table.

"Stephanie is in town," he said. "I think we ought to get a cup of coffee and talk about it."

Her key ring was on the table. If he had the keys, he could be heading for the Lincoln Tunnel. Years ago, they would be walking to the car hand in hand, in love. It would be her birthday. The car's odometer would have five miles on it.

One of Kirby's cats jumped up on the table and began to sniff at the butter dish there.

"Would you like to walk over to the Star Thrower and get a cup of coffee?" Nick said.

She got up slowly.

"Don't mind me," Kirby said.

"Would you like to come, Kirby?" she asked.

"Not me. No, no."

She patted Kirby's shoulder, and they went out.

"What happened?" she said, pointing to his hand.

"It's broken."

"How did you break it?"

"Never mind," he said. "I'll tell you when we get there."

When they got there it was not yet four o'clock, and the Star Thrower was closed.

"Well, just tell me what's happening with Stephanie," Karen said impatiently. "I don't really feel like sitting around talking because I haven't even unpacked yet."

"She's at my apartment, and she's pregnant, and she doesn't even talk about Sammy."

She shook her head sadly. "How did you break your hand?" she said.

"I was mugged. After our last pleasant conversation on the phone—the time you told me to come over immediately or not at all. I didn't make it because I was in the emergency room."

"Oh, Christ," she said. "Why didn't you call me?"

"I was embarrassed to call you."

"Why? Why didn't you call?"

"You wouldn't have been there anyway." He took her arm. "Let's find some place to go," he said.

Two young men came up to the door of the Star Thrower. "Isn't this where David had that great Armenian dinner?" one of them said.

"I *told* you it wasn't," the other said, looking at the menu posted to the right of the door.

"I didn't really think this was the place. *You* said it was on this street."

They continued to quarrel as Nick and Karen walked away.

"Why do you think Stephanie came here to the city?" Karen said.

"Because we're her friends," Nick said.

"But she has lots of friends."

"Maybe she thought we were more dependable."

"Why do you say that in that tone of voice? I don't have to tell you every move I'm making. Things went very well in Bermuda. He almost lured me to London."

"Look," he said. "Can't we go somewhere where you can call her?"

He looked at her, shocked because she didn't understand that Stephanie had come to see her, not him. He had seen for a long time that it didn't matter to her how much she meant to him, but he had never realized that she didn't know how much she meant to Stephanie. She didn't understand people. When he found out she had another man, he should have dropped out of her life. She did not deserve her good looks and her fine car and all her money. He turned to face her on the street, ready to tell her what he thought.

"You know what happened there?" she said. "I got sunburned and had a terrible time. He went on to London without me."

He took her arm again and they stood side by side and looked at some sweaters hanging in the window of Countdown.

"So going to Virginia wasn't the answer for them," she said. "Remember when Sammy and Stephanie left town, and we told each other what a stupid idea it was—that it would never work out? Do you think we jinxed them?"

They walked down the street again, saying nothing.

"It would kill me if I had to be a good conversationalist with you," she said at last. "You're the only person

I can rattle on with." She stopped and leaned into him. "I had a rotten time in Bermuda," she said. "Nobody should go to a beach but a sand flea."

"You don't have to make clever conversation with me," he said.

"I know," she said. "It just happened."

Late in the afternoon of the day that Stephanie had her abortion, Nick called Sammy from a street phone near his apartment. Karen and Stephanie were in the apartment, but he had to get out for a while. Stephanie had seemed pretty cheerful, but perhaps it was just an act for his benefit. With him gone, she might talk to Karen about it. All she had told was that it felt like she had caught an ice pick in the stomach.

"Sammy?" Nick said into the phone. "How are you? It just dawned on me that I ought to call and let you know that Stephanie is all right."

"She has called me herself, several times," Sammy said. "Collect. From your phone. But thank you for your concern, Nick." He sounded brusque.

"Oh," Nick said, taken aback. "Just so you know where she is."

"I could name you as corespondent in the divorce case, you know?"

"What would you do that for?" Nick said.

"I wouldn't. I just wanted you to know what I could do."

"Sammy—I don't get it. I didn't ask for any of this, you know."

"Poor Nick. My wife gets pregnant, leaves without a word, calls from New York with a story about how you had a broken hand and were having bad luck with women, so she went to bed with you. Two weeks later I get a phone call from you, all concern, wanting me to know where Stephanie is."

Nick waited for Sammy to hang up on him.

"You know what happened to you?" Sammy said.

"You got eaten up by New York."

"What kind of dumb thing is that to say?" Nick said. "Are you trying to get even or something?"

"If I wanted to do that, I could tell you that you have bad teeth. Or that Stephanie said you were a lousy lover. What I was trying to do was tell you something important, for a change. Stephanie ran away when I tried to tell it to her, you'll probably hang up on me when I say the same thing to you: you can be happy. For instance, you can get out of New York and get away from Karen. Stephanie could have settled down with a baby."

"This doesn't sound like you, Sammy, to give advice."

He waited for Sammy's answer.

"You think I ought to leave New York?" Nick said.

"Both. Karen *and* New York. Do you know that your normal expression shows pain? Do you know how much Scotch you drank the weekend you visited?"

Nick shared through the grimy plastic window of the phone booth.

"What you just said about my hanging up on you," Nick said. "I was thinking that you were going to hang up on me. When I talk to people, they hang up on me. The conversation just ends that way."

"Why haven't you figured out that you don't know the right kind of people?"

"They're the only people I know."

"Does that seem like any reason for tolerating that sort of rudeness?"

"I guess not."

"Another thing," Sammy went on. "Have you figured out that I'm saying these things to you because when you called I was already drunk? I'm telling you all this because I think you're so numbed out by your lousy life that you probably even don't know I'm not in my right mind."

The operator came on, demanding more money. Nick clattered quarters into the phone. He realized that he was not going to hang up on Sammy, and Sammy was not going to hang up on him. He would have to think of something else to say.

"Give yourself a break," Sammy said. "Boot them out. Stephanie included. She'll see the light eventually and come back to the farm."

"Should I tell her you'll be there? I don't know if—"

"I told her I'd be here when she called. All the times she called. I just told her that I had no idea of coming to get her. I'll tell you another thing. I'll bet—I'll *bet*—that when she first turned up there she called you from the airport, and she wanted you to come for her, didn't she?"

"Sammy," Nick said, staring around him, wild to get off the phone. "I want to thank you for saying what you think. I'm going to hang up now."

"Forget it," Sammy said. "I'm not in my right mind. Goodbye."

"Goodbye," Nick said.

He hung up and started back to his apartment. He realized that he hadn't told Sammy that Stephanie had had the abortion. On the street he said hello to a little boy—one of the neighborhood children he knew.

He went up the stairs and up to his floor. Some people downstairs were listening to Beethoven. He lingered in the hallway, not wanting to go back to Stephanie and Karen. He took a deep breath and opened the door. Neither of them looked too bad. They said hello silently, each raising one hand.

It had been a hard day. Stephanie's appointment at the abortion clinic had been at eight in the morning. Karen had slept in the apartment with them the night before, on the sofa. Stephanie slept in his bed, and he slept on the floor. None of them had slept much. In the morning they all went to the abortion clinic. Nick had intended to go to work in the afternoon, but when they got back to the apartment he didn't think it was right for him to leave Stephanie. She went back to the bedroom, and he stretched out on the sofa and fell asleep. Before he slept, Karen sat on the sofa with him for a while, and he told her the story of his second mugging. When he woke up, it was four o'clock. He called his office and told them he was sick. Later they all watched the television news together. After that, he offered to go out and get some food, but nobody was hungry. That's when he went out and called Sammy.

Now Stephanie went back into the bedroom. She said she was tired and she was going to work on a crossword puzzle in bed. The phone rang. It was Petra. She and Nick talked a little about a new apartment she was thinking of moving into. "I'm sorry for being so cold-blooded the other night," she said. "The reason I'm calling is to invite myself to your place for a drink, if that's all right with you."

"It's not all right," he said. "I'm sorry. There are some people here now."

"I get it," she said. "Okay. I won't bother you any more."

"You don't understand," he said. He knew he had not explained things well, but the thought of adding Petra to the scene at his apartment was more than he could bear, and he had been too abrupt.

She said goodbye coldly, and he went back to his chair and fell in it, exhausted.

"A girl?" Karen said.

He nodded.

"Not a girl you wanted to hear from."

He shook his head no. He got up and pulled up the blind and looked out to the street. The boy he had said hello to was playing with a hula hoop. The hula hoop was bright blue in the twilight. The kid rotated his hips and kept the hoop spinning perfectly. Karen came to the window and stood next to him. He turned to her, wanting to say that they should go and get the Thunderbird, and as the night air cooled, drive out of the city, smell honeysuckle in the fields, feel the wind blowing.

But the Thunderbird was sold. She had told him the news while they were sitting in the waiting room of the abortion clinic. The car had needed a valve job, and a man she met in Bermuda who knew all about cars had advised her to sell it. Coincidentally, the man—a New York architect—wanted to buy it. Even as Karen told him, he knew she had been set up. If she had been more careful, they could have been in the car now, with the key in the ignition, the radio playing. He stood at the window for a long time. She had been conned, and he was more angry than he could tell her. She had no conception—she had somehow never understood—that Thunderbirds of that year, in good condition, would someday be worth a fortune. She had told him this way: "Don't be upset, because I'm sure I made the right decision. I sold the car as soon as I got back from Bermuda. I'm going to get a new car." He had moved in his chair, there in the clinic. He had had an impulse to get up and hit her. He remembered the scene in New Haven outside the bar, and he understood now that it was as simple as this: he had money that the black man wanted.

Down the street the boy picked up his hula hoop and disappeared around the corner.

"Say you were kidding about selling the car," Nick said.

"When are you going to stop making such a big thing over it?" Karen said.

"That creep cheated you. He talked you into selling it when nothing was wrong with it."

"Stop it," she said. "How come your judgments are always right and my judgments are always wrong?"

"I don't want to fight," he said. "I'm sorry I said anything."

"Okay," she said and leaned her head against him. He draped his right arm over her shoulder. The fingers sticking out of the cast rested a little above her breast.

"I just want to ask one thing," he said, "and then I'll never mention it again. Are you sure the deal is final?"

Karen pushed his hand off her shoulder and walked away. But it was his apartment, and she couldn't go slamming around in it. She sat on the sofa and picked up the newspaper. He watched her. Soon she put it down and stared across the room and into the dark bedroom, where Stephanie had turned off the light. He looked at her sadly for a long time, until she looked up at him with tears in her eyes.

"Do you think maybe we could get it back if I offered him more than he paid me for it?" she said. "You probably don't think that's a sensible suggestion, but at least that way we could get it back."

# Distant Music

On Friday she always sat in the park, waiting for him to come. At one-thirty he came to this park bench (if someone was already sitting there, he loitered around it), and then they would sit side by side, talking quietly, like Ingrid Bergman and Cary Grant in *Notorious*. Both believed in flying saucers and health food. They shared a hatred of laundromats, guilt about not sending presents to relatives on birthdays and at Christmas, and a dog—part Weimaraner, part German shepherd—named Sam.

She was twenty, and she worked in an office; she was pretty because she took a lot of time with makeup, the way a housewife who really cared might flute the edges of a piecrust with thumb and index finger.

He was twenty-four, a graduate-school dropout (theater) who collaborated on songs with his friend Gus Greeley, and he wanted, he fervently wanted, to make it big as a songwriter. His mother was Greek and French, his father American. This girl, Sharon, was not the first woman to fall in love with Jack because he was so handsome. She took the subway to get to the bench, which was in Washington Square Park; he walked from the basement apartment he lived in. Whoever had Sam that day (they kept the dog alternating weeks) brought him. They could do this because her job required her to work only from eight to one, and he worked at home. They had gotten the dog because they feared for his life. A man had come up to them on West Tenth Street carrying a cardboard box, smiling, and saying, "Does the little lady want a kitty cat?" They peered inside. "Puppies," Jack said. "Well, who gives a fuck?" the man said, putting the box down, his face dark and contorted. Sharon and Jack stared at the man; he stared belligerently back. Neither of them was quite sure how things had suddenly turned ominous. She wanted to get out of there right away, before the man took a swing at Jack, but to her surprise Jack smiled at the man and dipped into the box for a dog. He extracted the scrawny, wormy Sam. She took the dog first, because there was a veterinarian's office close to her apartment. Once the dog was cured of his worms, she gave him to Jack to begin his training. In Jack's apartment the puppy would fix his eyes on the parallelogram of sunlight that sometimes appeared on the wood floor in the late morning—sniffing it, backing up, edging up to it at the border. In her apartment, the puppy's object of fascination was a clarinet that a friend had left there when he moved. The puppy looked at it respectfully. She watched the dog for signs of maladjustment, wondering if he was too young to be shuttling back and forth, from home to home. (She herself had been raised by her mother, but she and her sister would fly to Seattle every summer to spend two months with their father.) The dog seemed happy enough.

At night, in Jack's one-room apartment, they would sometimes lie with their heads at the foot of the bed, staring at the ornately carved oak headboard and the old-fashioned light attached to it, with the little sticker still on the shade that said "From home of Lady Astor. $4.00." They had found the lamp in Ruckersville, Virginia, on the only long trip they ever took out of the city. On the bed with them there were usually sheets of music—songs that he was scoring. She would look at the pieces of paper with lyrics typed on them, and read them slowly to herself, appraisingly, as if they were poetry.

On weekends they spent the days and nights together. There was a small but deep fireplace in his apartment, and when September came they would light a fire in the late afternoon, although it was not yet cold, and sometimes light a stick of sandalwood incense, and they would lean on each other or sit side by side, listening to Vivaldi. She knew very little about such music when she first met him, and much more about it by the time their first month had passed. There was no one thing she knew a great deal about—as he did about music—so there was really nothing that she could teach him.

"Where were you in 1974?" he asked her once.

"In school. In Ann Arbor."

"What about 1975?"

"In Boston. Working at a gallery."

"Where are you now?" he said.

She looked at him and frowned. "In New York," she said.

He turned toward her and kissed her arm. "I know," he said. "But why so serious?"

She knew that she was a serious person, and she liked it that he could make her smile. Sometimes, though, she did not quite understand him, so she was smiling now not out of appreciation, but because she thought a smile would make things all right.

Carol, her closest friend, asked why she didn't move in with him. She did not want to tell Carol that it was because she had not been asked, so she said that the room he lived in was very small and that during the day he liked solitude so he could work. She was also not sure that she would move in if he did ask her. He gave her the impression sometimes that he was the serious one, not she. Perhaps "serious" was the wrong word; it was more that he seemed despondent. He would get into moods and not snap out of them; he would drink red wine and play Billie Holiday records, and shake his head and say that if he had not made it as a songwriter by now, chances were that he would never make it. She hadn't really been familiar with Billie Holiday until he began playing the records for her. He would play a song that Billie had recorded early in her career, then play another record of the same song as she had sung it later. He said that he preferred her ruined voice. Two songs in particular stuck in her mind. One was "Solitude," and the first time she heard Billie Holiday sing the first three words, "In my solitude," she felt a physical sensation, as if someone were drawing something sharp over her heart, very lightly. The other record she kept thinking of was "Gloomy Sunday." He told her that it had been banned from the radio back then, because it was said that it had been responsible for suicides.

For Christmas that year he gave her a small pearl ring that had been worn by his mother when she was a girl. The ring fitted perfectly; she only had to wiggle it slightly to get it to slide over the joint of her finger, and when it was in place it felt as if she were not wearing a ring at all. There were eight prongs holding the pearl in place. She often counted things: how many panes in a window, how many slats in a bench. Then, for her birthday, in January, he gave her a silver chain with a small sapphire stone, to be worn on the wrist. She was delighted; she wouldn't let him help her fasten the clasp.

"You like it?" he said. "That's all I've got."

She looked at him, a little startled. His mother had died the year before she met him; what he was saying was that he had given her the last of her things. There was a photograph of his mother on the bookcase—a black-and-white picture in a little silver frame of a smiling young woman whose hair was barely darker than her skin. Because he kept the picture, she assumed that he worshiped his mother. One night he corrected that impression by saying that his mother had always tried to sing in her youth, when she had no voice, which had embarrassed everyone.

He said that she was a silent person; in the end, he said, you would have to say that she had done and said very little. He told Sharon that a few days after her death he and his father had gone through her possessions together, and in one of her drawers they came upon a small wooden box shaped like a heart. Inside the box were two pieces of jewelry—the ring and the chain and sapphire. "So she kept some token, then," his father had said, staring down into the little box. "You gave them to her as presents?" he asked his father. "No," his father said apologetically. "They weren't from me." And then the two of them had stood there looking at each other, both understanding perfectly.

She said, "But what did you finally say to break the silence?"

"Something pointless, I'm sure," he said.

She thought to herself that that might explain why he had not backed down, on Tenth Street, when the man offering the puppies took a stance as though he wanted to fight. Jack was used to hearing bad things— things that took him by surprise. He had learned to react coolly. Later that winter, when she told him that she loved him, his face had stayed expressionless a split

second too long, and then he smiled his slow smile and
gave her a kiss.

The dog grew. He took to training quickly and
walked at heel, and she was glad that they had saved
him. She took him to the veterinarian to ask why he
was so thin. She was told that the dog was growing
fast, and that eventually he would start filling out. She
did not tell Jack that she had taken the dog to the
veterinarian, because he thought she doted on him too
much. She wondered if he might not be a little jealous
of the dog.

Slowly, things began to happen with his music. A
band on the West Coast that played a song that he and
Gus had written was getting a big name, and they had
not dropped the song from their repertoire. In February
he got a call from the band's agent, who said that they
wanted more songs. He and Gus shut themselves in the
basement apartment, and she went walking with Sam,
the dog. She went to the park, until she ran into the
crippled man too many times. He was a young man,
rather handsome, who walked with two metal crutches
and had a radio that hung from a strap around his neck
and rested on his chest, playing loudly. The man always
seemed to be walking in the direction she walked in,
and she had to walk awkwardly to keep in line with
him so they could talk. She really had nothing to talk
to the man about, and he helped very little, and the
dog was confused by the crutches and made little leaps
toward the man, as though they were all three playing
a game. She stayed away from the park for a while,
and when she went back he was not there. One day in
March the park was more crowded than usual because
it was an unusually warm, springlike afternoon, and
walking with Sam, half dreaming, she passed a heavily
made-up woman on a bench who was wearing a polka-
dot turban, with a hand-lettered sign propped against
her legs announcing that she was Miss Sydney, a for-
tuneteller. There was a young boy sitting next to Miss
Sydney, and he called out to her, "Come on!" She smiled

slightly but shook her head no. The boy was Italian, she thought, but the woman was hard to place. "Miss Sydney's gonna tell you about fire and famine and early death," the boy said. He laughed, and she hurried on, thinking it was odd that the boy would know the word "famine."

She was still alone with Jack most of every weekend, but much of his talk now was about technical problems he was having with scoring, and she had trouble following him. Once, he became enraged and said that she had no interest in his career. He said it because he wanted to move to Los Angeles and she said she was staying in New York. She said it assuming at once that he would go anyhow. When he made it clear that he would not leave without her, she started to cry because she was so grateful that he was staying. He thought she was crying because he had yelled at her and said that she had no interest in his career. He took back what he said; he told her that she was very tolerant and that she often gave good advice. She had a good ear, even if she didn't express her opinions in complex technical terms. She cried again, and this time even she did not realize at first why. Later she knew that it was because he had never said so many kind things to her at once. Actually, very few people in her life had ever gone out of their way to say something kind, and it had just been too much. She began to wonder if her nerves were getting bad. Once, she woke up in the night disoriented and sweating, having dreamed that she was out in the sun, with all her energy gone. It was stifling hot and she couldn't move. "The sun's a good thing," he said to her when she told him the dream. "Think about the bright beautiful sun in Los Angeles. Think about stretching out on a warm day with a warm breeze." Trembling, she left him and went into the kitchen for water. He did not know that if he had really set out for California, she would have followed.

In June, when the air pollution got very bad and the air carried the smell that sidewalks get when they are baked through every day, he began to complain that it was her fault that they were in New York and not in California. "But I just don't like that way of life," she said. "If I went there, I wouldn't be happy."

"What's so appealing about this uptight New York scene?" he said. "You wake up in the night in a sweat. You won't even walk through Washington Square Park anymore."

"It's because of that man with the crutches," she said. "People like that. I told you it was only because of him."

"So let's get away from all that. Let's go somewhere."

"You think there aren't people like that in California?" she said.

"It doesn't matter what I think about California if I'm not going." He clamped earphones on his head.

That same month, while she and Jack and Gus were sharing a pot of cheese fondue, she found out that Jack had a wife. They were at Gus's apartment when Gus casually said something about Myra. "Who's Myra?" she asked, and he said, "You know—Jack's wife, Myra." It seemed unreal to her—even more so because Gus's apartment was such an odd place; that night Gus had plugged a defective lamp into an outlet and blown out a fuse. Then he plugged in his only other lamp, which was a sunlamp. It glowed so brightly that he had to turn it, in its wire enclosure, to face the wall. As they sat on the floor eating, their three shadows were thrown up against the opposite wall. She had been looking at that—detached, the way you would stand back to appreciate a picture—when she tuned in on the conversation and heard them talking about someone named Myra.

"You didn't know?" Gus said to her. "Okay, I want you both out. I don't want any heavy scene in my place. I couldn't take it. Come on—I really mean it. I want you out. Please don't talk about it here."

On the street, walking beside Jack, it occurred to

her that Gus's outburst was very strange, almost as strange as Jack's not telling her about his wife.

"I didn't see what would be gained by telling you," Jack said.

They crossed the street. They passed the Riviera Café. She had once counted the number of panes of glass across the Riviera's front.

"Did you ever think about us getting married?" he said. "I thought about it. I thought that if you didn't want to follow me to California, of course you wouldn't want to marry me."

"You're already married," she said. She felt that she had just said something very sensible. "Do you think it was right to—"

He started to walk ahead of her. She hurried to catch up. She wanted to call after him, "I would have gone!" She was panting.

"Listen," he said, "I'm like Gus. I don't want to hear it."

"You mean we can't even talk about this? You don't think that I'm entitled to hear about it?"

"I love you and I don't love Myra," he said.

"Where is she?" she said.

"In El Paso."

"If you don't love her, why aren't you divorced?"

"You think that everybody who doesn't love his wife gets divorced? I'm not the only one who doesn't do the logical thing, you know. You get nightmares from living in this sewer, and you won't get out of it."

"It's different," she said. What was he talking about?

"Until I met you, I didn't think about it. She was in El Paso, she was gone—period."

"Are you going to get a divorce?"

"Are you going to marry me?"

They were crossing Seventh Avenue. They both stopped still, halfway across the street, and were almost hit by a Checker cab. They hurried across, and on the other side of the street they stopped again. She looked at him, as surprised but as suddenly sure about something as he must have been the time he and his father had found the jewelry in the heart-shaped wooden box. She said no, she was not going to marry him.

It dragged on for another month. During that time, unknown to her, he wrote the song that was going to launch his career. Months after he had left the city, she heard it on her AM radio one morning, and she knew that it was his song, even though he had never mentioned it to her. She leashed the dog and went out and walked to the record shop on Sixth Avenue—walking almost the same route they had walked the night she found out about his wife—and she went in, with the dog. Her face was so strange that the man behind the cash register allowed her to break the rule about dogs in the shop because he did not want another hassle that day. She found the group's record album with the song on it, turned it over and saw his name, in small type. She stared at the title, replaced the record and went back outside, as hunched as if it were winter.

During the month before he left, though, and before she ever heard the song, the two of them had sat on the roof of his building one night, arguing. They were having a Tom Collins because a musician who had been at his place the night before had brought his own mix and then left it behind. She had never had a Tom Collins. It tasted appropriately bitter, she thought. She held out the ring and the bracelet to him. He said that if she made him take them back, he would drop them over the railing. She believed him and put them back in her pocket. He said, and she agreed, that things had not been perfect between them even before she found out about his wife. Myra could play the guitar, and she could not; Myra loved to travel, and she was afraid to leave New York City. As she listened to what he said, she counted the posts—black iron and shaped like arrows—of the fence that wound around the roof. It was

almost entirely dark, and she looked up to see if there
were any stars. She yearned to be in the country, where
she could always see them. She said she wanted him
to borrow a car before he left so that they could ride
out into the woods in New Jersey. Two nights later he
picked her up at her apartment in a red Volvo, with
Sam panting in the back, and they wound their way
through the city and to the Lincoln Tunnel. Just as
they were about to go under, another song began to
play on the tape deck. It was Ringo Starr singing "Oc-
topus's Garden." Jack laughed. "That's a hell of a fine
song to come on just before we enter the tunnel." Inside
the tunnel, the dog flattened himself on the back seat.
"You want to keep Sam, don't you?" he said. She was
shocked because she had never even thought of losing
Sam. "Of course I do," she said, and unconsciously
edged a little away from him. He had never said whose
car it was. For no reason at all, she thought that the
car must belong to a woman.

"I love that syrupy chorus of 'aaaaah' Lennon and
McCartney sing," he said. "They really had a fine sense
of humor."

"Is that a funny song?" she said. She had never
thought about it.

They were on Boulevard East, in Weehawken, and
she was staring out the window at the lights across the
water. He saw that she was looking, and drove slower.

"This as good as stars for you?" he said.

"It's amazing."

"All yours," he said, taking his hand off the wheel
to swoop it through the air in mock graciousness.

After he left she would remember that as one of the
little digs he had gotten in—one of the less than nice
things he had said. That night, though, impressed by
the beauty of the city, she let it go by; in fact, she would
have to work on herself later to reinterpret many of
the things he had said as being nasty. That made it
easier to deal with his absence. She would block out

the memory of his pulling over and kissing her, of the two of them getting out of the car, and with Sam between them, walking.

One of the last times she saw him, she went to his apartment on a night when five other people were there—people she had never met. His father had shipped him some 8mm home movies and a projector, and the people all sat on the floor, smoking grass and talking, laughing at the movies of children (Jack at his fourth birthday party; Jack in the Halloween parade at school; Jack at Easter, collecting eggs). One of the people on the floor said, "Hey, get that big dog out of the way," and she glared at him, hating him for not liking the dog. What if his shadow had briefly darkened the screen? She felt angry enough to scream, angry enough to say that the dog had grown up in the apartment and had the right to walk around. Looking at the home movies, she tried to concentrate on Jack's blunders: dropping an Easter egg, running down the hill after the egg, going so fast he stumbled into some blur, perhaps his mother's arms. But what she mostly thought about was what a beautiful child he was, what a happy-looking little boy. There was no sense in her staying there and getting sentimental, so she made her excuses and left early. Outside, she saw the red Volvo, gleaming as though it had been newly painted. She was sure that it belonged to an Indian woman in a blue sari who had been there, sitting close to Jack. Sharon was glad that as she was leaving, Sam had raised his hackles and growled at one of the people there. She scolded him, but out on the street she patted him, secretly glad. Jack had not asked her again to come to California with him, and she told herself that she probably would not have changed her mind if he had. Tears began to well up in her eyes, and she told herself that she was crying because a cab wouldn't stop for her when the driver saw that she had a dog. She ended up walking blocks and blocks back to her apartment that night; it made her more certain than ever that she loved the dog and that she did not love Jack.

About the time she got the first postcard from Jack, things started to get a little bad with Sam. She was afraid that he might have distemper, so she took him to the veterinarian, waited her turn and told the doctor that the dog was growling at some people and she had no idea why. He assured her that there was nothing physically wrong with the dog, and blamed it on the heat. When another month passed and it was less hot, she visited the veterinarian again. "It's the breeding," he said, and sighed. "It's a bad mix. A Weimaraner is a mean dog, and that cross isn't a good one. He's part German shepherd, isn't he?"

"Yes," she said.

"Well—that's it, I'm afraid."

"There isn't any medication?"

"It's the breeding," he said. "Believe me. I've seen it before."

"What happens?" she said.

"What happens to the dog?"

"Yes."

"Well—watch him. See how things go. He hasn't bitten anybody, has he?"

"No," she said. "Of course not."

"Well—don't say of course not. Be careful with him."

"I'm careful with him," she said. She said it indignantly. But she wanted to hear something else. She didn't want to leave.

Walking home, she thought about what she could do. Maybe she could take Sam to her sister's house in Morristown for a while. Maybe if he could run more, and keep cool, he would calm down. She put aside her knowledge that it was late September and already much cooler, and that the dog growled more, not less. He had growled at the teen-age boy she had given money to to help her carry her groceries upstairs. It was the boy's extreme reaction to Sam that had made it worse, though. You had to act calm around Sam when he got like that, and the boy had panicked.

She persuaded her sister to take Sam, and her brother-in-law drove into New York on Sunday and drove them out to New Jersey. Sam was put on a chain attached to a rope her brother-in-law had strung up in the backyard, between two huge trees. To her surprise, Sam did not seem to mind it. He did not bark and strain at the chain until he saw her drive away, late that afternoon; her sister was driving, and she was in the back seat with her niece, and she looked back and saw him lunging at the chain.

The rest of it was predictable, even to her. As they drove away, she almost knew it all. The dog would bite the child. Of course, the child should not have annoyed the dog, but she did, and the dog bit her, and then there was a hysterical call from her sister and another call from her brother-in-law, saying that she must come get the dog immediately—that he would come for her so she could get him—and blaming her for bringing the dog to them in the first place. Her sister had never really liked her, and the incident with the dog was probably just what she had been waiting for to sever contact.

When Sam came back to the city, things got no better. He turned against everyone and it was difficult even to walk him because he had become so aggressive. Sometimes a day would pass without any of that, and she would tell herself that it was over now—an awful period but over—and then the next morning the dog would bare his teeth at some person they passed. There began to be little signs that the dog had it in for her, too, and when that happened she turned her bedroom over to him. She hauled her mattress to the living room and let him have his own room. She left the door cracked so he would not think he was being punished. But she knew, and Sam knew, that it was best he stay in the room. If nothing else, he was an exceptionally smart dog.

She heard from Jack for over a year—sporadically, but then sometimes two postcards in a single week. He was doing well, playing in a band as well as writing music. When she stopped hearing from him—and when it became clear that something had to be done about the dog, and something had been done—she was twenty-two. On a date with a man she liked as a friend, she suggested that they go over to Jersey and drive down Boulevard East. The man was new to New York, and when they got there he said that he was more impressed with that view of the city than with the view from the top of the RCA Building. "All ours," she said, gesturing with her arm, and he, smiling and excited by what she said, took her hand when it had finished its sweep and kissed it, and continued to stare with awe at the lights across the water. That summer, she heard another song of Jack's on the radio, which alluded, as so many of his songs did, to times in New York she remembered well. In this particular song there was a couplet about a man on the street offering kittens in a box that actually contained a dog named Sam. In the context of the song it was an amusing episode—another "you can't always get what you want" sort of thing—and she could imagine Jack in California, not knowing what had happened to Sam, and, always the one to appreciate little jokes in songs, smiling.

# A Reasonable Man

She is waiting for the telephone to ring. It has not rung for at least six days, which is most unusual. Usually there would be a wrong number, or some sort of salesman trying to sell something she had never considered buying or that she did not know existed. In fact, it might be more than six days. At first she may not have been conscious that the phone was not ringing. You don't notice something being absent for a day or two: a mislaid pen, clouds. It may well not have rung for quite some time.

She tells the man this at dinner, remarking on how unusual it is. The man likes to know exactly why she mentions things because he often cannot follow her. So she is in the habit, now, of mentioning something and commenting on it, explaining why she mentioned it at all. Of course, this is often more trouble than it's worth, so their dinners are sometimes silent from beginning to end. They are good dinners. She is competent in that area. A home economics major, she fixes dinners that are not only good to eat, but balanced and nutritious. They rarely have colds. They have never had a major illness. Tonight they eat cream of asparagus soup, a salad of beans and pears on chopped lettuce, broiled chicken with mushrooms, a glass of white wine and baked custard.

"For heaven's sake," the man says. "It might have rung when you were out getting groceries. If you had been downstairs, it might have rung and you wouldn't have heard it." He raises a single green bean to his lips. She smiles at him. He chews, swallows and smiles. Everything he says is logical. She follows perfectly. She does not believe that the phone rang when she was out buying groceries, and anyway, she bought groceries three days ago. She was not downstairs today, or yesterday. She frowns. Did she go down there yesterday? He lifts another piece of food to his mouth. He notices that she is frowning. "You see that, don't you?" he says. Of course. She understands everything the man says.

The phone has not rung for seven days—assuming that it will not ring tonight. In a novel she is very fond of the main character tries to bring on her period by sleeping in white, on fresh bed sheets. She tries to think what she could do to make the phone ring. Perhaps make love to the man. That may be a little difficult, though, because he is still at a meeting and will be tired and hungry when he comes home. She will feed him and then seduce him. Another thing she might try, if this doesn't work, is showering.

The man comes home. He looks as though he has been in a windstorm. He confirms that it is very windy out. "Look," he says, pointing her toward the kitchen window. Leaves that they did not rake up during the winter blow across the yard. She is so glad! Usually her procrastination results in nothing good, but there are the leaves, blowing through the air and across the grass, which is already turning green.

"Didn't you go out today?" the man asks.

"No. I didn't go anywhere. I didn't have anywhere to go."

"But you went out yesterday, I presume."

"Yesterday?" (She is not a good liar.)

He nods again.

"I don't think I went out yesterday. No."

He sighs heavily. Seducing him will not be easy.

He brightens a bit at the table when she serves him marinated herring. He likes fish very much. The main course is beef stew, which he also seems to enjoy. They have oranges for dessert, coffee with milk.

"Tomorrow I guess you'll be going out to do some errands," he says. "Would you take my gray suit to the cleaners, please?"

"Certainly," she says. She will tell him that she forgot. That will work for one day. But the day after tomorrow she will have to go to the cleaners. That might not be so bad: the phone might ring tomorrow, and then the next day she would have no reason to wait home because the phone would have rung recently. She smiles.

"Aren't you going to answer me?" he says.

"I did answer. I said I would."

He looks at her blankly. His eyes are blank, but his mouth is a little tight.

"I didn't hear you," he says, with syrupy graciousness.

She thinks that she, too, might have a hearing problem. After dinner, alone in the kitchen, she puts down the dishtowel and goes to the phone, puts her ear against it. Shouldn't it hum like the refrigerator when it isn't ringing? There is always some slight noise, isn't there? She's had insomnia in the past and felt as though there were a war going on in the house, it was so noisy. The faint hum of electrical appliances, the glow in the little box in back of the television when it's not on. There must be something wrong with her hearing, or with the phone.

The next day she goes to the cleaners. There's a way to make the phone ring! Go out and leave it and surely it will ring in the empty house. She is not as happy as she might be about this, though, for the obvious reason that she will not have the satisfaction of hearing the phone. Driving home, she tries to remember the last phone conversation she had. She can't. It might have been with her neighbor, or with some salesman...a relative? If she kept a journal, she could check on this. Maybe now is the time to keep a journal. That way she could just flip back through the pages and check on details she has forgotten. She parks the car and goes into a drugstore and buys a blue tablet—actually it is called a theme book—and a special pen to write with: a black fountain pen, and a bottle of ink. She has to go back for the ink. She has never thought things through. At vacation time the man would stand at the front door saying, "Do you have beach shoes? Did you bring our toothbrushes? What about a hat for the sun? I know you brought suntan lotion, but what about Solarcaine?" She would run to her closet, to the bathroom, take down hatboxes, reopen her suitcase. "And Robby's raft—did you put that in the trunk?" Yes. She always thought a lot about Robby. He always had the correct clothes packed, his favorite toys included, comics to read in the car. She took very good care of Robby. She does not quite understand why he must live with his grandmother. Of all of them, she took the best care of Robby. She *does* understand why he is with the man's mother, but she does not like it, or want to accept it. She has been very honest with the man, has told him her feelings about this, and has not been converted to his way of thinking. She never did anything to Robby. He agrees with this. And she does not see why she can't have him. There they disagree. They disagree, and the man has not made love to her for months—as long as the disagreement has gone on.

She is so frustrated. Filling the pen is harder than she thought—to do it carefully, making sure not to spill the ink or put too much in. And what details, exactly, should she write down? What if she wanted to remember the times she went to the bathroom the day before? Should she include everything? It would take too long. And it would seem silly to write down the times she went to the bathroom. The journal is to make her feel better. What would be the point of flipping back through her journal and seeing things that would embarrass her? There are enough things that embarrass her around the house. All the bowls that the man likes so much are a tiny bit lopsided. He agrees with her there, but says no value should be placed on a perfect bowl. Once he became very excited and told her there was no such thing as perfection—it was all in the eye of the beholder. He went on to talk about molecules; fast, constantly moving molecules that exist in all things. She is afraid of the bowls now, and doesn't dust them. He wants her to dust them—to take pride in them. He talks and talks about the negative value of "perfection." He put the word in quotes. This, he explained, was because he, himself, did not think in those terms, but it was a convenient word. He left the note on the door one morning before leaving for work, and she found it when she went into the kitchen. She asked about it. It is established that they can ask about anything. Anything at all. And that the other has to answer. She would like to ask him if he has had the phone disconnected. She can ask, but she is frightened to.

The man's mother pays for her to take the crafts classes. In the summer, June through August, they spun the bowls (they could have made vases, plates, but she stuck with bowls); September through November they learned macramé, and for Christmas she gave all of it away—a useless tangle of knots. She had no plants to hang in them, and she did not want them hung on her walls. She likes plain walls. The one Seurat is enough. She likes to look at the walls and think. For the past four months they have been making silver jewelry. She is getting worse at things instead of better. Fatigue at having been at it so long, perhaps, or perhaps what she said to her teacher, which her teacher denied; that she is just too old, that her imagination is insufficient, that her touch is not delicate enough. She is used to handling large things: plates, vacuums. She has no feel for the delicate fibers of silver. Her teacher told her that she certainly *did*. He wears one of the rings she made—bought it from her and wears it to every class. She is flattered, although she has no way of knowing whether he is wearing it out of class. Like the garish orange pin Robby selected for her in the dime store, his gift to her for her birthday. He was four years old, and naturally the bright orange pin caught his eye. She wore it to the PTA meeting, on her coat, to show him how much she liked it. She took it off in the car and put it back on before coming in the house—just in case the baby-sitter had failed and he was still awake. Now, however, she would never consider taking off the pin. She wears it every day. It's as automatic as combing her hair. She's as used to seeing it on her blouse or dress as she is to waiting for the phone to ring.

The man says it is remarkable that they always have such good meals when she shops so seldom. She went out two days ago to the cleaners, and she showed him the stub, so he knows this, but he is still subtly criticizing her failure to go out every day. She gets tired of going out. She has to go to crafts classes Thursday, Friday and Saturday nights, and on Sunday she has to go to his mother's house. She says this to him by way of argument, but actually she *loves* to go to his mother's house. It is the best day of the week. She does not love, or even like, his mother, but she can be with Robby from afternoon until his bedtime. They can throw the ball back and forth on the front lawn (who cares if they spy on them through the window?), and she can brush his hair (she cuts it too short! Just a little longer. He's so beautiful that the short hair doesn't make him ugly, but he would be even more beautiful if it could grow an inch on the sides, on the top). He gives her pictures he has colored. He thinks that kindergarten should be more sophisticated and is a little embarrassed about the pictures, but he explains that he has to do what the teacher says. She nods. If he were older, she could explain that she *had* to make the bowls. He rebels by drawing sloppily, sometimes. "I didn't even try on that one," he says. She knows what he means. She says—as the man says to her about the bowls, as the crafts instructor says—that they are still beautiful. He likes that. He gives them all to her. There is not even one tacked up in his grandmother's kitchen. There are none on her walls, either, but she looks through the pile on the coffee table every day. She prefers the walls blank. When he comes with Grandma to visit, which hardly ever happens, she puts them up if she knows he's coming or points to the pile to show him that she has them close-by to examine. She never did anything to Robby, not one single thing. She argues and argues with the man about this. He goes to business meetings at night and comes home late. He does not fully enjoy the meals she prepares because he is so tired. This he denies. He says he does fully enjoy them. What can she say? How can you prove that someone is not savoring sweet-potato soufflé?

"How *do* you cook such delicious things when you shop so seldom?" he asks.

"I don't shop that infrequently," she says.

"Don't vegetables . . . I mean, aren't they very perishable?"

"No," she says. She smiles sweetly.

"You always have fresh vegetables, don't you?"

"Sometimes I buy them fresh and parboil them myself. Later I steam them."

"Ah," he says. He does not know exactly what she is talking about.

"Today I was out for a walk," she says. No way he can prove she wasn't.

"It's a late spring," he says. "But today it was very nice, actually."

They are having a civilized discussion. Perhaps she can lure him into bed. Perhaps if that works, the phone will also ring. Hasn't he noticed that it doesn't ring at night, that it hasn't for nights? That's unusual, too. She would ask what he makes of this, but talking about the phone makes him angry, and if he's angry, he'll never get into bed. She fingers her pin. He sees her do it. A mistake. It reminds him of Robby.

She sips her wine and thinks about their summer vacation—the one they already took. She can remember so little about the summer. She will not remember the spring if she doesn't get busy and write in her book. What, exactly, should she write? She thinks the book should contain feelings instead of just facts. Surely that would be less boring to do. Well, she was going to write something during the afternoon, but she was feeling blue, and worried—about the telephone—and it wouldn't cheer her up to go back and read about feeling blue and being worried. Her crafts teacher had given her a book of poetry to read: *Winter Trees* by Sylvia Plath. It was interesting. She was certainly interested in it, but it depressed her. She didn't go out of the house for days. Finally—she is glad she can remember clearly some details—he asked her to go to the cleaners and she went out. She did several errands that day. What was the weather like, though? Or does it really matter? She corrects herself: it does matter. It matters very much what season it is, whether the weather is typical or unusual. If you have something to say about the weather, you will always be able to make conversation with people, and communicating is very important. Even for yourself: you should know that you feel blue because the weather is cold or rainy, happy because it's a sunny day with high clouds. Tonight she feels blue. Probably it is cold out. She would ask, but she has already lied that she was out. It might have turned cold, however.

"I was out quite early," she says. "What was the weather like when you came home?"

"Ah," he says. "I called this morning."

She looks up at him, suddenly. He sees her surprise, knows she wasn't out.

"Just to say that I loved you," he says.

He smiles. It is not worth seducing him to make the phone ring. She will shower, wash her hair, stand there a long time, hoping, but she won't make love to the man. He is a rotten liar.

In the morning, when he is gone, she finds that she remembers her feelings of the night before exactly, and writes them down, at length, in the book.

On Friday night he no longer picks her up after crafts class. He has joined a stock club, and he has a meeting that night. The bus stop is only a block from where the class meets; it lets her off five minutes from where she lives. It is unnecessary for the man ever to pick her up. But he says that the streets are dangerous at night, and that she must be tired. She says that the bus ride refreshes her. She likes riding buses, looking at the people. There is good bus service. He smiles. But it is not necessary to ride them; and the streets are dangerous at night.

Tonight her instructor asks to speak to her when the class has ended. She has no interest in the thin silver filaments she is working with and says he can talk to her now. "No," he says. "Later is fine."

She remains when the others have left. The others are all younger than she, with one exception: a busty grandmother who is learning crafts hoping to ease her arthritis. The others are in their teens or early twenties. They have long hair and wear Earth shoes and are unfriendly. They are intense. Perhaps that's what it is. They don't talk because they're intense. They walk (so the ads for these shoes say) feeling clouds beneath them, their spines perfectly and comfortably straight, totally relaxed and enjoying their intensity. Their intensity results in delicate necklaces, highly glazed bowls—some with deer and trees, others with Mister Moon smiling. All but three are women.

When they have all left, he opens a door to a room at the back of the classroom. It opens into a tiny room, where there is a mattress on the floor, covered with a plaid blanket, two pairs of tennis shoes aligned with it, and a high narrow bookcase between the pipe and window. He wants to know what she thought of the Sylvia Plath book. She says that it depressed her. That seems to be the right response, the one that gets his head nodding—he always nods when he looks over her shoulder. He told her in November that he admired her wanting to perfect her bowls—her not moving on just to move on to something else. They nod at each other. In the classroom they whisper so as not to disturb anyone's intensity. It is strange now to speak to him in a normal tone of voice. When she sees her son, now, she also whispers. That annoys the man and his mother. What does she have to say to him that they can't all hear? They are noisy when they play, but when they are in the house—in his room, or when she is pouring him some juice from the refrigerator—she will kneel and whisper. A gentle sound, like deer in the woods. She made the bowl with the deer on it, gave it to the instructor because he was so delighted with it. He was very appreciative. He said that he meant for her to keep the book. But he would lend her another. Or two: *The Death Notebooks* and *A Vision*. The instructor puts his foot on the edge of the second shelf to get one of the books down from the top. She is afraid he will fall, stands closer to him, behind him, in case he does. She has a notion of softening his fall. He does not fall. He hands her the books. The instructor knows all about her, she is sure. The man's mother visited his studio before she suggested, firmly, that she enroll. The man's mother was charmed by the instructor. Imagine what she must have said to him about her. From the first, he was kind to her. When he gave her *Winter Trees*, he somehow got across the idea to her that many women felt enraged—sad and enraged. He said a few things to her that impressed her at the time. If only she had had the notebook then, she could have written them down, reread them.

He boils water in a pan for tea. She admires the blue jar he spoons the tea out of. He made it. Similarly, he admires her work. She sees that her bowl holds some oranges and bananas. She would like to ask what false or unfair things the man's mother said about her. That would cast a pall over things, though. The instructor would feel uncomfortable. It is not right to blurt out everything you feel like saying. People don't live like that in society. Talk about something neutral. Talk about the weather. She says to the instructor what the man always says to her: it is a late spring. She says more: she is keeping a journal. He asks again—the third time?—whether she writes poetry. She says, truthfully, that she does not. He shows her a box full of papers that he doodled on, wrote on, the semester he dropped out of Stanford. The doodles are very complex, heavily inked. The writing is sloppy, in big letters that were written with a heavy black pen. She understands from reading a little that he was unhappy when he dropped out of Stanford. He says that writing things down helps. Expressing yourself helps. Her attention drifts. When she concentrates again, he is saying the opposite: she must feel these classes are unpleasant, having been sentenced to them; all those books—he gestures to the bookcase—were written by unhappy people, and it's doubtful if writing them made them any happier. Not Sylvia Plath, certainly. He tells her that she should not feel obliged to act nicely, feel happy. He thumps his hand on the books he has just given her.

She tells him that the phone never rings anymore. She tells him that last, after the story about the summer vacation, how she and Robby set out to race through the surf, and Robby lagged behind, and she felt such incredible energy, she ran and ran. They got separated. She ran all the way to the end of the sand, to the rocks, and then back—walked back—and couldn't find Robby or the man anywhere. All the beach umbrellas looked the same, and so did the people. What exactly did Robby look like? Or the man? The man looked furious. He found her, came back for her in his slacks and shirt, having taken Robby back to the motel. His shoes were caked with wet sand, his face furious. She is not sure how to connect this to what she really wants to talk about, the inexplicably silent telephone.

# Shifting

The woman's name was Natalie, and the man's name was Larry. They had been childhood sweethearts; he had first kissed her at an ice-skating party when they were ten. She had been unlacing her skates and had not expected the kiss. He had not expected to do it, either—he had some notion of getting his face out of the wind that was blowing across the iced-over lake, and he found himself ducking his head toward her. Kissing her seemed the natural thing to do. When they graduated from high school he was named "class clown" in the yearbook, but Natalie didn't think of him as being particularly funny. He spent more time that she thought he needed to studying chemistry, and he never laughed when she joked. She really did not think of him as funny. They went to the same college, in their hometown, but he left after a year to go to a larger, more impressive university. She took the train to be with him on weekends, or he took the train to see her. When he graduated, his parents gave him a car. If they had given it to him when he was still in college, it would have made things much easier. They waited to give it to him until graduation day, forcing him into attending the graduation exercises. He thought his parents were wonderful people, and Natalie liked them in a way, too, but she resented their perfect timing, their careful smiles. They were afraid that he would marry her. Eventually, he did. He had gone on to graduate school after college, and he set a date six months ahead for their wedding so that it would take place after his first-semester final exams. That way he could devote his time to studying for the chemistry exams.

When she married him, he had had the car for eight months. It still smelled like a brand-new car. There was never any clutter in the car. Even the ice scraper was kept in the glove compartment. There was not even a sweater or a lost glove in the back seat. He vacuumed the car every weekend, after washing it at the car wash. On Friday nights, on their way to some cheap restaurant and a dollar movie, he would stop at the car wash, and she would get out so he could vacuum all over the inside of the car. She would lean against the metal wall of the car wash and watch him clean it.

It was expected that she would not become pregnant. She did not. It had also been expected that she would keep their apartment clean, and keep out of the way as much as possible in such close quarters while he was studying. The apartment was messy, though, and when he was studying late at night she would interrupt him and try to talk him into going to sleep. He gave a chemistry-class lecture once a week, and she would often tell him that overpreparing was as bad as underpreparing. She did not know if she believed this, but it was a favorite line of hers. Sometimes he listened to her.

On Tuesdays, when he gave the lecture, she would drop him off at school and then drive to a supermarket to do the week's shopping. Usually she did not make a list before she went shopping, but when she got to the parking lot she would take a tablet out of her purse and write a few items on it, sitting in the car in the cold. Even having a few things written down would stop her from wandering aimlessly in the store and buying things that she would never use. Before this, she had bought several pans and cans of food that she had not used, or that she could have done without. She felt better when she had a list.

She would drop him at school again on Wednesdays, when he had two seminars that together took up all the afternoon. Sometimes she would drive out of town then, to the suburbs, and shop there if any shopping needed to be done. Otherwise, she would go to the art museum, which was not far away but hard to get to by bus. There was one piece of sculpture in there that she wanted very much to touch, but the guard was always nearby. She came so often that in time the guard began to nod hello. She wondered if she could ever persuade the man to turn his head for a few seconds—only that long—so she could stroke the sculpture. Of course she would never dare ask. After wandering through the museum and looking at least twice at the sculpture, she would go to the gift shop and buy a few postcards and then sit on one of the museum benches, padded with black vinyl, with a Calder mobile hanging overhead, and write notes to friends. (She never wrote letters.) She would tuck the postcards in her purse and mail them when she left the museum. But before she left, she often had coffee in the restaurant: she saw mothers and children struggling there, and women dressed in fancy clothes talking with their faces close together, as quietly as lovers.

On Thursdays he took the car. After his class he would drive to visit his parents and his friend Andy, who had been wounded in Vietnam. About once a month she would go with him, but she had to feel up to it. Being with Andy embarrassed her. She had told him not to go to Vietnam—told him that he could prove his patriotism in some other way—and finally, after she and Larry had made a visit together and she had seen Andy in the motorized bed in his parents' house, Larry had agreed that she need not go again. Andy had apologized to her. It embarrassed her that this man, who had been blown sky-high by a land mine and had lost a leg and lost the full use of his arms, would smile up at her ironically and say, "You were right." She also felt as though he wanted to hear what she would say now, and that now he would listen. Now she had nothing to say. Andy would pull himself up, relying on his right arm, which was the stronger, gripping the rails at the side of the bed, and sometimes he would take her hand. His arms were still weak, but the doctors said he would regain complete use of his right arm with time. She had to make an effort not to squeeze his hand when he held hers because she found herself wanting to squeeze energy back into him. She had a morbid curiosity about what it felt like to be blown from the ground—to go up, and to come crashing down. During their visit Larry would put on the class-clown act for Andy, telling funny stories and laughing uproariously.

Once or twice Larry had talked Andy into getting in his wheelchair and had loaded him into the car and taken him to a bar. Larry called her once, late, pretty drunk, to say that he would not be home that night—that he would sleep at his parents' house. "My God," she said. "Are you going to drive Andy home when you're drunk?" "What the hell else can happen to him?" he said.

Larry's parents blamed her for Larry's not being happy. His mother could only be pleasant with her for a short while, and then she would veil her criticisms by putting them as questions. "I know that one thing that helps enormously is good nutrition," his mother said. "He works so hard that he probably needs quite a few vitamins as well, don't you think?" Larry's father was the sort of man who found hobbies in order to avoid his wife. His hobbies were building model boats, repairing clocks, and photography. He took pictures of himself building the boats and fixing the clocks, and gave the pictures, in cardboard frames, to Natalie and Larry for Christmas and birthday presents. Larry's mother was very anxious to stay on close terms with her son, and she knew that Natalie did not like her very much. Once she had visited them during the week, and Natalie, not knowing what to do with her, had taken her to the museum. She had pointed out the sculpture, and his mother had glanced at it and then ignored it. Natalie hated her for her bad taste. She had bad taste in the sweaters she gave Larry, too, but he wore them. They made him look collegiate. That whole world made her sick.

When Natalie's uncle died and left her his 1965 Volvo, they immediately decided to sell it and use the money for a vacation. They put an ad in the paper, and there were several callers. There were some calls on Tuesday, when Larry was in class, and Natalie found herself putting the people off. She told one woman that the car had too much mileage on it, and mentioned body rust, which it did not have; she told another caller, who was very persistent, that the car was already sold. When Larry returned from school she explained that the phone was off the hook because so many people were calling about the car and she had decided not to sell it after all. They could take a little money from their savings account and go on the trip if he wanted. But she did not want to sell the car. "It's not an automatic shift," he said. "You don't know how to drive it." She told him that she could learn. "It will cost money to insure it," he said, "and it's old and probably not even dependable." She wanted to keep the car. "I know," he said, "but it doesn't make sense. When we have more money, you can have a car. You can have a newer, better car."

The next day she went out to the car, which was parked in the driveway of an old lady next door. Her name was Mrs. Larsen and she no longer drove a car, and she told Natalie she could park their second car there. Natalie opened the car door and got behind the wheel and put her hands on it. The wheel was covered with a flaky yellow-and-black plastic cover. She eased it off. A few pieces of foam rubber stuck to the wheel. She picked them off. Underneath the cover, the wheel was a dull red. She ran her fingers around and around the circle of the wheel. Her cousin Burt had delivered the car—a young opportunist, sixteen years old, who said he would drive it the hundred miles from his house to theirs for twenty dollars and a bus ticket home. She had not even invited him to stay for dinner, and Larry had driven him to the bus station. She wondered if it was Burt's cigarette in the ashtray or her dead uncle's. She could not even remember if her uncle smoked. She was surprised that he had left her his car. The car was much more comfortable than Larry's, and it had a nice smell inside. It smelled a little the way a field smells after a spring rain. She rubbed the side of her head back and forth against the window and then got out of the car and went in to see Mrs. Larsen. The night before, she had suddenly thought of the boy who brought the old lady the evening newspaper every night; he looked old enough to drive, and he would probably know how to shift. Mrs. Larsen agreed with her—she was sure that he could teach her. "Of course, everything has its price," the old lady said.

"I know that. I meant to offer him money," Natalie said, and was surprised, listening to her voice, that she sounded old too.

She took an inventory and made a list of things in their apartment. Larry had met an insurance man one evening while playing basketball at the gym who told him that they should have a list of their possessions, in case of theft. "What's worth anything?" she said when he told her. It was their first argument in almost a year—the first time in a year, anyway, that their voices were raised. He told her that several of the pieces of furniture his grandparents gave them when they got married were antiques, and the man at the gym said that if they weren't going to get them appraised every year, at least they should take snapshots of them and keep the pictures in a safe-deposit box. Larry told her to photograph the pie safe (which she used to store linen), the piano with an inlaid mother-of-pearl decoration on the music rack (neither of them knew how to play), and the table with hand-carved wooden handles and a marble top. He bought her an Instamatic camera at the drugstore, with film and flash bulbs. "Why can't you do it?" she said, and an argument began. He said that she had no respect for his profession and no understanding of the amount of study that went into getting a master's degree in chemistry.

That night he went out to meet two friends at the gym, to shoot baskets. She put the little flashcube into the top of the camera, dropped in the film and closed the back. She went first to the piano. She leaned forward so that she was close enough to see the inlay clearly, but she found that when she was that close the whole piano wouldn't fit into the picture. She decided to take two pictures. Then she photographed the pie safe, with one door open, showing the towels and sheets stacked inside. She did not have a reason for opening the door, except that she remembered a *Perry Mason* show in which detectives photographed everything with the doors hanging open. She photographed the table, lifting the lamp off it first. There were still eight pictures left. She went to the mirror in their bedroom and held the camera above her head, pointing down at an angle, and photographed her image in the mirror. She took off her slacks and sat on the floor and leaned back, aiming the camera down at her legs. Then she stood up and took a picture of her feet, leaning over and aiming down. She put on her favorite record: Stevie Wonder singing "For Once in My Life." She found herself wondering what it would be like to be blind, to have to feel things to see them. She thought about the piece of sculpture in the museum—the two elongated mounds, intertwined, the smooth gray stone as shiny as sea pebbles. She photographed the kitchen, bathroom, bedroom and living room. There was one picture left. She put her left hand on her thigh, palm up, and with some difficulty—with the camera nestled into her neck like a violin—snapped a picture of it with her right hand. The next day would be her first driving lesson.

He came to her door at noon, as he had said he would. He had on a long maroon scarf, which made his deep-blue eyes very striking. She had only seen him from her window when he carried the paper in to the old lady. He was a little nervous. She hoped that it was just the anxiety of any teen-ager confronting an adult. She needed to have him like her. She did not learn about mechanical things easily (Larry had told her that he would have invested in a "real" camera, except that he did not have the time to teach her about it), so she wanted him to be patient. He sat on the footstool in her living room, still in coat and scarf, and told her how a stick shift operated. He moved his hand through the air. The motion he made reminded her of the salute spacemen gave to earthlings in a science-fiction picture she had recently watched on late-night television. She nodded. "How much—" she began, but he interrupted and said, "You can decide what it was worth when you've learned." She was surprised and wondered if he meant to charge a great deal. Would it be her fault and would she have to pay him if he named his price when the lessons were over? But he had an honest face. Perhaps he was just embarrassed to talk about money.

He drove for a few blocks, making her watch his hand on the stick shift. "Feel how the car is going?" he said. "Now you shift." He shifted. The car jumped a little, hummed, moved into gear. It was an old car and didn't shift too easily, he said. She had been sitting forward, so that when he shifted she rocked back hard against the seat—harder than she needed to. Almost unconsciously, she wanted to show him what a good teacher he was. When her turn came to drive, the car stalled. "Take it easy," he said. "Ease up on the clutch. Don't just raise your foot off of it like that." She tried it again. "That's it," he said. She looked at him when the car was in third. He sat in the seat, looking out the window. Snow was expected. It was Thursday. Although Larry was going to visit his parents and would not be back until late Friday afternoon, she decided she would wait until Tuesday for her next lesson. If he came home early, he would find out that she was taking lessons, and she didn't want him to know. She asked the boy, whose name was Michael, whether he thought she would forget all he had taught her in the time between lessons. "You'll remember," he said.

When they returned to the old lady's driveway, the car stalled going up the incline. She had trouble shifting. The boy put his hand over hers and kicked the heel of his hand forward. "You'll have to treat this car a little roughly, I'm afraid," he said. That afternoon, after he left, she made spaghetti sauce, chopping little pieces of pepper and onion and mushroom. When the sauce had cooked down, she called Mrs. Larsen and said that she would bring over dinner. She usually ate with the old lady once a week. The old lady often added a pinch of cinnamon to her food, saying that it brought out the flavor better than salt, and that since she was losing her sense of smell, food had to be strongly flavored for her to taste it. Once she had sprinkled cinnamon on a knockwurst. This time, as they ate, Natalie asked the old-lady how much she paid the boy to bring the paper.

"I give him a dollar a week," the old lady said.

"Did he set the price, or did you?"

"He set the price. He told me he wouldn't take much because he has to walk this street to get to his apartment anyway."

"He taught me a lot about the car today," Natalie said.

"He's very handsome, isn't he?" the old lady said.

She asked Larry, "How were your parents?"

"Fine," he said. "But I spent almost all the time with Andy. It's almost his birthday, and he's depressed. We went to see Mose Allison."

"I think it stinks that hardly anyone else ever visits Andy," she said.

"He doesn't make it easy. He tells you everything that's on his mind, and there's no way you can pretend that his troubles don't amount to much. You just have to sit there and nod."

She remembered that Andy's room looked like a gymnasium. There were handgrips and weights scattered on the floor. There was even a psychedelic pink hula hoop that he was to put inside his elbow and then move his arm in circles wide enough to make the hoop spin. He couldn't do it. He would lie in bed with the hoop in back of his neck, and holding the sides, lift his neck off the pillow. His arms were barely strong enough to do that, really, but he could raise his neck with no trouble, so he just pretended that his arms pulling the loop were raising it. His parents thought that it was a special exercise that he had mastered.

"What did you do today?" Larry said now.

"I made spaghetti," she said. She had made it the day before, but she thought that since he was mysterious about the time he spent away from her ("in the lab" and "at the gym" became interchangeable), she did not owe him a straight answer. That day she had dropped off the film and then she had sat at the drugstore counter to have a cup of coffee. She bought some cigarettes, though she had not smoked since high school. She smoked one mentholated cigarette and then threw the pack away in a garbage container outside the drugstore. Her mouth still felt cool inside.

He asked if she had planned anything for the weekend.

"No," she said.

"Let's do something you'd like to do. I'm a little ahead of myself in the lab right now."

That night they ate spaghetti and made plans, and the next day they went for a ride in the country, to a factory where wooden toys were made. In the showroom he made a bear marionette shake and twist. She examined a small rocking horse, rhythmically pushing her finger up and down on the back rung of the rocker to make it rock. When they left they took with them a catalogue of toys they could order. She knew that they would never look at the catalogue again. On their way to the museum he stopped to wash the car. Because it was the weekend there were quite a few cars lined up waiting to go in. They were behind a blue Cadillac that seemed to inch forward of its own accord, without a driver. When the Cadillac moved into the washing area, a tiny man hopped out. He stood on tiptoe to reach the coin box to start the washing machine. She doubted if he was five feet tall.

"Look at that poor son of a bitch," he said.

The little man was washing his car.

"If Andy could get out more," Larry said. "If he could get rid of that feeling he has that he's the only freak . . . I wonder if it wouldn't do him good to come spend a week with us."

"Are you going to take him in the wheelchair to the lab with you?" she said. "I'm not taking care of Andy all day."

His face changed. "Just for a week was all I meant," he said.

"I'm not doing it," she said. She was thinking of the boy, and the car. She had almost learned how to drive the car.

"Maybe in the warm weather," she said. "When we could go to the park or something."

He said nothing. The little man was rinsing his car. She sat inside when their turn came. She thought that Larry had no right to ask her to take care of Andy. Water flew out of the hose and battered the car. She thought of Andy, in the woods at night, stepping on the land mine, being blown into the air. She wondered if it threw him in an arc, so he ended up somewhere away from where he had been walking, or if it just blasted him straight up, if he went up the way an umbrella opens. Andy had been a wonderful ice skater. They all envied him his long sweeping turns, with his legs somehow neatly together and his body at the perfect angle. She never saw him have an accident on the ice. Never once. She had known Andy, and they had skated at Parker's pond, for eight years before he was drafted.

The night before, as she and Larry were finishing dinner, he had asked her if she intended to vote for Nixon or McGovern in the election. "McGovern," she said. How could he not have known that? She knew then that they were farther apart than she had thought. She hoped that on Election Day she could drive herself to the polls—not go with him and not walk. She planned not to ask the old lady if she wanted to come along because that would be one vote she could keep Nixon from getting.

At the museum she hesitated by the sculpture but did not point it out to him. He didn't look at it. He gazed to the side, above it, at a Francis Bacon painting. He could have shifted his eyes just a little and seen the sculpture, and her, standing and staring.

After three more lessons she could drive the car. The last two times, which were later in the afternoon than her first lesson, they stopped at the drugstore to get the old lady's paper, to save him from having to make the same trip back on foot. When he came out of the drugstore with the paper, after the final lesson, she asked him if he'd like to have a beer to celebrate.

"Sure," he said.

They walked down the street to a bar that was filled with college students. She wondered if Larry ever came to this bar. He had never said that he did.

She and Michael talked. She asked why he wasn't in high school. He told her that he had quit. He was living with his brother, and his brother was teaching him carpentry, which he had been interested in all along. On his napkin he drew a picture of the cabinets and bookshelves he and his brother had spent the last week constructing and installing in the house of two wealthy old sisters. He drummed the side of his thumb against the edge of the table in time with the music. They each drank beer, from heavy glass mugs.

"Mrs. Larsen said your husband was in school," the boy said. "What's he studying?"

She looked up, surprised. Michael had never mentioned her husband to her before. "Chemistry," she said.

"I liked chemistry pretty well," he said. "Some of it."

"My husband doesn't know you've been giving me lessons. I'm just going to tell him that I can drive the stick shift, and surprise him."

"Yeah?" the boy said. "What will he think about that?"

"I don't know," she said. "I don't think he'll like it."

"Why?" the boy said.

His question made her remember that he was sixteen. What she had said would never have provoked another question from an adult. The adult would have nodded or said, "I know."

She shrugged. The boy took a long drink of beer. "I thought it was funny that he didn't teach you himself, when Mrs. Larsen told me you were married," he said.

They had discussed her. She wondered why Mrs. Larsen wouldn't have told her that, because the night she ate dinner with her she had talked to Mrs. Larsen about what an extraordinarily patient teacher Michael was. Had Mrs. Larsen told him that Natalie talked about him?

On the way back to the car she remembered the photographs and went back to the drugstore and picked up the prints. As she took money out of her wallet she remembered that today was the day she would have to pay him. She looked around at him, at the front of the store, where he was flipping through magazines. He was tall and he was wearing a very old black jacket. One end of his long thick maroon scarf was hanging down his back.

"What did you take pictures of?" he said when they were back in the car.

"Furniture. My husband wanted pictures of our furniture, in case it was stolen."

"Why?" he said.

"They say if you have proof that you had valuable things, the insurance company won't hassle you about reimbursing you."

"You have a lot of valuable stuff?" he said.

"My husband thinks so," she said.

A block from the driveway she said, "What do I owe you?"

"Four dollars," he said.

"That's nowhere near enough," she said and looked over at him. He had opened the envelope with the pictures in it while she was driving. He was staring at the picture of her legs. "What's this?" he said.

She turned into the driveway and shut off the engine. She looked at the picture. She could not think what to tell him it was. Her hands and heart felt heavy.

"Wow," the boy said. He laughed. "Never mind. Sorry. I'm not looking at any more of them."

He put the pack of pictures back in the envelope and dropped it on the seat between them.

She tried to think what to say, of some way she could turn the pictures into a joke. She wanted to get out of the car and run. She wanted to stay, not to give him the money, so he would sit there with her. She reached into her purse and took out her wallet and removed four one-dollar bills.

"How many years have you been married?" he asked.

"One," she said. She held the money out to him. He said "Thank you" and leaned across the seat and put his right arm over her shoulder and kissed her. She felt his scarf bunched up against their cheeks. She was amazed at how warm his lips were in the cold car.

He moved his head away and said, "I didn't think you'd mind if I did that." She shook her head no. He unlocked the door and got out.

"I could drive you to your brother's apartment," she said. Her voice sounded hollow. She was extremely embarrassed, but she couldn't let him go.

He got back in the car. "You could drive me and come in for a drink," he said. "My brother's working."

When she got back to the car two hours later she saw a white parking ticket clamped under the windshield wiper, flapping in the wind. When she opened the car door and sank into the seat, she saw that he had left the money, neatly folded, on the floor mat on his side of the car. She did not pick up the money. In a while she started the car. She stalled it twice on the way home. When she had pulled into the driveway she looked at the money for a long time, then left it lying there. She left the car unlocked, hoping the money would be stolen. If it disappeared, she could tell herself that she had paid him. Otherwise she would not know how to deal with the situation.

When she got into the apartment, the phone rang.

"I'm at the gym to play basketball," Larry said. "Be home in an hour."

"I was at the drugstore," she said. "See you then."

She examined the pictures. She sat on the sofa and laid them out, the twelve of them, in three rows on the cushion next to her. The picture of the piano was between the picture of her feet and the picture of herself that she had shot by aiming into the mirror. She picked up the four pictures of their furniture and put them on the table. She picked up the others and examined them closely. She began to understand why she had taken them. She had photographed parts of her body, fragments of it, to study the pieces. She had probably done it because she thought so much about Andy's body and the piece that was gone—the leg, below the knee, on his left side. She had had two bourbon-and-waters at the boy's apartment, and drinking always depressed her. She felt very depressed looking at the pictures, so she put them down and went into the bedroom. She undressed. She looked at her body—whole, not a bad figure—in the mirror. It was an automatic reaction with her to close the curtains when she was naked, so she turned quickly and went to the window and did that. She went back to the mirror; the room was darker now and her body looked better. She ran her hands down her sides, wondering if the feel of her skin was anything like the way the sculpture would feel. She was sure that the sculpture would be smoother—her hands would move more quickly down the slopes of it than she wanted—that it would be cool, and that somehow she could feel the grayness of it. Those things seemed preferable to her hands lingering on her body, the imperfection of her skin, the overheated apartment. If she were the piece of sculpture and if she could feel, she would like her sense of isolation.

This was in 1972, in Philadelphia.

# La Petite Danseuse
# De Quatorze Ans

His father was Joseph Berridge, the painter. Her father was Horace Cragen, the poet (to be distinguished from Cragen the pianist, his brother Philip). They met in Cambridge, just after he had dropped out of Harvard at the end of the fall term. She was sharing a one room apartment with a girl who went to B.U. The girl was the one who introduced them; she had gone to high school with Griffin, and he had looked her up when he moved to Cambridge. In the short time since high school he had changed a great deal, and she no longer felt very comfortable with him. Had he not literally stumbled into her table, where she sat with Diana, just before Jacks bar closed, she would have avoided talking to him. She certainly would not have introduced him to Diana. She had nothing on her mind about introducing the children of famous men to one another—he pitched into her table, and when the boy he was with pushed him by the shoulders so that he slumped into a vacant chair at the table, she tried to make the best of the situation by pretending that he was not as drunk as he was by introducing him. Or perhaps part of the lurch into the table was show to begin with: outside, he had not been too drunk to ask for, and scribble down, Diana's phone number. "I lost yours," he said to Louise. "I know hers is the same, but if I don't have yours—" Griffin's friend clapped his hand around his neck and began to move him away from the two girls. "His father's Joseph Berridge," Louise said to Diana when they turned to begin the walk back to their apartment. "And Griffin decided to be fucked up about it all of a sudden and dropped out of Harvard. I think he's faking—I knew him in high school, and there was nothing wrong with him. When he got here he started drinking and not going to classes. He's just doing it to spite his father."

Louise answered the phone when Griffin called. She said, "One moment," and handed the phone to Diana and went into the kitchen. She thought that Griffin had a nasty streak, and had even in high school, when he was usually fun to be with, and it irritated her that now he was pretending they were not even friends. On the phone he had only asked her formally to speak to Diana.

She listened as Diana hesitated, then agreed to see him over the weekend. She was glad that even though Diana was shy, when put in a bad position, she would fight for her rights. She thought that Diana could—and would probably have to—handle Griffin.

"We're going to the movies," Diana told Louise, coming into the kitchen and grinning like a girl who had just been asked on a first date.

"What are you going to see?"

She shrugged. "Whatever's at the movies."

Louise had to smile. Not to have smiled would have looked as if she were sulking.

Louise was average in height and a little overweight, with hair that was pretty and wavy, even though it was no special shade of brown. Next to Diana she looked almost petite; Diana was a little taller than five nine, and her hips and shoulders were broad, so that people thought of her as a big person, even though she was slender. When Diana was depressed, Louise remembered not to stand by a mirror with her. She had done that once, inadvertently, walked up to Diana slumped in the hallway and tried to cheer her by insisting that she was pretty and Diana had turned and stood facing forward, next to Louise, the mirror in front of them, and said simply, "See?" Louise had seen. Mirrors seemed to distort Diana's body in some way, so that she actually did look taller than she was.

The "Griffin Berridge" that Diana scrawled on the bathroom mirror with lipstick was a real shock to Louise. And because she knew the message had not been left for her, she did not know whether it was all right to wash it off. She decided to be good-humored about it—even though it was her tube of lipstick.

On Saturday they went to the movies, and on Sunday afternoon he drove to her apartment in his black Volvo. It was a first-floor apartment, so Diana went to the window when the honking started. Diana thought it was hilarious that he sat outside blowing the horn, and grabbed her sweater and keys, and calling goodbye to Louise, ran to the car.

They went to the Museum of Fine Arts, and kept getting lost as they searched for the modern paintings. He said that Monet's haystacks were his favorites. He knew so much more than she about all the paintings, but had she not commented or occasionally asked a question, she was sure he would have said nothing. She asked how he knew so much, forgetting, momentarily, who his father was, and he told her that instead of bedtime stories, he had heard about the lives of painters.

"And my father read me Blake's poetry to put me to sleep," she said. "When I was very young, the *Songs of Innocence* and *Experience*. When I was a little older—six, maybe—he jumped right into *The Marriage of Heaven and Hell*."

"Yeah," he said. "That's hardly a normal childhood."

She was a little startled by how quickly he answered, cutting her off, because from the fond way she spoke about Blake she thought that Griffin understood that those memories were pleasant.

"He used to roller-skate with me," she said—wondering herself at the *non sequitur,* saying it only to let Griffin know how pleasant and interesting a relationship she had had with her father.

"My father used to compensate like mad, too. He'd go on tirades against Kandinsky, actually standing over my shoulder and pointing to tiny spots of color with a pencil, when he knew I didn't give a damn. Then the next minute he'd be pulling a baseball cap on my head and throwing me my catcher's mitt, wanting us to go off to the game. My mother thought that was so wonderful, but I knew he didn't care about baseball, and that he was suspicious because I liked it so much."

They wandered into another room of paintings, and she went up to a piece of sculpture she had not noticed the other time she came to the museum: a statue by Degas, of a young dancer, foot delicately extended, head held high, tilted back.

"Snob," he said.

"No she isn't. She's fourteen years old and she can dance, and she's proud."

He started to walk away.

"Not proud, I guess, but she feels regal. She can do something and she's poised for a moment before she moves."

"Are you kidding?" Griffin said.

"No. I'm serious."

"You really like that?"

"I like it a lot."

"Well, don't sound challenging. Is it an important issue?"

"You don't like it?" she said.

"No. I don't like it much."

They moved away, went to one of the seats in the room and sat down, looking at the large dark painting in front of them.

"I don't know why I spend so much time at museums," he said. "I thought that the minute I got away from home I'd never look at a painting if it wasn't in a book, but I end up here all the time."

She said nothing, wanting to look at the ballerina again, but not wanting to shut him out, either.

"That was quite a scene back in Rye, New York: my father always pretending to be happy when the Yankees had home games, my mother always pretending excitement about the different shows at the galleries in Manhattan, the dog probably pretending she enjoyed playing tug of war with the stick."

She said nothing. She was wondering if she could have been wrong—if he might have not liked roller-skating.

"It's freaky," he said. "That I'd end up taking a dive into the table of Horace Cragen's daughter."

She hated being spoken of as Horace Cragen's child. Her image of her father, which was always in the back of her mind when she was not actually thinking of him, dimmed a little. She moved her head to get the picture back: her father, in his baggy slacks and cardigan, smiling down at her, poised on the edge of her bed with his large hands turning the pages of a book as delicately as if the paper were feathers.

Her eyes came to rest on the sculpture.

"You like it," he said, looking at her looking at it, "becuase you were an aspiring ballerina when you were little. Right?"

"No," she said. "I never took dancing lessons."

"What did you do? You didn't have a treehouse and play touch football, did you?"

She laughed at the notion. No—her father had always seen to it that she wore a ribbon in her hair and that she was a feminine little girl; if she had taken dancing lessons, she would have been like the statue. But she told him that she had taken lessons in nothing. She had belonged to the Brownies, until she got sick of it, but you could not really call that taking lessons.

"Then tell me what you did," he said.

"Oh—I didn't do so much. I was very shy when I was a child. I stayed home a lot of the time." She smiled at him. He continued to look at her, not challenging, but interested: he wanted more. "I went sleigh-riding in the winter and I roller-skated a lot—sometimes at roller rinks. My father and I used to play tennis."

"But you weren't a little ballerina, huh?"

"No," she said.

"They made me go to dancing class. Ballroom dancing. Can you imagine that? They wanted me to be a proper gentleman. My father always used to wear a jacket to dinner. He even painted in an old paint-smeared corduroy jacket. We went to the ball game and I'd wear my baseball cap and he'd sit beside me in his sport coat, with one of those porkpie hats on. It used to embarrass the hell out of me. He must have been embarrassed, too, to have been so handsome and to have such an ordinary-looking son. What he wore looked stylish, and whatever I wore looked wrong. At the time, I thought his hat was embarrassing, but he looked good in it—he was the sort of man who can look *more* serious because he's wearing something silly and it doesn't look funny on him. Do you know what I mean? He was six feet tall, and here I am, not even as tall as you."

She felt uneasy again; she hated to have her height talked about. She had been a tall child, and that was part of her reason for being so shy. What she had always wanted was to fade in, to be like everybody else.

When they left the museum he talked no more about his father, or her father. She was glad, because some of the things he had said had disturbed her. And then when he kissed her, at the bottom of the museum steps, she smiled widely. She had started to be depressed, and then he had made her forget it.

Neither of them was sure it was not a mistake, but still they decided before Christmas to live together. Louise, who suspected it would happen, already knew a person who would share the apartment. Diana had made it clear that she would not move out until Louise could find someone to take her place, but that was accomplished quickly, much to Diana's joy and Louise's dismay. Louise had even spent a Saturday loading books into cartons and taking them by car to Griffin's apartment.

When Diana and Griffin got back from New York, where they had gone to the wedding of Griffin's good friend Charlie to a girl named Inez, they were going to stop at Louise's and pick up Diana's clothing. Everything else had been moved out. Driving back, Louise felt sure that Griffin would send Diana alone. It must be, she thought, that he knew she disapproved of his leaving school and drinking, that she did not like it when he called her when he got to town, and then saw her once and never called again. She did not think he was a nice person anymore, and she hoped that he would not be unkind to Diana.

For Christmas, Diana and Griffin went to Rye to stay with his parents, and on Christmas Day drove into the city to have dinner with her parents. Both places were loud and festive, with relatives from both sides sizing up the new person: Chopin waltzes were played at Griffin's house as the family sipped afternoon wine, and at Diana's parents' apartment in the Village the radio was tuned to the *Messiah,* and Caroline—her fa-

vorite aunt—gave them a bottle of champagne and tall
etched pink glasses and made them promise that they
would visit her at her farm in Pennsylvania.

Above the mantle hung a poem of Horace Cragen's,
hand-lettered on parchment and framed in an old wal-
nut frame—a gift to Horace from Diana's mother. The
poem was lovely, but as she admired it she also had
the uneasy feeling that her mother should have given
her father something else. Was it appropriate to—in
a sense—give someone back what he had already
given?

She wondered, at dinner, what her family thought
of Griffin. She knew that her mother did not approve
of her living with him, but she also knew that her
mother would not allude to it. And her father? She
looked at him across the table, eating roast goose,
seeming happy but preoccupied, as he so often did. He
had asked if the Griffin Berridge she was dating (he
called it "dating") was Joe Berridge's son. He had called
him Joe, so naturally she had asked if he knew him.
"No," he had said. "Know of him." In conversation he
did not mind speaking bluntly: his poems, though, were
full of surprises and confusions. No matter how many
poems were framed and hung in the house, she understood that where her father really lived was not there,
but somewhere in the cloudy, starry world of poetry.
"How is the roast goose?" her mother asked. "It's fine
with me," her father replied. She and Griffin and Caroline nodded assent. "Very good," Griffin said. Her
mother nodded approval, and again they cut their meat
and ate. The meal was more restrained than usual—
because Griffin was there?

"What was wrong?" she asked. They were walking
down Fifth Avenue, having wandered far from the
apartment after dinner. She had asked it not so much
because she was convinced that Griffin was bothered
by something, but rather because she was wondering
aloud.

"Nothing's wrong. You don't like it when I'm moody, and when I'm not you act as though I am."

"I didn't mean to criticize you. I was wondering aloud, really. That's all I meant."

"Was it like other Christmases?"

"No. It was quieter."

"Do they usually get along?"

"Who?" she said.

"Your mother and father."

"They've always gotten along."

He was swinging her hand, answering but not paying too much attention to the conversation.

"They're always like that?" he said.

"Yes."

"Then they don't get along. Or they get along, but there's something wrong."

"What's wrong?" she said, trying to remember if it was true that they always acted that way.

"It's obvious, isn't it? He's a famous man and she's his wife, and she's in awe of him but also resents him."

For the first time she lifted her head from staring at the sidewalk to look at him.

"Let's not be serious on Christmas," he said.

"I'm sorry," she said.

Later, on the walk home, she thought uncomfortably about her response to Griffin. It had been too deferential. Her mother, all her life, had been too deferential to her father. As they walked farther she thought that there was some logic to that at least: her father was Horace Cragen. But Griffin was only Griffin, and he shouldn't declare her moods. Sorry that she had said she was sorry, she eased her hand out of his and plunged it into the deep silk-lined pocket of her coat.

They had just begun to live together.

In February her father sent her a new poem. Much of it she did not understand, but the allusions to their days roller-skating—the parts of the poem about her—

she understood well. She left it on the table, with the morning mail, along with the letter from her father.

"What's this?" he said, sitting at the kitchen table and trying to rub some life into his body. He had gotten little sleep, in spite of the fact that it was almost eleven o'clock, because he had gone to a jazz club with his friend Tony and then gone drinking at another friend's apartment after the bars closed.

"Go ahead and read it," she answered.

When he had come back at four in the morning, drunk, they had quarreled: hadn't he said he wouldn't drink to get drunk anymore? Didn't he think she might worry—couldn't he have called? He picked up the poem and read it, and then the letter, too. The letter asked her if she would come to her father's favorite cousin's remarriage on February 25—just the time she and Griffin had planned to visit friends up north.

"So what are you telling him?" he said. He shook the coffee jar but did not get up to make coffee.

"I think I should go, if you don't mind delaying the trip a week."

"Charlie and Inez will have to be out of the house then. They only rent it for February. The weekend after that is March."

"I'm sorry," she said, "but I still think I ought to go. I haven't seen them since Christmas, and he's been depressed because his back has been bothering him."

"I haven't seen my parents since Christmas either."

"I get along with my parents, and you don't get along with yours."

"Oh, I don't know about that," he said. "I sit like a stone with my parents, and you sit like a stone with yours."

"That's untrue! What are you talking about?"

"Forget it," he said. "Go to the wedding. I'm going to Charlie and Inez's."

"Since you prefer getting drunk to being with me, I don't see why you're sulking."

"Because I'm sorry for you, goddamn it. Because he's

ordering you around, and I don't like that. Because he sent that sentimental poem about his baby girl, and after stroking her with the pen stabbed her in the heart and told her to come home."

She looked at him to see if he could be serious. He looked very serious.

"You're wrong," she said.

"You are," he said.

He went into the bedroom and dressed, and left the apartment without saying goodbye. Either he was crazy, or she was crazy. And *she* was sorry for *him*—he had looked so sick when he came into the kitchen. He had been sick from the night before. Since he was not there to talk to, she talked to herself. Through clenched teeth she said, "They are a poem and a letter." She took them both with her when she went back to the bedroom and stretched out on the still-unmade bed. She did not go to class.

March was a good month for them, and April was, too, until late in the month when he lost his job at the library. His friend Tony got him a job selling shoes, and he needed the money (he no longer would accept anything from his parents), but he found the job unbearable. All day women would come in and try to fit into shoes that were too small and that the store did not have in their size, and Griffin was supposed to tell them that he would take the shoes in the back and put them on the shoe stretcher. The shoe stretcher was a mop handle which he inserted in the shoe, then whomped down hard: the pressure would break the lining in the shoe, and the women would have a fraction of an inch more room. Tony, who worked in the store part-time and was always stoned, thought it was hilarious. But after a week Griffin was miserable and began to drink again—this time topping off the evening by smoking grass with Tony. He went back to the apartment and fought with her, and she went into a rage, throwing clothes into a suitcase, saying that she was not going to live with him any longer. But she looked back and saw him, pale-faced and probably sorry for what he had said—he told her so often that he was sorry for blaming her for things she couldn't help and to please forgive him—and she threw the things from the suitcase to the floor, shaking her head at him and at herself: if she was leaving, why would she take the Equadorian sweater but not a nightgown? Throwing things so randomly into the suitcase, she could not even have appeared serious to him about going.

"I think about what my father did to me—about how he implied it was all right not to consider women's feelings—the way he was to my mother, taking her along, taking her hand the same way he took mine—on *his* outings. And it's no wonder it's taking me so long to know how to act."

He lit a cigarette. When he drank, or was hung-over, he had begun to smoke cigarettes.

"You're obsessed with your father," she said. Before, she had screamed that, but now it was such a familiar line that she said it quietly, perturbed but stating the obvious. "Forget about your father and live your life."

"You know that can't be done," he said. "You know it. You know it when you pick up a magazine and read your father's poetry, or when you see his picture in a bookstore window. And I know it when I read interviews with my father, when he sends me brochures about gallery openings and I read about the facts of his life. You know that you can't forget that."

She stood amid the scattered clothes, wondering if it could be true.

They broke up in May, but it didn't last. Griffin went to stay with Tony but came back at the end of the week, and she agreed to try again. He came back sober and, he said, sorry for being the cause of so much of their unhappiness. She could tell even as he spoke that he still believed she did not realize how much her father had her under his thumb, but if he would only not say that, then she knew she could stand it.

She was surprised when, in June, he told her he wanted to marry her. Their relationship had always been up and down, and when he came back after their separation they did not come together with the closeness they had had early on. So she tried to tell him no as gently as possible.

"God," he said. "Your loyalty is still with him."

"Don't start that," she said. "Please."

"It's so easy for me to see. It's so clear, and sometimes I know you see it. I know you do, and sometimes you've even agreed with me. If you see it, then break away. Break the tie."

"Griffin, I haven't called or written my father for nearly a month."

"But you don't have to. That's what's so insidious about it. During that month he reminded you of who he was and how he was because his long poem was printed in the magazine you subscribe to. He was on your mind, even if you didn't call, even if he didn't call you. Jesus—at least admit the truth."

"What do you want me to say? That I hate my father?"

"Admit you'll never leave him—or you'll leave him for somebody he approves of. Some man he'll find for you."

"Griffin, he has never told me who to date."

"He has to approve, though, doesn't he? And he doesn't approve of me, does he? Did he like me there at Christmas, eating roast goose across the table from him, sitting next to his only daughter in his classy Village apartment? Did you think he radiated warmth?"

"He had just met you," she said.

"And did he want to meet me again? You got the phone calls. Did he?"

"He's never told me who to bring there and who—"

"He didn't. Just give a simple answer."

"Don't tell me how to answer you. Answer yourself if you know all the answers."

"Please," he said, bowing his head and coming toward her with his arms outstretched. "Do you think I asked you to marry me because I hate you? Do you think I'm saying this because I only want to hurt? I've been through this too. Once you face it, you can get away from it."

"I'm not going to let you make me hate my father," she said. She was so confused, wondering now what her father had thought, why even her mother had not said what he thought. But maybe her father and mother weren't getting along—Griffin had said they weren't—and it had to be true that he was not saying these things because he hated her. He was standing and holding her, very sad; he was a least doing what he thought was right.

"It's all so simple," he said. His arms closed around her.

These were the things in their apartment: a sofa with two usable cushions, the other cushion ripped to shreds; one large pillow for floor seating; draperies at the window left by the former tenants; a kitchen table and two chairs, one of which always needed gluing; a bed in the bedroom and a bureau they shared. Nothing else. The clutter was not the result of trying to cram large furniture into small spaces, but piles of books, clothers, shoes and boots. They threw out little, keeping almost all the mail, stacked first into piles of a dozen envelopes or so, the piles later cascading, being walked over—letters getting littered across the floor. So when they were in the apartment and wanted to be close to each other, they gravitated toward the bed, the sofa with two cushions too small to stretch on comfortably.

Tonight they were on the bed—he at the far end, his feet under her thigh for warmth, she with a pillow behind her head, looking down at him. She was recovering from a cold and did not have much energy.

She had been asleep when he came in, but had roused herself to ask about his day, to talk to another human being in the hopes that if she stopped drifting in and out of sleep, she might feel less sick. He had gone out with Tony two nights before and had come home sober. She had been grateful and happy, sure that he was changing. He hardly ever talked about Joseph Berridge, and she wondered if she had finally gotten through to him. But, to keep peace, she hardly ever mentioned Horace Cragen either, and she felt ridiculous omitting mention of someone she cared for and thought about. Her mother had sent her a letter saying that his back still bothered him, after two doctor appointments, and that he was not working well, and growing despondent. She had meant to call, but each time she thought of it Griffin was in the apartment.

"If you got a job," he said, "with my dividend checks and my job, and your income, too, you wouldn't have to take money from him."

She held up a hand, palm toward him, to tell him to stop talking. His words flowed right through it.

"And you're being childish not to do it," he said.

"You don't want me to take my parents' money, and you drive around in a new Volvo your father gave you," she said.

Whether because she was sick and he was sorry for her, or because she had just effectively silenced him, he said nothing more. In retrospect, she would continue to think just what she thought at the time: that he had shrugged off what she said. When he and Tony, drunk again, were in the accident—when Griffin, going thirty miles over the limit, went off the road and crashed the Volvo into a tree, she did not even think of their conversation in the bed two nights before. Tony was cut and scraped; Griffin, with a broken arm and a concussion, was pulled out of the car by Tony. She got the call about the accident from the hospital. She had no money to get a cab to go get him, so she called Louise. "Let him wrestle with his own demons," Louise said, her own foot heavy on the pedal. "I'm glad you weren't in the car." That must have been what started her thinking about the conversation in which she accused him of accepting the car from his parents. But surely crashing it into a tree at high speed was an extreme response. He seemed almost desperately happy to see her, and was very polite to Louise, thanking her over and over for putting herself out for him. He did not seem disturbed—not disturbed the way a person who crashes into a tree would act. It was probably foolish to keep wondering if it had been deliberate. But if it had been, she should be more careful about what she said to him. He was more upset than she knew, if it had been deliberate. She would have asked him if he meant it to happen, but he seemed so peaceful after the accident that she didn't speak. She was also afraid that he would admit to doing it to spite her, even if the car had really gone out of control. He was sneaky sometimes—or a better way to put it was that he was an actor: Louise had been right the time she told her who Griffin Berridge was when she said that he *decided* to be fucked up about his father's fame.

A week later when her mother called, she felt guilty for not having called or written. She told her mother about Griffin's car accident, by way of explanation, and her mother said only, "I'm sorry." Her mother was calling to tell her that her father was suffering, that he would not take the pain pills the doctor had given him because they made his mind fuzzy, but that he couldn't work or, some days, even go out, because the disc in his back bothered him so. She said that she had thought that Diana's coming home might cheer him—or perhaps Diana could talk him into taking the pills.

Alarmed, she called the airline, forgetting she could not reserve a seat on the shuttle, even before she spoke to Griffin. Then she went into the bedroom and told him she had to go home, and why. She hoped that it would not result in a tirade—that for once he would be reasonable and see it as the simple situation it was.

He said, "That's where your parents live. This is home," and went back to his reading.

Her father was not very pleasant to her, which surprised her and disappointed her mother, she knew. He was glad to see her, but brooded that his wife had summoned her, when she had a life of her own. Did he protest too much—could he be doing it to make his wife feel badly? Diana was ashamed for wondering. Here was her father, depressed and hurting, and she was wondering if mind games were being played.

She stayed for three days, and once each day—as much as she thought he would tolerate—she tried to talk him into taking the pills. When, at the end of the third day, he still would not, she resented his iron will, his thundering "I will not!," which made her back off, so far that she backed over the threshold to the living room, where she found her mother weeping. "He's so damn stubborn," her mother said, brushing away the tears. And it was not like her mother ever to disagree with her father; when her mother disagreed, you knew it by her blank face.

That night, when she left, a neighbor drove her to the airport. His name was Peter Jenkins—everyone called him Jenkins—and he could afford to live in the Village because of the money he got when his parents were killed in a plane crash. She could not remember how she got that information, but from the time she was small she had known it, and because people in the neighborhood talked about it often, she was able now to understand that they liked Jenkins, but they also looked down on him. Even calling him by his last name indicated that he was a little apart from them.

All Peter Jenkins wanted to talk about was her father (a great man, he always said—talented and also kind) and his difficulties, and what difficulties she might be having adjusting to life in Boston. She felt hypocritical presenting her life as interesting and peaceful. She knew that he would want to hear the truth, and she did not mean to be condescending to him—it was just that she did not want to think about the truth herself. She was doing badly in school and the man she lived with might have deliberately smashed up his car, and she had found her father remote, obstinate, wanting sympathy rather than help. She had felt sorry for her mother.

"Ever go rowing on the Charles?" he asked, weaving through traffic.

She told him she hadn't.

"You jog?" he said. "Last time I was there it looked like a marathon was going on, there were so many people running."

She said that she didn't run.

"If you ran, you might make it to the airport faster than I'm getting you there."

"Don't worry about that," she said. "If I miss one flight I can get another."

When they got to the airport he smiled at her and got out to lift her bag to the sidewalk.

"You take care," he said. "Everything's going to work out all right."

"Thank you very much for bringing me," she said.

To fill an awkward moment of silence he said, "You know, your father is really a fine man. I don't understand every word of what he writes, but God—the tone of those poems—the mood he can create. And he never has his head in the clouds. The week before he got sick he came around to see if he couldn't steady the ladder for me so I could fix the shutter on the second floor that had blown loose in the storm."

She thanked him again and walked into the airport. She was sad to leave with nothing resolved. She was depressed because she knew Griffin was going to be waiting with some sarcastic comment, or something to be said in the guise of enlightening her. She was going back to Griffin, and everything in that world seemed so complicated, yet so vague, and the man who had just brought her to the airport was so nice and sensible. But

neither did it cross her mind to get something going
with Peter Jenkins. Griffin was, as Louise had said,
obsessed with his own demons, and that did not make
it easy to live with him, but she respected that intensity. In the long run, someone like Griffin was important, in spite of his faults. Peter Jenkins was even a
little dull, although he was a very kind and caring
man. If she had had to talk to him longer than the car
ride, what would she have said?

Getting into the plane, she thought she might have
asked him for help—or made some move toward him,
to break his exterior. Then she settled into her seat,
convinced her thoughts were crazy—she was imagining
a whole situation in her mind that did not, and would
not, exist. She was like Griffin.

No one, including Horace Cragen, imagined he
would die. When they operated they found a malignant
tumor, and the cancer had already spread through his
lymphatic system. Diana had not even gone to New
York for the operation. She had talked to him the day
before he was hospitalized, and tried to cheer him by
promising to go with him to Paris in the spring, to a
conference he wanted to attend. Before the operation
he had started to care again about poetry, and an old
friend—another famous poet who was the subject of a
week-long conference in Paris in June—had invited
Horace to attend with him. And Horace Cragen did go
to the conference, taking along his medicine and check-
ing in with an American doctor. When Diana and her
mother showed delight with his progress and told him
they would both go with him to Paris, he said—and not
even nicely—that he would go with William, alone.

William, besieged by reporters and having had
enough of listening to himself talked about, having
shaken enough hands, left Paris for the States two days
before Horace was to leave. Horace waited two days,
did not cancel his flight, talked in the morning to a
reporter and gave him information about his youth

with William at Princeton, ordered dinner to be sent to his room, ate it, then shot himself in the head, the radio playing music he did not understand because he had adamantly refused to learn French.

"Oh, parley-voo and fuck these Frogs," Horace had said to William as they stood in the lobby of the big hotel, William having checked out and lingering for a final cigarette before he left for Charles de Gaulle Airport. William had laughed at that; Horace had been profane in his youth, but he had become—both of them had become—so dignified, so cultured. William himself did not even use bad language, with the exception of "goddamn it." Or, as Horace told the interviewer who came two days later, on the morning of the day he was to kill himself, "He became a gentleman." The interviewer, wondering if Cragen's phrasing was not perhaps a subtle way to indicate something about the other poet's character, and used to interviewing writers who knifed other writers in the back, wrote simply that Horace Cragen considered William Duvall a true gentleman. He took the last photograph of Horace Cragen alive. Cragen was pictured, thin from his recent medical treatments but still strikingly handsome, sitting in a tufted chair in the hotel lobby, an uncharacteristic cigarette in his hand. (The pack was given to him by William, who said that now that he was leaving the tension behind, he was leaving the cigarettes too—Horace Cragen reached out and took them and, to William's surprise, lit one. Then they embraced for a slap on the back, shook hands, and William left for the airport.)

Back in the States, William did not even hear the news the day it happened. He heard it days later and flew to New York. The apartment was full of mourners, including Diana and Griffin, and the only order was kept by Peter Jenkins, who, after a little time had passed in which the mourners expressed their sorrow to the family, would walk up to them and thank them kindly for coming, and slowly edge them toward the door. Peter Jenkins did not do that to William Duvall, or to a couple of other old friends. They sat with Diana and Griffin, in silence mostly, and stared about the room as if the ceiling might go at any second, or the floor. Most of them seemed to be betting on the floor.

Griffin took Diana for a walk when Peter Jenkins suggested it. Peter took Diana's mother for a walk, too, putting her sweater around her and leading her, unprotesting, out the door. They locked the apartment and went outside, Peter indicating to Griffin that he was walking left and that he and Diana should go right. Griffin, shocked by the death and still remembering Diana's first cry of pain, was very glad that Peter Jenkins was there to manage instead of him. He did everything the man said, and hoped that Diana would stay as calm as she had become. He meant to do nothing wrong—he had left town with her, even though he thought it meant he would lose his job. He intended only kindness, but walking down the street and seeing her sorrow, and thinking that he understood its peculiar quality, he said to her that one time when his own father had been ill with hepatitis and he had seen him losing strength, he had been amazed that as his father lost weight, as he got slighter in the hospital bed, he had nevertheless grown larger in proportion. "It was as though even in death—and although nobody else thought it, at least I thought he was dying—he was becoming larger than life, rather than shrinking. He was a famous man, and that was getting *more* intense, he was . . ."

"Shut up, you son of a bitch," she said. "You don't understand anything, and I'm not going to let you rage against my father the day after he's been buried."

He looked at her, shocked that she would call him that, sorry for having said the wrong thing. She had let go of his arm and stood there, her face firm and challenging, and he could see that she did not want to do anything more than kill him. He looked at the sidewalk and muttered an apology, reached again for her arm. She snapped it to her side and began to walk, and he walked at her side, thinking, for the first time, My God—she's bigger than I am. He looked up at her, a large girl, even taller than usual in the high-heeled black boots she had worn to the funeral. She would never understand. Horace Cragen *had* been larger than life, he was right about that, and she was larger than life too, though she would never admit it. Didn't his own father disparage the constant photo-taking, the constant reporting on, analysis of, his work? Great men didn't want to think they were great all the time—only when they needed confidence, or when they felt like playing the role. But he squinted hard here: she was not great in that she was accomplished, she was just large and silent—her father and not her father.

He squinted again, this time looking at her: she had admitted that she was shy as a child. He was that way, too, and he understood it: he had quit Harvard because he did not want to let people know he was bright and talented, just another rich man's son making it big. He would rather be passive, lie low, carry out the pointed-toe shoes to the fan-shaped feet of the women who came into the store. It was no wonder she had admired the statue so—she had envied the young dancer, poised to take her step. Like him, Diana had no clear ambition. He knew more than he ever had before, and he wanted to explain it to her, but there was no way to do it. She was walking ahead of him, still furious. He trailed beside her, but her face was set. If a man walking along had not touched Griffin's sleeve to ask what time it was, the intensity of his own thoughts might not have been interrupted and he might have continued to walk with her—she clearly did not know where she was going, but was getting breathless going there—across the city for even longer. Griffin looked at his watch and was shocked to see that they had already been walking for almost two hours, that he must get her back to the apartment.

She lived with Griffin in the month following her father's death, not hating him for his problems or even for what he had said so coldly on the walk in New York to leave him instantly, but unhappy still, in spite of their occasional compatibility and even happiness, now knowing she would have to leave soon. She asked Louise if she would be able to stay with her and her roommate until she could find an apartment to share, and Louise, of course, said yes.

Since coming back, she had had recurring dreams: grotesque in their comicness, dreams clearly planted in her mind by Griffin (the way her mother had planted the word "home" and she had innocently repeated it to him) in which she would approach her father's tombstone and it would grow higher and higher, blocking everything from her view. She would finally be standing before a wall of total gray, and this is the point in the dream at which she would wake up. Lately the dream had become even more horrible, with a loud noise—a confusion of voices—that augmented as the tombstone rose: the voice of her father reading fragments from his long poem, the voices of a Lion and a Wolf talking with human voices, a shout from Lyca, even the landscape of the cemetery—the softly-out-of-focus bushes but the bright tall sunflowers bordering the path she walked to her father's headstone—all put in her head by her father.

Her father had told her that she didn't do well in literature classes because she knew more than the teachers; Griffin told her that because her father was a literary man, naturally she resisted competing with him. Why did Griffin stubbornly insist that her father was such a dominant force in her life? He had been a gentle man, not overbearing at all, the man she skated with in the warm weather, who brushed her hair and told her bedtime stories like any father. But then why—if he had not been that force—why the nightmares? Because anyone would have nightmares when a parent died. Louise had said so.

She told Griffin she was leaving, and he was very unhappy. So unhappy that he rose from the bed before her—she heard the faint music from the other room when she awoke from the nightmare and reached out to touch only tangled blankets. She listened and could pick it up faintly: "Little boy lost, he takes himself so seriously . . ." And she pursed her lips until she realized that this time she was making too much of it; he would surely not have been able to time the singing of that phrase with her awakening if he had wanted to. So she went out to the living room and put her arms around him.

She saw him hardly at all after she left, then not at all, and when he called her in late September she was surprised to hear that he was back at Harvard. She knew from Louise that he had called there wanting to find out about her—he had called drunk one night and demanded that Louise tell him if she had another boyfriend.

"I'm sorry," Diana sighed. "What did you say?"

"I didn't want to say no, so I hinted that you did."

"That was silly. You should have just said that I didn't."

"You will," Louise said. "You will."

"I don't want a boyfriend," Diana said. "I just want to be left alone."

"You're still upset about your father," Louise said, laying her hand on Diana's in sympathy.

And it was only because she knew Louise meant to be kind that she didn't yank away her hand. How many times would she have to endure hearing how her father's life and her father's death had to do with her life?

Not long after hearing from Louise about Griffin's call, he called her himself. She was going to berate him for drinking and for bothering her friend, but thought better of it. He had said enough to her, and she had said enough to him—she should just let it go.

She was glad that she had not criticized him for anything when he said that he was back in school, with money on loan from his mother. She was glad that he had gone back—she thought that he was wasting his time working, and had told him that all along. She was glad she had not been critical (and would not be critical, as he would have been, about the semantics of taking money from his mother but not from his father) because he sounded happy, and he seemed to know he had made a sensible decision. He had called her for approval, and she gave it to him. He had also called to see if she would have dinner with him, and she said that she would.

"Do you have night classes Monday?" he asked.

"I don't have any classes. I'm working on Newbury Street from nine to five, and I love it. I go home at night and read a book or go to the movies."

"You're kidding," he said.

"No. I know it's ironic, your going back to Harvard and my dropping out of school, but you made the right decision, and I did too. I wasn't getting anything out of it."

"Christ," he said. "You didn't make the right decision."

She let that go, too. The last thing she wanted was another argument with him.

The dinner was nice: the food was good, he had only one glass of wine, and it made her a little sad that she was no longer with him. She knew that she had done something to him that she had not meant to do—she knew it at the time, when she awoke to hear him listening to sad songs late at night. But it was inadvertent—at least she could say that; he had continued his drinking and badgering her, when he knew she could not stand it, but she had only lingered with him a little time before deciding to go. And now that she was gone, he seemed better. She was so glad that he had gone back to school. They left the restaurant and took a walk before she went back to her apartment and he went back to his when, swinging her hand and speaking very kindly, he said, "I guess Louise told you what I did. My apologies to you for acting so stupid, but no apologies to her—if anything, it put a little excitement in her life."

"She's a nice person," Diana said. "Why don't you care about her feelings?"

"I do—it's just that we're so different that we can't come close to understanding each other. Look, it's simple: Louise didn't have a famous father, so she doesn't know what it's like. I've missed you so much because we could talk, we could know things and not have to say them, couldn't we?"

She could not believe that he had said that. And because he had ruined her evening, she spoke without thinking that it did no good to argue. "No, Griffin. All our time together should have taught you that I didn't agree with you, that we didn't have that common bond."

"You know we did," her persisted. "The nightmares told you that, didn't they? That wasn't me putting thoughts in your head; that was your head telling thoughts to you."

"Why did you call to put me through this again?"

"Because you have to know it. You have to know that it's all right, and that you've got me—you can have me again in a second—that you can work through it. He's going to vanish. He might expand from a tombstone to a tower, but eventually the tower will topple. But don't give in—don't quit school and not come back to me. Don't—"

"Stop it!" she said, so loudly that people turned to stare at them.

"Please," he said, taking her arm. "I didn't tell you that day in New York when Peter sent us off on a walk, but I thing about it every day, and it's still clear in my head and I can still tell you about it."

"Tell me what?" she said. She began to wonder, as she had after the car crash, as she did so often when they argued, if he might really be crazy.

"What I was trying to say before: that your father's dead—"

She threw off his arm and ran, praying he wouldn't follow. And by the time she had gone several blocks she felt free, his voice had stopped ringing in her head. She looked back, thinking that she would see him, but she had left him behind. She had missed him, in spite of his obsession, and it angered her that that was so, because of what he had just done. She remembered what her father had told her one time when she came home crying from grade school because she wasn't selected to be on anybody's team: "It's hard, but that's what life is like, and you're very special, so you'll see that sooner. You know, I'm an outsider too—if I hadn't been a poet, I wouldn't have been fit for much of anything else. And even outsiders hate other outsiders: poets hate novelists, painters look down on sculptors . . . " The rest of what he said was blurry, but she remembered the feel of his hand on her shoulder, felt it there as she moved down the street and walked more than twenty blocks home because as she looked down at the sidewalk, remembering, she didn't think to take a bus or a cab—she just kept putting one foot in front of the other, as the sidewalk kept lengthening.

# Octascope

We live in a house divided into five rooms, heated by a wood stove. When Carlos finished building his house, a friend gave him furniture: three beds, so there are three bedrooms and a living room and a bathroom. In one of the bedrooms is a refrigerator and a sink and a hotplate on top of cinder blocks.

The marionette-maker, Carlos, supports us. IIis friends Nickel and Dime come by and leave cigarettes and fiddle strings and Jordan almonds (lint-specked from the pockets of their flannel shirts). The baby puts all of these things in her mouth, and when she has nothing else, sucks her finger until the corner of her mouth is raw. She sleeps on a mat by the wood stove, far enough away so that the cats are closest to the warmth. The cats, five of them, belonged to Dime, but one by one Dime brought them to live with us. There is also an old mutt, thirteen years old, part hound and part coyote, legend has it, with a missing tail. This dog is devoted to the baby as is the sleek gray cat, who looks too noble to be in this house, but whose specialty is killing bats.

Nickel's real name is Nick. His best friend, Dominic, had been nicknamed Dime before he met Nick. Because they were best friends, the rest of the joke seemed inevitable.

Nickel brought me here to live. I was living with my aunt, and the baby, and waitressing the night shift at a restaurant. I lived with her when I was pregnant and for nearly a year after the baby was born, with her caring for the baby while I worked, until she told me she was getting married.

Nick came for me in his old Mercedes, with a velvet-covered, foam-padded board for a front seat, and drove us to Carlos' house. All the time I was hoping he'd tell me to come to his house—that his large, scarred hand would shyly slip into mine, and that I would go with him. The wind chimes dangled from the handle of the glove compartment and the baby kept lunging for them. Our cat was in the back seat, pacing, meowing. She didn't like living with the gray cat and ran away our first week at Carlos' house. Inside the car were little square mirrors. There was a full moon, and when the trees were not dense along the road I could cock my head and see my profile in the mirror glued on the passenger-side window, or bend forward to take the chimes out of the baby's sticky fist and see my eyes in the mirror on the dashboard. Nick was grumbling about what a bad thing it was that the Mass was no longer said in Latin. The front left headlight had burned out, and he smoked grass and drove seventy all the way there. No cop had ever stopped the car.

I first met Nick at the restaurant about a month

before. He was there trying to sober up Dominic. It was
the end of my shift. When I got off, I went out to my
aunt's car, which I parked in the field behind the place,
and saw the two of them, in the Mercedes, doors thrown
open, weeping. Dominic was alcohol-sick, and Nick was
sick of being called from bars to round him up. I talked
to them, and pretty soon we started to laugh. Dominic
passed out in the back seat, and Nick and I drove for
hours, going in circles, because he was a strange man
I had just met and I was afraid to go anywhere with
him. I told him about my baby, my aunt. He told me
that he had lived with a woman named Julie for seven
years. He had met her when he went to college in the
Hudson Valley in 1965. Her father gave them money.
They always had money. Every Valentine's day she cut
hearts out of red paper and wrote love messages on
them and glued them together in a circle, points touching. He took his hands off of the wheel, curling his
fingers and looking into the empty circle between them.
We went to a bar, had three drinks apiece and danced.
We went back to the car and he opened the door for me.
I sat down and put my hands beside me, bracing myself
already for his fast driving, and it shocked me to feel
the material: I was confused and thought that it was
something living that I was sitting on—soft, chilly
moss. The dome light came on again when his door
opened, and I looked down to see the royal-blue velvet.
In the back seat Dominic was very still, no expression
on his face, his hand cupped over his fly.

We drove a long way without speaking, until a big
black dog ran in front of the car.

"Do you have a dog?" I said.

He shook his head no. "Dime's got five cats."

"Does she really love you?"

"I don't know. I guess so."

"Should I stop asking questions?"

"I'm not giving very good answers."

"Aren't you afraid to drive so fast?"

"I used to work in the pits, repair race cars." He turned his scarred hand toward me. "I don't have any awe of cars.

"There," he said, pointing across a field. "That's where I live."

The silhouette of a big barn, no house nearby. No lights on in the barn.

"I could take you in," he said.

"No," I said, afraid for the first time. "I don't want to go in there."

"Neither do I," he said.

We drove to the end of that road and turned and began to climb a mountain. There were more stars, suddenly. Out of habit, I looked for the Big Dipper. It was as though the small mirror was a magnet—I kept looking into my own eyes.

We went to Dominic's house. There was no phone to call my aunt, and in my sleepy confusion, as I watched Nick load logs into the wood stove, I held my hand over my heart and sent her telepathic messages that I was all right. He put on a light and we helped Dominic to bed and pulled the cold covers over him. I saw the scar clearly then—a thick jagged scar still deep-pink and not very old, from thumb to fourth finger.

"You want to know about my life?" he said. "I was born in China. No kidding. My father was with the embassy—you don't believe me? I don't remember anything about it, though. We left before I was three."

My eyes moved from Dominic's bed in the corner of the room to a row of vacuum cleaners lined as straight as soldiers, and from there to the only table in the room where there was a mannequin head with a wide-brimmed black hat.

"He repairs vacuum cleaners," Nick said. "He's been my friend since we were twelve years old. Really. Don't you believe that?" He struck a long wooden match on the side of the stove and held the flame over the bowl of a small ivory pipe.

When I woke up it was getting dark. Nick was

breathing into my hair. Dominic was sitting on the floor surrounded by his tools, repairing a vacuum cleaner, able to concentrate as though he'd never passed out the night before.

"I thought you should wake up," Nick said, his hand on mine as though he were consoling a patient. I was sprawled in a pile of blankets and quilts that seemed about three feet high. "You've been asleep for almost fourteen hours."

When I told him my aunt was getting married, he told me I should go live with the marionette-maker. They call him that instead of calling him by his real name because his profession interests them. Formerly he was in medical school. Formerly a fiddle player.

His marionettes are made of cherry wood and peach wood, some of birch. They are unicorns and bears and huntsmen. He has passed some on to a friend, a silversmith, to sink eyes of silver into them. There is a green-jacketed huntsman with silver eyes, and there is a shapeless cow with a ridge of fox fur down its back and amber beads for eyes Sometimes he hangs them on strings from the ceiling beams, and the slits and circles of eyes glow at night like the eyes of nightmare demons. The baby is not afraid of any of them. She has broken pieces of some of them and understands their fragility—a bit of unicorn horn, a sliver of claw.

It is sad when Kirk comes the last Saturday of every month and collects them for the drive to New York. The ones that have been around a long time seem like friends, and it reminds me of a funeral when they are laid in layers of white towel in boxes and carried to Kirk's VW bus.

"It would be good if you could make more people and less animals," Kirk says. But he knows that Carlos will carve whatever he pleases. He lingers by our stove, accepts a mug of tea with cloves and honey.

"What do I want to drive to New York for?" he always says. It is his mother's shop that sells the marionettes.

Carlos' father was Mexican, his mother Scandinavian. Carlos does not look as if he belongs to any nationality. He is six three, almost too tall for his house, with thick curly red hair and a blond beard streaked with gray. The baby watches him move around the house, watches him carving and painting. It is clear from her expression that she already understands that men are to be respected. He is fond of her and will sometimes call her "my baby," although he has never asked who her father is.

We came to Carlos' because Nick told me Carlos was a kind person who wanted a woman to live with him. I went feeling like a prostitute, but it was weeks before he touched me. The cats and the dog were more affectionate—and he tried to keep the animals away, afraid that they would overwhelm us. The baby missed her cat when it ran away, though, and quickly befriended all of them.

I looked for clues about him in the old cabinet above the bathroom sink that he used for a medicine cabinet. I found gauze and adhesive, a pair of socks folded small, and a card decorated with a pressed yellow field flower—the sort of card you'd scotch-tape to a gift—with nothing written inside. There was a box of Cepacol throat lozenges. There was a paperback book about megavitamin therapy.

That was the end of my first week in his house, and it frightened me the way I felt about him, as though I could love any man.

Kirk is apologetic. I have heard people described as shrinking before, but this is the first time I have understood what a person who is shrinking looks like. He opens his mouth, clenching his teeth; his neck disappears into his sweater like a turtle's neck.

He has not been to New York. Before he got ten miles down the road, his bus was stopped by the cops. At first he is so funny, cringing, hating the cops, that Carlos is amused. There were all those bumper stickers: NO NUKES; I AM A COON HUNTER; HONK IF IT'S MY BIRTHDAY. And on the side of his bus Kirk's brother had painted gypsy women, dancing in a field with blue smoke blowing through it. Kirk's headlight was burned out. The cops went mad looking for drugs, with Kirk telling them his rights all along: they couldn't search the bus unless they saw something, or they had a warrant (cocky because he had nothing with him).

They lifted the lid of the cardboard box and smiled to each other as they saw the packages of white towels. The tall old cop was furious when he unwrapped the towel and saw a smirking bear in a painted vest. His partner smelled it. Nothing. They made Kirk walk— to see if he could walk a straight line. He thought then that they would pretend that he had failed and run him in. But when he turned, they were huddled together, no longer even watching. The tall old cop stayed where he was and the other one—who looked to Kirk as if he was a little stoned himself—went to the cop car and opened the trunk and came back with an ax. They placed the bear between them as Kirk watched. Then the young funny-faced cop whomped the ax through the center of it. The bear split into two halves, exposing the pale peach wood inside, where it had not been oiled. The funny-faced cop bent over it, squinted and picked up one half, sniffed again. They gave him a warning ticket to get the headlight fixed and drove away.

Carlos listened, transfixed as if a guru were speaking, the expression on his face somewhere between joy and wonder. That expression never meant that he was feeling good.

We followed Kirk out of the house, walking single file on the shoveled path, the baby taking clumsy baby steps beside me. They had not disturbed the swathed marionettes in the rest of the box. On the front seat of the van, along with a horseshoe-shaped mirror Kirk was taking to his mother and an unopened bag of licorice, lay the bear. It had been neatly chopped, exactly in the middle. The pieces lay side by side. Before I saw that, I hadn't been as awed by Carlos' profession as the others, but when I saw it destroyed, I was as moved as if he had created something that was living, that they had cut open.

Kirk's teeth were chattering. He wanted both of them to sue the cops. Cops couldn't ax your possessions at will.

Carlos stared through the window sadly. He didn't open the door or touch the bear.

Kirk, neck still hunched into his shoulders, said he couldn't get it together to go to New York now.

We sat by the stove, as lost in our own silences as if we were stoned.

When the baby cried, Kirk went out to the bus and got the licorice. She sucked a piece and spit it out. He took a circle of licorice from the bag and skipped it across the floorboards. She watched it and smiled. He flipped another out of his fingers and she smiled and went for it.

It has made Carlos more sure that he is right: there is nowhere in the United States safe to bring up a baby.

He is so good to us that I hardly ever think about Nick anymore, though tonight Nick is coming to the house, and they are going to shoot pool at the bar where Nick and I once danced.

I am reading a book on ant societies. I am learning to type on a tall Royal typewriter lent to me by Kirk's brother. The baby, asleep in the cocoon of Carlos' coat, with Bat the Cat curled against her, sucks her first finger (she has never sucked her thumb). I part the material because she is too warm, her forehead pale-pink and sweaty. She has a small blue vein just at her temple. When we lived at my aunt's house I could hear, at night, her whispered prayers: "Please God, please King Christ, she's a girl—make the vein in her face go away." Her voice at night was nice to listen to—the prayers were so logical, all the things I would have forgotten to ask for, and she breathed them in a rhythm that came fast and slow, like a music-box song.

Carlos made my aunt two marionettes: a bride and a groom, with pointed silk shoes on the bride and rabbit-fur slippers on the groom. They both wrote letters to thank him. They have never asked us, since I came here, to come to visit.

At dusk Nick comes, a bottle of beer in his hand, his gray knit stocking cap lowered over his eyebrows. I am always happy to see him. I never see him alone, and I have never properly thanked him for bringing me here. The last time he came, when he got a sliver of wood in his thumb from stroking an unfinished marionette and I tweezed it out, I wanted to hold his hand longer than necessary to tweeze; I thought that I'd close the bathroom door and say thank you, but he was eager to be back in the living room, embarrassed to have cried out.

From the front window I watch them go down the plank from door to field, and over to Nick's car. The baby waves, and they wave back. The car starts and fishtails out of the snowy driveway. The baby looks to me for amusement. I settle us by the fire, baby on my lap, and do what she likes best: I seat her facing me and bend my head until my lips graze the top of her head, and softly sing songs into her hair.

He does not know what childhood diseases he has had. He thinks he remembers itching with the measles.

He has lost his passport, but has extra passport photographs in a jar that once was filled with Vaseline.

With Nick and Dominic he plays Go on Mondays.

He washes his own sweaters, and shapes them.

He can pare radishes into the shape of rosebuds.

The woman he lived with five years before, Marguerite, inspired him to begin making the marionettes because she carved and painted decoys. Once he got furious at her and pulled all her fennel out of the garden before it was grown, and she came at him screaming, punching him and trying to push him over with the palms of her hands.

I practice typing by typing these facts about him. He nods his head only—whether to acknowledge that these are facts (some told to me by Nick) or because my typing is improving, I don't know. Sometimes I type lies, or what I think are lies, and that usually makes him laugh:

He secretly likes Monopoly better than Go.

He dreams of lactobaccilli.

He wants a Ferrari.

I have typed a list for him that says I was born to parents named Toni and Tony, and that they still live in Virginia, where I grew up. That I have no brothers or sisters who can console them for their wild child, who wanted to run away to New York at seventeen. When I was eighteen, they sent me to live with my aunt in Vermont, and I went through a year and a half of college at Bennington. I fell in love with a musician. We skied cross-country (I was more timid than my parents knew), and in the spring he taught me to drive a car. I learned to like Mexican food. I learned to make cheese, and to glaze windows. I ended the list here; I wanted him to ask if this man was the baby's father, where he went, what my life was really like before I met that man, if I was happy or sad living in my aunt's house. I have told him a lot about myself. Sometimes I've talked for so long that we are both left exhausted. He is so good to us that I want him to remember these facts: height and weight and age, and details of my childhood, color preferences, favorite foods. Sometimes, in his quiet way, he'll ask a question, say he understands. Last week, after I had rambled on for hours, I stopped abruptly. He knew he had to give something. He was painting a unicorn white; it was suspended from the beam with fishline so he could paint it all at once and let it air-dry, steadying it only at the last beneath a hoof, then dabbing paint on the last spot of bare wood. He took a deep breath, sighed and began: Should he raise chickens? Do we want our own eggs, so we will not have to rely on Dime?

Tonight, or tomorrow, or the next day or night, we have to talk.

I have to know if we are to stay always, or for a long time, or a short time.

When he talked to me about eggs, I went along with his conversation. I said we shoud get another hive, make more honey.

We are thinking about the spring.

I pick up the baby's Christmas present from Nick: an Octascope (a kaleidoscope without the colored glass), which she uses as a toy to roll across the floor. I hold it and feel as powerful raising it to my eye as a captain with his periscope. I aim it at the two toys suspended from the beams, a camel and a donkey, and watch them proliferate into a circular zoo. I put on my jacket and go to the door and open it. It closes behind me with a tap. I have never before lived where there is no lock on the door. I thought that a baby would make demands until I was driven crazy. When I step out, she is silent inside, dog curled beside her, waiting. I raise the Octascope to eye level, and in floods the picture: the fields, spread white with snow, the palest ripple of pink at the horizon—eight triangles of the same image, as still as a painted picture when my hand is steady on the Octascope.

Bat the Cat darts from under a juniper bush to crouch between my legs. It will rain, or snow. Pink blurs to pearly gray.

This is the dead of winter.

# Weekend

On Saturday morning Lenore is up before the others. She carries her baby into the living room and puts him in George's favorite chair, which tilts because its back legs are missing, and covers him with a blanket. Then she lights a fire in the fireplace, putting fresh logs on a few embers that are still glowing from the night before. She sits down on the floor beside the chair and checks the baby, who has already gone back to sleep—a good thing, because there are guests in the house. George, the man she lives with, is very hospitable and impetuous; he extends invitations whenever old friends call, urging them to come spend the weekend. Most of the callers are his former students—he used to be an English professor—and when they come it seems to make things much worse. It makes *him* much worse, because he falls into smoking too much and drinking and not eating, and then his ulcer bothers him. When the guests leave, when the weekend is over, she has to cook bland food: applesauce, oatmeal, puddings. And his drinking does not taper off easily anymore; in the past he would stop cold when the guests left, but lately he only tapers down from Scotch to wine, and drinks wine well into the week—a lot of wine, perhaps a whole bottle with his meal—until his stomach is much worse. He is hard to live with. Once when a former student, a woman named Ruth, visited them—a lover, she suspected—she overheard George talking to her in his study, where he had taken her to see a photograph of their house before he began repairing it. George had told Ruth that she, Lenore, stayed with him because she was simple. It hurt her badly, made her actually dizzy with surprise and shame, and since then, no matter who the guests are, she never feels quite at ease on the weekends. In the past she enjoyed some of the things she and George did with their guests, but since overhearing what he said to Ruth she feels that all their visitors have been secretly told the same thing about her. To her, though, George is usually kind. But she is sure that is the reason he has not married her, and when he recently remarked on their daughter's intelligence (she is five years old, a girl named Maria) she found that she could no longer respond with simple pride; now she feels spite as well, feels that Maria exists as proof of her own good genes. She has begun to expect perfection of the child. She knows this is wrong, and she has tried hard not to communicate her anxiety to Maria, who is already, as her kindergarten teacher says, "untypical."

At first Lenore loved George because he was untypical, although after she had moved in with him and lived with him for a while she began to see that he was not exceptional but a variation on a type. She is proud of observing that, and she harbors the discovery—her silent response to his low opinion of her. She does not know why he found her attractive—in the beginning he did—because she does not resemble the pretty, articulate young women he likes to invite, with their lovers or girl friends, to their house for the weekend. None of these young women have husbands; when they bring a man with them at all they bring a lover, and they seem happy not to be married. Lenore, too, is happy to be single—not out of conviction that marriage is wrong but because she knows that it would be wrong to be married to George if he thinks she is simple. She thought at first to confront him with what she had overheard, to demand an explanation. But he can weasel out of any corner. At best, she can mildly fluster him, and later he will only blame it on Scotch. Of course she might ask why he has all these women come to visit, why he devotes so little time to her or the children. To that he would say that it was the quality of the time they spent together that mattered, not the quantity. He has already said that, in fact, without being asked. He says things over and over so that she will accept them as truths. And eventually she does. She does not like to think long and hard, and when there is an answer—even his answer—it is usually easier to accept it and go on with things. She goes on with what she has always done: tending the house and the children and George, when he needs her. She likes to bake and she collects art postcards. She is proud of their house, which was bought cheaply and improved by George when he was still interested in that kind of work, and she is happy to have visitors come there, even if she does not admire them or even like them.

Except for teaching a night course in photography at a junior college once a week, George has not worked since he left the university two years ago, after he was denied tenure. She cannot really tell if he is unhappy working so little, because he keeps busy in other ways. He listens to classical music in the morning, slowly sipping herbal teas, and on fair afternoons he lies outdoors in the sun, no matter how cold the day. He takes photographs, and walks alone in the woods. He does errands for her if they need to be done. Sometimes at night he goes to the library or goes to visit friends; he tells her that these people often ask her to come too, but he says she would not like them. This is true—she would not like them. Recently he has done some late-night cooking. He has always kept a journal, and he is a great letter writer. An aunt left him most of her estate, ten thousand dollars, and said in her will that he was the only one who really cared, who took the time, again and again, to write. He had not seen his aunt for five years before she died, but he wrote regularly. Sometimes Lenore would find notes that he has left for her. Once, on the refrigerator, there was a long note suggesting clever Christmas presents for her family that he had thought of while she was out. Last week he scotch-taped a slip of paper to a casserole dish that contained leftover veal stew, saying: "This was delicious." He does not compliment her verbally, but he likes to let her know that he is pleased.

A few nights ago—the same night they got a call from Julie and Sarah, saying they were coming for a visit—she told him that she wished he would talk more, that he would confide in her.

"Confide what?" he said.

"You always take that attitude," she said. "You pretend that you have no thoughts. Why does there have to be so much silence?"

"I'm not a professor anymore," he said. "I don't have to spend every minute *thinking*."

But he loves to talk to the young women. He will talk to them on the phone for as much as an hour; he walks with them through the woods for most of the day when they visit. The lovers the young women bring with them always seem to fall behind; they give up and return to the house to sit and talk to her, or to help with the preparation of the meal, or to play with the children. The young woman and George come back refreshed, ready for another round of conversation at dinner.

A few weeks ago one of the young men said to her, "Why do you let it go on?" They had been talking lightly before that—about the weather, the children—and then, in the kitchen, where he was sitting shelling peas, he put his head on the table and said, barely audibly, "Why do you let it go on?" He did not raise his head, and she stared at him, thinking that she must have imagined his speaking. She was surprised—surprised to have heard it, and surprised that he had said nothing after that, which made her doubt that he had spoken.

"Why do I let what go on?" she said.

There was a long silence. "Whatever this sick game is, I don't want to get involved in it," he said at last. "It was none of my business to ask. I understand that you don't want to talk about it."

"But it's really cold out there," she said. "What could happen when it's freezing out?"

He shook his head, the way George did, to indicate that she was beyond understanding. But she wasn't stupid, and she knew what might be going on. She had said the right thing, had been on the right track, but she had to say what she felt, which was that nothing very serious could be happening at that moment because they were walking in the woods. There wasn't even a barn on the property. She knew perfectly well that they were talking.

When George and the young woman had come back, he fixed hot apple juice, into which he trickled rum. Lenore was pleasant, because she was sure of what had not happened; the young man was not, because he did not think as she did. Still at the kitchen table, he ran his thumb across a pea pod as though it were a knife.

This weekend Sarah and Julie are visiting. They came on Friday evening. Sarah was one of George's students—the one who led the fight to have him rehired. She does not look like a troublemaker; she is pale and pretty, with freckles on her cheeks. She talks too much about the past, and this upsets him, disrupts the peace he has made with himself. She tells him that they fired him because he was "in touch" with everything, that they were afraid of him because he was so in touch. The more she tells him the more he remembers, and then it is necessary for Sarah to say the same things again and again; once she reminds him, he seems to need reassurance—needs to have her voice, to hear her bitterness against the members of the tenure committee. By evening they will both be drunk. Sarah will seem both agitating and consoling, Lenore and Julie and the children will be upstairs, in bed. Lenore suspects that she will not be the only one awake listening to them. She thinks that in spite of Julie's glazed look she is really very attentive. The night before, when they were all sitting around the fireplace talking, Sarah made a gesture and almost upset her wineglass, but Julie reached for it and stopped it from toppling over. George and Sarah were talking so energetically that they did not notice. Lenore's eyes met Julie's as Julie's hand shot out. Lenore feels that she is like Julie: Julie's face doesn't betray emotion, even when she is interested, even when she cares deeply. Being the same kind of person, Lenore can recognize this.

Before Sarah and Julie arrived Friday evening, Lenore asked George if Sarah was his lover.

"Don't be ridiculous," he said. "You think every student is my lover? Is Julie my lover?"

She said, "That wasn't what I said."

"Well, if you're going to be preposterous, go ahead and say that," he said. "If you think about it long enough, it would make a lot of sense, wouldn't it?"

He would not answer her question about Sarah. He kept throwing Julie's name into it. Some other woman might then think that he was protesting too strongly—

that Julie really was his lover. She thought no such thing. She also stopped suspecting Sarah, because he wanted that, and it was her habit to oblige him.

He is twenty-one years older than Lenore. On his last birthday he was fifty-five. His daughter from his first marriage (his *only* marriage; she keeps reminding herself that they are not married, because it often seems that they might as well be) sent him an Irish country hat. The present made him irritable. He kept putting it on and putting it down hard on his head. "She wants to make me a laughable old man," he said. "She wants me to put this on and go around like a fool." He wore the hat all morning, complaining about it, frightening the children. Eventually, to calm him, she said, "She intended *nothing*." She said it with finality, her tone so insistent that he listened to her. But having lost his reason for bitterness, he said, "Just because you don't think doesn't mean others don't think." Is he getting old? She does not want to think of him getting old. In spite of his ulcer, his body is hard. He is tall and handsome, with a thick mustache and a thin black goatee, and there is very little gray in his kinky black hair. He dresses in tight-fitting blue jeans and black turtleneck sweaters in the winter, and old white shirts with the sleeves rolled up in the summer. He pretends not to care about his looks, but he does. He shaves carefully, scraping slowly down each side of his goatee. He orders his soft leather shoes from a store in California. After taking one of his long walks—even if he does it twice a day—he invariably takes a shower. He always looks refreshed, and very rarely admits any insecurity. A few times, at night in bed, he has asked, "Am I still the man of your dreams?" And when she says yes he always laughs, turning it into a joke, as if he didn't care. She knows he does. He pretends to have no feeling for clothing, but actually he cares so strongly about his turtlenecks and shirts (a few are Italian silk) and shoes that he will have no others. She has noticed that the young women who visit are always vain. When Sarah arrived, she was wearing a beautiful silk scarf, pale as conch shells

Sitting on the floor on Saturday morning, Lenore watches the fire she has just lit. The baby, tucked in George's chair, smiles in his sleep, and Lenore thinks what a good companion he would be if only he were an adult. She gets up and goes into the kitchen and tears open a package of yeast and dissolves it, with sugar and salt, in hot water, slushing her fingers through it and shivering because it is so cold in the kitchen. She will bake bread for dinner—there is always a big meal in the early evening when they have guests. But what will she do for the rest of the day? George told the girls the night before that on Saturday they would walk in the woods, but she does not really enjoy hiking, and George will be irritated because of the discussion the night before, and she does not want to aggravate him. "You are unwilling to challenge anyone," her brother wrote her in a letter that came a few days ago. He has written her for years—all the years she has been with George—asking when she is going to end the relationship. She rarely writes back because she knows that her answers sound too simple. She has a comfortable house. She cooks. She keeps busy and she loves her two children. "It seems unkind to say *but*," her brother writes, "but . . . " It is true; she likes simple things. Her brother, who is a lawyer in Cambridge, cannot understand that.

Lenore rubs her hand down the side of her face and says good morning to Julie and Sarah, who have come downstairs. Sarah does not want orange juice; she already looks refreshed and ready for the day. Lenore pours a glass for Julie. George calls from the hallway, "Ready to roll?" Lenore is surprised that he wants to leave so early. She goes into the living room. George is wearing a denim jacket, his hands in the pockets.

"Morning," he says to Lenore. "You're not up for a hike, are you?"

Lenore looks at him, but does not answer. As she stands there, Sarah walks around her and joins George in the hallway and he holds the door open for her. "Let's walk to the store and get Hershey bars to give us energy for a long hike," George says to Sarah. They are gone. Lenore finds Julie still in the kitchen, waiting for the water to boil. Julie says that she had a bad night and she is happy not to be going with George and Sarah. Lenore fixes tea for them. Maria sits next to her on the sofa, sipping orange juice. The baby likes company, but Maria is a very private child; she would rather that she and her mother were always alone. She has given up being possessive about her father. Now she gets out a cardboard box and takes out her mother's collection of postcards, which she arranges on the floor in careful groups. Whenever she looks up, Julie smiles nervously at her; Maria does not smile, and Lenore doesn't prod her. Lenore goes into the kitchen to punch down the bread, and Maria follows. Maria has recently gotten over chicken pox, and there is a small new scar in the center of her forehead. Instead of looking at Maria's blue eyes, Lenore lately has found herself focusing on the imperfection.

As Lenore is stretching the loaves onto the cornmeal-covered baking sheet, she hears the rain start. It hits hard on the garage roof.

After a few minutes Julie comes into the kitchen. "They're caught in this downpour," Julie says. "If Sarah had left the car keys, I could go get them."

"Take my car and pick them up," Lenore says, pointing with her elbow to the keys hanging on a nail near the door.

"But I don't know where the store is."

"You must have passed it driving to our house last night. Just go out of the driveway and turn right. It's along the main road."

Julie gets her purple sweater and takes the car keys. "I'll be right back," she says.

Lenore can sense that she is glad to escape from the house, that she is happy the rain began.

In the living room Lenore turns the pages of a magazine, and Marja mutters a refrain of "Blue, blue, dark blue, green blue," noticing the color every time it appears. Lenore sips her tea. She puts a Michael Hurley record on George's stereo. Michael Hurley is good rainy-day music. George has hundred of records. His students used to love to paw through them. Cleverly, he has never made any attempt to keep up with what is currently popular. Everything is jazz or eclectic: Michael Hurley, Keith Jarrett, Ry Cooder.

Julie comes back. "I couldn't find them," she says. She looks as if she expects to be punished.

Lenore is surprised. She is about to say something like "You certainly didn't try very hard, did you?" but she catches Julie's eye. She looks young and afraid, and perhaps even a little crazy.

"Well, we tried," Lenore says.

Julie stand in front of the fire, with her back to Lenore. Lenore knows she is thinking that she is dense—that she does not recognize the implications.

"They might have walked through the woods instead of along the road," Lenore says. "That's possible."

"But they would have gone out to the road to thumb when the rain began, wouldn't they?"

Perhaps she misunderstood what Julie was thinking. Perhaps it has never occurred to Julie until now what might be going on.

"Maybe they got lost," Julie says. "Maybe something happened to them."

"Nothing happened to them," Lenore says. Julie turns around and Lenore catches that small point of light in her eye again. "Maybe they took shelter under a tree," she says. "Maybe they're screwing. How should I know?"

It is not a word Lenore often uses. She usually tries

not to think about that at all, but she can sense that Julie is very upset.

"Really?" Julie says. "Don't you care, Mrs. Anderson?"

Lenore is amused. There's a switch. All the students call her husband George and her Lenore; now one of them wants to think there's a real adult here to explain all this to her.

"What am I going to do?" Lenore says. She shrugs.

Julie does not answer.

"Would you like me to pour you tea?" Lenore asks.

"Yes," Julie says. "Please."

George and Sarah return in the middle of the afternoon. George says that they decided to go on a spree to the big city—it is really a small town he is talking about, but calling it the big city gives him an opportunity to speak ironically. They sat in a restaurant bar, waiting for the rain to stop, George says, and then they thumbed a ride home. "But I'm completely sober," George says, turning for the first time to Sarah. "What about you?" He is all smiles. Sarah lets him down. She looks embarrassed. Her eyes meet Lenore's quickly, and jump to Julie. The two girls stare at each other, and Lenore, left with only George to look at, looks at the fire and then gets up to pile on another log.

Gradually it becomes clear that they are trapped together by the rain. Maria undresses her paper doll and deliberately rips a feather off its hat. Then she takes the pieces to Lenore, almost in tears. The baby cries, and Lenore takes him off the sofa, where he has been sleeping under his yellow blanket, and props him in the space between her legs as she leans back on her elbows to watch the fire. It's her fire, and she has the excuse of presiding over it.

"How's my boy?" George says. The baby looks, and looks away.

It gets dark early, because of the rain. At four-thirty George uncorks a bottle of Beaujolais and brings it into the living room, with four glasses pressed against his chest with his free arm. Julie rises nervously to extract the glasses, thanking him too profusely for the wine. She gives a glass to Sarah without looking at her.

They sit in a semicircle in front of the fire and drink the wine. Julie leafs through magazines—*New Times, National Geographic*—and Sarah holds a small white dish painted with gray-green leaves that she has taken from the coffee table; the dish contains a few shells and some acorn caps, a polished stone or two, and Sarah lets these objects run through her fingers. There are several such dishes in the house, assembled by George. He and Lenore gathered the shells long ago, the first time they went away together, at a beach in North Carolina. But the acorn caps, the shiny turquoise and amethyst stones—those are there, she knows, because George likes the effect they have on visitors; it is an expected unconventionality, really. He has also acquired a few small framed pictures, which he points out to guests who are more important than worshipful students—tiny oil paintings of fruit, prints with small details from the unicorn tapestries. He pretends to like small, elegant things. Actually, when they visit museums in New York he goes first to El Grecos and big Mark Rothko canvases. She could never get him to admit that what he said or did was sometimes false. Once, long ago, when he asked if he was still the man of her dreams, she said, "We don't get along well anymore." "Don't talk about it," he said—no denial, no protest. At best, she could say things and get away with them; she could never get him to continue such a conversation.

At the dinner table, lit with white candles burning in empty wine bottles, they eat off his grandmother's small flowery plates. Lenore looks out a window and sees, very faintly in the dark, their huge oak tree. The rain has stopped. A few stars have come out, and there are glints on the wet branches. The oak tree grows very close to the window. George loved it when her brother once suggested that some of the bushes and trees should be pruned away from the house so it would not always be so dark inside; it gave him a chance to rave about the beauty of nature, to say that he would never tamper with it. "It's like a tomb in here all day," her brother had said. Since moving here, George has learned the names of almost all the things growing on the land: he can point out abelia bushes, spirea, laurels. He subscribes to *National Geographic* (although she rarely sees him looking at it). He is at last in touch, he says, being in the country puts him in touch. He is saying it now to Sarah, who has put down her ivory-handled fork to listen to him. He gets up to change the record. Side two of the Telemann record begins softly.

Sarah is still very much on guard with Lenore; she makes polite conversation with her quickly when George is out of the room. "You people are so wonderful," she says. "I wish my parents could be like you."

"George would be pleased to hear that," Lenore says, lifting a small piece of pasta to her lips.

When George is seated again, Sarah, anxious to please, tells him, "If only my father could be like you."

"Your father," George says. "I won't have that analogy." He says it pleasantly, but barely disguises his dismay at the comparison.

"I mean, he cares about nothing but business," the girl stumbles on.

The music, in contrast, grows lovelier.

Lenore goes into the kitchen to get the salad and hears George say, "I simply won't let you girls leave. Nobody leaves on a Saturday."

There are polite protests, there are compliments to Lenore on the meal—there is too much talk. Lenore has trouble caring about what's going on. The food is warm and delicious. She pours more wine and lets them talk.

"Godard, yes, I know . . . panning that row of honking cars *so* slowly, that long line of cars stretching on and on."

She has picked up the end of George's conversation. His arm slowly waves out over the table, indicating the line of motionless cars in the movie.

"That's a lovely plant," Julie says to Lenore.

"It's Peruvian ivy," Lenore says. She smiles. She is supposed to smile. She will not offer to hack shoots off her plant for these girls.

Sarah asks for a Dylan record when the Telemann finishes playing. White wax drips onto the wood table. George waits for it to solidify slightly, then scrapes up the little circles and with thumb and index finger flicks them gently toward Sarah. He explains (although she asked for no particular Dylan record) that he has only Dylan before he went electric. And "Planet Waves"—"because it's so romantic. That's silly of me, but true." Sarah smiles at him. Julie smiles at Lenore. Julie is being polite, taking her cues from Sarah, really not understanding what's going on. Lenore does not smile back. She has done enough to put them at ease. She is tired now, brought down by the music, a full stomach, and again the sounds of rain outside. For dessert there is homemade vanilla ice cream, made by George, with small black vanilla-bean flecks in it. He is still drinking wine, though; another bottle has been opened. He sips wine and then taps his spoon on his ice cream, looking at Sarah. Sarah smiles, letting them all see the smile, then sucks the ice cream off her spoon. Julie is missing more and more of what's going on. Lenore watches as Julie strokes her hand absently on her napkin. She is wearing a thin silver choker and—Lenore notices for the first time—a thin silver ring on the third finger of her right hand.

"It's just terrible about Anna," George says, finishing his wine, his ice cream melting, looking at no one in particular, although Sarah was the one who brought up Anna the night before, when they had been in the

house only a short time—Anna dead, hit by a car,
hardly an accident at all. Anna was also a student of
his. The driver of the car was drunk, but for some reason charges were not pressed. (Sarah and George have
talked about this before, but Lenore blocks it out. What
can she do about it? She met Anna once: a beautiful
girl, with tiny, childlike hands, her hair thin and
curly—wary, as beautiful people are wary.) Now the
driver has been flipping out, Julie says, and calling
Anna's parents, wanting to talk to them to find out
why it has happened.

The baby begins to cry. Lenore goes upstairs, pulls
up more covers, talks to him for a minute. He settles
for this. She goes downstairs. The wind must have af-
fected her more than she realizes; otherwise, why is
she counting the number of steps?

In the candlelit dining room, Julie sits alone at the
table. The girl has been left alone again; George and
Sarah took the umbrellas, decided to go for a walk in
the rain.

It is eight o'clock. Since helping Lenore load the
dishes into the diswasher, when she said what a beautiful house Lenore had, Julie has said very little. Lenore is tired, and does not want to make conversation.
They sit in the living room and drink wine.

"Sarah is my best friend," Julie says. She seems
apologetic about it. "I was so out of it when I came back
to college. I was in Italy, with my husband, and suddenly I was back in the States. I couldn't make friends.
But Sarah wasn't like the other people. She cared
enough to be nice to me."

"How long have you been friends?"

"For two years. She's really the best friend I've ever
had. We understand things—we don't always have to
talk about them."

"Like her relationship with George," Lenore says.

Too direct. Too unexpected. Julie has no answer.

"You act as if you're to blame," Lenore says.

"I feel strange because you're such a nice lady."

A nice lady! What an odd way to speak. Has she been reading Henry James? Lenore has never known what to think of herself, but she certainly thinks of herself as being more complicated than a "lady."

"Why do you look that way?" Julie asks. "You *are* nice. I think you've been very nice to us. You've given up your whole weekend."

"I always give up my weekends. Weekends are the only time we socialize, really. In a way, it's good to have something to do."

"But to have it turn out like this . . ." Julie says. "I think I feel so strange because when my own marriage broke up I didn't even suspect. I mean, I couldn't act the way you do, anyway, but I—"

"For all I know, nothing's going on," Lenore says. "For all I know, your friend is flattering herself, and George is trying to make me jealous." She puts two more logs on the fire. When these are gone, she will either have to walk to the woodshed or give up and go to bed. "Is there something . . . *major* going on?" she asks.

Julie is sitting on the rug, by the fire, twirling her hair with her finger. "I didn't know it when I came out here," she says. "Sarah's put me in a very awkward position."

"But do you know how far it has gone?" Lenore asks, genuinely curious now.

"No," Julie says.

No way to know if she's telling the truth. Would Julie speak the truth to a lady? Probably not.

"Anyway," Lenore says with a shrug, "I don't want to think about it all the time."

"I'd never have the courage to live with a man and not marry," Julie says. "I mean, I wish I had, that we hadn't gotten married, but I just don't have that kind of . . . I'm not secure enough."

"You have to live somewhere," Lenore says.

Julie is looking at her as if she does not believe that

she is sincere. Am I? Lenore wonders. She has lived with George for six years, and sometimes she thinks she has caught his way of playing games, along with his colds, his bad moods.

"I'll show you something," Lenore says. She gets up, and Julie follows. Lenore puts on the light in George's study, and they walk through it to a bathroom he has converted to a darkroom. Under a table, in a box behind another box, there is a stack of pictures. Lenore takes them out and hands them to Julie. They are pictures that Lenore found in his darkroom last summer; they were left out by mistake, no doubt, and she found them when she went in with some contact prints he had left in their bedroom. They are high-contrast photographs of George's face. In all of them he looks very serious and very sad; in some of them his eyes seem to be narrowed in pain. In one, his mouth is open. It is an excellent photograph of a man in agony, a man about to scream.

"What are they?" Julie whispers.

"Pictures he took of himself," Lenore says. She shrugs. "So I stay," she says.

Julie nods. Lenore nods, taking the pictures back. Lenore has not thought until this minute that this may be why she stays. In fact, it is not the only reason. It is just a very demonstrable, impressive reason. When she first saw the pictures, her own face had become as distorted as George's. She had simply not known what to do. She had been frightened and ashamed. Finally she put them in an empty box, and put the box behind another box. She did not even want him to see the horrible pictures again. She does not know if he has ever found them, pushed back against the wall in that other box. As George says, there can be too much communication between people.

Later, Sarah and George come back to the house. It is still raining. It turns out that they took a bottle of brandy with them, and they are both drenched and drunk. He holds Sarah's finger with one of his. Sarah, seeing Lenore, lets his finger go. But then he turns— they have not even said hello yet—and grabs her up, spins her around, stumbling into the living room, and says, "I am in love."

Julie and Lenore watch them in silence.

"See no evil," George says, gesturing with the empty brandy bottle to Julie. "Hear no evil," George says, pointing to Lenore. He hugs Sarah closer. "I speak no evil. I speak the truth. I am in love!"

Sarah squirms away from him, runs from the room and up the stairs in the dark.

George looks blankly after her, then sinks to the floor and smiles. He is going to pass it off as a joke. Julie looks at him in horror, and from upstairs Sarah can be heard sobbing. Her crying awakens the baby.

"Excuse me," Lenore says. She climbs the stairs and goes into her son's room, and picks him up. She talks gently to him, soothing him with lies. He is too sleepy to be alarmed for long. In a few minutes he is asleep again, and she puts him back in his crib. In the next room Sarah is crying more quietly now. Her crying is so awful that Lenore almost joins in, but instead she pats her son. She stands in the dark by the crib and then at last goes out and down the hallway to her bedroom. She takes off her clothes and gets into the cold bed. She concentrates on breathing normally. With the door closed and Sarah's door closed, she can hardly hear her. Someone taps lightly on her door.

"Mrs. Anderson," Julie whispers. "Is this your room?"

"Yes," Lenore says. She does not ask her in.

"We're going to leave. I'm going to get Sarah and leave. I didn't want to just walk out without saying anything."

Lenore just cannot think how to respond. It was really very kind of Julie to say something. She is very close to tears, so she says nothing.

"Okay," Julie says, to reassure herself. "Good night. We're going."

There is no more crying. Footsteps. Miraculously, the baby does not wake up again, and Maria has slept through all of it. She has always slept well. Lenore herself sleeps worse and worse, and she knows that George walks much of the night, most nights. She hasn't said anything about it. If he thinks she's simple, what good would her simple wisdom do him?

The oak tree scrapes against the window in the wind and rain. Here on the second floor, under the roof, the tinny tapping is very loud. If Sarah and Julie say anything to George before they leave, she doesn't hear them. She hears the car start, then die out. It starts again—she is praying for the car to go—and after conking out once more it rolls slowly away, crunching gravel. The bed is no warmer; she shivers. She tries hard to fall asleep. The effort keeps her awake. She squints her eyes in concentration instead of closing them. The only sound in the house is the electric clock, humming by her bed. It is not even midnight.

She gets up, and without turning on the light, walks downstairs. George is still in the living room. The fire is nothing but ashes and glowing bits of wood. It is as cold there as it was in the bed.

"That damn bitch," George says. "I should have known she was a stupid little girl."

"You went too far," Lenore says. "I'm the only one you can go too far with."

"Damn it," he says, and pokes the fire. A few sparks shoot up. "Damn it," he repeats under his breath.

His sweater is still wet. His shoes are muddy and ruined. Sitting on the floor by the fire, his hair matted down on his head, he looks ugly, older, unfamiliar.

She thinks of another time, when it was warm. They were walking on the beach together, shortly after they met, gathering shells. Little waves were rolling in. The sun went behind the clouds and there was a momentary illusion that the clouds were still and the sun was racing ahead of them. "Catch me," he said, breaking away from her. They had been talking quietly, gathering shells. She was so surprised at him for breaking away that she ran with all her energy and did catch him, putting her hand out and talking hold of the band of his swimming trunks as he veered into the water. If she hadn't stopped him, would he really have run far out into the water, until she couldn't follow anymore? He turned on her, just as abruptly as he had run away, and grabbed her and hugged her hard, lifted her high. She had clung to him, held him close. He had tried the same thing when he came back from the walk with Sarah, and it hadn't worked.

"I wouldn't care if their car went off the road," he says bitterly.

"Don't say that," she says.

They sit in silence, listening to the rain. She slides over closer to him, puts her hand on his shoulder and leans her head there, as if he could protect her from the awful things he has wished into being.

# Colorado

Penelope was in Robert's apartment, sitting on the floor, with the newspaper open between her legs. Her boots were on the floor in front of her. Robert had just fixed the zipper of one of the boots. It was the third time he had repaired the boots, and this time he suggested that she buy a new pair. "Why?" she said. "You fix them fine every time." In many of their discussions they came close to arguments, but they always stopped short. Penelope simply would not argue. She thought it took too much energy. She had not even argued with Robert's friend Johnny, whom she had been living with, moved out on her, taking twenty dollars of her money. Still, she hated Johnny for it, and sometimes Robert worried that even though he and Penelope didn't argue, she might be thinking badly of him, too. So he didn't press it. Who cared whether she bought new boots or not?

Penelope came over to Robert's apartment almost every evening. He had met her more than a year before, and they had been nearly inseparable ever since. For a while he and Penelope and Johnny and another friend, Cyril, had shared a house in the country, not far from New Haven. They had all been in graduate school then. Now Johnny had gone, and the others were living in New Haven, in different apartments, and they were no longer going to school. Penelope was living with a man named Dan. Robert could not understand this, because Dan and Penelope did not communicate even well enough for her to ask him to fix her boots. She hobbled over to Robert's apartment instead. And he couldn't understand it back when she was living with Johnny, because Johnny had continued to see another girl, and had taken Penelope's money and tried to provoke arguments, even though Penelope wouldn't argue. Robert could understand Penelope's moving in with Dan at first, because she hadn't had enough money to pay her share of the house rent and Dan had an apartment in New Haven, but why had she just stayed there? Once, when he was drunk, Robert had asked her that, and she had sighed and said she wouldn't argue with him when he'd been drinking. He had not been trying to argue. He had just wanted to know what she was thinking. But she didn't like to talk about herself, and saying that he was drunk had been a convenient excuse. The closest he ever got to an explanation was when she told him once that it was important not to waste your energy jumping from one thing to another. She had run away from home when she was younger, and when she returned, things were only worse. She had flunked out of Bard and dropped out of Antioch and the University of Connecticut, and now she knew that all colleges were the same—there was no point in trying one after another. She had traded her Ford for a Toyota, and Toyotas were no better than Fords.

She was flipping through the newspaper, stretched out on her side on the floor, her long brown hair blocking his view of her face. He didn't need to look at her: he knew she was beautiful. It was nice just to have her there. Although he couldn't understand what went on in her head, he was full of factual information about her. She had grown up in Iowa. She was almost five feet nine inches tall, and she weighed a hundred and twenty-five pounds, and when she was younger, when she weighed less, she had been a model in Chicago. Now she was working as a clerk in a boutique in New Haven. She didn't want to model again, because that was no easier then being a salesperson; it was more tiring, even if it did pay better.

"Thanks for fixing my boots again," she said, rolling up her pants leg to put one on.

"Why are you leaving?" Robert said. "Dan's student won't be out of there yet."

Dan was a painter who had lost his teaching job in the South. He moved to New Haven and was giving private lessons to students three times a week.

"Marielle's going to pick me up," Penelope said. "She wants me to help her paint her bathroom."

"Why can't she paint her own bathroom? She could do the whole thing in an hour."

"I don't want to help her paint," Penelope said, sighing. "I'm just doing a favor for a friend."

"Why don't you do me a favor and stay?"

"Come on," she said. "Don't do that. You're my best friend."

"Okay," he said, knowing she wouldn't fight over it anyway. He went to the kitchen table and got her coat. "Why don't you wait till she gets here?"

"She's meeting me at the drugstore."

"You sure are nice to some of your friends," he said.

She ignored him. She did not totally ignore him; she kissed him before she left. And although she did not say that she'd see him the next day, he knew she'd be back.

When Penelope left, Robert went into the kitchen and put some water on to boil. It was his habit since moving to this apartment to have a cup of tea before bed and to look out the window into the brightly lit alley. Interesting things appeared there: Christmas trees, large broken pieces of machinery, and, once, a fireman's uniform, very nicely laid out—a fireman's hat and suit. He was an artist—or, rather, he had been an artist until he dropped out of school—and sometimes he found that he still arranged objects and landscapes, looking for a composition. He sat on the kitchen table and drank his tea. He often thought about buying a kitchen chair, but he told himself that he'd move soon and he didn't want to transport furniture. When he was a child, his parents had moved from apaprtment to apartment. Their furniture got more and more battered, and his mother had exploded one day, crying that the furniture was worthless and ugly, and threatening to chop it all up with an ax. Since he moved from the country Robert had not yet bought himself a bed frame or curtains or rugs. There were roaches in the apartment, and the idea of the roaches hiding—being able to hide on the underside of curtains, under the rug—disgusted him. He didn't mind them being there so much when they were out in the open.

The Yale catalogue he had gotten months before when he first came to New Haven was still on the kitchen table. He had thought about taking a course in architecture, but he hadn't. He was not quite sure what to do. He had taken a part-time job working in a picture-framing store so he could pay his rent. Actually, he had no reason for being in New Haven except to be near Penelope. When Robert lived in the house with Johnny and Cyril and Penelope, he had told himself that Penelope would leave Johnny and become his lover, but it never happened. He had tried very hard to get it to happen; they had often stayed up later than any of the others, and they talked—he had never talked so much to anybody in his life—and sometimes they fixed food before going to bed, or took walks in the snow. She tried to teach him to play the recorder, blowing softly so she wouldn't wake the others. Once in the summer they had stolen corn, and Johnny had asked her about it the next morning. "What if the neighbors find out somebody from this house stole corn?" he said. Robert defended Penelope, saying that he had suggested it. "Great," Johnny said. "The Bobbsey Twins." Robert was hurt because what Johnny said was true—there wasn't anything more between them than there was between the Bobbsey Twins.

Earlier in the week Robert had been sure that Penelope was going to make a break with Dan. He had gone to a party at their apartment, and there had been a strange assortment of guests, almost all of them Dan's friends—some Yale people, a druggist who had a Marlboro cigarette pack filled with reds that he passed around, and a neighbor woman and her six-year-old son, whom the druggist teased. The druggist showed the little boy the cigarette pack full of pills, saying, "Now, how would a person light a cigarette like this? Which end is the filter?" The boy's mother wouldn't protect him, so Penelope took him away, into the bedroom, where she let him empty Dan's piggy bank and count the pennies. Marielle was also there, with her hair neatly braided into tight corn rows and wearing glasses with lenses that darkened to blue. Cyril came late, pretty loaded. "Better late than never," he said, once to Robert and many times to Penelope. Then Robert and Cyril huddled together in a corner, saying how dreary the party was, while the druggist put pills on his tongue and rolled them sensually across the roof of his mouth. At midnight Dan got angry and tried to kick them all out—Robert and Cyril first, because they were sitting closest to him—and that made Penelope angry because she had only three friends at the party, and the noisy ones, the drunk or stoned ones, were all

Dan's friends. Instead of arguing, though, she cried. Robert and Cyril left finally and went to Cyril's and had a beer, and then Robert went back to Dan's apartment, trying to get up the courage to go in and insist that Penelope leave with him. He walked up the two flights of stairs to their door. It was quiet inside. He didn't have the nerve to knock. He went downstairs and out of the building, hating himself. He walked home in the cold, and realized that he must have been a little drunk, because the fresh air really cleared his head.

Robert flipped through the Yale catalogue, thinking that maybe going back to school was the solution. Maybe all the hysterical letters his mother and father wrote were right, and he needed some order in his life. Maybe he'd meet some other girls in classes. He did not want to meet other girls. He had dated two girls since moving to New Haven, and they had bored him and he had spent more money on them than they were worth.

The phone rang; he was glad, because he was just about to get very depressed.

It was Penelope, sounding very far away, very knocked out. She had left Marielle's because Marielle's boyfriend was there, and he insisted that they all get stoned and listen to "Trout Mask Replica" and not paint the bathroom, so she left and decided to walk home, but then she realized she didn't want to go there, and she thought she'd call and ask if she could stay with him instead. And the strangest thing. When she closed the door of the phone booth just now, a little boy had appeared and tapped on the glass, fanning out a half circle of joints. "Ten dollars," the boy said to her. "Bargain City." *Imagine* that. There was a long silence while Robert imagined it. It was interrupted by Penelope, crying.

"What's the matter, Penelope?" he said. "Of course you can come over here. Get out of the phone both and come over."

She told him that she had bought the grass, and that

it was powerful stuff. It was really the wrong thing to do to smoke it, but she lost her nerve in the phone booth and didn't know whether to call or not, so she smoked a joint—very quickly, in case any cops drove by. She smoked it too quickly.

"Where are you?" he said.

"I'm near Park Street," she said.

"What do you mean? Is the phone booth on Park Street?"

"Near it," she said.

"Okay. I'll tell you what. You walk down to McHenry's and I'll get down there, okay?"

"You don't live very close," she said.

"I can walk there in a hurry. I can get a cab. You just take your time and wander down there. Sit in a booth if you can. Okay?"

"Is it true what Cyril told me at Dan's party?" she said. "That you're secretly in love with me?"

He frowned and looked sideways at the phone, as if the phone itself had betrayed him. He saw that his fingers were white from pressing so hard against the receiver.

"I'll tell you," she said. "Where I grew up, the cop cars had red lights. These green things cut right through you. I think that's why I hate this city—damn green lights."

"Is there a cop car?" he said.

"I saw one when you were talking," she said.

"Penelope. Have you got it straight about walking to McHenry's? Can you do that?"

"I've got some money," she said. "We can go to New York and get a steak dinner."

"Christ," he said. "Stay in the phone booth. Where is the phone booth?"

"I told you I'd go to McHenry's. I will. I'll wait there."

"Okay. Fine. I'm going to hang up now. Remember to sit in a booth. If there isn't one, stand by the bar. Order something. By the time you've finished it, I'll be there."

"Robert," she said.

"What?"

"Do you remember pushing me in the swing?"

He remembered. It was when they were all living in the country. She had been stoned that day, too. All of them—stoned as fools. Cyril was running around in Penelope's long white bathrobe, holding a handful of tulips. Then he got afraid they'd wilt, so he went into the kitchen and got a jar and put them in that and ran around again. Johnny had taken a few Seconals and was lying on the ground, saying that he was in a hammock, and cackling. Robert had thought that he and Penelope were the only ones straight. Her laughter sounded beautiful, even though later he realized it was wild, crazy laughter. It was the first really warm day, the first day when they were sure that winter was over. Everyone was delighted with everyone else. He remembered very well pushing her in the swing.

"Wait," he said. "I want to get down there. Can we talk about this when I get there? Will you walk to the bar?"

"I'm not really that stoned," she said, her voice changing suddenly. "I think it's that I'm sick."

"What do you mean? How do you feel?"

"I feel too light. Like I'm going to be sick."

"Look," he said. "Cyril lives right near Park. What if you give me the number of the phone booth, and I call Cyril and get him down there, and I'll call back and talk to you until he comes. Will you do that? What's the phone number?"

"I don't want to tell you."

"Why not?"

"I can't talk anymore right now," she said. "I want to get some air." She hung up.

He needed air too. He felt panicked, the way he had the day she was in the swing, when she said, "I'm going to jump!" and he knew it was going much too fast, much too high—the swing flying out over a hill that rolled steeply down to a muddy bank by the creek. He had had the sense to stop pushing, but he only stood there, waiting, shivering in the breeze the swing made.

He went out quickly. Park Street—somewhere near there. OK, he would find her. He knew he would not. There was a cab. He was in the cab. He rolled down the window to get some air, hoping the driver would figure he was drunk.

"What place you looking for again?" the driver said.

"I'm looking for a person, actually. If you'd go slowly..."

The cabdriver drove down the street at ordinary speed, and stopped at a light. A family crossed in front of the cab: a young black couple, the father with a child on his shoulders. The child was wearing a Porky Pig mask.

The light changed and the car started forward. "Goddamn," the driver said. "I knew it."

Steam had begun to rise from under the hood. It was a broken water hose. The cab moved into the next lane and stopped. Robert stuffed two one-dollar bills into the driver's hand and bolted from the cab.

"Piece of junk!" he heard the driver holler, and there was the sound of metal being kicked. Robert looked over his shoulder and saw the cabdriver kicking the grille. Steam was pouring out in a huge cloud. The driver kicked the cab again.

He walked. It seemed to him as if he were walking in slow motion, but soon he was panting. He passed several telephone booths, but all of them were empty. He felt guilty about not helping the cabdriver, and he walked all the way to McHenry's. He thought—and was immediately struck with the irrationality of it— that New Haven was really quite a nice town, architecturally.

Penelope was not at McHenry's. "Am I a black dude?" a black man said to him as Robert wedged his way through the crowd at the bar. "I'm gonna ask you straight, look at me and tell me: Ain't I a black dude?" The black man laughed with real joy. He did not seem to be drunk. Robert smiled at the man and headed toward the back of the bar. Maybe she was in the bath-room. He stood around, looking all over the bar, hoping she'd come out of the bathroom. Time passed. "If I was drunk," the black man said as Robert walked toward the front door, "I might try to put some rap on you, like I'm the king of Siam. I'm not saying nothing like that. I'm asking you straight: Ain't I a black dude, though?"

"You sure are," he said and edged away.

He went out and walked to a phone booth and dialed Dan's number. "Dan," he said, "I don't want to alarm you, but Penelope got a little loaded tonight and I went out to look for her and I've lost track of her."

"Is that right?" Dan said. "She told me she was going to sleep over at Marielle's."

"I guess she was. It's a long story, but she left there and she got pretty wrecked, Dan. I was worried about her, so—"

"Listen," Dan said. "Can I call you back in fifteen minutes?"

"What do you mean? I'm at a phone booth."

"Well, doesn't it have a number? I'll be right back with you."

"She's wandering around New Haven in awful shape, Dan. You'd better get down here and—"

Dan was talking to someone, his hand covering the mouthpiece.

"To tell you the truth," Dan said, "I can't talk right now. In fifteen minutes I can talk, but a friend is here."

"What are you talking about?" Robert said. "Haven't you been listening to what I've been saying? If you've got some woman there, tell her to go to the toilet for a minute, for Christ's sake."

"That doesn't cut the mustard anymore," Dan said. "You can't shuffle women off like they're cats and dogs."

Robert slammed down the phone and went back to McHenry's. She was still not there. He left, and out on the corner the black man from the bar walked up to him and offered to sell him cocaine. He politely refused, saying he had no money. The man nodded and walked down the street. Robert watched him for a minute, then looked away. For just a few seconds he had been interested in the way the man moved, what he looked like walking down the street. When he had lived at the house with Penelope, Robert had watched her, too; he had done endless drawings of her, sketched her on napkins, on the corner of the newspaper. But paintings—when he tried to do anything formal, he hadn't been able to go through with it. Cyril told him it was because he was afraid of capturing her. At first he thought Cyril's remark was stupid, but now—standing tired and cold on the street corner—he had to admit that he'd always been a little afraid of her, too. What would he have done tonight if he'd found her? Why had her phone call upset him so much—because she was stoned? He thought about Penelope—about putting his head down on her shoulder, somewhere where it was warm. He began to walk home. It was a long walk, and he was very tired. He stopped and looked in a bookstore window, then walked past a dry cleaner's. The last time he'd looked, it had been a coffee shop. At a red light he heard Bob Dylan on a car radio, making an analogy between time and a jet plane.

She called in the morning to apologize. When she hung up on him the night before, she got straight for a minute—long enough to hail a cab—but she had a bad time in the cab again, and didn't have the money to pay for the ride . . . To make a long story short, she was with Marielle.

"Why?" Robert asked.

Well, she was going to tell the cabdriver to take her to Robert's place, but she was afraid he was mad. No—that wasn't the truth. She knew he wouldn't be mad, but she couldn't face him. She wanted to talk to him, but she was in no shape.

She agreed to meet him for lunch. They hung up. He went into the bathroom to shave. A letter his father had written him, asking why he had dropped out of graduate school, was scotch-taped to the mirror, along with other articles of interest. There was one faded clipping, which belonged to Johnny and had been hung on the refrigerator at the house, about someone called the California Superman who had frozen to death in his Superman suit, in his refrigerator. All of Robert's friends had bizarre stories displayed in their apartments. Cyril had a story about a family that had starved to death, in their car at the side of the highway. Their last meal had been watermelon. The clipping was tacked to Cyril's headboard. It made Robert feel old and disoriented when he realized that these awful newspaper articles had replaced those mindless Day-Glo pictures everybody used to have. Also, people in New Haven had begun to come up to him on the street—cops, surely; they had to be cops—swinging plastic bags full of grass in front of his nose, bringing handfuls of ups and downs out of their pockets. Also, the day before, he had got a box from his mother. She sent him a needlepoint doorstop, with a small white-and-gray Scottie dog on it, and a half-wreath of roses underneath it. It really got him down.

He began to shave. His cat walked into the bathroom and rubbed against his bare ankle, making him jerk his leg away, and he cut his cheek. He put a piece of toilet paper against the cut, and sat on the side of the tub. He was angry at the cat and angry at himself for being depressed. After all, Dan was out of the picture now. Penelope had been found. He could go get her, the way he got groceries, the way he got a book from the library. It seemed too easy. Something was wrong.

He put on his jeans—he had no clean underwear; forget about that—and a shirt and his jacket, and walked to the restaurant. Penelope was in the first booth, with her coat still on. There was a bottle of beer on the table in front of her. She was smiling sheepishly, and seeing her, he smiled back. He sat next to her and put his arm around her shoulder, hugging her to him.

"Who's the first girl you ever loved?" she said.

Leave it to her to ask something like that. He tried to feel her shoulder beneath her heavy coat, but couldn't. He tried to remember loving anyone but her. "A girl in high school," he said.

"I'll bet she had a tragic end," she said.

The waitress came and took their orders. When she went away, Penelope continued, "Isn't that what usually happens? People's first loves washing up on the beach in Mexico?"

"She didn't finish high school with me. Her parents yanked her out and put her in private school. For all I know, she did go to Mexico and wash up on the beach."

She covered her ears. "You're mad at me," she said.

"No," he said, hugging her to him. "I wasn't too happy last night, though. What did you want to talk to me about?"

"I wanted to know if I could live with you."

"Sure," he said.

"Really? You wouldn't mind?"

"No," he said.

While she was smiling at the startled look on his face, the waitress put a cheeseburger in front of him. She put an omelette in front of Penelope, and Penelope began to eat hungrily. He picked up his cheeseburger and bit into it. It was good. It was the first thing he had eaten in more than a day. Feeling sorry for himself, he took another bite.

"I just took a few drags of that stuff, and I felt like my mind was filling up with clouds," she said.

"Forget about it," he said. "You're okay now."

"I want to talk about something else, though."

He nodded.

"I slept with Cyril," she said.

"What?" he said. "When did you sleep with Cyril?"

"At the house," she said. "And at his place."

"Recently?" he said.

"A couple of days ago."

"Well," he said. "Why are you telling me?"

"Cyril told Dan," she said.

That explained it.

"What do you expect me to say?" he said.

"I don't know. I wanted to talk about it."

He took another bite of his cheeseburger. He did not want her to talk about it.

"I don't know why I should be all twisted around," she said. "And I don't even know why I'm telling you."

"I wouldn't know," he said.

"Are you jealous?"

"Yes."

"Cyril said you had a crush on me," she said.

"That makes it sound like I'm ten years old," he said.

"I was thinking about going to Colorado," she said.

"I don't know what I expected," he said, slamming his hand down on the table. "I didn't expect that you'd be talking about screwing Cyril and going to Colorado." He pushed his plate away, angry.

"I shouldn't have told you."

"Shouldn't have told me what? What am I going to do about it? What do you expect me to say?"

"I thought you felt the way I feel," she said. "I thought you felt stifled in New Haven."

He looked at her. She had a way of sometimes saying perceptive things, but always when he was expecting something else.

"I have friends in Colorado," she said. "Bea and Matthew. You met them when they stayed at the house once."

"You want me to move out to Colorado because Bea and Matthew are there?"

"They have a big house they're having trouble paying the mortgage on."

"But I don't have any money."

"You have the money your father sent you so you could take courses at Yale. And you could get back into painting in Colorado. You're not a picture framer—you're a painter. Wouldn't you like to quit your lousy job framing pictures and get out of New Haven?"

"Get out of New Haven?" he repeated, to see what it felt like. "I don't know," he said. "It doesn't seem very reasonable."

"I don't feel right about things," she said.

"About Cyril?"

"The last five years," she said.

He excused himself and went to the bathroom. Scrawled above one of the mirrors was a message: "Time will say nothing but I told you so." A very literate town, New Haven. He looked at the bathroom window, stared at the ripply white glass. He thought about crawling out the window. He was not able to deal with her. He went back to the booth.

"Come on," he said, dropping money on the table.

Outside, she began to cry. "I could have asked Cyril to go, but I didn't," she said.

He put his arm around her. "You're bats,[2] he said.

He tried to get her to walk faster. By the time they got back to his apartment, she was smiling again, and talking about going skiing in the Rockies. He opened the door and saw a note lying on the floor, written by Dan. It was Penelope's name, written over and over, and a lot of profanity. He showed it to her. Neither of them said anything. He put it back on the table, next to an old letter from his mother that begged him to go back to graduate school.

"I want to stop smoking," she said, handing him her cigarette pack. She said it as if it were a revelation, as if everything, all day, had been carefully leading up to it.

It is a late afternoon in February, and Penelope is painting her toenails. She had meant what she said about moving in with him. She didn't even go back to Dan's apartment for her clothes. She has been borrowing Robert's shirts and sweaters, and wears his pajama bottoms under his long winter coat when she goes to the laundromat so she can wash her one pair of jeans. She has quit her job. She wants to give a farewell party before they go to Colorado.

She is sitting on the floor, and there are little balls of cotton stuck between her toes. The second toe on each foot is crooked. She wore the wrong shoes as a child. One night she turned the light on to show Robert her feet, and said that they embarrassed her. Why, then, is she painting her toenails?

"Penelope," he says, "I have no interest in any damn party. I have very little interest in going to Colorado."

Today he told his boss that he would be leaving next week. His boss laughed and said that he would send his brother around to beat him up. As usual, he could not really tell whether his boss was kidding. Before he goes to bed, he intends to stand a Coke bottle behind the front door.

"You said you wanted to see the mountains," Penelope says.

"I know we're going to Colorado," he says. "I don't want to get into another thing about that."

He sits next to her and holds her hand. Her hands are thin. They feel about an eighth of an inch thick to him. He changes his grip and gets his fingers down toward the knuckles, where her hand feels more substantial.

"I know it's going to be great in Colorado," Penelope says. "This is the first time in years I've been sure something is going to work out. It's the first time I've been sure that doing something was worth it."

"But why Colorado?" he says.

"We can go skiing. Or we could just ride the lift all day, look down on all that beautiful snow."

He does not want to pin her down or diminish her enthusiasm. What he wants to talk about is the two of them. When he asked if she was sure she loved him she said yes, but she never wants to talk about them. It's very hard to talk to her at all. The night before, he asked some questions about her childhood. She told him that her father died when she was nine, and her mother married an Italian who beat her with the lawn-mower cord. Then she was angry at him for making her remember that, and he was sorry he had asked. He is still surprised that she has moved in with him, surprised that he has agreed to leave New Haven and move to Colorado with her, into the house of a couple he vaguely remembers—nice guy, strung-out wife.

"Did you get a letter from Matthew and Bea yet?" he says.

"Oh, yes, Bea called this morning when you were at work. She said she had to call right away to say yes, she was so excited."

He remembers how excited Bea was the time she stayed with them in the country house. It seemed more like nervousness, really, not excitement. Bea said she had been studying ballet, and when Matthew told her to show them what she had learned, she danced through the house, smiling at first, then panting. She complained that she had no grace—that she was too old. Matthew tried to make her feel better by saying that she had only started to study ballet late, and she would have to build up energy. Bea became more frantic, saying that she had no energy, no poise, no future as a ballerina.

"But there's something I ought to tell you," Penelope says. "Bea and Matthew are breaking up."

"What?" he says.

"What does it matter? It's a huge state. We can find a place to stay. We've got enough money. Don't always be worried about money."

He was just about to say that they hardly had enough money to pay for motels on the way to Colorado.

"And when you start painting again—"

"Penelope, get serious," he says. "Do you think that all you have to do is produce some paintings and you'll get money for them?"

"You don't have any faith in yourself," she says.

It is the same line she gave him when he dropped out of graduate school, after she had dropped out herself. Somehow she was always the one who sounded reasonable.

"Why don't we forget Colorado for a while?" he says.

"Okay," she says. "We'll just forget it."

"Oh, we can go if you're set on it," he says quickly.

"Not if you're only doing it to placate me."

"I don't know. I don't want to stick around New Haven."

"Then what are you complaining about?" she says.

"I wasn't complaining. I was just disappointed."

"Don't be disappointed," she says, smiling at him.

He puts his forehead against hers and closes his eyes. Sometimes it is very nice to be with her. Outside he can hear the traffic, the horns blowing. He does not look forward to the long drive West.

In Nebraska they get sidetracked and drive a long way on a narrow road, with holes so big that Robert has to swerve the car to avoid them. The heater is not working well, and the defroster is not working at all. He rubs the front window clear with the side of his arm. By early evening he is exhausted from driving. They stop for dinner at Gus and Andy's Restaurant, and are served their fried-egg sandwiches by Andy, whose name is written in sequins above his shirt pocket. That night, in the motel, he feels too tired to go to sleep. The cat is scratching around in the bathroom. Penelope complains about the electricity in her hair, which she has just washed and is drying. He cannot watch television because her hair dryer makes the picture roll.

"I sort of wish we had stopped in Iowa to see Elaine," she says. Elaine is her married sister.

She drags on a joint, passes it to him.

"You were the one who didn't want to stop," he says. She can't hear him because of the hair dryer.

"We used to pretend that we were pregnant when we were little," she says. "We pulled the pillows off and stuck them under our clothes. My mother was always yelling at us not to mess up the beds."

She turns off the hair dryer. The picture comes back on. It is the news; the sportscaster is in the middle of a basketball report. On a large screen behind him, a basketball player is shown putting a basketball into a basket.

Before they left, Robert had gone over to Cyril's apartment. Cyril seemed to know already that Penelope was living with him. He was very nice, but Robert had a hard time talking to him. Cyril said that a girl he knew was coming over to make dinner, and he asked him to stay. Robert said he had to get going.

"What are you going to do in Colorado?" Cyril asked.

"Get some kind of job, I guess," he said.

Cyril nodded about ten times, the nods growing smaller.

"I don't know," he said to Cyril.

"Yeah," Cyril said.

They sat. Finally Robert made himself go by telling himself that he didn't want to see Cyril's girl.

"Well," Cyril said. "Take care."

"What about you?" he asked Cyril. "What are you going to be up to?"

"Much of the same," Cyril said.

They stood at Cyril's door.

"Seems like we were all together at that house about a million years ago," Cyril said.

"Yeah," he said.

"Maybe when the new people moved in they found dinosaur tracks," Cyril said.

In the motel that night, in his dreams Robert makes love to Penelope. When the sun comes through the drapes, he touches her shoulder and thinks about waking her. Instead, he gets out of bed and sits by the dresser and lights the stub of the joint. It's gone in three tokes, and he gets back into bed, cold and drowsy.

Going to sleep, he chuckles, or thinks he hears himself chuckling. Later, when she tries to rouse him, he can't move, and it isn't until afternoon that they get rolling. He feels tired but still up from the grass. The effect seems not to have worn off with sleep at all.

They are at Bea and Matthew's house. It was cloudy and cold when they arrived, late in the afternoon, and the sides of the roads were heaped high with old snow. Robert got lost trying to find the house and finally had to stop in a gas station and telephone to ask for directions. "Take a right after the feed store at the crossroads," Matthew told him. It doesn't seem to Robert that they are really in Colorado. That evening Matthew insists that Robert sit in their one chair (a black canvas butterfly chair) because Robert must be tired from driving. Robert cannot get comfortable in the chair. There is a large photograph of Nureyev on the wall across from Robert, and there is a small table in the corner of the room. Matthew has explained that Bea got mad after one of their fights and sold the rest of the living room furniture. Penelope sits on the floor at Robert's side. They have run out of cigarettes, and Matthew and Bea have almost run out of liquor. Matthew is waiting for Bea to drive to town to buy more; Bea is waiting for Matthew to give in. They are living together, but they have filed for divorce. It is a friendly living-together, but they wait each other out, testing. Who will turn the record over? Who will buy the Scotch?

Their dog, Zero, lies on the floor listening to music and lapping apple juice. He pays no attention to the stereo speakers but loves headphones. He won't have them put on his head, but when they are on the floor he creeps up on them and settles down there. Penelope points out that one old Marianne Faithfull record seems to make Zero particularly euphoric. Bea gives him apple juice for his constipation. She and Matthew dote on the dog. That is going to be a problem.

For dinner Bea fixes beef Stroganoff, and they all sit on the floor with their plates. Bea says that there is honey in the Stroganoff. She is ignoring Matthew, who stirs his fork in a circle through his food and puts his plate down every few minutes to drink Scotch. Earlier Bea told him to offer the bottle around, but they all said they didn't want any. A tall black candle burns in the center of their circle; it is dark outside, and the candle is the only light. When they finish eating, there is only one shot of Scotch left in the bottle and Matthew is pretty drunk. He says to Bea, "I was going to move out the night before Christmas, in the middle of the night, so that when you heard Santa Claus, it would have been me instead, carrying away Zero instead of my bag of tricks."

"Bag of *toys*," Bea says. She has on a satin robe that reminds Robert of a fighter's robe, stuffed between her legs as she sits on the floor.

"And laying a finger aside of my nose . . ." Matthew says. "No, I wouldn't have done that, Bea. I would have given the finger to you." Matthew raises his middle finger and smiles at Bea. "But I speak figuratively, of course. I will give you neither my finger nor my dog."

"I got the dog from the animal shelter, Matthew," Bea says. "Why do you call him your dog?"

Matthew stumbles off to bed, almost stepping on Penelope's plate, calling over his shoulder, "Bea, my lovely, please make sure that our guests finish that bottle of Scotch."

Bea blows out the candle and they all go to bed, with a quarter inch of Scotch still in the bottle.

"Why are they getting divorced?" Robert whispers to Penelope in bed.

They are in a twin bed, narrower than he remembers twin beds being, lying under a brown-and-white quilt.

"I'm not really sure," she says. "She said that he was getting crazier."

"They both seem crazy."

"Bea told me that he gave some of their savings to a Japanese woman who lives with a man he works with, so she can open a gift shop."

"Oh," he says.

"I wish we had another cigarette."

"Is that all he did?" he asks. "Gave money away?"

"He drinks a lot," Penelope says.

"So does she. She drinks straight from the bottle." Before dinner Bea had tipped the bottle to her lips too quickly and the liquor ran down her chin. Matthew called her disgusting.

"I think he's nastier than she is," Penelope says.

"Move over a little," he says. "This bed must be narrower than a twin bed."

"I *am* moved over," she says.

He unbends his knees, lies straight in the bed. He is too uncomfortable to sleep. His ears are still ringing from so many hours on the road.

"Here we are in Colorado," he says. "Tomorrow we'll have to drive around and see it before it's all under snow."

The next afternoon he borrows a tablet and walks around outside, looking for something to draw. There are bare patches in the snow—patches of brown grass. Bea and Matthew's house is modern, with a sundeck across the back and glass doors across the front. For some reason the house seems out of place; it looks Eastern. There are no other houses nearby. Very little land has been cleared; the lawn is narrow, and the woods come close. It is cold, and there is a wind in the trees. Through the woods, in front of the house, distant snow-covered mountains are visible. The air is very clear, and the colors are too bright, like a Maxfield Parrish painting. No one would believe the colors if he painted them. Instead he begins to draw some old fence posts, partially rotted away. But then he stops. Leave it to Andrew Wyeth. He dusts away a light layer of snow and sits on the hood of his car. He takes the pencil out of his pocket again and writes in the sketchbook: "We are at Bea and Matthew's. They sit all day. Penelope sits. She seems to be waiting. This is happening in Colorado. I want to see the state, but Bea and Matthew have already seen it, and Penelope says that she cannot face one more minute in the car. The car needs new spark plugs. I will never be a painter. I am not a writer."

Zero wanders up behind him, and he tears off the piece of sketch paper and crumples it into a ball, throws it in the air. Zero's eyes light up. They play ball with the piece of paper—he throws it high, and Zero waits for it and jumps. Finally the paper gets too soggy to handle. Zero walks away, then sits and scratches.

Behind the house is a ruined birdhouse, and some strings hang from a branch, with bits of suet tied on. The strings stir in the wind. "Push me in the swing," he remembers Penelope saying. Johnny was lying in the grass, talking to himself. Robert tried to dance with Cyril, but Cyril wouldn't. Cyril was more stoned than any of them, but showing better sense. "Push me," she said. She sat on the swing and he pushed. She weighed very little—hardly enough to drag the swing down. It took off fast and went high. She was laughing—not because she was having fun, but laughing at him. That's what he thought, but he was stoned. She was just laughing. Fortunately, the swing had slowed when she jumped. She didn't even roll down the hill. Cyril, looking at her arm, which had been cut on a rock, was almost in tears. She had landed on her side. They thought her arm was broken at first. Johnny was asleep, and he slept through the whole thing. Robert carried her into the house. Cyril, following, detoured to kick Johnny. That was the beginning of the end.

He walks to the car and opens the door and rummages through the ashtray, looking for the joint they had started to smoke just before they found Bea and Matthew's house. He has trouble getting it out because his fingers are numb from the cold. He finally gets it and lights it, and drags on it walking back to the tree with the birdhouse in it. He leans against the tree.

Dan had called him the day before they left New Haven and said that Penelope would kill him. He asked Dan what he meant. "She'll wear you down, she'll wear you out, she'll kill you," Dan said.

He feels the tree snapping and jumps away. He looks and sees that everything is OK. The tree is still there, the strings hanging down from the branch. "I'm going to jump!" Penelope had called, laughing. Now he laughs, too—not at her, because here he is, leaning against a tree in Colorado, blown away. He tries speaking, to hear what his speech sounds like. "Blown away," he says. He has trouble getting his mouth into position after speaking.

In a while Matthew comes out. He stands beside the tree and they watch the sunset. The sky is pale-blue, streaked with orange, which seems to be spreading through the blue sky from behind, like liquid seeping through a napkin, blood through a bandage.

"Nice," Matthew says.

"Yes," he says. He is never going to be able to talk to Matthew.

"You know what I'm in the doghouse for?" Matthew says.

"What?" he says. Too long a pause before answering. He spit the word out, instead of saying it.

"Having a Japanese girl friend," Matthew says, and laughs.

He does not dare risk laughing with him.

"And I don't even *have* a Japanese girl friend," Matthew says. "She lives with a guy I work with. I'm not interested in her. She needed money to go into business. Not a lot, but some. I loaned it to her. Bea changes facts around."

"Where did you go to school?" he hears himself say.

There is a long pause, and Robert gets confused. He thinks he should be answering his own question.

Finally: "Harvard."

"What class were you in?"

"Oh," Matthew says. "You're stoned, huh?"

It is too complicated to explain that he is not. He says, again, "What class?"

"1967," Matthew says, laughing. "Is that your stuff or ours? She hid our stuff."

"In my glove compartment," Robert says, gesturing.

He watches Matthew walk toward his car. Sloped shoulders. Something written across the back of his jacket, being spoken by what looks like a monster blue bird. Can't read it. In a while Matthew comes back smoking a joint, Zero trailing behind.

"They're inside, talking about what a pig I am," Matthew exhales.

"How come you don't have any interest in this Japanese woman?"

"I do," Matthew says, smoking from his cupped hand. "I don't have a chance in the world."

"I don't guess it would be the same if you got another one," he says.

"Another what?"

"If you went to Japan and got another one."

"Never mind," Matthew says. "Never mind bothering to converse."

Zero sniffs the air and walks away. He lies down on the driveway, away from them, and closes his eyes.

"I'd like some Scotch to cool my lungs," Matthew says. "And we don't have any goddamn Scotch."

"Let's go get some," he says.

"Okay," Matthew says.

They stay, watching the colors intensify. "It's too cold for me," Matthew says. He thrashes his arms across his chest, and Zero springs up, leaping excitedly, and almost topples Matthew.

They get to Matthew's car. Robert hears the door close. He notices that he is inside. Zero is in the back seat. It gets darker. Matthew hums. Outside the liquor store Robert fumbles out a ten-dollar bill. Matthew declines. He parks and rolls down the window. "I don't want to walk in there in a cloud of this stuff," he says. They wait. Waiting, Robert gets confused. He says, "What state is this?"

"Are you kidding?" Matthew asks. Matthew shakes his head. "Colorado," he says.

# Starley

His full name was Dickie Ray Starley, but he was Starley to everyone but his wife. She called him Dickie, and told close friends that even though it was a silly, little-boy name for a tall grown man, at least it was better than calling him Starley. She didn't like Starley's friends, and would have resented anything they called him. She liked Starley's best friend, Donald, better than the rest, because years before, when their daughter Anita was four, and they were all together for a weekend at the beach at Ocean City, Maryland, he had been very attentive to Anita, brushing sand from her knees before she got on the towel, taking her by the hand and walking with her to the cold gray sand where the water washed in. Alice knew that Donald was nice to Anita not so much because he liked her, but because he liked Starley. She didn't care what his motives were. Anita was very disagreeable that year. She had held her hand out to Donald, staring up at him and saying, "Kiss me here." "Wrong side," he said, and turned the hand over and kissed the palm. "It is not! You kiss the back of the hand! Now kiss it right!" He hated to be ordered around. The only way he knew how to deal successfully with kids was to tease them, and she didn't want to be teased. She had no sense of humor. He told her about "step on a crack, break your mother's back" and she squinted and said, "That's awful. And it's not true. Anybody can walk wherever they want." "That's true," he said. "This is a democracy, isn't it? Can you spell democracy?" He had few ways of getting back at her. He knew she was a poor speller.

Donald was not married. He had a son, Bobby, eight years old, living with his mother in North Miami, Florida. He did not get along with him any better than he got along with Anita, although he did not try to antagonize him. He brought his son gloxinia tubers, bubble-blowing liquid with a six-loop blower, a bird's nest with a speckled blue egg broken into four neat pieces lying inside. He bought him a plastic bird to clip onto the nest, a flower pot for the gloxinia tubers, walked up and down the beach with him as he blew bubbles at the sea gulls, rushing them and shouting between each blow. At seafood restaurants he carefully picked through his son's filet of sole for those tiny, invisible bones, worrying all through dinner that he might choke and die. Donald and Bobby were both Pisces.

Things started to change in Donald's life the summer of 1976. He had a girl friend, Marilyn, who was excessively kind. She made a lobster stew that made his eyes water with pleasure, and when they walked down the street together, she held his hand. She wore perfume that smelled like spice. She had a son from her first marriage, named Joshua, who was a problem: wouldn't eat fish of any sort, and sat at the table as Marilyn ate her boiled lobster and Donald ate his lobster stew (Marilyn liked plain things), crossing his eyes, shaping his hands into opening and closing lobster claws. He disapproved of Donald. He was fifteen years old and he built big rockets that he launched from a hilltop in the park on the weekends—rockets so big that they shook and whistled in a frightening way when they were ignited and took off in a split second and vanished from sight. Joshua demanded that his mother come along on these outings. With Joshua there, Marilyn was embarrassed to hold Donald's hand. They would sit side by side, she calling out approval to Joshua, Joshua grinning like mad and jumping up and down as rocket after rocket disappeared. It was a perfect place to hold hands, but she wouldn't.

In July, Donald had a two-week vacation, and Marilyn's vacation (ten days) coincided with it. Joshua was in summer school because he had failed plane geometry, so they had every afternoon alone together. Donald had promised to go fishing with Starley on Chesapeake Bay, but he never got around to calling him. Joshua's absence allowed them time to make love listening to music, go to the swimming pool in back of her apartment, walk slowly, holding hands, to the fish market for lobster.

Things changed at the end of the month when it turned out that Joshua had again failed plane geometry. By this time Donald was staying at her apartment most nights, so he was there when Joshua came home crying. The two of them stood in the hallway weeping. She tried to embrace him and he shoved her away. That made her cry so loudly that she bellowed. Joshua swore that he had done his best, that the teacher was a witch who punished a student even when he tried and failed. He said that he didn't care about the two sides of an isosceles triangle, and he would stab himself in the

heart with the point of a compass if he had to take the
course again. He ran out, slamming the door. Marilyn
went around the house, moving in patterns that made
no sense, trying to round up all the compasses. They
were all around the apartment: rusted compasses, compasses bent out of shape, compasses empty of pencils;
they looked ugly and evil, like something the Nazis
would use. She eventually found four of them and held
them out to Donald, the metal instruments shaking in
her hand louder than dice, and told him to bury them.
He buried them under a mock orange bush near the
swimming pool, dropping a stub of a pencil that had
been in one of them on top of the grave as a marker.
He had not buried anything since his pet turtle died
when he was twelve. When he went back to comfort
Marilyn, things started to come apart: he told her that
she was a good mother, and she turned on him and
said, "How can you give advice when you know nothing
about parenting? When you haven't seen your son all
year, except for one day last December?" Later that
week she went to see the school counselor. She came
home and told Donald that Joshua was "disturbed" by
their living together, that he would have to go. "You're
going to let a fifteen-year-old tell you how to live?"
Donald said. "What would you know, when you have
a child you completely ignore? If you loved that child,
and if he was suffering, and if you could help him, and
if you . . . if you ever cared enough to help him, then
you'd know, you'd . . ." She stood there, trembling, Lobster stew was bubbling on the stove. That night Donald
had two hamburgers at a drive-in restaurant and went
home and waited for her to call and apologize. She
didn't call that night or the next night, and each night
when the phone did not ring, Donald went to sleep
praying that Joshua would have to repeat the course.
At night he would awaken, sweating, stomach heavy,
having been fooled by some slight noise into thinking
that the phone was ringing. With only three days of

vacation left, knowing he had to get himself together, he did what he always did when he was in trouble or feeling blue—he called Starley. Starley had been his best friend in college; he had taught him how to take apart a carburetor, had patiently tutored him in logic. Starley had taught him, late in life, to whistle. After college, they had gone to New York together.

That night Starley and Alice met him for drinks at My Blue Heaven. They were late, so at the time Donald was to meet them, he crossed the street and went into the bar. He had almost finished his gin-and-tonic when they came in. He was sucking on the wedge of lime, and liking its greenness. The booths were padded in blue plastic, and there were silver-flecked blue Formica tabletops. Up near the ceiling were tiny twinkling blue lights. On the wall in back of the bar was a big cutout of Rita Hayworth, in a striped bathing suit; it had been stuck on a piece of board lettered "The One That Got Away," which had formerly held the huge plastic fish that was now hanging at the other end of the bar, its snout pointed up the skirt of Marilyn Monroe, who was pouting and pushing her full white skirt down as if, unexpectedly, a wind storm had just started up between her knees. There was, next to this, an anatomically correct baby-boy doll, painted Day-Glo blue.

"None of this would have happened if you had gone to the beach for your vacation," Alice said to Donald.

"I wanted to be with her. Her kid was in school. Everything was going fine until the little bastard flunked plane geometry."

"Get him a calculator," Alice said.

"Plane geometry isn't the sort of course that a calculator would help in," Starley said.

"Give me a light, Dickie," Alice said.

He lit her cigarette.

"I don't think this place is as funny as I used to," Alice said.

Nobody said anything.

"I'm in a bad mood, and I apologize for it," Alice said. "All week I've been trying to give up smoking by smoking these cigarettes that are made of lettuce."

"Why don't you call Marilyn and see if she won't come have a drink with us?" Starley said.

"I don't know."

"Why do we have to be here if he's going to have a drink with her, Dickie? I'd feel awkward. I already feel sick to my stomach."

"Then put that thing out."

"I can't. I need to smoke in social situations."

Years before, in New York, Starley had told Donald that his only misgiving about marrying Alice was her chain-smoking. The smoke made him cough. At the wedding reception there had been little silver trays with pastel-colored Nat Sherman cigarettes.

They sat looking at the tabletop. The waiter was avoiding them. The waiter had apple-pink puckered cheeks like Howdy Doody.

"Do you think you would do us a favor?" Alice said. "Dickie and I haven't been out to dinner in so long that I can't remember it, and the sitter could only come for an hour tonight. Do you think you could go stay with Anita?"

"Alice!" Starley said. "He doesn't want to be our baby-sitter."

"That's okay, Starley," Donald said. "It doesn't matter where I brood. You go out and have dinner. I'll go over to your place and watch Anita."

"Thank you," Alice said.

Starley rolled his eyes dramatically. He stood up, and then Alice bumped out of the booth. She looked heavier. Her skirt was wrinkled. Mascara had smudged under one eye. The summer before, he and Starley had picked up a whore after a day of fishing on Chesapeake Bay, and while he went at it with her, Donald had sat drunkenly on the floor across the room, casting his line into her hair. There was a little plastic worm attached to the fishing pole, and once he missed and she reached

down and pushed the thing off of her breast, saying,
"Ugh! Make him stop!" "She says she wants you to stop,
Starley," Donald said. Then the whore started giggling,
and Starley frowned at him. "She says she wants you
to quit it," he said. He was drunk. He was naked. Earlier (this was in a Howard Johnson's Motor Lodge) he
had put his underpants on his head and marched
around saying he was Ponce de Leon (Florida was on
his mind; his son was on his mind). They played tag.
The whore was easy to catch because she didn't want
to play tag in the first place, so she never really tried
to get away. When she bumped into a table and nicked
her shin, she refused to play anymore. They all sat
around drinking gin-and-tonics. She flipped a coin to
see who got her first. Whoever got "tails" got her. Much
later the three of them stood, in towels, on the tiny
balcony outside their room. In the parking lot a family
was unloading their station wagon. There was a wind-
blown mother, and a husband not quite as tall as she
was who carried an infant in a baby seat, and a little
girl, about five, who sat on the gravel and made demands as her father removed suitcases. The little girl
started crying, and her mother fumbled her up in her
arms, and they all marched into the Howard Johnson's
and disappeared.

Donald held the door of the bar open for Alice and
Starley. He shook hands with Starley and kissed Alice
on the cheek, and then he walked to Starley's to baby-
sit Anita, thinking all the way of the whore's legs—
kissing her scraped shin to make it well.

An hour later Donald was going out to eat chicken
with a kid who had never liked him, his relationship
with Marilyn over, the fan belt in Alice's car squealing.
Nothing he had ever done had made his own son like
him. Joshua hated him, failed his course to get even
with him, no kid *ever* liked him. He even had trouble
making friends with other kids when he was a kid.
Starley had been his first close friend. He drove, in the
rush hour, brooding, wanting to put the silent Anita

out of the car and go back to My Blue Heaven and make the waiter wait on him until he had had all the drinks he wanted.

Two summers before, the whore in the Howard Johnson's had asked: "Were you guys in Vietnam?"

"No," Starley said. "We're too old."

"Do we act like we were in Vietnam?" Donald asked her.

"How old are you?" she asked Starley.

He made her guess. She guessed wrong, by almost ten years.

"Thirty-five," he said.

"You're his age?" she said.

Donald nodded.

They were eating crabs. The crabs came in a black bucket and the waitress rolled out thick paper on the table and gave them a pile of napkins, but no plates. The whore was having crab cakes, which were very expensive. As they drank beer she drank a Coke. She sipped it through a straw, like a little girl.

"How old are you?" Donald asked her.

"Twenty-three," she said. She looked twenty-seven or -eight.

"Are you married?" she asked Donald.

"No," he said.

"Are you?" she asked Starley.

He squinched up his face and waved his hand from side to side—a gesture that meant "so-so."

"Do you have kids?" she asked him.

"One kid."

"I've got a friend who's a Vietnamese woman," she said, "and she told me about soldiers who came into the village who pushed her down and one of them fucked her while the other one held the rifle underneath his friend, touching her asshole."

She finished her Coke, sucking in mostly air. Donald thought that maybe she was twenty-three. It was just that she had sweated and not washed her face, and the make-up had caked on her cheeks.

"If you two want to do it again after dinner, you'll have to pay me more," she said. She looked into her empty Coke glass. "I guess it would have been only fair to tell you that before I let you take me to dinner." She put her finger in the glass and brought out a piece of ice and sucked it. "I just didn't think of it," she said. "I honestly didn't think of it."

When it happened, Donald had just recently begun to feel happy—happy for the first time in months. (Marilyn never called; when he called her, she wouldn't see him. Not any of the four times he called.) It was the first of November—the same day he had half a cord of wood delivered, which was stacked in what used to be a closet in the living room (door now removed). A fire was burning. Getting close to midnight, alone (but there had been someone earlier), having a cup of coffee that would keep him awake, but what the hell—the next day was Saturday—the phone rang. He crossed the room and picked up the phone and heard the voice of a stranger telling him, in a flat voice, that his friend Starley was dead.

Starley and Alice had been having a party—a party to which Alice had invited her important friends and to which Donald had not been invited—and Starley went out to get ice cubes. They were drinking mint juleps. (This gets crazier: they had all brought beach towels, were sitting around wrapped up in them with the heat turned up, pretending they were Arabs in the desert.) It was nine o'clock, around there, and Starley said they were running out of ice. (Correction: *Alice* said they were running out of ice, for which she will never forgive herself; yes, she realized that he, too, would eventually have noticed it. But if he had noticed five seconds later—probably *one* second later—the truck that went out of control would have passed that stretch of street Starley was crossing.) Starley had put on his black jacket and taken Alice's scarf and, cold as it was, decided that the store was two blocks away, so he'd walk. (Alice, later, was sure that he had opened the door of the Fiat—his car was in the garage—and looked for the key under the floor mat—the one time she had left her key in the kitchen instead of in the usual hiding place. She was sure that he had tried to drive, had not found the key, had then and only then decided to walk. If he had taken the Fiat, he would be alive.)

The truck, a United Van Lines truck, its brakes not working properly as it came down the hill, and then the ice patch that threw it off course, right into him, on his way to buy ice cubes...

Donald heard all this when he picked up the phone. He could not really focus on the fact that Starley was dead; he could think only of himself, and the guilt he felt thinking, Hey—he's dead and I'm alive. The guilt he felt thinking that if he had been invited to the party, he would probably have been the one to go for ice.

After Donald put down the phone (the anonymous voice having said, two times: "Come to the hospital for *what?*") and he was standing there, disbelieving, the memory of the summer before with the whore making him smile and encroaching on his sorrow, the phone rang again. It was the woman who had been at his house earlier. It was Susan with her lovely, soft voice, calling to tell him she loved him. A few seconds after she hung up, wandering through his apartment, Donald was not clear what he had said to her. He knew that he should call her back, but he had no time. He was on the road, sad but full of purpose, an hour after both phone calls, headed for North Miami.

The drive took several days. The last night before he got there, he slept in a Howard Johnson's, wanting to indulge all his maudlin instincts and be done with them. But this motel was not like the other one. The only room they had had one twin bed, and the room they had rented on the fishing trip had been much larger, with two double beds. This motel was loud. People in the next room sang along with a singer on television, other people joined them, they had a party. Donald stood staring out the window (no balcony off this room) at the pool, flat and blue, just a little too far away to be inviting, the night a little too cool for swimming.

From a phone booth on the highway that afternoon he had called his boss. His boss had met Starley at a party at his apartment once, but said he didn't remember him.

"I flipped," Donald said. "It made me realize that while I was alive there were things I had to do. Please don't fire me."

There was static on the line; a bad connection. His boss was placating: of course he wouldn't fire him, but when did he think—(cars roared by). They hung up, both joking about Florida oranges.

He had tried to call Joanna from another phone later on, to say he was coming. There was no answer. He tried to call Susan, but of course she was at work, no answer there either. With the back of his arm he wiped the sweat off his forehead. What the hell had his boss been joking about—what was funny about Florida oranges?

Joanna's house was only a ten-minute drive from the highway. It was a small pale-green house. The lawn was full of exotic bushes. In front of the house a pink 1955 Cadillac convertible was parked. The upholstery inside was white, in perfect condition. Whose was it?

He went up the walk and knocked on the doorframe of the screen door. A girl came to the door when he knocked.

"What do you want?" she said.

"Does Joanna still live here?"

"Yeah. Who are you?"

"I'm Bobby's father."

"What do you mean?" She looked confused. She put her face closer to the screen. Her eyes were large, like Anita's. She was prettier. Older.

"I'm his father. I came to visit him."

He snapped his arms into his sides. He had been standing there like a bear, leaning forward, arms away from his body.

"What does he look like?" she said.

"He has medium-length brown hair. He has braces. Wait a minute—he was getting braces when I was last here, but I don't know if he got them. He looks like me. Don't you see the resemblance?"

"Yeah," she said. "Come on in."

"Who are you?" Donald said. "Where are they?"

"Bobby's gone over to a friend's house. I'm waiting for him to get back. Your wife is playing volleyball."

"Where?" he said.

"Do you know the Orrs?"

"No."

"She's there."

They stood facing each other. She had a cigarette in her mouth and was about to light the filter.

"It's to surprise them," he said. "They didn't know I was coming."

"Oh," she said.

"Wrong end," he said, reaching out to touch her hand before she could touch the lighted match to the cigarette.

The television was on, but she had turned down the volume before opening the door. Red Skelton was gesticulating, his face expanding and contracting as if it were made of putty.

"If you're going to be here," she said, "I might as well go."

He nodded. She was going down the walk when he remembered about paying her. She turned around when he called after her and cocked her head. "Pay me?" she said. "Joanna's my friend. I watch Bobby and she watches my daughter."

"You have a daughter?" he said.

"Yes. I have a four-year-old daughter." She smiled, deciding to be more friendly. "Her father is watching her. They went to the beach. I just live three streets over."

She waved. She went out to the car and started it. The radio came on when the car started. It was a fine car: in perfect shape, motor idling quietly, paint sparkling. She waved again. Donald waved. She was gone.

He walked into the kitchen to look for a drink, realizing that he was not only tired but depressed. Depressed that he didn't know one friend of Joanna's and that the one he had just met was by accident. Maybe it wasn't one of her close friends. How could she be a close friend if she didn't even know that Joanna had never married. But maybe Joanna had told people she was divorced, for Bobby's sake. For Bobby's sake he would have married her, but she wouldn't do it. They had argued about it, but he couldn't change her mind. She lived in an apartment in New York with three other girls—a tiny apartment on the East Side. When she was three months pregnant she started bleeding. She called the doctor and he told her to go to bed. She and Donald jogged around Central Park. They danced the Virginia reel in his apartment as best they could, because that apartment was only slightly larger than hers. They sat in a bar and she said, "Everything's okay. Everything's going to be okay." The bleeding stopped. They jogged again, every night for a week, running like maniacs. Bobby was born six months later, in Florida. She had gone there because she had friends in Florida, and because he would not stop pestering her to marry him. Bobby was born one week before Donald's birthday. One of her friends called him at work to tell him. Ironically, after she described the baby, she said, "Everything's okay." She told him that Joanna did not want to see him, that when she was ready she would call. No call.

Most houses that look small outside are a little larger inside. This one was not. He found rum to drink and walked around the house sipping it. He went from the kitchen back to the living room to the bedroom adjoining it and went in. It was her room. There was no bedspread, and the bed was made with white sheets. He sat on it, realizing how tired he was, then got up and smoothed out the wrinkles. The room was almost empty. There was a wicker chair in front of a big antique mirror, an ugly high white-painted dresser. He walked out and into Bobby's room. There was a pile of clothes on the floor. On his dresser was a letter. It was addressed to someone named Robert Winter. It could have been anybody. Robert Winter lived in Pennsylvania. Who would Bobby know in Pennsylvania? He looked in the bathroom (Jean Naté on the glass shelf above the sink, a sand dollar, a tube of toothpaste, coiled like a snake), then walked exactly three steps and went back to the kitchen, where he put down his drink because he didn't want it, and stepped down one step into the living room. He hoped that Bobby would come home first. Then she would be cordial if Bobby was glad to see him. If she came first, there was little chance of her being friendly. On a table by the sofa was a pile of pictures. Most of them were of Bobby, in uniform, playing baseball. There was one of her father hugging Bobby, in the snow, outside his big house in Massachusetts. Probably they had gone there for Christmas. There was one of Joanna in a long yellow skirt and a white blouse, and she was standing stiffly, as she always did in photographs. She looked as if she was going out for a big evening. Who was she going with? Robert Winter?

"Starley," he had said, years ago in New York, "Joanna is pregnant and she won't marry me."

"I wouldn't marry you either," he said.

"Why wouldn't you?"

"Because I'm a man."

"Christ—what are you joking about? This is serious. She's going to have a baby, and she won't get married."

"I'm sorry," he said.

"You're sorry she won't marry me, or what?"

"What's the cross-examination?" he said. "I'm sorry about everything."

They were walking past the reservoir, where he and Joanna had run the week before.

"Give her time, she'll change her mind."

He took big steps when he walked. Donald took big steps with him.

"What do you want to get married for, anyway?" he said.

Four months later Starley was married to Alice.

He sat quietly with his hands in his lap until he heard her car in the drive—the VW she insisted on driving, even though he had patiently explained each time he saw her how unsafe a car it was. He fidgeted, now knowing whether to get up and open the door, or just sit there. Either way, he would probably frighten her. While he sat thinking, he lost the opportunity to move. She opened the door a crack, put her head around the corner, and her eyes met his.

"Oh God," she sighed. "I wondered why the door was hanging open."

Her hair was pulled back in a rubber band. She was carrying a tennis racket. She had on white shorts and a black T-shirt. She wiped her hair out of her face.

"Okay," she said. "What are you doing here? I assume it got too cold for you up north."

"It did," he said. "It really did."

"Where's Deena?" she said.

"Is that her name? The woman with the four-year-old daughter?"

"She didn't have her with her, did she? Am I crazy or something?"

"No, she . . . she told me. She said she had a daughter. I didn't know her name."

"Deena," she said. "Now, what are you doing here?"

She sat in a wicker chair. He thought, If I can still be so attracted to her, I can't love Susan. If I had reached Susan on the phone, what would I have said?

"Who's Robert Wilson?" he said.

"I don't know. Who?"

"Isn't that his name?" He got up and went to Bobby's room. He came back. "I mean Robert Winter," he said.

"A friend of his who moved to Pennsylvania," she said. "Did you count the silverware to make sure it was all there too?"

"Joanna," he said. He locked his fingers together. "Do you remember Starley?"

She sighed, obviously exasperated. They had all been constant companions in New York; the three of them—later the four of them—had gone dancing together at night.

"He died," he said. "He was run over by a truck."

Her mouth came open. She slowly pulled the rubber band out of her hair and rubbed it into a ball between her fingers. "Starley's dead?" she said. "I just got a letter from Starley."

"No you didn't. What would he write you a letter for?"

"He wrote me." She shrugged.

"What did he write you?"

"Stay here," she said. She crossed the room, stepped up, turned into her bedroom.

"What is it?" he said, following her.

The letter was about a picture that Starley could get her a print of from the National Gallery of Art. She must have written to ask him if he could get it. At the end of the letter he had written: "P.S. Why don't you let bygones be bygones and marry him, Joanna? He shacks up with one dreary woman after another, the latest of which dumped him because her fifteen-year-old son wouldn't do his math homework as long as she had him around."

"Imagine thinking that after all this time I'm going to marry you," she said. "When I knew you I was eighteen years old, and I thought that you were hot stuff. I thought New York was a big, impressive place. I was eighteen years old."

Past her, outside the window, was a bush with bright-green leaves and lavender flowers that looked very bright in the half-light.

"That's pretty," he said, pointing over her shoulder. "What kind of bush is that?"

"Hibiscus," she said. "But look—what are you doing here?"

He was sitting by her on the bed. Her skin was cool, on top of her arm where his arm touched hers. The bed linen was cool, too, because the window had been open and the bush outside had shaded it from the sun. It was summer in Florida, and winter back north. He was holding her hand. Years ago he had held her hand when she was eighteen. He rubbed his thumb over her knuckles. He picked up the letter with the other hand and dropped it to the floor.

"Starley's dead," he said. "A truck hit him. It was an accident."

He was surprised to be saying out loud what he had been thinking for days. In the apartment she had shared with the three other girls in New York they had gotten used to whispering, in the bedroom, behind the closed door (a sign that her roommates were to stay in the living room or, preferably, go out). They had whispered, she had whispered that she loved him.

He ran his hand along the sheet, then rested it on top of her leg. As he tried to clear his mind he heard the hum of the highway, the faint static that had made it difficult to talk when he made the phone call earlier. He was talking to himself, but she was answering him.

"Wait," he said, his voice no louder than the sound his hand made stroking the sheet. "Wait a minute," he said. "Wait."

"Wait for what?" she whispered.

# Deer Season

There had been very few times in their lives when they lived apart, and now, for almost three years, Margaret and Elena had shared the cottage in the Adirondacks. In all that time, things had gone smoothly. The only time in their lives things had not gone well was the time before the sisters moved to the cottage. Elena and Tom, the man Elena had been living with, had broken up, and Tom had begun to date Margaret. But Tom and Margaret had not dated long, and now it had become an episode the sisters rarely mentioned. Each understood that the other had once loved him.

Elena had lived with Tom in his brother's high rise on the East Side of Manhattan, but when Tom's brother came back from Europe they had to leave the borrowed apartment, and Tom suggested that it might be a good idea if they lived apart for a while. It had not come as a surprise to Elena, but Tom's dates with Margaret had.

Margaret had never lived with Tom; she had dated him when she was going to nursing school, telling Elena that she knew living with a man would be a great distraction from her work, and once she had decided what she wanted to do, she wanted to concentrate hard. It hurt Elena that Tom would prefer Margaret's company to her own, and it hurt her more that Margaret did not seem to really love him—she preferred her work to him. But Margaret had always been the lucky one.

Tom visited every year, around Christmas. The first year he came he talked about a woman he was dating: a college professor, a minor poet. If the news hurt either of them, the sisters didn't show it. But the next year— they were surprised that he would come again, since the first year he came his visit seemed more or less perfunctory—he talked to Elena after Margaret had gone to bed. He told her then that it had been a mistake to say that they should live apart, that he had found no one else, and would find no one else: he loved her. Then he went into her bedroom and got into bed. She thought about telling him to get out, that she didn't want to start anything again and that it would be embarrassing with Margaret in the next bedroom. But she counted back and realized that she had not slept with anyone in almost a year. She went to bed with him. After that visit, a sentence in one of his letters might have been meant as a proposal, but Elena did not allude to that in her letter to him, and Tom said nothing more. Finally his letters became less impassioned. The letters stopped entirely for almost six months, but then he wrote again, and asked if he could come for what he called his "annual visit." He also wrote Margaret, and Margaret said to Elena, "Tom

wants to visit. That's all right with you, isn't it?" They
were standing in the doorway to the kitchen, where
Elena was putting down a saucer of milk for the cat.

"What are you thinking about so seriously?" Margaret said.

"We need a new kettle," Elena said. "One that
doesn't whistle." She lifted the kettle off the burner.

"Is that what you were really thinking about? I
thought you might have been thinking about the visit."

"What would I be thinking? I don't care if he comes
or not."

"I don't either. Maybe next year we should just say
no. It does sort of stir up memories."

Margaret poured water into a cup and added instant
coffee and milk. She put the kettle down and Elena
picked it up. It irritated Elena that Margaret always
added the coffee after she had put the water in. It also
irritated her that she had time to be bothered by such
things. She thought that as she got older, she was becoming more and more petty. She had a grant, this
year, to write about Rousseau's paintings, and she kept
bogging down in details. After a few hours' work she
would be bored and leave the house. Sometimes she
would see no one but Margaret from week to week,
except for the regulars at the village store and an occasional hunter walking through the woods, or along
the roads. In the summer she had dated an older man
named Peter Virrell, one of the summer people who
had stayed on, but they had very little to say to each
other. He was a painter, so they could talk about art,
but she got tired of researching and writing and then
talking all night about the same subject, and he drank
more than she liked and embarrassed her the next day
by calling and begging forgiveness. She found excuses
not to see him. Once, when she did, he drank too much
and insisted on holding her when she didn't want to be
held, and with his lips softly against her ear whispered,
"Stop pretending, stop pretending..." She had been

afraid that when he stopped whispering, he was going
to strike her. He looked angry when he let go of her
and stood there staring. "Pretending what?" she said,
trying to keep her voice even. "You're the one who
knows," he said. He sat in front of his open fireplace,
tossing in bits of paper that he had shredded and
worked into little balls.

"I don't have to explain myself to you," she said.

"I'm forty years old and I drink too much," he said.
"I don't blame you for not being interested in me. You
don't intend to sleep with me, do you?"

She had not been asked that so bluntly since college,
when a few crazy boys she knew talked that way. She
didn't know whether to resent it or to try to answer
him.

"That's what I thought," he said. "Next do you say
that you want to go home, and do I drive you?"

"You're trying to make me a puppet," she said.
"You're making a mockery of me before I even speak."

"I'm sorry," he said. He got up and put his coat on,
and she heard his keys jingle as he lifted them from
the table. She was humiliated to be sent home, like a
child being sent from the room after it has cutely performed for all the guests. She continued to stand by
the fire, but he continued to stand in the hallway.

"I didn't know you were dating me for sex," she heard
herself say.

"I wasn't," he said.

That was in August, and she had not seen him since.
Sometimes when she was depressed she would think
of Peter and wonder whether she shouldn't have tried
harder so that she and Margaret wouldn't end up together forever. They seemed to Elena to be old people
already, the way they carried on about the cat: how
clever it was, how much personality it had.

Tom came at eight o'clock, as Elena and Margaret
were finishing dinner. Tom's hair had grown long. He

wore a black coat and black boots. He had a friend with him, a fellow named Max, who stood by shyly. Max was taller than Tom, and nowhere as good-looking. He had on a denim jacket with layers of sweaters underneath, and his face was mottled pink from the cold. Tom brought him forward and introduced him. Tom presented his usual assortment of odd gifts: a basil plant, a jar of macadamia nuts, a book of poetry called *Gathering the Bones Together*, a poster of Donald O'Connor and Debbie Reynolds and Gene Kelly from *Singin' in the Rain*. After the admiring, and the laughing, and Margaret adopting Debbie Reynold's posture and expression, no one seemed to know what to say. Margaret offered to show Max the house. Elena told Tom how much he had changed. She didn't think that she would have recognized him on the street. When they lived together he had been thin, with a beard and short hair. Now, she saw, as he took off the coat, he had put on weight. His hair was as long as hers.

"Would you like a drink or a cup of coffee?" Elena said.

"Where have Margaret and Max gone?" Tom said.

They were silent, and could hear talking in the far room, the room where Margaret grew plants under lights in the winter.

"I might have a beer," he said. "There are some in that bag Max carried in."

They bent together to pick up the bag. Their heads bumped. She thought again, that this was going to be an impossible visit.

"Have one?" he said.

"No thank you."

"Okay if I get a fire going? You're the only person I know who's got a fireplace."

He went to the fireplace and crumpled newspaper and stuffed it in and began building a pile of kindling and logs. Elena sat on the floor, holding the box of matches. She thought back to the night in August when she had last seen Peter.

"You said you were writing about Rousseau," Tom said. "How's it coming?"

"Not very well. I think I might have chosen the wrong topic."

"What's your topic?" he said, striking a match and putting it to the newspaper. She had told him in the letter what it was.

"Ah, beautiful," Tom said. "Look at it go." He sat beside her and smiled at the flames. "Are you going to take a walk with me later? I want to talk to you."

"What about?"

"Max has talked me into going to the West Coast. I want to talk you into going with us."

"You come to visit once a year, and this time you want me to move to the West Coast with you."

"I don't have the nerve to visit you more than once a year. I treated you like hell."

"That just occurred to you."

"It didn't just occur to me. My shrink said to tell you."

"Your shrink said to tell me."

"You sound like my shrink," Tom said. "I say something, and he repeats it."

By the time they went for a walk, several records had been played and they had all eaten cheese and crackers, and then Margaret and Max had wandered out of the room again, back to the plant room to get stoned. Elena and Tom sat drinking the last two cans of beer. She admitted defeat—she told him all the problems she had with writing, the problem she had concentrating. He confessed that he had no intention of going away with Max, but that he thought if he told her that, she might come back.

"I'm nuts. I admit I'm nuts," Tom said.

He was beginning to seem more familiar to her. Underneath the black coat had been a plaid shirt she remembered. The shoes were the same black motorcycle boots, polished.

Tom stood and pulled her up with one hand. Then, weaving, he headed for the chair to get his coat. Elena went to the closet for hers. The temperature gauge outside the door read thirty-four degrees. There was a full moon.

"Rousseau," Tom said, looking at the moon. "I think that gypsy's sleeping just to flip out the wolf."

He buried their clasped hands in the pocket of his coat. He didn't let go as he unbuttoned his coat and turned sideways to urinate on the leaves. Elena stared at him with amazement. When he finished, he buttoned his coat with one hand.

"Hang on!" Max called, running with Margaret down the field to the edge of the woods. Elena saw that Margaret had put on the white poncho their grandmother had sent her as an early Christmas present. Max and Margaret were laughing, close enough now to see their breath, running so fast that they passed Tom and Elena and stumbled toward the woods.

"I've got the tape!" Max called back, holding a cassette.

"He has a tape he borrowed from a hunter friend," Tom said.

"Recording of a dying rabbit!" Max called to Elena. "Once I get this thing going, we can hide and see if a fox comes."

Max put the machine down and clicked the cassette into place, and was hurrying them into the woods and whispering for them to be quiet, although his loud whisper was the only noise. Max crouched next to Margaret, with his arm around her. Tom took Elena's hand and plunged it into his pocket again. Elena was spellbound by the noise from the cassette player: it was a rabbit in pain, shrieking louder and louder.

"You see a fox?" Max whispered.

Soon an owl landed in a small peach tree in the middle of the field. It sat there, silhouetted by the moon, making no noise. Max pointed excitedly, cupped his hands over his eyes (though there was no reason for it) to look at the owl, which sat, not moving. The screeching on the cassette player reached a crescendo and stopped abruptly. The owl stayed in the tree.

"Well," Max said. "We got an owl. Don't anybody move. Maybe there's something else out there."

They sat in silence. Elena's hand was sweaty in Tom's pocket. She got up and said, "I'm going to finish my walk." Tom rose with her and followed her out of the woods. When they had gone about a hundred feet they heard, again, the sounds of the dying rabbit.

"Is he serious?" Elena said.

"I guess so," Tom said.

They were walking toward the moon, and toward the end of the field. There was a road to the left that went to the pump house. She was thinking about going there, sitting on one of the crates inside, and telling him she would come back to him. Imagining it, Elena felt suddenly elated. Just as quickly, her mood changed. He was the one who had broken off their relationship. Then he had begun to date her sister.

"Let's go to the pump house," Tom said.

"No," Elena said. "Let's go back to the house and get warm."

Their indecision had been a joke between them when they lived together; it got so bad that they could not decide which movie to see, which restaurant to eat at, whom to invite over for an evening. Tom's solution had been to flip a coin, but even after the flip, he'd say, "Of course, we could still do the other. Would you rather do that?"

They talked for hours that night before they went to bed. They were squeezed into a chair he had hauled in front of the fireplace, both sitting on one hip to fit in.

"How could you think you're not on my mind when I write you a letter a week?" Tom said, kissing her hair.

"You only come once a year."

"When have you invited me?"

"I don't know."

"You never have. I've asked you to visit me."

"You asked Margaret, too."

"I did when I thought that you wouldn't come under any other circumstances."

"Does Max like Margaret?"

"I guess so. Max is a real charmer. Max likes women. I don't know many of his women friends. I just know he likes them, period." Tom lit a cigarette. He threw the match in the fireplace. "And anyway, you're not Margaret's keeper."

"The lease on the house goes until June," Elena said.

"They can find somebody. And if they don't, we can pay for it until then."

"You're being so matter-of-fact. It's a little strange, don't you agree? I don't know. Let me think about it."

"We'll flip a coin."

"Be serious," Elena said.

Tom stood and got a nickel out of his pocket. He tossed it, turned the coin upside down on the back of his hand. "Heads. You come back," he said.

"How do I know it was heads?"

"Okay, I'll flip again. If it's heads, you agree to believe that I was honest about the flip."

He flipped the coin again. "Heads," he said. "You believe me."

He came back to the chair.

Elena laughed. "What have you been doing the last three years?"

"I put it all in my letters."

"You never told me about the women you were seeing."

"I was seeing women. Tall women. Short women. What do you want to know?"

He took out his pocket watch and opened it. Two o'clock. Margaret and Max had been asleep for about an hour. The front of the gold watch was embossed with a hunting scene: a hunter taking aim on a deer leaping toward the woods. He pushed the watch back into his pants pocket.

"I think you want to stay here out of some crazy responsibility to Margaret," he said, "and there's no reason for it. Margaret wrote me."

"What did she write you?"

"That things weren't going well out here, and neither of you would admit it. And, as a matter of fact, I wasn't lying about the coin, either. It came up heads both times."

"Does Max like her?"

"We just discussed that."

"But does he?"

"Max charms, and screws, every woman who has a pretty face. Look: I asked her in a letter what she'd do if you went back with me, and she said she'd stay on with her job at the hospital until the lease ran out."

The fire was dying out. The side of Elena's body that was not turned toward Tom was cold.

"Come on," he said and pulled her out of the chair. Walking down the hallway to the bedroom, he stopped and turned her toward the mirror. "You know what you're looking at?" he said.

"A sheep in wolf's clothing. In the morning you just say, 'Goodbye, Margaret,' and drive away with me."

She said it, but a bit more elaborately. Max and Tom took a walk while Margaret and Elena had coffee. She told Margaret that she was going to spend the week with Tom, that after the week was up, she would be back, to decide what to do.

Margaret nodded, as if she hadn't really heard. Just as Elena was about to repeat herself, Margaret looked up and said, "I always thought that Daddy liked me best. Although maybe he didn't, Elena. Maybe he teased you so much because you were his favorite."

Max came into the kitchen, followed by Tom.

"We ought to get moving," Tom said. "Thank you, Margaret, for your hospitality." He held out his hand.

Margaret shook his hand.

"Snow forecast," Max said. "I heard it on the radio when I was warming up the car."

The car was running. Elena could hear it. This departure was too abrupt. Earlier Tom had carried out two boxes of books and her papers. Max was swinging her suitcase.

Max kissed Margaret's cheek. Perhaps earlier he had said he would call her. Perhaps Margaret already understood that, and it wasn't as bad as it looked. After all, Margaret had been pretty silent about other things. Hadn't Tom made that clear?

Max held open the back door. Elena hugged Margaret and told her again that she'd be back.

"Stay put if you're happy," Margaret said. It was hard to tell with what tone she said it.

They walked single file to the car. Elena sat between them. The radio was on, and Max turned up the volume. Margaret disappeared from the door, then reappeared, waving, wind blowing the white poncho away from her body. Elena could not tell who was singing on the radio because she never listened to country music. When the song ended, she changed stations. There was a weather forecast for snow before evening. She looked up through the tinted glass of the windshield and saw that the snow would start any minute; it wasn't only the gray glass that made the sky look that ominous.

"God, I'm happy," Tom said and hugged her. Max moved the dial back to the country-music station and began to sing along with the song. She looked at him to see if that was deliberate, but he was looking out the window. As he sang she looked at him again, to make sure that he wasn't teasing her. Her father had loved to tease her. When she was small, her father used to toss her in the air, to the count of three. Usually he gave one toss for each count. Sometimes, though, he would throw her high and run the words together "onetwothree." That frightened her. She told him that it did, and one time she cried. Her mother yelled at her

father then for going too far: "How is she going to be
an acrobat if she's afraid of height?" her father said.
He always tried to turn things into a joke. She could
still close her eyes and see him clearly, in his silk bathrobe with his black velvet slippers monogrammed in
silver, coming for her to toss her in the air.

They stopped at a restaurant for lunch. Max put a
quarter in the jukebox and played country songs. Elena
was beginning to dislike him. She already regretted
leaving her sister so abruptly. But everything Tom said
had been the truth. Margaret probably wanted her to
go.

"Your shrink would be happy to see that smile on
your face," Max said to Tom. "He'd know that he was
worth the money."

"How long have you been seeing a shrink?" she
asked.

"I don't know," Tom said. "Six months, maybe. Is
that about right, Max?"

"His ladylove left him," Max said, "almost six
months to the day."

"What the hell's the matter with you?" Tom said.
"What did you say that for?"

"Was it a secret?"

"It wasn't a secret. It's just that I hadn't discussed
it with her yet."

"Sorry," Max said. "I'll wash out my mouth with
soap. Believe me, I intended nothing by it. If you knew
how lousy my own love life was, you'd know I wasn't
passing judgment."

The snow started as they ate. Elena looked toward
the window because there was such a draft she thought
it might be open a crack, saw that it was closed, saw
the snow.

"I guess we'd better hit the road while the road's
still visible," Max said, waving to the waitress. Tom
took Elena's hand and kissed her knuckles. She had
left almost all of her sandwich.

Outside, they all stopped. They stood staring at a van, with a deer strapped to the top. Elena looked down and fingered the buttons on her coat. When she looked up, the deer was still there, on its side on the rack on top of a blue van. Tom went over to the van. He took a piece of paper out of his pocket and wrote "Murdering Motherfucker" and swung open the door and dropped the paper on the driver's seat.

"Let's get out of here before he comes out and starts a fight," Max said.

Tom took a turn at the wheel. Max stretched out in the back seat. The driving was getting more difficult, so Tom let go of Elena's hand to drive with both hands on the wheel. She turned off the radio, and nobody said anything. "That bastard was the one who should have been shot," Max said. She turned around and saw him: eyes closed, knees raised so his feet would fit on the seat. She no longer hated him. She hoped that Margaret had taken in wood before the snow started. The place where it was stacked was hardly sheltered at all.

When the car started to swerve, she grabbed Tom's arm—the worst thing she could have done—and sucked in her breath. Max sat up and started cursing. She watched as the car drifted farther and farther to the right, onto the shoulder of the road. It bumped to a stop. "Goddamn tire," Max said, and opened the back door and got out. Tom got out on his side, leaving the door open. Snow blew into the car. No cars had been behind them when it happened. They had been lucky. Elena heard Tom complaining that there was a jack, but no spare tire. "I'll walk back," Max said and kicked his foot in the gravel. "There's got to be somebody who'll come out, snow or not. I'll call somebody." He did not sound as if he believed what he was saying.

Tom got back in the car and slammed the door. "How stupid can we be, to take this trip without a spare?" he said. "Now we sit here and freeze, like a couple of idiots." He looked up into the rear-view mirror, at Max walking back to where they had come from. No cars

came along the road. Elena took his hand, but he withdrew it.

"We'll get going again," she said.

"But I can't believe how stupid we were."

"It's Max's car," she said. "He should have had the
spare with him."

"It's Max's car, but we're all in the same boat. You
took that I-am-not-my-brother's-keeper lecture too
much to heart."

"You believed what you told me, didn't you?"

"Oh, leave me alone. I've had to argue and discuss
all weekend."

She turned the rear-view mirror toward her to see
what progress Max was making, but the back window
was entirely covered with snow. The light was dim-
ming. She took Tom's hand again and this time he let
her, but didn't look at her.

"You'll hate me again," he said, "because I never
change."

"I won't," she said.

"What about what Max said in the restaurant? You
don't want to hear about all that crap, do you?"

"I guess not."

"If I bullied you into leaving Margaret, you can go
back. I wouldn't hate you for it. Maybe I said too much.
It just struck me that I'm not the best one to be giving
advice."

"What are you trying to do?" Elena said. "Are you
trying to get me to back out?"

Tom sighed. Elena moved over next to him for
warmth. As they sat huddled together, a car pulled up
behind them. Tom opened the door to get out. Elena
looked around him, hoping to see a policeman. She saw
a short man with a camouflage hat that buckled under
the chin. Tom pushed the door shut behind him, but
it didn't click and slowly swung open as the man talked.
Elena reached across the seat to close the door, and as
she did that she looked farther than she had the first
time and saw that it was the blue van with the deer

on top. She was terrified. Certainly the man had seen, from the restaurant, who put the note in the van. She took her hand off the handle and leaned across the seat to watch the conversation. In a while the man in the camouflage hat laughed. Tom laughed too. Then he walked to the man's van with him. Elena moved into the driver's seat and stuck her head out the door. She felt the snow soaking her hair. Max was nowhere to be seen. Tom and the man were nodding at the deer. Then Tom turned and came back to the car, and Elena moved into her seat again.

"Did he know it was us?" she said.

"How would he know?" Tom said.

"He could have looked out the restaurant window."

"No," Tom said. "He didn't know it was us."

"I thought something awful was going to happen."

"Don't be silly," Tom said, but she could tell from his voice that he had been frightened too.

"Did he make you look at it?"

"No. He was nice about stopping. I thought I'd take a look at his deer and say something about it."

"What did you say?"

"Nothing," Tom said.

Elena stared ahead, into the falling snow.

When they were on the road again, Max made small talk about how smart it had been to stop to eat, because otherwise they would have starved as well as frozen. On the highway, guide lights had been turned on. Elena rubbed her window clear of fog so that she could see a little, and made a game of silently counting the lights. She got no farther than the third one before the one-two-three she had counted reminded her of her father throwing her in the air, hollering "onetwothree, onetwothree." She could remember how light, how buoyant, she had felt being tossed high in the air, and thought that perhaps being powerless was nice, in a way. She stared at the guide lights without counting, as the car moved slowly along the highway.

# The Lawn Party

I said to Lorna last night, "Do you want me to tell you a story?" "No," she said. Lorna is my daughter. She is ten and a great disbeliever. But she was willing to hang around my room and talk. "Regular dry cleaning won't take that out," Lorna said when she saw the smudges on my suede jacket. "Really," she said. "You have to take it somewhere special." In her skepticism, Lorna assumes that everyone else is also skeptical.

According to the Currier & Ives calendar hanging on the back of the bedroom door, and according to my watch, and according to my memory, which would be keen without either of them, Lorna and I have been at my parents' house for three days. Today is the annual croquet game that all our relatives here in Connecticut gather for (even some from my wife's side). It's the Fourth of July, and damn hot. I have the fan going. I'm sitting in a comfortable chair (moved upstairs, on my demand, by my father and the maid), next to the window in my old bedroom. There is already a cluster of my relatives on the lawn. Most of them are wearing little American flags pinned somewhere on their shirts or blouses or hanging from their ears. A patriotic group. Beer (forgive them: Heineken's) and wine (Almadén Chablis) drinkers. My father loves this day better than his own birthday. He leans on his mallet and gives instructions to my sister Eva on the placement of the posts. Down there, he can see the American flags clearly. But if he is already too loaded to stick the posts in the ground, he probably isn't noticing the jewelry.

Lorna has come into my room twice in the last hour—once to ask me when I am coming down to join what she calls "the party," another time to say that I am making everybody feel rotten by not joining them. A statement to be dismissed with a wave of the hand, but I have none. No right arm, either. I have a left hand and a left arm, but I have stopped valuing them. It's the right one I want. In the hospital, I rejected suggestions of a plastic arm or a claw. "Well, then, what do you envision?" the doctor said. "Air," I told him. This needed amplification. "Air where my arm used to be," I said. He gave a little "Ah, so" bow of the head and left the room.

I intend to sit here at the window all day, watching the croquet game. I will drink the Heineken's Lorna has brought me, taking small sips because I am unable to wipe my mouth after good foamy sips. My left hand is there to wipe with, but who wants to set down his beer bottle to wipe his mouth?

Lorna's mother has left me. I think of her now as Lorna's mother because she has made it clear that she no longer wants to be my wife. She has moved to another apartment with Lorna. She, herself, seems to be

no happier for having left me and visits me frequently.
Mention is no longer made of the fact that I am her
husband and she is my wife. Recently Mary (her name)
took the ferry to the Statue of Liberty. She broke in on
me on my second day here in the room, explaining that
she would not be here for the croquet game, but with
the news that she had visited New York yesterday and
had taken the ferry to the Statue of Liberty. "And how
was the city?" I asked. "Wonderful," she assured me.
She went to the Carnegie Delicatessen and had cheese
cake. When she does not visit, she writes. She has a
second sense about when I have left my apartment for
my parents' house. In her letters she usually tells me
something about Lorna, although no mention is made
of the fact that Lorna is my child. In fact, she once slyly
suggested in a bitter moment that Lorna was not—but
she backed down about that one.

Lorna is a great favorite with my parents, and my
parents are rich. This, Mary always said jokingly, was
why she married me. Actually, it was my charm. She
thought I was terrific. If I had not fallen in love with
her sister, everything would still be fine between us.
I did it fairly; I fell in love with her sister before the
wedding. I asked to have the wedding delayed. Mary
got drunk and cried. Why was I doing this? How could
I do it? She would leave me, but she wouldn't delay the
wedding. I asked her to leave. She got drunk and cried
and would not. We were married on schedule. She had
nothing more to do with her sister. I, on the other
hand—strange how many things one cannot say anymore—saw her whenever possible. Patricia—that was
her name—went with me on business trips, met me for
lunches and dinners, and was driving my car when it
went off the highway.

When I came to, Mary was standing beside my hospital bed, her face distorted, looking down at me. "My
sister killed herself and tried to take you with her,"
she said.

I waited for her to throw herself on me in pity.

"You deserved this," she said, and walked out of the room.

I was being fed intravenously in my left arm. I looked to see if my right arm was hooked up to anything. It hurt to move my head. My right arm was free—how free I didn't know at the time. I swear I saw it, but it had been amputated when I was unconscious. The doctor spoke to me at length about this later, insisting that there was no possibility that my arm was there when my wife was in the room and gone subsequently— gone when she left. No, indeed. It was amputated at once, in surgery, and when I saw my wife I was recovering from surgery. I tried to get at it another way, leaving Mary out of it. Wasn't I conscious before Mary was there? Didn't I see the arm? No, I was unconscious and didn't see anything. No, indeed. The physical therapist, the psychiatrist and the chaplain the doctor had brought with him nodded their heads in fast agreement. But soon I would have an artificial arm. I said that I did not want one. It was then that we had the discussion about air.

Last Wednesday was my birthday. I was unpleasant to all. Mrs. Bates, the cook, baked me chocolate-chip cookies with walnuts (my favorite), but I didn't eat any until she went home. My mother gave me a red velour shirt, which I hinted was unsatisfactory. "What's wrong with it?" she said. I said, "It's got one too many arms." My former student Banks visited me in the evening, not knowing that it was my birthday. He is a shy, thin, hirsute individual of twenty—a painter, a true *artiste*. I liked him so well that I had given him the phone number at my parents' house. He brought with him his most recent work, a canvas of a nude woman, for my inspection. While we were all gathered around the birthday cake, Banks answered my question about who she was by saying that she was a professional model. Later, strolling in the backyard, he told me that he had picked her up at a bus stop, after convincing her that she did not want to spend her life waiting for buses, and brought her to his apartment, where he fixed a steak dinner. The woman spent two days there, and when she left, Banks gave her forty dollars, although she did not want any money. She thought the painting he did of her was ugly, and wanted to be reassured that she wasn't really that heavy around the hips. Banks told her that it was not a representational painting; he said it was an Impressionist painting. She gave him her phone number. He called; there was no such number. He could not understand it. He went back to the bus stop, and eventually he found her again. She told him to get away or she'd call the police.

Ah, Banks. Ah, youth—to be twenty again, instead of thirty-two. In class, Banks used to listen to music on his cassette player through earphones. He would eat candy bars while he nailed frames together. Banks was always chewing food or mouthing songs. Sometimes he would forget and actually sing in class—an eerie wail, harmonizing with something none of the rest of us heard. The students who did not resent Banks's talent resented his chewing or singing or his success with women. Banks had great success with Lorna. He told her she looked like Bianca Jagger and she was thrilled. "Why don't you get some platform shoes like hers?" he said, and her eyes shriveled with pleasure. He told her a couple of interesting facts about Copernicus; she told him about the habits of gypsy moths. When he left, he kissed her hand. It did my heart good to see her so happy. I never delight her at all, as Mary keeps telling me.

They have written me from the college where I work, saying that they hope all is well and that I will be back teaching in the fall. It is not going to be easy to teach painting, with my right arm gone. Still, one remembers Matisse in his last years. Where there's a will, et cetera. My department head has sent flowers twice (mixed and tulips), and the dean himself has written a message on

a get-well card. There is a bunny on the card, looking
at a rainbow. Banks is the only one who really tempts
me to go back to work. The others, Banks tells me, are
"full of it."

Now I have a visitor. Danielle, John's wife, has come
up to see me. John is my brother. She brings an opened
beer and sets it on the windowsill without comment.
Danielle is wearing a white dress with small porpoises
on it, smiling as they leap. Across that chest, no wonder.

"Are you feeling blue today or just being rotten?"
she asks.

The beginnings of many of Danielle's sentences often
put me in mind of trashy, romantic songs. Surely someone has written a song called "Are You Feeling Blue?"

"Both," I say. I usually give Danielle straight answers. She tries to be nice. She has been nice to my
brother for five years. He keeps promising to take her
back to France, but he never does.

She sits on the rug, next to my chair. "Their rotten
lawn parties," she says. Danielle is French, but her
English is very good.

"Pull up a chair and watch the festivities," I say.

"I have to go back," she says, pouting. "They want
you to come back with me."

Champagne glasses clinking, white tablecloth, single carnation, key of A: "They Want You Back with
Me."

"Who sent you?" I ask.

"John. But I think Lorna would like it if you were
there."

"Lorna doesn't like me anymore. Mary's turned her
against me."

"Ten is a difficult age," Danielle says.

"I thought the teens were difficult."

"How would I know? I don't have children."

She has a drink of beer, and then puts the bottle in
my hand instead of back on the window sill.

"You have beautiful round feet," I say.

She tucks them under her. "I'm embarrassed," she says.

"Our talk is full of the commonplace today," I say, sighing.

"You're insulting me," she says. "That's why John wouldn't come up. He says he gets tired of your insults."

"I wasn't trying to be insulting. You've got beautiful feet. Raise one up here and I'll kiss it."

"Don't make fun of me," Danielle says.

"Really," I say.

Danielle moves her leg, unstraps a sandal and raises her right foot. I take it in my hand and bend over to kiss it across the toes.

"Stop it," she says, laughing. "Someone will come in."

"They won't," I say. "John isn't the only one tired of my insults."


I have been taking a little nap. Waking up, I look out the window and see Danielle below. She is sitting in one of the redwood chairs, accepting a drink from my father. One leg is crossed over the other, her beautiful foot dangling. They all know I am watching, but they refuse to look up. Eventually my mother does. She makes a violent sweep with her arm—like a coach motioning the defensive team onto the field. I wave. She turns her back and rejoins the group—Lorna, John, Danielle, my Aunt Rosie, Rosie's daughter Elizabeth, my father, and some others. Wednesday was also Elizabeth's birthday—her eighteenth. My parents called and sang to her. When Janis Joplin died Elizabeth cried for six days. "She's an emotional child," Rosie said at the time. Then, forgetting that, she asked everyone in the family why Elizabeth had gone to pieces. "Why did you feel so bad about Janis, Elizabeth?" I said. "I don't know," she said. "Did her death make you feel like killing yourself?" I said. "Are you unhappy the way she was?" Rosie now speaks to me only perfunctorily.

On her get-well card to me (no visit) she wrote: "So sorry." They are all sorry. They have been told by the doctor to ignore my gloominess, so they ignore me. I ignore them because even before the accident I was not very fond of them. My brother, in particular, bores me. When we were kids, sharing a bedroom, John would talk to me at night. When I fell asleep he'd come over and shake my mattress. One night my father caught him doing it and hit him. "It's not my fault," John hollered. "He's a goddamn snob." We got separate bedrooms. I was eight and John was ten.

Danielle comes back, looking sweatier than before. Below, they are playing the first game. My father's brother Ed pretends to be a majorette and struts with his mallet, twirling it and pointing his knees.

"Nobody sent me this time," Danielle says. "Are you coming down to dinner? They're grilling steaks."

"He's so cheap he'll serve Almadén with them," I say. "You grew up in France. How can you drink that stuff?"

"I just drink one glass," she says.

"Refuse to do it," I say.

She shrugs. "You're in an awful mood," she says.

"Give back that piggy," I say.

She frowns. "I came to have a serious discussion. Why aren't you coming to dinner?"

"Not hungry."

"Come down for Lorna."

"Lorna doesn't care."

"Maybe you're mean to her."

"I'm the same way I always was with her."

"Be a little extra nice, then."

"Give back that piggy," I say, and she puts her foot up. I unbuckle her sandal with my left hand. There are strap marks on the skin. I lick down her baby toe and kiss it, at the very tip. In turn, I kiss all the others.

It's evening, and the phone is ringing. I think about answering it. Finally someone else in the house picks it up. I get up and then sit on the bed and look around. My old bedroom looks pretty much the way it looked when I left for college, except that my mother has added a few things that I never owned, which seem out of place. Two silver New Year's Eve hats rest on the bedposts, and a snapshot of my mother in front of a Mexican fruit stand (I have never been to Mexico) that my father took on their "second honeymoon" is on my bureau. I pull open a drawer and take out a pack of letters. I pull out one of the letters at random and read it. It is from an old girl friend of mine. Her name was Alison, and she once loved me madly. In the letter she says she is giving up smoking so that when we are old she won't be repulsive to me. The year I graduated from college, she married an Indian and moved to India. Maybe now she has a little red dot in the middle of her forehead.

I try to remember loving Alison. I remember loving Mary's sister, Patricia. She is dead. That doesn't sink in. And she can't have meant to die, in spite of what Mary said. A woman who meant to die wouldn't buy a big wooden bowl and a bag of fruit, and then get in the car and drive it off the highway. It is a fact, however, that as the car started to go sideways I looked at Patricia, and she was whipping the wheel to the right. Maybe I imagined that. I remember putting my arm out to brace myself as the car started to turn over. If Patricia were alive, I'd have to be at the croquet game. But if she were alive, she and I could disappear for a few minutes, have a kiss by the barn.

I said to Lorna last night that I would tell her a story. It was going to be a fairy tale, all about Patricia and me but disguised as the prince and the princess, but she said no, she didn't want to hear it, and walked out. Just as well. If it had ended sadly it would have been an awful trick to pull on Lorna, and if it had ended happily, it would have depressed me even more. "There's nothing wrong with coming to terms with your depression," the doctor said to me. He kept urging me to see a shrink. The shrink came, and urged me to talk to him. When he left, the chaplain came in and urged me to see *him*. I checked out.

Lorna visits a third time. She asks whether I heard the phone ringing. I did. She says that—well, she finally answered it. "When you were first walking, one of your favorite things was to run for the phone," I said. I was trying to be nice to her. "Stop talking about when I was a baby," she says, and leaves. On the way out, she says, "It was your friend who came over the other night. He wants you to call him. His number is here." She comes back with a piece of paper, then leaves again.

"I got drunk," Banks says on the phone, "and I felt sorry for you."

"The hell with that, Banks," I say, and reflect that I sound like someone talking in *The Sun Also Rises*.

"Forget it, old Banks," I say, enjoying the part.

"You're not loaded too, are you?" Banks says.

"No, Banks," I say.

"Well, I wanted to talk. I wanted to ask if you wanted to go out to a bar with me. I don't have any more beer or money."

"Thanks, but there's a big rendezvous here today. Lorna's here. I'd better stick around."

"Oh," Banks says. "Listen. Could I come over and borrow five bucks?"

Banks does not think of me in my professorial capacity.

"Sure," I say.

"Thanks," he says.

"Sure, old Banks. Sure," I say, and hang up.

Lorna stands in the doorway. "Is he coming over?" she asks.

"Yes. He's coming to borrow money. He's not the man for you, Lorna."

"You don't have any money either," she says. "Grandpa does."

"I have enough money," I say defensively.

"How much do you have?"

"I make a salary, you know, Lorna. Has your mother been telling you I'm broke?"

"She doesn't talk about you."

"Then why did you ask how much money I had?"

"I wanted to know."

"I'm not going to tell you," I say.

"They told me to come talk to you," Lorna says. "I was supposed to get you to come down."

"Do you want me to come down?" I ask.

"Not if you don't want to."

"You're supposed to be devoted to your daddy," I say.

Lorna sighs. "You won't answer any of my questions, and you say silly things."

"What?"

"What you just said—about my daddy."

"I am your daddy," I say.

"I know it," she says.

There seems nowhere for the conversation to go.

"You want to hear that story now?" I ask.

"No. Don't try to tell me any stories. I'm ten."

"I'm thirty-two," I say.


My father's brother William is about to score a victory over Elizabeth. He puts his foot on the ball, which is touching hers, and knocks her ball down the hill. He pretends he has knocked it an immense distance and cups his hand over his brow to squint after it. William's wife will not play croquet; she sits on the grass and frowns. She is a dead ringer for the woman behind the cash register in Edward Hopper's "Tables for Ladies."

"How's it going?" Danielle asks, standing in the doorway.

"Come on in," I say.

"I just came upstairs to go to the bathroom. The cook is in the one downstairs."

She comes in and looks out the window.

"Do you want me to get you anything?" she says. "Food?"

"You're just being nice to me because I kiss your piggies."

"You're horrible," she says.

"I tried to be nice to Lorna, and all she wanted to talk about was money."

"All they talk about down there is money," she says.

She leaves and then comes back with her hair combed and her mouth pink again.

"What do you think of William's wife?" I ask.

"I don't know, she doesn't say much." Danielle sits on the floor, with her chin on her knees. "Everybody always says that people who only say a few dumb things are sweet."

"What dumb things has she said?" I say.

"She said, 'Such a beautiful day,' and looked at the sky."

"You shouldn't be hanging out with these people, Danielle," I say.

"I've got to go back," she says.

Banks is here. He is sitting next to me as it gets dark. I am watching Danielle out on the lawn. She has a red shawl that she winds around her shoulders. She looks tired and elegant. My father has been drinking all afternoon. "Get the hell down here!" he hollered to me a little while ago. My mother rushed up to him to say that I had a student with me. He backed down. Lorna came up and brought us two dishes of peach ice cream (handmade by Rosie), giving the larger one to Banks. She and Banks discussed *The Hobbit* briefly. Banks kept apologizing to me for not leaving, but said he was too strung out to drive. He went into the bathroom and smoked a joint and came back and sat down and rolled his head from side to side. "You make sense," Banks says now, and I am flattered until I realize that I have not been talking for a long time.

"It's too bad it's so dark," I say. "That woman down there in the black dress looks just like somebody in an Edward Hopper painting. You'd recognize her."

"Nah," Banks says, head swaying. "Everything's basically different. I get so tired of examining things and finding out they're different. This crappy nature poem isn't at all like that crappy nature poem. That's what I mean," Banks says.

"Do you remember your accident?" he says.

"No," I say.

"Excuse me," Banks says.

"I remember thinking of *Jules and Jim*."

"Where she drove off the cliff?" Banks says, very excited.

"Umm."

"When did you think that?"

"As it was happening."

"Wow," Banks says. "I wonder if anybody else flashed on that before you?"

"I couldn't say."

Banks sips his iced gin. "What do you think of me as an artist?" he says.

"You're very good, Banks."

It begins to get cooler. A breeze blows the curtains toward us.

"I had a dream that I was a raccoon," Banks says. "I kept trying to look over my back to count the rings of my tail, but my back was too high, and I couldn't count past the first two."

Banks finishes his drink.

"Would you like me to get you another drink?" I ask.

"That's an awful imposition," Banks says, extending his glass.

I take the glass and go downstairs. A copy of *The Hobbit* is lying on the rose brocade sofa. Mrs. Bates is sitting at the kitchen table, reading *People*.

"Thank you very much for the cookies," I say.

"It's nothing," she says. Her earrings are on the table. Her feet are on a chair.

"Tell them we ran out of gin if they want more," I say. "I need this bottle."

"Okay," she says. "I think there's another bottle, anyway."

I take the bottle upstairs in my armpit, carrying a glass with fresh ice in it in my hand.

"You know," Banks says, "they say that if you face things—if you just get them through your head—you can accept them. They say you can accept anything if you can once get it through your head."

"What's this about?" I say.

"Your arm," Banks says.

"I realize that I don't have an arm," I say.

"I don't mean to offend you," Banks says, drinking.

"I know you don't."

"If you ever want me to yell at you about it, just say the word. That might help—help it sink in."

"I already realize it, Banks," I say.

"You're a swell guy," Banks says. "What kind of music do you listen to?"

"Do you want to hear music?"

"No. I just want to know what you listen to."

"Schoenberg," I say. I have not listened to Schoenberg for years.

"Ahh," Banks says.

He offers me his glass. I take a drink and hand it back.

"You know how they always have cars—car ads—you ever notice . . . I'm all screwed up," Banks says.

"Go on," I say.

"They always put the car on the beach?"

"Yeah."

"I was thinking about doing a thing with a great big car in the background and a little beach up front." Banks chuckles.

Outside, the candles have been lit. A torch flames from a metal holder—one of the silliest things I have ever seen—and blue lanterns have been lit in the trees.

Someone has turned on a radio, and Elizabeth and some man, not recognizable, dance to "Heartbreak Hotel."

"There's Schoenberg," Banks says.

"Banks," I say, "I want you to take this the right way. I like you, and I'm glad you came over. Why did you come over?"

"I wanted you to praise my paintings." Banks plays church and steeple with his hands. "But also, I just wanted to talk."

"Was there anything particularly—"

"I thought you might want to talk to me."

"Why don't you talk to me, instead?"

"I've got to be a great painter," Banks says. "I paint and then at night I smoke up or go out to some bar, and in the morning I paint . . . All night I pray until I fall asleep that I will become great. You must think I'm crazy. What do you think of me?"

"You make me feel old," I say.

The gin bottle is in Banks' crotch, the glass resting on the top of the bottle.

"I sensed that," Banks says, "before I got too wasted to sense anything."

"You want to hear a story?" I say.

"Sure."

"The woman who was driving the car I was in—the Princess . . ." I laugh, but Banks only nods, trying hard to follow. "I think the woman must have been out to commit suicide. We had been out buying things. The back seat was loaded with nice antiques, things like that, and we had had a nice afternoon, eaten ice cream, talked about how she would be starting school again in the fall—"

"Artist?" Banks asks.

"A linguistics major."

"Okay. Go on."

"What I'm saying is that all was well in the kingdom. Not exactly, because she wasn't my wife, but she should have been. But for the purpose of the story, what I'm saying is that we were in fine shape, it was a fine day—"

"Month?" Banks says.

"March," I say.

"That's right," Banks says.

"I was going to drop her off at the shopping center, where she'd left her car, and she was going to continue on to her castle and I'd go to mine ..."

"Continue," Banks says.

"And then she tried to kill us. She did kill herself."

"I read it in the papers," Banks says.

"What do you think?" I ask.

"Banks's lesson," Banks says. "Never look back. Don't try to count your tail rings."

Danielle walks into the room. "I have come for the gin," she says. "The cook said you had it."

"Danielle, this is Banks."

"How do you do," Banks says.

Danielle reaches down and takes the bottle from Banks. "You're missing a swell old time," she says.

"Maybe a big wind will come along and blow them all away," Banks says.

Danielle is silent a moment, then laughs—a laugh that cuts through the darkness. She ducks her head down by my face and kisses my cheek, and turns in a wobbly way and walks out of the room.

"Jesus," Banks says. "Here we are sitting here and then this weird thing happens."

"Her?" I say.

"Yeah."

Lorna comes, very sleepy, carrying a napkin with cookies on it. She obviously wants to give them to Banks, but Banks has passed out, upright, in the chair next to mine. "Climb aboard," I say, offering my lap. Lorna hesitates, but then does, putting the cookies down on the floor without offering me any. She tells me that her mother has a boyfriend.

"What's his name?" I ask.

"Stanley," Lorna says.

"Maybe a big wind will come and blow Stanley away," I say.

"What's wrong with him?" she says, looking at Banks.

"Drunk," I say. "Who's drunk downstairs?"

"Rosie," she says. "And William, and, uh, Danielle."

"Don't drink," I say.

"I won't," she says. "Will he still be here in the morning?"

"I expect so," I say.

Banks has fallen asleep in an odd posture. His feet are clamped together, his arms are limp at his sides, and his chin is jutting forward. The melting ice cubes from the overturned glass have encroached on the cookies.

At the lawn party, they've found a station on the radio that plays only songs from other years. Danielle begins a slow, drunken dance. Her red shawl has fallen to the grass. I stare at her and imagine her dress disappearing, her shoes kicked off, beautiful Danielle dancing naked in the dusk. The music turns to static, but Danielle is still dancing.

# Friends

Perry had just walked into Francie's living room, headed toward the table for the bowl of anchovy-stuffed olives. Dickie, who had called earlier to say he was too stoned to come, looked up and raised two fingers to his sweaty forehead in salute. Before Perry could say anything but hello, the phone rang, and he answered. The woman Perry used to live with, Beth Ann, used to complain that Perry should have been a robot—he was programmed to answer the phone and would talk politely to whatever wasted friend it might be, at whatever ridiculous hour.

"Delores?" he said.

"I'm in Miami," she said over the static in the line, "but I'm coming your way. I came to round up Meagan from my parents' place." Static cut off her next sentence. "I haven't talked to you for so long. How are you, Perry? I heard you were winterizing your place in Vermont."

"Yeah, I am. I can live in half the house now. I came down to Francie's this weekend for a party. It gets lonesome up there. I broke my goddamn foot. I had on sneaks, and I turned my ankle jumping off a wall."

"Your hand was broken the last time I saw you."

"Only two broken bones I've ever had in my life," he said.

Dickie had picked up the bowl of olives and was having one. He held the bowl out to Perry. Perry took two, and with his tongue rolled one to either side of his mouth.

"I'd *love* to come up there."

"There's plenty now that's livable. Come on up. Bring Meagan."

"Thanks, Perry. I think I really might. Is Francie there?"

"This may sound crazy, but Francie is passed out with her head under the bed."

"Everybody's drunk?"

"I'm not drunk, Delores. Is there anything I can tell Francie tomorrow?"

"Maybe you'd know." (He waves away the olives.) "I wanted to know if my oak table is still there. The one with the wideboard top."

"I don't think so."

"Would you look in the kitchen for me? I think she piles cookbooks on it."

"Sure."

He walked down the hallway to the kitchen. T.W. and Katie were putting the make on each other in a corner of the kitchen. The Scandinavian rock-'n'-roll record Daryl Freed had brought to the party was playing for the fifth or sixth time. He looked for the table and it wasn't there. He remembered the table now. He was sure it wasn't in the house.

"Hey, Delores? It's not there."

"No?" she said. "Thanks for looking."

In the other room the needle scratched across the record, somebody cursed loudly, and Chuck Berry started singing.

"Jump a wave for me," he said.

"Sure," she said. "Stick your finger in some maple syrup."

He put the phone down in time to face his fate: Dickie coming at him, ski mask pulled over his head, fireplace poker extended. He laughed a little more than he felt like laughing and stepped aside so that when Dickie stumbled and tripped, the poker jabbed the wall.

"It's all sexual," Dickie said. He pulled off the ski mask and smiled widely. "I put a hole in her wall," he said. "Hey, I saw you had two poems published. Congratulations."

Perry tilted his head like an obsequious maître d'.

"They were good, too," Dickie said. "I read them in one of those free magazines on the airplane."

Perry frowned, confused.

"No I didn't. I read them in the magazine. Francie gave it to me. Where *is* our hostess, anyway? Did I hear you say she was about, but indisposed?"

"Why don't you go check on her?" Perry said.

This time Dickie did the courtly bow. He turned with a military pivot—long ago he and Dickie had gone to the same boys' school—and headed out the door just as the needle was scratched across another record and Daryl Freed cursed. After a long silence the London Bach Choir began to sing. "Cut that shit!" somebody hollered. "I mean it—cut the shit." The London Bach Choir was silent. T.W. and Katie, arms around each other's waists, walked down the hallway, past the door. He knew they were going to bed. He looked down at his foot. The cast looked larger than he remembered. He had not put on his sock, and his toes were lavender from the cold. Francie never heated the house well enough in the winter. When he was partying he didn't notice it, but when he stood still, he noticed both the cold and the slight pain across his instep. He looked at the glass of Scotch he had left on the table and decided to leave it there. He took an olive, picked up the Scotch only for a second, to wash away the salty taste, and left-right-left-right, without his crutch went into the living room. Nick and Anita were dancing. Roger Dewey and Daryl Freed were sitting on the floor in earnest conversation, bobbing heads at each other like plastic birds dipping for water. Somebody Perry had never met before—a man (a teen-ager?) with white streaks fanning out from his temples whom Freed had brought to the party—sat next to Roger Dewey. It looked as if he was mocking Roger's gestures.

"Hi," Anita said.

"Hi," he said. He hobbled out of the room. He went down the hall to Francie's room and found her conscious, flat on her back, Dickie seated behind her, brushing her hair.

"Good night," he said to both of them. "I'm going up to the attic to go to sleep."

Dickie raised the brush to his forehead in salute. Perry took the afghan draped over Francie's mattress and headed for the attic stairs.

"He drilled a hole in your wall, Francie," Dickie said, making his words come slowly, in time with the brush strokes. "In the other room, he crouched down and concentrated all his energy, and his right eye bored a hole about half an inch deep in the wall."

He climbed the stairs to the attic slowly and carefully, wishing there were a handrail. The afghan was draped around his neck like a towel.

Francie painted, and the attic was where she usually went to do it, although it was cold in the winter and hot in the summer. He groped for the light bulb at the top of the stairs and fumbled for the switch on the side of it. The attic lit up. To his left was the mattress, under the window, flecked with oil paint. It was the mattress the cat had had a litter on when he and Beth Ann and Francie, Dickie and Gus lived together in Connecticut. He sat down awkwardly because of the cast, sighing as he sank down because he would just have to get up in another minute to turn off the light. In front of him was a stool with a piece of material draped over it. On top of the fabric was a conch shell. Little tubes of paint were scattered on the floor like cigarette butts. He always liked to sleep in Francie's attic, and went there by choice instead of to the spare bedroom. In the morning the light came through the four-over-four windows and made a crosshatch pattern on the floor.

He lay back on the mattress, pulling the afghan over him, and tried to block out the noise from the party. He heard rock-'n'-roll, pretty clearly. Then he opened his eyes and concentrated on the music; it was rock-'n'-roll, and he could hear it clearly.

He took off his belt and watch and unbuttoned his jeans. There was a slight odor of cat about the mattress. He got up and put off the light and went back to bed. The bass downstairs was turned up so high that he could feel the reverberation through the mattress, and it made him think of one of those motel beds that vibrate when you deposit a quarter. The last time he had been in one of those beds it was in a room he shared with Francie, after he drove to Francie's sister's house to pick her up and bring her back to this house. Francie had been married to a lawyer for a year, and when the marriage broke up, she flew to her sister's. She missed the house and wanted to come back to it, but she was afraid that she might cry in public. She called him because she said that she did not want to cry on an airplane or train. They could have made the ride from her sister's to Francie's house in New Hampshire without spending the night in a motel. Stopping had been Francie's idea. She wanted to spend the night in a motel and go back in the morning, when the house wouldn't look as nice, when the sunlight would make all the dust visible, when she wouldn't be sentimental for the good times she and her husband had had in the house. They sat in the motel on their twin beds and each drank a Coke from the machine outside their door. Francie had been going to pay for the motel with her American Express Card, but then she realized that the bill would go to her husband. She didn't have any money, so he paid for the room. They had each put quarters in the boxes attached to the headboards and been shaken off to sleep. At least they had pretended that, because it wasn't the right night to sleep together. The next morning when they woke up it was raining, and when they got to her house it looked even more depressing than she had hoped it would. He was never clear on why Francie and her husband divorced, except that Francie did not want children and wanted to be a painter.

Before he fell asleep he heard the silence. He was conscious of it not because he heard the music die out or voices get quiet, but because he heard a car starting outside. It sounded as if everybody downstairs had gone home. Waiting to fall asleep, he thought about what Francie had told him recently: that he was her best friend. "A woman should have another woman for her best friend," Francie said and shrugged, "but you're it." "Why would you have to have a woman for a best friend?" he said. She shrugged again. "It's hard for men and women to be best friends," she said. He nodded and she thought he understood, but all he meant to acknowledge was that they were close, but there was also something hard about that. What it was, was that it had never been the right time to go to bed with her, and if he did it after all this time, he would have been self-conscious.

Beth Ann was in Albuquerque.

Delores—spacy Delores—had traveled from Palo Alto to Miami and was headed north.

Drifting off to sleep, he thought about being on the

subway in Boston, where he had stopped on the way
to Francie's earlier in the day to pick up some things
for her at Charrette. An old lady had struck up a conversation with him, saying that she was a rarity, a
native Bostonian. She asked him where he was from.
"Michigan," he said, although he was not from there.
He hated talking to strangers, and he felt that there
must be something wrong with him because so many
old ladies thought he was a nice young man; they
talked to him in spite of his long hair and leather
jacket, with the leather so old it was flaking off like
scabs. But she had a friend in Michigan, so she went
on and on about it. "Then I moved with my family to
Fort Worth," he said, "and then we lived in Germany
until I was a teen-ager, and then we moved to New
Jersey, and Iowa, and Los Angeles." She nodded,
greatly interested. "How long have you been in Boston?" she asked. "Six days," he told her. Then she
caught on—something told her he was putting her on,
or crazy. He could see her narrowing her focus on the
rotting leather, raise her head a bit to look at where
his hair edged over the shoulder of the jacket. "Tomorrow I'm going to Mexico," he said. She didn't speak
the rest of the ride, from Charles Street to Harvard
Square.

In the morning he went downstairs, looking for coffee. The door to Francie's room was closed. In place of
a DO NOT DISTURB sign was a sign that Delores had
taken from the pool at the condominium where her
parents lived: POR FAVOR PONGA LES TOALLAS EN EL
CESTO. He thought that he could use a shower, and
wondered if there would be towels. His friends' bath-
rooms never had towels, and he could not imagine how
they dried off. He got distracted by the odor of bacon,
walked into the kitchen to find a plate of half-eaten
eggs and bacon, and Daryl Freed slumped over it.

"Fucking creep stole my car," Freed said.

"What are you talking about?"

Freed had pulled his cardigan sweater over the top

of his head. He looked like a mad nun. He looked as if he had been awake all night.

"What are you talking about, Freed? Who stole your car?"

"He fucking ate breakfast, and *then* he stole my car."

"Who did?"

"The kid I brought to the party. Didn't you see that kid with the skunk streaks down both sides of his hair?" Freed pulled the cardigan back to his shoulders and gestured toward his temples. His hair was full of electricity.

"Yeah. I think I saw him talking with you. Who was he? How do you know he stole your car?"

"He was a hitchhiker. He was going to your home state of Vermont. Put on a big push to come to the party with me when I told him what I was doing. I brought him over here with me, and he tried to put the make on T.W. You missed T.W. taking a swing at him, too. Kid woke me up this morning when I was sleeping in there on the rug and said he wanted cigs, where were my car keys? I didn't even know what time it was, but I thought it was morning. Pulled my keys out of my pocket and handed them up to him. Must have been about four in the morning because when I got up I realized it was still dark. So I came in here and waited for him and he never showed."

"What time is it now?"

Freed pointed to the clock in the stove. It was grease-covered, so he got up to peer into it. It was close to eleven o'clock.

"You tell me how it takes seven hours to go to the corner store for cigs."

"Did you call the cops?"

"I don't like the cops."

"I'll ride you down to the store. We can find out if he went there."

"He didn't go there. He stole my car."

"You'll get your car back, Freed. Come on—let's go to the store."

"Wait'll I explain to the cops why I have a Virginia driver's license and New Hampshire plates and live in Maine."

"Come on, Freed."

"I don't know where my jacket is. He stole my jacket."

Perry pointed to something behind Freed. Freed turned and stared down at the thick red nylon jacket hanging from the chair.

"Yeah. That's my jacket. Now where's my car? He fucking stole my car. I handed him the keys like I knew him, and he got my car."

"Come on, Freed. Let's go down to the store."

Freed stood and pulled on the jacket. It was an exceptionally thick ski jacket, and Freed looked as if he should have a hose trailing out of it and be walking on the moon.

"I hate it when somebody makes a fool of me," Freed said. "It makes me want to kill. I don't mean that as a generalization—I mean it really makes me insanely angry and I want to kill the person."

"Come on, Freed. The door's this way."

"I know where the door is. Don't tell me anything. Just take me to the store so I can make a fool of myself asking if some faggot stopped there for cigs and drove off in a black Pontiac. Watch how friendly that guy at the store's going to be."

He left the front door open a crack, since he didn't have a key to get back in. Freed walked beside him, his huge red-jacketed arms folded over his chest.

"How are things in Maine?" he asked. Freed taught English, French and German at a private school there.

"Cold. And the little ladies in my class look at me while I'm talking with that same vacant look chickens have when they lay eggs."

"So are you going to stay there?"

Freed shrugged. "I'm looking around." Freed picked up a cassette from the floor and studied the label and pushed it into the machine. It was a live recording of

Gatemouth Brown playing "Take the 'A' Train."

The store was coming up at the bottom of the hill. He pulled in beside a Ford truck. Freed looked at the store with incomprehension. During the summer, when he first bought the house in Vermont, Freed and several of the others had come up and they had played hide-and-seek. When it came Freed's turn to count, he counted out loud very slowly and then never went looking for anyone. Eventually Francie's laugh boomed through the woods, and all of them peered out from behind trees or bushes or wherever they were hiding, and there stood Freed, stark naked, waiting to be discovered himself.

"You ask," Freed said.

"It's your car."

"I'm a Jew. The guy who runs the store doesn't like Jews."

"Are you putting me on? What has he ever said?"

"I know he doesn't," Freed said.

"Get in there, Freed. Go on."

Freed got out of the car and slammed the door behind him and walked into the store. He was out almost as fast as he went in.

"He doesn't know who bought cigarettes there this morning. He was sick and his mother was at the register, and his mother is eighty-eight and he won't call her at home to ask because she went home to go to sleep. It's stolen," Freed said, looking around. "It's obvious that it's stolen. How am I going to get back to Maine?"

"Maybe back at the house you ought to get some sleep and then call the cops."

"I told you, I don't want to call the cops."

"What do you intend to do—just forget about the car?"

"I need cigarettes myself," Freed said, "and I forgot to buy them."

Perry made a U-turn and went back to the store.

Freed didn't thank him for doing it. He got out and slammed the door again. He came back with a newspaper and a pack of Trues. Perry backed out and headed for Francie's house, suddenly remembering clearly the large canvases Francie had painted recently, in greens and grays, of herself, naked. He had come down the weekend she showed them to him determined to sleep with her, but as usual something happened—the showing of the paintings happened—and he thought that it would be crass if he asked her after she showed him her work.

"What do you hear from Beth Ann?"

"I don't hear anything. Her sister sent me part of a letter Beth Ann sent her, about how she and Zack had managed to borrow the money for a restaurant and how they'd just found a building. It was about a quarter of a piece of paper that her sister cut off for me with pinking shears. On the back was some drivel about the Grand Canyon."

"That was a surprise to you she left," Freed said.

"I thought she was going to New York. I didn't know she was going to Albuquerque, and I had no idea she had any interest in Zack."

Freed shrugged. "None of my business to have brought it up."

"It's okay. I'm not that touchy."

"Yes you are. You've always been touchy. You were pissed off at me for months after we went to the baseball game and I rooted for the Red Sox."

"I was just kidding."

"No you weren't. You care a lot about sports and you don't approve of my taste."

He turned onto the unpaved road that went to Francie's house and parked his car beside three bushes that were trimmed in the shape of triangles. Francie had had them shaped a few summers before because she thought it was funny. Nothing else on the property was pruned. "They're pyramids," she said, making her eyes look crazy. "You can walk up to the bushes and derive power from them."

Going into the house, he noticed that T.W.'s car was in the driveway.

The front door was closed, but when he rapped quietly on it, Francie answered. She was wearing her blue nightgown, and somebody's plaid shirt in place of a robe.

"My car was stolen," Freed said.

"What do you mean? Somebody took your car from here?"

"The kid I brought to the party stole it. I've got to call the cops."

"Oh hell," Francie said. "Do they have to come here? Have I got to have cops in the house?"

"No. I'll call them from the store and sit there and have a cup of coffee with them while I tell the story."

"Oh Christ," Francie said. "Who was that guy, anyway?"

"Somebody who was hitching. I don't know who he was."

"What did you pick him up for?" Francie said. When Francie first woke up she was always argumentative.

"Because I'm stupid," Freed said. "Did you know that T.W. was here in the bedroom?"

"Yeah. He said he was going to come back after he took Katie home."

"Maybe we ought to wake him up. It's noon, isn't it?"

"Go ahead and call the cops," Perry said. "They're going to wonder why it took you so long to report it."

"Good morning," Francie said to Perry.

"Hi," he said.

Freed sighed and unzipped his jacket and went to the kitchen phone.

"Maybe you should wait," Francie called. "Maybe he'll come back with it."

Freed came into the living room and sighed and sat

down. He and Francie both saw the puddle of red wine that had seeped into the rug at the same time.

"I don't know why I have parties," Francie said.

Perry remembered Delores' phone call, and wondered if there was any point in mentioning it to Francie. Francie went over to the wine stain and looked down at it. "How do you get wine out of a rug?" she said.

"Don't you transform the wine into blood and the rug into a turnip?" Freed said. "Francie, if you didn't have such drunken parties, my car never would have been stolen."

"I guess you should call them," Francie said. "If he really stole it, he's not going to bring it back."

"Delores called last night from Miami," Perry said. "She was looking for her oak table."

"What oak table?"

"That one with the wide-board top. You used to have it, didn't you?"

"I never had it here. I think it was in my room in the house we rented."

"I think T.W. has that table," Freed said.

Francie took one of Freed's Trues and sat down by the stain. She had on black knee socks that were covered in lint, and she sat so that he could almost see between her legs.

"Or maybe I did have it here. Maybe it's the table I used to stack things on in the kitchen, that Delores took out of here and traded Beth Ann for a chair she wanted. Yeah, that's what happened to it: Beth Ann has it."

"Oh goddamn it," Freed said. "Goddamn it to hell. It's freezing out and I've got to start discussing how my fucking car was stolen with a bunch of New Hampshire cops."

"Let's have some music," Francie said. "Does anybody have a headache, or can we have music?"

The music got T.W. out of bed. He came looking for

his shirt, and when Francie had to hand it over, she decided to get dressed herself. Before long they were all dressed, and Freed was down at the store, and Francie and T.W. and Perry were eating eggs Benedict that T.W. fixed and drinking leftover champagne mixed with ginger ale.

"I've got to drive all the way to a job in Stowe," T.W. sighed. "But that's not until tomorrow."

Perry looked out the window and saw his own car gone from the drive. Freed had taken it to go to the store after he called the cops. It had started to snow.

"Why don't we have another party tonight and invite your other set of friends, Francie? There's food left over."

"What other set of friends?"

"Just kidding," T.W. said.

Perry and T.W. went out to the shed and loaded in kindling and wood for the fire.

Nick and Anita came back that night, bringing with them a huge pan of Anita's fried chicken. Francie got out the last gallon of Chablis and they sat by the fire talking about the snow storm and eating and drinking. T.W. and Freed were talking about architecture. They both knew more than Perry, and he kept entering into their conversation, hoping they could tell him some things he needed to know about fixing his house. He had hired people to fix the heating system, but he was doing the carpentry work himself. It was a large house, oddly shaped because it had been added onto without much thought for aesthetics at least twice, and probably three times. T.W. and his band had been up a lot on the weekends, and T.W. had been a lot of help.

"You lonesome up there in the woods?" Anita asked Perry.

"Sometimes."

"Ought to come back to the city," Nick said. (He was kidding; he and Anita lived in a town with a population of three hundred.)

"Bring your dirty pictures out," Anita said to Francie.

Francie laughed, embarrassed, knowing that Anita meant the canvases.

"Don't you freeze your butt standing in here naked?" Freed said.

"Maybe I *should* have asked my other friends," Francie said to Perry. He smiled at her, no longer interested in T.W. and Freed's talk about architecture. He was thinking about Francie, in the big house, painting herself.

"Aren't we an artsy bunch?" T.W. said. "Perry a poet and Anita a photographer and Perry a poet—or did I say that?—Francie a painter..."

Freed moved the jug of wine away from T.W.

"To say nothing of our music maker," T.W. said, touching his chest. He reached for the jug of wine, but Freed was pouring the last of it in his glass.

"I need it more than you do," Freed said. "My car was stolen."

The phone rang and Francie got up to answer it. Perry saw her turn on the kitchen light. Things looked better in the living room, where it was dark except for the fire. The clutter from the party the night before was still all over the room, but sitting and looking into the fire, he could forget about it. He intended to help her pick it up on Sunday, before he left to give Freed a ride to his house in Maine. He looked back to the kitchen, where Francie stood with her back to him, talking on the phone. Sometimes it bothered him that he was just one of the people she liked to have around all the time, although it meant a lot to him that they had all been friends for so long.

As they sat silently they could hear Francie talking on the phone. Perry heard the name Beth Ann twice and concentrated on the log crackling in the fire. He had gotten so he didn't think about her much, and that day he had had to listen to her spoken about too much.

"That was odd," Francie said, coming back and sitting next to Perry. "That was Delores' mother, and she said she wanted me to know that Delores and Meagan were coming to my house—that they had left yesterday in a hurry and had asked her to call. Did Delores say that to you?"

"I think she said she was coming this way, but she didn't say she was about to leave."

"And her mother said that Delores is going to live with Carl in New Hampshire. Do you know anything about that?"

"No," he said.

"We ought to get going," Nick said. "We've got to go to Anita's mother's tomorrow."

Anita groped behind her for her cowboy boots. They were fine boots, her Christmas present, with red roses painted on the sides and pointy toes and high heels.

"You ever want to borrow these, you could add a little kink to your dirty pictures," Anita said, and Francie smiled in embarrassment. Anita rolled her white wool slacks down over the boots and pushed herself up with a groan. Nick stood with her, holding the pan that had once held chicken but now held bones.

"Thanks for the good dinner," Perry said. "Thanks for cooking it, Anita."

"Oh, it was nothing," Anita said, fanning out her fingers and pushing her fingertips into her chest. She had on a cashmere sweater that looked electrified in the firelight. Her belly protruded because she was four months pregnant.

"Good night," Nick said, kissing Francie on the forehead. Freed reached up and silently shook hands with both of them. T.W. got up and walked them to the door. When he had waved them off, the door closed and the draft stopped. T.W.'s hair was dusted with snow when he came back to the fire.

"I'm going to bed down in your spare room, Francie. You're welcome to share the bed, Freed," he said.

"I think I'll sleep in the attic," Freed said.

"I'm sleeping there," Perry said.

"I know it, asshole. I was just kidding."

Freed and T.W. walked out of the living room, clowning, with arms around each other's waists, swaying their hips with all the grace of cows walking on ice. Francie looked after them without saying good night.

"What's the matter?" he said.

"I'm annoyed is what's the matter."

"Why?"

"First of all, that phone call. People's mothers calling me and informing me of what's going to happen to me—some woman I've never met calling to tell me that her crazy daughter and grandchild are headed for my house to stay with me."

"Come on," he said. "You've always felt sorry for Delores."

"And all that talk about her oak table. I never asked for the damn table to begin with—she put it in my house and then she took it out, and now she wants me to track it down."

"It's sad," he said. "It's sad if she's so crazy that she's trying to track down a table nobody has seen for years."

"And I'm touchy about Anita, and her talking about my dirty pictures. She's trying to embarrass me because she resents it that I have a career, when she's pregnant."

He remembered going to Francie's house once when Francie was still married, and he and Francie's husband had sat on the mattress playing checkers while she painted. The radio was playing. People and noise didn't distract her, usually. He liked it that when she painted, she acted like a painter: she backed up from the canvas, tilted her head from side to side, moved forward to put a small blot of paint on the canvas, stood back, smiled. He lost the game of checkers. Winning had never been very important to him, but it would have pleased him if Francie had known that he had won—if the "Aha!" had come from him instead of from Francie's husband. Francie herself was both casual about her art and competitive. She would paint quietly, showing nothing, for many months. But if she entered a show and didn't win first prize, she would be furious, drag out all her canvases to show her friends, pointing out how good they were. Sometimes there was some doubt in her mind—you could tell by the way her enthusiasm came out with a questioning tone—but most of the time failure made her angry, and she resisted the idea of it by talking about all the things that were done right, with originality, in her work. The first time she did that it had taken him aback—all his friends were humble, if not self-deprecating, and he had thought at first that Francie was putting him on. He probably listened to her talk about her work for half an hour with a silly smile on his face before he realized that his expression was inappropriate. Though when other people said, occasionally, that she was an egomaniac, he defended her, saying that it was mature to believe in yourself. Sometimes even Francie knew that she went on about the importance of what she was doing too much; she had a sense of humor about it, and would mock herself: she had a long gray apron she painted in, with GREAT ARTIST stenciled across the back.

He looked at Francie, slumped by the fire.

"You're in a bad mood," he said.

"You don't think Anita said that to embarrass me?"

"I don't know," he said. He threw a chip of wood into the fire.

"Anita and her hundred-dollar boots she walks around in the snow in."

"Go to bed," he said. "You've tolerated all of us for long enough today."

"Everybody has to be so teasing. Nobody can talk straight. Freed has to pretend he's taking the attic. T.W. and Freed have to pretend they're gay because they're sleeping in the same double bed. Everybody's got their act down."

"What's the matter with you?" he said again.

"What's the matter is that it will be six months before I have a show, and *nothing happens*. I sit around here all day alone and I paint. When people come they want to make jokes about my being my own model, as though I'm narcissistic."

"Your paintings are good," he said. "You know they are. Nobody else paints the way you do."

"You like them?"

"I admire them. They're very good. I think you should hang them on the walls."

In the living room there was one picture—a photograph taken by Anita of oil drums in the snow in New Jersey the winter before. It was a large 11" × 14" photograph hanging on the longest wall of the room. When Francie's husband left, she took down the drapes and gave him the pictures from the walls. Perry didn't ask about it because he thought he understood.

"Put some up," he said. "You shouldn't just lean them against your bedroom wall."

She bent her knee and put her forehead to it. "I guess I am in a bad mood," she mumbled. "I guess I might hang some of them up. But the earlier ones—not the ones of me."

"Loan me one," he said. "I'd like to hang one in my house."

"Seriously?"

"Seriously."

"Then I'll give you one. Which one do you want?"

She got up and went toward her bedroom. He walked behind her and noticed, as they passed the kitchen, that she had left the phone off the hook.

There was a mattress on the floor of Francie's room. There were hooks shaped like eagles on the wall in front of the bed, on which she hung clothes. There were bamboo curtains, and in the corner there was a tall plant with four leaves at the top. He thought the room was even more depressing than the one she had lived in, in the house they had shared. Her husband had taken the furniture when he went, and although she had gone to auctions and replaced some of the furniture

in some of the rooms, she had put only a mattress back
in the bedroom. Seeing the clothes on hooks reminded
him of the way coats were hung in his schoolroom in
the winter when he was young. In place of the line of
yellow boots beneath them were Francie's self-portraits.

"This one?" she said. The painting she propped
against her side was one of her best; she had painted
it in front of the fire, and the pink glow of the firelight
on her bare legs was just right. He looked from the
picture to Francie, wanting to say that what he would
like was the person propping up the painting, but the
expression on her face (shy but earnest; it was easy to
see that she took her painting seriously) kept him from
saying anything except that it was one of her best, she
should keep that one and give him another.

She shook her head. "I'll leave it in front, and you
can take it when you go."

He touched his lips to the top of her head with a
small kiss and gave her a hug and went out of the room
for a drink of water, then climbed the stairs to bed. His
foot felt sore, and too large for the cast. He put the
light on in the attic and went over to the stool with the
piece of fabric and the shell on it. He stroked the fabric
and held the shell to his ear to listen to the roar, carefully holding his free hand on the material so he
wouldn't disturb her still-life arrangement. The sound
inside the shell was very loud in the attic. He put it
back and turned off the light bulb and lay on the bed.
Like a child, he scrawled "Francie" on the fogged win-
dowpane above the mattress, then, before falling
asleep, erased it with the side of his hand.

Nobody could understand how Delores and Carl had
made such good time driving, but they said they were
speeding the whole way, and that one slept while the
other drove. They came to Francie's door late Sunday
night—early Monday morning, actually—with Meagan thrown like a sack over Carl's shoulder. "She had

hiccups half the way here," Carl sighed, sinking down in the nearest chair with Meagan still sprawled up against him.

"But what are you doing with your coats on?" Delores asked. "What's going on?"

"We were on our way out. Freed has got to teach school tomorrow."

"Freed!" Delores said, running over to him and throwing her arms around his neck.

"Do I know this woman?" Freed said, rubbing the palm of his hand down her spine after he hugged her. Freed and Delores had been lovers ten years before.

"My Pontiac was stolen," Freed said. "Ask anybody."

"What?" Delores said, looking around. "What's the joke?"

"His car was stolen," Perry shrugged.

"Do you want some coffee, Delores? Do you, Carl?" Francie said.

"I don't care," Carl said. "I'll do anything."

"I can't let you two take off when I just got here," Delores said.

"I'll write out directions to my house," Perry said. "The three of you can come up and stay with me."

"That's right," Delores said. "You have that big house now."

"Francie," Carl said, "you look freakishly beautiful. You've kinked up your hair and your butt is unnaturally shapely."

"T.W. was here," Francie said to Carl, ignoring what he had just said. "He would have stayed around if he had known you would be here so soon, I know."

"How's your ex-husband, Francie? It looks like you decided to go on living after he pulled out. Last time I was here there wasn't a chair to sit in. How's Beth Ann, Perry? Might as well state all the shit that's in my mind and calm myself down."

Delores broke in, saying, "She has nightmares," to Francie and pointing to Meagan. "They took her to Disney World and she screams in the night."

Carl picked up a small bottle from the table and shook it back and forth absently. Meagan shifted on him and was still again. The bottle was Hard As Nails, which T.W. coated the middle fingernail of his right hand with, to keep the nail in good shape; to relax, when he was not playing electric music with the band, T.W. played the banjo.

"Did Anita have her kid yet?" Delores asked.

"No—she's just four months pregnant," Freed said. "How did you know about that?"

"She wrote me."

"What did you do to your foot, Perry?" Carl said, standing.

"I broke it."

"I can see that your foot is broken. Forgive me for speaking imprecisely: *how* did you break your foot, Perry?"

"I fell down. I was stepping off of a stone wall in the woods and my foot went out from under me in wet leaves beneath the wall."

"Oh Christ, I've got to teach in the morning," Freed said. "I hate to bust things up, but are we about to move?"

"I'll spread out the sleeping bag for Meagan," Perry said. He went down the hall and turned the radiator all the way on in the bedroom, unrolled the sleeping bag at the foot of the bed. He went back to the living room and got Meagan, who flopped into his arms without waking up. He carried her to the sleeping bag and put her inside and closed the top over her without zipping it. If she had nightmares, it wouldn't do to zip her in. There were little flecks of dried skin on her eyelids, and beneath her eyes were bluish circles. Her face was a little sunburned from Florida. "Do you remember me, Meagan?" he whispered. He smiled at her and turned off the light. Meagan never moved.

"How's T.W.'s band?" Carl asked when he came back into the room.

"Are you giving me a ride home or not?" Freed said.

"What are you going to do without a car?" Delores asked.

"I can borrow my neighbor's truck. I don't know," Freed said. "Hopefully they'll find it and it won't be wrecked."

"T.W. says they're making money. He had a new demo tape down here that was very good."

"Come on," Freed said, pulling at the sleeve of his leather jacket.

"One minute," Perry said. He went into Francie's bedroom and got the painting and hobbled out to the car with it. Freed came out the door behind him, and then Francie, carrying his crutches, saying, "Aren't you even going to say goodbye?"

"I'm just carrying this out to the car."

"I'm sitting in the car," Freed said. "I'm sitting in the car until you decide to start driving it."

"I hope they find your car, Freed," Francie said.

"Del looks great," Freed sighed, and pushed around the snow with the toe of his boot. "That's all I need to see."

"Oh—are you giving them directions to your house?" Francie asked Perry.

He closed the trunk and wiped the snow off his hands on his jeans.

"Just one second," he said to Freed.

"Thank you for the weekend, Francie," Freed said. "I'm going to sit here and freeze until he decides to get going."

"He has to give directions—"

"I understand what's being said, Francie." He closed the car door, opened the window a crack to let the smoke from his cigarette leave the car. Freed was talking to himself in the car about how he was going to sit there until they got going.

Perry went into the house and found a piece of paper and wrote directions and a map. He gave it to Carl, who pocketed it and said, "Thanks. When are we welcome?"

"Any time," he said. "Come up as soon as you can."

"Thank you," Delores said. "We can help you work on the house."

He nodded. He could not remember ever seeing Delores do anything with her hands.

"Goodbye, Francie," he said, giving her a hug. "Stop entertaining people and do your painting."

"I can't see," Carl said. "I'm going to bed."

"Go ahead," Francie said. "Goodbye, Perry. Let me know where you hang the picture."

He hugged her again and stepped to the side, still holding her. He was clowning, clumping in his cast to do the box step. The walkway was covered with snow. The flagstones underneath the snow were slick with ice, so he hopped down the grass, feeling the snow edging over the top of his low boots.

"It's an odd match," Freed said, shivering in the car. "Delores and Carl. I don't get it."

"Come on, close that window," Perry said, starting the car.

"I'm smoking."

"Wait'll I get the heat on."

Freed pitched the cigarette into the snow. "You think he's still on reds?" Freed said. Before Perry could answer, Freed changed his voice. "You have to feel sorry for the little children," he said, wobbling his head at Perry. "What will become of the little ones?" With the hood of his parka covering his head, he looked enough like a little old lady to make Perry laugh. "What the fuck did I do to deserve having my car stolen?"

Freed lit another cigarette. "Tonight when I saw Del I wished I had her back," he said. "It makes me sad that I still don't have any sense."

"Delores is okay now."

"She might look it, but she'll never be okay. You think Carl is still swallowing pills?"

"If he is, they aren't keeping him too alert."

"They looked good. Tired, but okay. Del looked

good." Freed sighed. He pushed the tape into the tape deck, listened a second, then rewound to Gatemouth Brown doing "Take the 'A' Train."

"You forgive me for cheering for the Red Sox?" Freed said. He opened the window a crack. "Where's my car?" he said. "It could be anywhere."

(They finally went to Alexandria, Virginia, to get Freed's car. The police found it after four days. At the start of the ride Freed had said, "Thank you very much for doing this," but Freed had let him pay for his own coffee in the machines along the highway, and Freed had not thanked him again. It was true that when Freed saw the car parked on the lot behind the police station he reached out and grabbed the crook of Perry's arm, but that was almost certainly happiness at seeing the car rather than silent thanks to Perry. Yet on the ride back to Vermont without Freed, he had been lonesome. He and Freed had shared a motel room the night they got the car. They had eaten soggy fried shrimp in the motel dining room, and wandered around Alexandria. Freed, who always had a lot of energy, had tried to talk him into going across the bridge into Georgetown, but he wouldn't do it, and Freed had had the nerve to sulk. He had told Freed that he didn't feel like dragging his broken foot around that night—actually, it didn't bother him very much, and by that time he was hardly able to remember what it had felt like not to have a broken foot. Reading a letter he had written Francie at that time but forgot to mail—a letter he found in a book—he could read between the lines of his petulance that he was already becoming antisocial.)

In June, Beth Ann came back from Albuquerque. She found out from Francie where Perry was living and wrote down his phone number, and took a bus to the town nearest him in Vermont. He picked up his phone one night when the band was practicing—everyone's instrument was instantly silent—and he stood there wishing they would make noise again when he realized who was on the phone. "Whether you want me or not, I'm almost to your house," Beth Ann said. "Will you come get me?"

He went to the drugstore where the bus had left her off, and got her. She had on a black cap and a trench coat. Her eyes were bloodshot, and her skin was filmed with sweat, as if she had walked to Vermont instead of taking the bus. They walked back to his car without touching. "I actually knew your number," she said. "The reason I called Francie first was to see if she was still living in New Hampshire, or if she had moved here with you."

"She's still in New Hampshire," he said. "What made you think she'd be with me?"

"Everybody knows how you feel about Francie except Francie. Or maybe she pretends not to know. I don't know."

"Francie's having a show in New York next month," he said.

"I don't want to be filled in on the news."

"Should I talk about politics?"

"Do you read the newspaper?" she said. "What's the point of being so isolated if you pick up the paper?"

"What are you doing here?" he said.

They drove without speaking all the way back to the house. He was glad that T.W.'s band was there because that would give him something to do other than listen to whatever she had to say. They would be eating dinner by the time they got back—he could sit down and eat, and not talk much.

"T.W.'s band is at my place," he said.

When they got inside, T.W. was on the phone. "Here he is, wait a minute," T.W. said, holding the phone out to Perry. "There's Beth Ann!" T.W. said, giving her a kiss on the forehead. "Good to see you."

Perry was talking to Nick, who had just become a father—a long, blurted story about how Anita was all right and how they had an *enormous* baby that Anita and the midwife hadn't been able to deliver at home. "They took her out in the ambulance bent like a boomerang," Nick said. It sounded as if he was crying. "This kid is eleven pounds and some ounces, I can't remember how many. One, I think. The kid looks like he's ready to take off crawling."

"Well, congratulations, Nick. What are you naming him?"

"I don't know. We haven't written down anything yet. Call me back if you think of a good name."

He hung up. "Nick and Anita had a baby," he said to Beth Ann.

"Hey," said T.W., "you ought to see Delores' kid now, Beth Ann. She's the prettiest little girl I've ever seen. Delores is living in New Hampshire with Carl Fellows, on a farm his grandfather used to run. I think they're getting married. Is that right, Perry?"

Perry shrugged.

"Hey, what happened to Zack?" T.W. asked.

Perry rolled his eyes, and not wanting to hear, he started for the kitchen, where two people from the band were cooking spaghetti sauce. He heard her say, "Zack is dead."

"What are you talking about?" T.W. said.

"He fell off a rock in the Sandia Range. I'm not kidding you."

"What did you say?" Dickie said, coming out of the kitchen, dripping tomato sauce from a spoon.

"He really is," Beth Ann said. "He's dead."

"Is he buried?" T.W. said. Perry looked at T.W., wondering why he asked such a thing.

"Of course," Beth Ann said.

"Where?" T.W. said.

"In Albuquerque."

"He is not dead," Dickie said. "Look at her: she's smiling."

"I'm smiling because it's so horrible, and because I told you in such an awful way." She was no longer smiling. She went over to the sofa where Perry had just sat down and slumped beside him. "He's been dead for four months," she said.

"Fuck it!" Dickie said. "Fuck it—he didn't fall off a mountain."

"I don't know," Roger said. Roger had just come out of the kitchen. He had joined the band a little while before and hadn't known Zack.

"Oh fuck it!" Dickie said, and walked to the front door and went outside. Roger went after him and looked out the door for a minute, then quietly closed it.

"Why didn't you call us?" Perry said.

"I wasn't thinking. It didn't even hit me that I had no reason to be in Albuquerque until a few days ago. I sat around a rented room for four months. I called his parents, and they came out and put on a funeral. It was horrible. His mother was taking sedatives, and we all had to hold her up for three days so she wouldn't fall over. When she left she said to me, 'I'm not even going to see you again, ever in my life,' as though I was her kid."

The phone rang. Perry picked it up. "We're naming her Belinda," Nick said. "This is really embarrassing, but the baby's a girl. I don't know what I was talking about. I haven't had any sleep for almost two days."

"Tell Anita we're happy," Perry said. "T.W. and the band are here. We'll come around soon and inspect the kid and see for ourselves if it has a penis."

"What's he talking about?" T.W. said to Beth Ann.

Perry hung up. He sat on the floor by the phone, thinking of all the times he'd cursed Zack. He hoped that he had never said that he wished he would fall off a mountain.

"I'm going to eat dinner," Roger said. "If anybody else can eat, they're welcome."

They sat in the living room, smelling the sauce. T.W. pulled a guitar slide out of his case. Joints were tightly packed inside it. He looked at it and said, "I guess that's not the thing to do," put it in his pocket, and got up and went into the kitchen. Perry and Beth Ann could hear Roger, feigning cheerfulness, saying, "Would you like me to get you some spaghetti?"

"Maybe I ought to go after Dickie," Beth Ann said.

Dickie came back, with leaves and mud and bark sticking to him, as they were finishing dinner. He bit into a piece of cold garlic bread. He tore a square of paper towel from the roll that was in the center of the table and rubbed it over his face. "What was that spastic asshole doing climbing mountains?" he said.

The phone rang, and no one got up to answer it.

Roger went to the door the next evening, when Delores and Carl showed up. The others had organized a softball game on a neighbor's field, but Roger had been feeling sick to his stomach, and he had stayed around for Borka's arrival. Borka played electric bass with the band, and he was thinking about moving in on her. He loved her wavy gold hair and the little pierced earrings she wore, a moon in one ear and a star in the other. She had won his heart when she did an imitation of Viva in *Bike Boy* for an audience in a bar between sets, calling *Bike Boy* an "old movie." When he went to answer the door, he thought it was her. It was Delores and Carl, and he didn't know who they were. They introduced themselves and came in and sprawled on the sofa, and alternately commented on how nice the house was and argued about whether it was wrong to have left Meagan with Francie. Carl said it was, and Delores said that Meagan knew very well who Francie was, and was just bluffing when they left. Roger told them that he would have to excuse himself (he had been lying on the couch before they took it over) to go stretch out because his stomach felt funny. "Papaya leaf tea," Delores said and instantly pulled a box from her canvas bag. She went into the kitchen and brewed it for him. Roger began to formulate questions to find out who they were.

"Who are you?" Carl finally said to him.

"I'm Roger. I play trumpet with the band."

"You look familiar," Carl said. "Did I see you some other time with another band?"

"I doubt it," Roger said. "I haven't played with a group for a long time." What he didn't tell Carl was that he had been in the seminary. He realized that that always stopped conversation, and he had been trying hard not to say it to people.

"Who are you?" Roger said to Carl.

"Hello, look at this," Perry said, coming into the house. There was a grass stain down the side of his khakis and he had torn the knee of his pants.

"Is there room for us?" Delores called from the kitchen. "We tried to call you twice this morning, but everybody must have been out."

"Sure," Perry said.

He looked around. "Where's Meagan?" he said.

"We were visiting Francie and we left her there. Carl thinks I'm a bad mother."

Carl looked away and said nothing.

"She's with Francie?" Perry echoed. "Well, have you two eaten? We were going to drive into town and get a pizza."

"Perry, this house is as big as a barn. Doesn't it get depressing here in the winter?" Delores said, coming into the living room.

"Did you go to Bard?" Carl asked Roger.

"Yeah," Roger said. "I was there for a couple of years."

"In 'sixty-five or 'sixty-six?"

"'Sixty-six, sure," Roger said, his face lighting up. He and Carl shook hands and laughed.

"Gordon Liddy was the fucking Assistant D.A. of Duchess County," Carl said to everybody. "Did you know Inez?" Carl asked Roger.

"Was she the tall girl who hung out with Little Ruthie?"

"No—she was a musician."

"Right, right."

Delores sighed. She had not gone to college, and Carl

was always running into people from Bard, which bored
her. She asked Perry if she could use the phone and
went into the kitchen. Suddenly Carl stopped reminisc-
ing. He hollered, "Who are you calling?"

"I'm calling Freed. I thought we'd stay here a couple
of days and look around and then go see him in Maine."

"I'm not going to Maine to see Freed," Carl said.

"Why not?"

"Why don't you call and see if your kid stopped sulking?" Carl said. "That's what I think you ought to do."

They could hear her dialing.

"Delores," Carl said. "If you're calling Freed, don't
tell him I'm going there, because I'm not."

"Inez used to go to Adolph's and drive everybody
crazy playing 'Heat Wave' on the jukebox over and
over," Roger said.

"Don't be that way," Delores said, coming out of the
kitchen. "He wrote us that nice letter."

"I don't give a shit what he writes us. If you want
to go visit Freed, I'm not stopping you."

"I suppose you're going to give me your car too."

"If it really means that much to you to visit him,
Delores, you can take the car."

"I'm going to stretch out," Roger said. "Excuse me."

Delores watched Roger walk out of the room and go
up the stairs. "You seriously won't go to Maine?" she
said.

"That's right."

She went back into the kitchen. Perry sat in a chair
and waited for the fight. As he waited, Beth Ann and
T.W. came back to the house. "Carl!" Beth Ann said.
"What are you doing here?"

"Hey!" Carl said and stood to hug her. "How are you,
T.W.?" he said.

"Hey, Carl," T.W. said. "Are you going to fill in on
bass if our bass player doesn't show?"

"I'd throw you off—I'm not good enough," Carl said.
He looked toward the kitchen. "In every respect," he
said.

"Is Roger still sick?" T.W. said, looking around the room. He saw his slide on the floor and took out a joint and offered it around. Only Beth Ann would have any of it.

"Is that Delores in there?" Beth Ann said.

"Yeah," Perry said.

Beth Ann went to the door and waved to Delores and stood by the door, waiting for her to finish. When Delores kept whispering on the phone, she walked away and sat by T.W. and asked where the band was playing. He started naming names of bars.

Carl took a hit off of T.W.'s joint and walked into the kitchen. He came out with a beer.

T.W. offered the joint again and Carl had another hit. "I'm very tempted to go get in my car and drive off," he said.

"Sit down, Carl," Perry said. "We're all going to go get pizza in a minute."

"This is humiliating," Carl said. "Why did she have me bring her to your place if what she wanted was to be in Maine with Freed?"

"I don't know," Perry said. "Sit down."

"I'm going," Carl said. "This is ridiculous."

"Where are you going?" Beth Ann said.

"I'm just going. I apologize for making a scene. I'm just going."

He stood in the middle of the room for a minute, then pulled his wallet and sunglasses out of Delores' bag and went outside. He sat in the car for quite a while. Then they heard the car start.

"Who is she talking to?" Beth Ann said. "She's talking to Freed?"

"Let's get Dickie and go eat," T.W. said.

"Maybe there's something here to eat," Beth Ann said.

"There isn't," Perry said.

"I'm willing to spring for pizza," T.W. said. "I want to eat so we can start practicing. We've got to get up early to drive to the job."

Delores came out of the kitchen, seeming oblivious to Carl's departure. She went over to Beth Ann and rumpled her hair. "What are *you* doing here?" she said.

"Don't tell her," T.W. said. "We're going for pizza. Want to come?"

"Sure," Delores said. "Did Carl stalk out?"

"He drove off. In the car."

"Did you ever see anybody have a temper tantrum like that?" Delores said. "Don't you think that was irrational?"

"I want pizza with mushrooms and onions," T.W. said. "Will you split that kind of a pizza with me, Beth Ann?"

All of them got up and followed him out of the house.

"We can take my bus," T.W. said. "Come on—pile in the back."

"How far do we have to go?" Beth Ann said.

"Come on, get in. Should we ask Roger if he's feeling better?"

"He's sick," Perry said. "Let's just go."

"Tell me about Meagan," Beth Ann said to Delores. "Does she still have skin like porcelain?"

"You can see the veins in it," Delores said. "It scares me sometimes. It looks like silk instead of human skin."

"Where is she?"

"She's with Francie. Francie's taking her to a dog show."

"Bring her to see us," Beth Ann said.

Perry wondered if the "us" was inadvertent. He wondered how long she intended to stay, and what Delores intended to do about getting out of the house with Carl gone.

"It's so beautiful here," Beth Ann sighed as they rolled down the driveway.

They were sitting on wood seats on opposite sides of the van, facing one another. The floor of the van had been painted with a picture of the sun coming up over the mountains. T.W. drove with the dome light on, and the painting was positioned right under it; that made it seem as if the sun was actually glowing.

"Where's Borka?" Perry called to T.W.

"I don't know. If she doesn't show this time, I'm firing her."

"It'll break Roger's heart," Perry said.

"Roger doesn't have a heart. Roger's got religion."

T.W. put on the brakes. Dickie was standing up to his knees in the stream, clearing rocks out of it.

"There's Dickie," T.W. said. "Hey, Dickie! You going to eat with us?"

"I can eat mud," Dickie said, stumbling around in the stream and making a wild face and holding a cupped hand of mud in front of his face.

"You want us to bring you a pizza?" T.W. called.

"I eat mud!" Dickie screamed.

"What's that all about?" Perry said.

T.W. shrugged. They pulled out of the driveway and T.W. headed toward town.

"Somebody remind me to call my mother," T.W. said.

T.W., as usual, set two alarms, and at nine in the morning they left in the van, taking Delores with them and dropping her at the bus stop so she could get the bus to Maine. Perry didn't know she was going until she tiptoed into his room to say that she was going to Freed's and that if Carl came back, he could tell him whatever he wanted. Perry sat up in bed and smiled at her and said, "It was good to see you." When she tiptoed out, he couldn't sleep because that had been such a lame thing to say. Beth Ann had left late the night before, with Roger, who was going to drop her at the train station so she could go to her parents' house in Westport. It crossed his mind that she and Roger would get something going. He could remember his anger and outrage when she pulled out for Albuquerque, and was surprised when she came to him again that he felt very little hostility. That was because, as Freed had been telling him for a long time, the person he was interested in was Francie. He thought that he

should call her because she might not know where
Delores had gone. Her line was busy when he called,
though, so he forgot about that for a while and went
outside and looked at the new paint on his house. He
walked down to the brook and inspected and approved
of the work Dickie had done clearing it. In spite of
smoking dope too much, Dickie got a lot of work done.
He sat on a mossy rock and thought about Zack's death
and wondered if there might not have been one split
second during the fall that was pleasurable, when perhaps his body was weightless and his mind clear. He
tossed a pebble into the stream below him and it hit
the water unremarkably—it just fell and went plop. He
smiled at himself in dismay: he would have to do better
than that if he was going to be a poet. Writing poetry
was still an embarrassing idea to him, and Francie was
the only one he thought really approved of it and urged
him on. He thought that the more practical thing to
aim for would be to repair houses. It seemed that this
might be a part of the world where he could establish
himself as a carpenter, now that he had some experience. He and T.W. had even tossed around the idea of
a partnership, with T.W. working when it was more
profitable to do that than play music.

He thought again of what Dickie had said; Dickie
had been right to wonder what gawky Zack had been
doing scaling mountains. The truth was that there was
something very debilitating about being with Beth
Ann—Zack had said that to him, which was why he
assumed Zack didn't like her—and probably Zack had
felt the urge to break out to do something physical and
in that way escape her. The last time he saw Zack,
before Zack picked up Beth Ann, they had played a
quiet game of poker. He could not remember at whose
house they had played, but he remembered that Zack
had won the game. Later, in his journal, he noted that
as a nice irony and as a neat little foreshadowing of
what was to come. Zack had always been quiet and
clumsy, and while a lot of people came around to liking

him, he didn't have one close friend in the group. It occurred to him that Beth Ann might have picked Zack the way she had picked out the runt of the litter when they went their separate ways when the lease was up on the house they all rented, and she had to take a kitten from the litter. He could remember Zack's ornate denim jacket, with a mandala embroidered on the back. Since his parents had arranged the funeral, it was certain that he wasn't buried in that. Zack claimed that he got the jacket by trading a Porky Pig bank to a friend named Famous Malcolm he had since lost track of.

He walked back to the house and took off all his clothes but his underwear and stretched out on the chaise longue. It was missing several strips, so his body sank low to the ground and he could feel the cool of the earth on his buttocks. He sat there enjoying the quiet, listening to the birds. Then after a while he got up to call Francie and stopped on the way in to study an ant war in the grass by the front door. That was when he heard the unfamiliar car in the driveway and looked up to see Borka in a beat-up Chevrolet.

"They're all gone," he said.

"They can't be. We have to practice."

"The job is today. The practice was yesterday."

"You're putting me on," she said. "Are they inside?"

"I'm not putting you on. They're gone." He was pulling his jeans on.

She put her hand to her face and was about to sink down in the grass, but he took her by the arm and steered her away; she had been about to sit where the ants were having their war.

"T.W. is never going to believe this wasn't on purpose," she said.

Borka had on a scarf tied around her breasts and several necklaces: one that looked like a little magnifying glass, a necklace of tiny silver birds, and a necklace with a large moon dangling from it that seemed to be made out of pottery. She had on cut-off lavender jeans and black spike-heeled shoes. She was eighteen. It was T.W.'s opinion, Perry knew, that she dressed that way because she was a virgin.

"What am I going to do?" she said. "You can even look at the book I wrote the date down in—it says today,. not yesterday. Maybe he told me the wrong day."

She was upset, and it was unlike her; he was used to her silence, or her mockery.

"I know the name of the bar they're playing at. Why don't you call the bar—or you could even make it there in about three hours."

"He'd kill me. I don't have the nerve to call him." Borka went over to her car and sat on the hood and stared into the woods. "I blew it," she said.

He went inside to call Francie. If Borka was going to cry, he didn't want to have to watch. Before he got to the phone, it started ringing. He answered the phone, and it was Freed.

"Let me talk to Del," Freed said.

"She left hours ago. She was on her way to Maine."

"Yeah, well, Carl called and told me he was going to slit my throat, and I really don't want that to happen, and I'm very willing not to have that woman here if Carl is going to kill me over the issue."

"Freed. What have I got to do with it?"

"Do you think I should call the cops? Does he know where I live? What have I suddenly got to be involved with the cops all the time for? I'm growing grass in my garden this summer, and the cops are going to take a liking to me and stop around for fucking coffee."

Borka came into the house and got a Coke from the refrigerator. She had been crying.

"Leave your house," Perry said.

"Leave. That's fine, except that he specifically said that he was coming to the school to slit my throat in front of my class so that I would be embarrassed before I died. I mean, I know Carl isn't going to kill me, but I really don't want to deal with Carl." Freed coughed. "Carl is jealous because I have a job and he doesn't."

"I don't think Carl will even show up, Freed."

"I've got to hang up," Freed said. "My phone bill was a hundred and forty dollars last month."

He said goodbye to Freed and sat down opposite Borka. "T.W.'s temper always cools off," he said to her.

"No, I think he really dislikes me. And I keep making mistakes like this, and that makes him dislike me more."

"You like him?"

She nodded.

"I don't think he knows that," he said.

"He isn't interested in knowing it. All he cares about is music. Anyway—he told me if I fucked up again, he was throwing me out of the band."

"I think what you ought to do is drive to the place in New York State and go on stage with them. You'll do okay without practicing, and they'll be relieved to see you, even if they're pissed off."

She hung her head. Perry could see the dark hair down her center part; it became golden again about an inch from the scalp.

"Thank you," she said.

"For what?"

"For the Coke," she said and hit the edge of the empty can on the table.

When she left he picked up the things the band had thrown around, and emptied the ashtrays and sat at the kitchen table again, listening to the birds and to the sound of a dog barking far away. It was too much for him when the house was full of people, but when everybody was gone he felt a little depressed. He was grating cheese and sprinkling it over a can of pinto beans for an early supper when the phone rang.

"You wouldn't know where Delores is, would you?" Francie said.

"Yeah. Carl left and Delores went to Freed's."

"Freed's?"

"Freed's. What the hell."

"Where's Carl?"

"He was supposed to go there too. I heard from Freed that Carl called and threatened to kill him."

"This is wearing me down. I'm going to call Maine. Meagan is coming down with a cold and she wants her mother."

"Did you get your paintings crated?" he asked.

"Some of them. I'm going to fix Meagan and me some supper and go back to it."

"I put your painting—" He cut himself off from what he was going to say: that the painting was hanging in his bedroom. "I put it up, and it looks wonderful, Francie."

"Thanks," she said. "When I become famous, don't sell it."

He wandered around the house. He wondered if this was what someone who was going crazy would be like. Then he berated himself for thinking about that again, and for still believing in the back of his mind that the most honorable activity was working from nine to five. He put on a John Coltrane record and sat in his favorite Morris chair to calm down. After he had sat there quietly for a while, he started to get his perspective back: the house was a wreck, after all, not because he didn't care enough to live decently, but because his friends had taken it over and wrecked it. When Dickie sat in a chair, it seemed to come unglued. Pieces of paper on which T.W. had scrawled words and chord symbols were scattered everywhere, amid tangles of broken strings. Cigarette butts were floating in half-empty glasses of bourbon. He knew that it was Francie again when the phone rang.

"I can't reach Delores," she said. "If you hear from her, tell her to call me." Francie hesitated. "Is it because I'm a Capricorn? What is it about me that makes people drop their kids with me and come stay with me, and why is everything always so confused?"

"People take advantage of you."

"It's such a nice night out," Francie sighed. "Meagan has a cold and I'm going to get it. I don't think that's fair. I was going to go for a walk, but I can't drag her along when she's so droopy, and I don't feel right about leaving her." Francie lowered her voice to a whisper. "I don't think much of Delores walking out on Meagan to take a vacation. I only took Meagan because I felt sorry for her."

"Call her at Freed's and tell her to come back."

"I have to cut aspirin in half and give her a half aspirin," Francie whispered. "I called my doctor."

"Would you like me to come there to be with you?"

Francie waited a minute before answering. "I'd like it, but that would be silly."

"I'm coming. It's only an hour's drive."

Another hesitation. "Are you sure you want to?"

"I want to. I don't have anything I have to do here."

Going down the driveway, Perry felt elated. It was the right time, and he knew what he was going to say to Francie. The realization of it, the weight of it, came as inevitably as pressure builds around a diver.

Francie was talking on the phone to Delores' mother. She was assuring her that Meagan's voice was odd only because she was coming down with a cold, and lied that Delores was out but would be back soon.

Francie hung up and greeted him with "Wait'll you hear this: Freed and Delores have decided to go away and live together. Carl went to the house and threw firecrackers at the windows, apparently, and scared them to death. Then Carl drove off and they got some things into suitcases. He's just left his job a week before the term ends and he's going south, he says, to live with Delores. I hinted that I didn't want them to come here just now, but they're coming anyway. I think Delores is cracking up. She was crying and laughing on the phone."

"Let's lock the door and turn out all the lights," he said.

"No, I'm just going to tell them that they can spend the night, but that I'm not going to put up with any shit. And if Carl follows them down here and makes a scene, I'm going to call the police."

She was too preoccupied for him to ask her to go to bed. He looked at her and looked away. There was a smudge of yellow paint on her cheek she did not know was there.

"Why don't we take Meagan and get out of here?" he said.

"Delores would arrest us for kidnapping."

"If she could remember where she left her," he said.

She followed him to the living room. It was June, and too warm for a fire, but Francie loved the wood burning, and when the evenings were a little cold, she lit a fire. The fire was dying in the fireplace. He sat on the sofa and patted the cushion for her to sit beside him. There was a big box on the sofa, addressed to T.W. c/o Francie.

"What's that?" he said.

"Worms. Honest to God. He's going to start raising worms for profit."

"What are you doing with the worms?"

"He had them delivered here because I'm usually home in the day and he's out of town so often."

He put the box of worms on the floor. In this context, how could he talk about going to bed with her?

"You shouldn't put up with it," he said.

"You know what T.W. said that time about my other set of friends? It was just a joking remark, but he was right: I don't have any other friends. I know a few other people, but I don't care anything about them. Sometimes when all of us are together we have good times. I don't want to make them all go away."

"What if you were just with me? What if we did what Freed and Delores are doing?"

"What do you mean?"

"I mean, what if we went away?"

"Where would we go?"

He had not thought about where they would go. "You could come live in my house in Vermont."

"What would I do with my house?" she said.

He sat by the fire, staring into the peaks of flames, and looked at her. He saw that she did not want to live with him. She shifted on the sofa and looked somewhere else, embarrassed.

"You told me before that I was your best friend," he said.

"You are. We don't have to live together because of that, do we?"

"You don't even have to speak to me. You can entertain yourself with T.W. and his worms, or you can hold down the fortress while Carl rockets firecrackers at your windows, or you can have a big party and study the Rorschach blots of wine on your rug. You could do most any of those things."

"I'm sorry I hurt your feelings," she said.

"I'm your best friend, Francie. Say something kinder to me."

"I don't know how to talk," she said.

"What do you mean?"

"I mean that I'm either alone and it's silent here all day, or my friends are around, and I don't really talk to them."

"You can talk to me."

"I've already hurt your feelings. I don't want to do anything worse."

"Well, what are you holding out that might really do me in? How little do you think of me?"

Francie drew up her knees and clasped her hands around them. "I want to be a painter," she said.

"You are a painter."

"I want to be an important painter."

He stared at her, waiting for more.

"I don't know what I want," Francie said. "When Anita had her baby I wanted to be a mother. I want to be left alone, but I need to have people around."

"When I was a kid my parents made me take dancing lessons, and the boys had to go up to the girls and ask them to dance. I asked, and the girl stomped my foot."

"That didn't really happen."

"If I wanted to make you feel sorry for me, I could have thought of something more dramatic."

"You mean *just* live with you in the house?" Francie said.

"No," he said.

Francie heaved out a sigh. "Was that horrible to ask?"

"No. It's okay that you asked."

"But I mean—do you understand?" Her voice was softer then the crackling fire.

"No," he said.

She let her legs hang down and stroked the top of the box with one foot, looking away from him.

"I just don't think of us that way," she said.

"Would you think about it for a while?" he said.

Francie got off the sofa and went to sit by him. "Have I not understood all along?" she said.

"I love mattresses thrown in attics, Francie."

"I'm sorry," she said.

"I'm sorry I said anything. I can't keep sitting here being embarrassed."

Perry got up. He was tired and hungry, and he knew that he had made a mistake. He went into the kitchen and headed for the refrigerator to see if there was a beer. One of her canvases of herself was propped up in the kitchen, and he looked away from it and went back to the living room with nothing to drink.

"Forget I said it," he said. "Are you willing to forget it?"

She smiled at him. "Sure," she said.

"It's none of my business," he said, "but who do you sleep with?"

"Nobody," she said.

That came as a harder blow than the little-girl's shoe on the top of his foot.

"I don't want to talk about it," she said. "Don't embarrass me."

She looked terrible, as if she was about to cry.

"Get rid of the worms," he said. "Let's get rid of the worms."

"What are you talking about?"

"Yes. Come on. I'm dumping them."

He took the box and went outside. It was just starting to get dark. The sky was deep-purple at the horizon. He pried open the box while Francie watched. The worms were packed in something that looked like straw, but darker brown. When he lifted that out of the big box, Francie stepped back, wincing. You could see the worms squirming in the packing. He pulled it apart into about five gobs and threw them into the bushes. Then he went inside and ripped up the box and threw it into the fire.

They sat in front of the fire for a long time, neither of them saying anything, until the car came into the drive. They both got up and went to the window and looked out. Delores got out of the car first and came weaving toward the house without waiting for Freed. Perry almost grabbed Francie and stopped her from going to the door.

"How's my baby?" he heard Delores say. There was something wrong with her voice. He heard Freed's voice. The three of them came into the living room. Freed shook his head. "I thought you were in Vermont," he said. He came over to where Perry stood by the window. Freed was sweating.

"What do you think I found?" Delores said. Perry looked at her, forcing a smile. Delores was stoned; her eyes were red, and she wasn't focusing.

"I found my *table*," Delores said. "I thought it was lost, and Freed had it all the time. It was there in his living room."

"I thought all this time that I'd gotten the table from Anita," Freed said. Then he looked self-conscious because obviously nobody cared how he got the table.

"Meagan's sleeping," Francie said. "She has a cold."

"Does she have the hiccups again?"

"What?" Francie said. "I said she has a cold."

"Where's my poor baby?" Delores said and walked out of the living room toward the bedroom.

"What the hell are you doing?" Perry said to Freed.

"I don't know," Freed said and hung his head. "Either I've always loved Del or I never have."

Francie looked disgusted when he said that and walked out of the room to find Delores.

"What's the matter?" Freed said. "Why does everybody look so funny?"

"Freed, you can't take them out of here like this. Delores is stoned and probably has no idea of what's going on."

"I'm not stoned," Freed said. "I can't help it if she got herself smashed." His clothes smelled of grass, and he kept tugging at his shirt hanging out of his pants but not tucking it in. "Listen," he said. "This is the end."

"The end of what?"

"It's just the end! We're taking Meagan to her grandparents and we're going to try to have a life. She knows what she's doing. Don't insult me by saying she's just going with me because she's not in her right mind."

"Okay," Perry said. "You do what you want."

"Well, I want to be friends," Freed said, dipping his hand toward Perry's. "Aren't you going to be my friend?"

"I didn't say I wasn't your friend, Freed. You do what you want."

"Then shake my hand," Freed said. "You shake it." He shook Freed's hand firmly.

"Jesus Christ!" Freed said. "What happens when a handshake doesn't mean anything?"

"I shook your fucking hand, Freed."

"You like me! Cut it out, Perry. You drove me to fucking Alexandria to get my Pontiac."

"It's okay, Freed. Calm down."

"You don't think she knows what's going on, do you?"

"What about Meagan? Are you going to take her when she's sick?"

"We've got my two pillows in the back seat. She can lie back there. What's wrong with that?"

"Nothing. Nothing's wrong with it."

"Then what's happening?" Freed said. "You're acting this way and Carl flipped out and tried to bomb my house. Is it because you're jealous that I've got Delores?"

"No," he said. "I just think you're both upset and you oughtn't to do this."

Delores was standing in the doorway holding Meagan, with Meagan's head fallen off of her shoulder, and Francie beside her. Freed stood with his back to the fire, tilting the clock on the mantel back and forth absent-mindedly. He tilted it too far and had to turn around and set it back in place.

"We don't want to have a fight," Francie said. "Let's talk about this some other time."

"He doesn't think we can get to Florida!" Freed said. "What's he talking about?"

Nobody sat down. They stood awkwardly until Meagan began to squirm, and then Delores whispered to Francie and the two of them walked out to the car. Freed looked at Perry and didn't say anything more. He put out his hand, and Perry shook it again, this time taking care not to shake it firmly. Freed mumbled something that Perry couldn't catch; it sounded as though he was saying "How do you know?"

Perry sat on the sofa and waited for the inevitable starting of the motor and the car driving away. Francie came in, shaking her head. "I forgot to tell her that her mother called," she said.

Perry remembered, suddenly, what T.W. had asked to be reminded of in the car.

"I feel like a criminal letting them go," she said.

"What could you do? They'll probably wake up in the morning and forget the plan. You can expect one or both of them by tomorrow night."

"I don't want them. I've really had it."

He felt sorry for her, and sorry for himself that he wasn't what she wanted. He thought about what she had told him a long time ago about how she had been a fat kid, and the last one picked to be on teams. Of course it would be important to her to be the center of things. She was slender now, and pretty in spite of her frizzed hairdo. He had thought all the time he was repairing his house that eventually he would have the nerve to ask Francie to live there. He had not thought beyond that—that Francie would say no.

"Some days I think I'm going to be famous," Francie was saying.

He got up and looked out the window. There was a three-quarter moon shining on the pyramid bushes, and he sighed because he suddenly felt that he couldn't derive power from them or anything else.

"I'm sure you will," he said. "I'll see you in the morning, Francie."

At the top of the stairs he stepped on a little twisted tube of paint, and orange oozed out on the floorboards. He sat on the mattress and listened to her walking downstairs. He heard her put on the tape of T.W.'s band. He got up and took off his belt and his watch and put them beside the mattress. In a little while he heard her walking again.

"Listen," Francie called up the stairs. "I'd like to come live in Vermont."

"You don't have to," he said.

"I know it. I want to."

He waited to hear her foot on the stairs.

"Is that all right?" she said. "I can live in Vermont and be a painter."

He thought that she sounded like Meagan, who liked to tell stories back to people as well as have them read to her.

"Okay?" she said. She was climbing the stairs as she spoke.


"It's morning," she said.

He opened and closed his eyes several times; the crosshatching on the floor drew his attention. He looked at Francie and saw that she was already awake.

"I think I have bad news for you. I think Carl's poking around here."

"Carl?" he said.

"I'm not going to answer the door," she whispered.

His arm had gone dead stretched under her neck during the night. He withdrew it and put it outside the covers. Lying together, they drifted off to sleep again. They slept for about an hour, until the crosshatching began to slant and grow pale. He heard a noise and woke up.

"What's that?" she said.

"I don't know. Is Carl hanging around because he thinks Delores is here?"

She pushed herself up and looked out the window. She didn't see Carl's car, or any car but hers and Perry's.

"Be quiet," he said. "Listen."

But there was no more noise downstairs. He lay back, waiting for another sound. It came, eventually, in the form of faint radio music.

"Who's down there?" Francie whispered to him. She curled into him and didn't move.

He was curious now, so he got up and pulled on his jeans. "Hey—who's downstairs?" he called.

The radio continued to play.

Francie got up after him and put on her jeans. She picked up his sweater from the floor and pulled it over her head. Barefoot, they went down the stairs.

"Carl?" Francie yelled. It was the first time that Perry was frightened; her voice echoed in the house, and there was no answer, just the radio music. They saw him at the same time, and both drew back a little.

It was the boy from the party—the boy who had stolen Freed's car. He had on a stocking cap, but his face, which had seemed unremarkable before, seemed unforgettable now. There was what looked like a large mole on his temple. Perry took one step forward and saw that it was a fly, but not a real fly—a little black plastic fly, with glue smeared underneath it.

"How did you get in here?" Perry asked. Francie took one step forward to stand beside him.

"I'm not here. You just think I'm here. You're sleep-walking." When he said the last thing, his voice changed from mocking to serious. "This is a very nice house, but I'm not interested in comfortable furniture or nice oil paintings. What I'm interested in is money, and that's what I haven't found. Where's your money, Francie?"

They were both shocked that the boy knew Francie's name.

The boy said, "I have a hunting knife with a fat straight blade, and I have a Swiss army knife with little corkscrews and curved blades. What I don't have is *money*, and I know that there has to be money, Francie, because this is a very fancy house you have here."

Perry reached in his back pocket and took out his billfold and tossed it at the boy. He did it because he was afraid to walk up to him, and he hoped that money was all he wanted.

The boy looked inside and saw the money: about forty dollars, although he didn't count it. He threw the wallet back.

"Let's play 'Mother May I,'" the boy said.

Perry turned to walk for the phone, but stopped. The gleam he saw out of the corner of his eye was the knife: not the Swiss army knife, but the other one—a knife you would use for skinning animals.

"I know your brother," the boy said to Francie.

Perry heard her voice as if it were filtering through something. "You do?" Francie said.

"And I know your friend Freed better than he told you. I slept with your friend Freed. That's why I can't understand his pretending I was just some hitchhiker at your party. He was going to give me the car. The plan was, he was going to buy a car from your brother, and he was going to sell me his car." The boy's voice changed. "His car wasn't worth anything," he said.

Francie looked at Perry. He was too frightened to do what he wanted to do and look back at her reassuringly.

"I don't understand," Francie said.

Perry held out the wallet again but didn't throw it.

"Do you think I'm lying?" the boy said. "You didn't know that he picked me up hitching two days before he brought me here? I was on my way somewhere else, but he took me home with him and then he brought me to your party."

"We don't know anything about it," Perry said. "You can have any money we have if you'll get out."

"Where's your brother's car?" the boy said to Francie.

"I don't—" Francie broke off, not wanting to say that she had no brother. "I don't know anything about what Freed told you."

Francie saw that Perry was staring at something and followed his line of vision. She saw the sofa cushion, sliced down the middle.

"I wanted to come here and be friendly, but you know, I didn't think you'd feel friendly toward me. I thought maybe you'd act like you were, and that you might be liberal-minded about the mistake with your friend Freed's car—particularly if I showed you this— but I thought, you understand—that I wanted your money more than I wanted your friendship. But then I thought I'd serenade you and you'd come downstairs and we might be friendly too. I thought I could explain to you about Freed."

Francie looked at Perry, her hands clenched in front of her; the ladylike gesture seemed grotesque in context.

"I see what you're saying about Freed," Perry said.

The boy smiled what looked like a genuine smile. "Then you understand about the car."

"Sure," Perry said.

"Do you know that game, 'Mother May I?'" the boy said to Francie.

She looked again to Perry. He stood there with his arms at his side, his billfold in one hand, the other hand making a fist and releasing it.

"Does she know the game?" he said to Perry.

"No," Perry said. He was wondering why some of their friends who were always around didn't show up.

"It's such an easy game!" the boy said. "I tell you to do something, Francie, and you have to ask, 'Mother may I?' before doing it. You lose if you do something without asking permission. You see? It's a fucked-up game."

The boy was the only one who smiled at this.

"If you want our money, you can have it," Perry said again.

"I'm not talking about *money* now," the boy said. "I'm talking about a game. If, for instance, you wish to ask, 'Mother may I give you my money?,' and then wait for me to give an answer, I might say yes."

"Mother may I give you our money?" Perry said quickly. He held out his billfold.

"I'm not your mother, you blind son of a bitch," the boy said, and turned his smile into a laugh. "I used to work in a restaurant and carve centerpieces out of ice."

"Please," Perry said. "Take our money and whatever else you want from the house and go."

"Why aren't we playing the game?" the boy said. He seemed to be genuinely puzzled. "Are you too fucked-up to play this game?"

They stood there silently.

"I was Freed's friend, but I'm not good enough to be your friend, am I? Do you think your brother doesn't like me, Francie, and that's why the car deal fell through?"

Perry held out his billfold again.

"You're a fucking coward," the boy said. "I don't want to see that again."

Perry put it in his pocket.

"Take out the money," the boy said then.

Perry removed his billfold and took the money out of it. He couldn't throw the bills at the boy because they wouldn't reach him, and he didn't want to go closer.

"Say, 'Mother may I give you the money?'."

Perry didn't say it. He took a few steps closer and held out his hand. When the boy made no move, Perry said what the boy wanted.

"No!" the boy said and laughed.

"Make him get out," Francie said to Perry.

"And then you'd be so happy!" the boy said suddenly. "You'd have no money, and one of you would have lost a car, but they'd find the car for you, and I might not even have wrecked it, and you could get more money and you could buy a deadbolt lock for your door—that's what you're supposed to have, Francie, not leave your door swinging open."

"I didn't," Francie said to Perry. She stared at him, wanting him to agree with her.

"You want to lock your doors," the boy said. "There are so many crazy people. Your friend, for instance— Freed. I could tell from the way he was acting toward me that you didn't understand what was going on. I came back to set you straight. I know you probably think I came back to kill you, but the truth is, I decided I needed a car and some money for gas, and I thought I'd turn on the radio while I waited. If you wanted to give me your car keys, Francie, and if you wanted to get your money, I'd be grateful."

Francie turned toward the backpack that hung from one strap on the doorknob, and the knife whizzed past her shoulder and stuck in the door. Perry was going to dive for it, but the knife was in too deeply; he would never get it out in time.

"Mother may I?" the boy said.

Francie sucked in her breath. It was a long time

before she spoke, and said, "Mother may I get my money?"

"I'll get it," the boy said. He got up and Francie jumped back, next to Perry. The boy looked at the two of them and nodded politely. He had the Swiss army knife drawn, and as he spoke he began clicking out the parts; Perry looked at the corkscrew snap out. With his free hand the boy groped through her backpack for her wallet, found it and put it in his shirt pocket.

"Just like that," the boy said, "I got everything I wanted, and now I can be going. Only I want your assurance that you won't call the police."

"No," Francie said. "We won't."

"We won't call," Perry said, his voice overlaying hers.

"Do you think you'll get a bolt for your door, Francie?" the boy said.

Francie was looking at the sofa cushion.

"She learns fast," the boy said to Perry. "She learned the game and she knows what to do now. I've actually performed quite a service for you, Francie."

The boy's T-shirt said NATIONAL HOTEL, BLOCK ISLAND, R.I. When he got up to cross the room, the fly fell off his temple. Under the smeared glue Perry could see blood—the fly had been glued there to cover a sore.

"Of course, I could stay much longer," the boy said. He paused dramatically. "But I hate to drive in rush hour," he said.

Then he was gone. Neither of them moved toward the door. All the time he had been pulling knives out of his pocket, Perry had seen the butt of a gun sticking out of his pants pocket. Except for coming together, neither of them moved again until they heard the car screeching out of the driveway. Then Francie exhaled and he put his arm around her. He noticed for the first time that his hands were trembling. When he locked his fingers together, he could feel the joints vibrating against each other.

"It's the first time I ever wanted to be old," Francie said. "I thought I was going to die."

They went to the kitchen to call the police, but the boy had cut the phone cord. The receiver, with a stub of cord, was placed on the top of the refrigerator, in a basket of apples. He had also slashed through one of Francie's self-portraits, the one that had been propped in the kitchen for months. He had slashed her head until it was unrecognizable, but the body was untouched. Francie put her hand over her mouth when she saw that. And since there was no way to call the police, Perry went back to her.

"What if Meagan had been there?" she whispered. "And what was he saying about Freed—was there any sense to that?"

Perry snapped off the radio. For the first time since coming down the stairs and seeing the boy, Francie was crying. She was crying as hard as she had been the night before, when she got to the top of the stairs.

"All right, let's take it from the top," T.W. said, banging a Bic pen instead of a baton on Perry's table instead of on a conductor's podium.

The band started up, perfectly together, until suddenly Roger, swaying back and forth, wearing his Harvard letter sweater and a pair of cut-offs, lifted his trumpet and blared out the first bars of "Young At Heart."

"Thank you, ladies and gentlemen," Borka said. She cupped her hand and pretended to be speaking into a microphone. "And now I'd like to do an old favorite of mine: 'As Time Goes By.'" Borka leaned into her hand again.

Everybody in the band was convulsed except T.W., who said, "All right, you piss-holes, we get the song down right or we practice all night."

Borka stepped back behind the bass. Roger put down his trumpet.

"Here we go," T.W. said, tapping the pen.

The band started playing, perfectly together. Less than ten seconds into the song, Roger picked up his trumpet and loudly blew the beginning of "Young At Heart" again.

"Oh fuck," T.W. said, shouting above everyone's laughter. "Somebody take his pipe away from him."

Borka leaned her bass against the wall and lifted the ashtray with the pipe of grass burning in it from the floor and put it on the table by T.W. Roger glared at her.

"If you screw us up again, I'm going to stab your eyes out," T.W. said, holding out the Bic pen to Roger. Roger looked humble. T.W. was in a bad mood because he had agreed to play for a bar mitzvah, on Long Island, and he hated things like that. Nobody in the band wanted to do it either, except that they all needed the money. Halfway through the next song, there was more activity. Dickie was wrestling with Roger. They all turned and saw Roger's horn lifted in the air. Dickie had gotten it away from him and was handing it to Borka.

"You're all a bunch of fucking imbeciles," T.W. said and threw the pen into the center of the group and slammed out of the house.

"I got his horn! He's going to sit this song out!" Dickie called after T.W., but it was no use. The door slammed before Dickie had finished speaking. Dickie sighed and handed Roger his horn back.

"What's going on?" Perry said, coming downstairs. Everybody looked at him gloomily, and no one answered. "What?" Perry said.

"Roger made T.W. mad," Borka said.

"'You *must* remember this,'" Roger boomed, a capella.

"'A kiss is just a kiss,'" Borka sang, in an unnaturally high voice.

Roger picked up his trumpet. He thrust out his hips

and raised his horn high, over his head, playing "As Time Goes By."

"I think he's getting not very funny," Dickie said, brushing past Perry to get a beer in the kitchen. "I think Roger's acting like a moron."

The rest of the band sat slumped on the floor, enduring Roger's song.

"All right!" T.W. screamed, rushing back into the house. "On your feet. Roger, you put your horn away and go sit across the room. We're going to do this practice so we can do the job and get it over with."

"Why do we have to play at a circumcision?" Roger said.

"Shut up, Roger," T.W. said.

"I'm going to play 'As Time Goes By' at the circumcision."

"Go sit in that chair, Roger," T.W. said, pointing to Perry's Morris chair. "If we have to tie you into it and stuff your sweater into your mouth, we're going to do that."

Roger skulked off to the chair. Everybody stared at him, and nobody smiled.

"Now let's play this fucking song," T.W. said.

Perry sighed and wandered into the kitchen to see if there was any meatloaf left over from dinner the night before. There was a small end slice, and he picked it up in his fingers and ate it. He thought about taking part of it to Francie but ate it all himself. For the past several days, not at all distracted by the band, she had been making a sketch for a huge painting she wanted to do of all her friends. They were going to be standing on the canvas holding hands, like paper dolls. It was a realistic painting except that Francie had sketched a horn in place of Roger's arm, and she had put a fox's head on T.W.'s body and a chicken head on Borka's body. T.W. and Borka were sleeping together.

It was August, and hot in the house. Several of the screens were ripped, and there were a lot of flies buzz-

ing around. At dawn the flies would dive-bomb everybody. The last several nights, Perry had bought the
newspaper so he could roll it up and hunt flies.

Francie had put her house up for sale. Nobody had
made a good offer yet, and she was anxious for it to be
sold: she didn't feel right about taking Perry's money,
and all the money she had now was what she had made
from the sales at the gallery in New York where her
show had opened. The show had been a success, and
Francie was getting what she wanted—she was going
to be famous, all of them were sure. That afternoon a
man who was writing about contemporary women art-
ists was coming to Vermont to interview her. She had
gone upstairs to sketch because all of them had been
teasing her. Roger had said that when the man came,
he was going to open the door naked. Perry worried
that Roger might really do it now that he was so stoned,
but he didn't say that to Francie. He just listened carefully for the car so he could be the one who opened the
door. He figured that if Roger started to throw off his
clothes, the band would tackle him.

On the calendar in the kitchen was penciled: "Miner—
*Village Voice.*" It was hard to believe that someone was
coming to interview Francie—that Francie was living
in his house, in the first place, and that someone was
coming here to interview her. He wanted to stay with
her when the interview took place, but she had already
told him that she didn't want him there; she didn't
want any protection and, it was true, she didn't need
any.

He was very proud of her. Some days he thought
that his importance in life was to take care of other
people—that he would be remembered as the person
who housed them and looked after them: T.W.'s band
was going to be famous, he was sure, and when Miner's
piece came out in the *Voice*, Francie was going to be
interviewed much more, and have more shows. It made
him slightly sorry for himself that there was nothing

he excelled at. He had done a good job finishing the inside of his house, but there were a lot of people who did good carpentry work.

He wanted to ask her to marry him now, before she was famous, but he didn't dare. She had had nothing but withering things to say about marriage since her own marriage had gone bad, and although she liked Nick and Anita, she also thought their togetherness was a little ridiculous. He was embarrassed at what he wanted lately: to have T.W. and the band go away, to have the house to him and Francie, to marry her.

He went upstairs. She was where he had left her, painting.

"What are you doing?" he said.

She laughed at him; they both knew he was being petulant, that he was more nervous about the interview than she was. He was standing and admiring the work she had done that day when they heard the car in the driveway. Francie pretended indifference and went on painting. He looked out the window and saw the old Saab pull into the drive, and the man, the interviewer, get out of the car. He had a backpack that he put on, nudging away Perry's neighbor's puppy with his foot. The puppy kept yapping, so finally the man bent and patted it. He stood outside his car a minute, stroking the puppy's ear, not realizing that anyone was watching. He stood there, sizing everything up: the rainbow Borka had painted on the front door, the cars in the drive, the puppy running in circles, the loud music from T.W.'s band. Then he came toward the house, one hand smoothing down his hair in the back, amused—Perry was suddenly sure, from the slight smile on his face— that he was about to interview someone in a commune.

Perry turned away from the window to answer the door; the phone rang.

# A Clever-Kids Story

The two clever kids are Jane and Joseph. The names alliterate. Our parents planned that—two cute kids with alliterating names, born two and a half years apart.

The summer that I was five and Joseph was seven and a half he began to tell me the clever-kids stories when we were put to bed. We lived in what had been our grandparents' house in New Hampshire—a huge barn of a house with high ceilings and rose-splotched wallpaper. My parents moved there when Joseph was four and a half and I was two. He claimed to remember New York City. It was one of the many things I envied him for: he had been born in a hospital as high as a skyscraper; I had been born in a bed in the house in

New Hampshire. When my grandfather died, my parents sold their furniture and my father quit his job, and they moved to the woods of New Hampshire, into the house where our family had spent the summer. My grandmother, after my grandfather's death, moved to the warmer weather in Georgia and was able to live with a cousin whose husband had died a few years before. My grandmother came to New Hampshire in June and stayed until the first of September.

The first clever-kids story I remember was about her: the grandmother was chewing gum, and she blew a bubble so big that you could see things in it, like a mirror. The clever kids looked into the bubble and saw a robber coming in the door, and as the grandmother began to breathe in and retract the bubble they saw the robber getting smaller and smaller, but coming closer. The grandmother didn't see anything because she was squinting, concentrating on making the bubble disappear. Just as the bubble was about to disappear, the clever kids whirled around and overpowered the robber. They took out their guns and shot him dead.

Nothing about the stories seemed odd to me. That we would have real guns seemed perfectly possible. Anything Joseph said seemed reasonable and likely. He told me that he could fly, and I believed him. Partly it was because when he told me the stories late at night—when he crept into my bed and awed or scared me and then ended the stories in some satisfactory way—he seemed so authoritative that I couldn't help but believe him. His whispering made the stories more emphatic. The secret ritual of climbing into my bed made them something we shared privately, and things privately shared must be important—and therefore true. When he told me he could fly I didn't challenge him. I had never heard of Peter Pan, and had never even been to a circus to see the trapeze performers, but I could believe that a person, particularly my brother Joseph, could fly. "Where do you fly?" I whispered. He thought about it. "I fly by the lake," he said. "I've flown on the main beach. One Sunday when it rained and there was nobody around."

I remembered the day he was talking about. It was a Sunday in springtime and it had rained for three days, but the rain was really pouring down that Sunday. And Joseph put on his black rubber boots and his raincoat and said he was going to the beach. My mother grabbed him by the arm and said he was not. My father told Joseph to go ahead, then turned to my mother and said he admired his son's spirit. Sebastian was visiting, and she started to argue but backed down when Sebastian asked them please not to fight. In many ways Sebastian was like one of us: he put his hands over his ears if someone said something harsh. Once when he hit his finger with a hammer, I saw him cry. Sebastian had left New York the same year my parents did; my father worked as a carpenter with two other men, and Sebastian kept the books.

My grandmother did not like Sebastian. My father liked him very much, and my mother tolerated him. Joseph and I had mixed emotions: he was always kind to us, but when he was with adults he seemed childish, so we didn't respect him as we'd respect an adult, but when he played with us he seemed reserved—the way an adult would. When I was seven, when I saw him cry after he hit his thumb, my father took me aside and told me that sometimes Sebastian's reactions were a little out of whack because in New York he had had a breakdown. He explained to me what a breakdown was. I was fascinated and wanted to tell Joseph, but somehow I knew that he was the storyteller. In fact, I started to tell him, but he interrupted with his own Sebastian story: in the Bible they shot him full of arrows, for being evil, but a beautiful lady pulled out all the arrows, without causing him any pain. "What happened to the holes?" I said. "All the arrows were shot into his face. She pulled them out so carefully that they just left little holes. Whiskers grew out of them."

As Joseph was fabricating stories that spring, strange

things were happening that we didn't know about. We knew things were going on, but we were involved in collecting seashells from the main beach, playing hide and seek in the woods with Billy LaPierre, whose family had the camp next to ours, and the secret nighttime stories. We knew our mother was irritable and our father silent. We knew that Sebastian didn't come around very often. We did not know that our mother had had an abortion, and that Sebastian had driven her to Montreal, where she had it performed illegally, and against my father's wishes. I overheard her, one night, saying to him, "Where would we get the money for another baby? You won't commit yourself to anything. You could have worked for a prosperous business, but you hooked up with Frankie and Phil Renshaw. I'm already *surrounded* by babies: Sebastian in tears every time I turn around, you bumming around, your mother coming every summer and expecting me to do everything but wipe her chin."

I don't think that my mother loved Sebastian—just that after the abortion, when he felt she and Sebastian had both turned against him, they began to spend more time with each other, discussing it. Then my father became jealous, and my mother laughed at him for thinking anything so stupid, and her taunting made my father bitter, and finally silent. Things were so bad that my grandmother came in June and left before the month was over, pretending that she felt guilty for having left her cousin.

Sebastian and Joseph and I drove her to Boston to get a plane. Everyone knew that it was strange my parents didn't go. My father said that he had to work, and my mother offered to go along for the ride, looking very ashamed, but my grandmother said no—she wanted some time alone with her two favorite children. As I recall, she hardly talked to us, but she gave us both money. On the way back, Sebastian bought us large vanilla ice cream cones. We sat on the grass beside the ice cream stand, bees swarming around the trash can, Joseph more interested in watching them than in licking his cone. He got ice cream all down his shirt, and when we got home my mother complained about that instead of thanking Sebastian for what he had done. We ran outside as soon as we could and hid our five-dollar bills in an old tackle box and buried the box in the nook of a tree, because Joseph said we should.

At dinner my mother asked if Grandma had given us a treat before she left. It was all she said about her having left. Joseph tried to evade the question.

"Because your father has stopped speaking doesn't · mean that you should stop, Joseph," she said. She laid down her fork and Sebastian laid his down too.

"I think she gave them both some money," Sebastian said, looking at me because he knew I'd never have the courage to avoid a direct question.

"Yes," I said.

My mother smiled. "She said she was going to give you money to buy a treat when she and I had breakfast this morning."

Sebastian picked up his fork and began to eat his salad.

"Did you put it somewhere safe?" she said.

Joseph looked at me—a warning look.

"What's the big secret?" my mother said.

"Look," my father said, "it isn't necessary to fill us in on little details. We don't need to know everything. They should just do whatever they feel like doing."

My mother frowned. "That's unfair," she said, "to challenge me in the guise of protecting the children."

"I was aiming it at you. I love children. I wouldn't put the children on the spot."

"Stop it," she said, "or I'm going to leave the table."

"Take Sebastian with you. There's nearly a full moon tonight—good night for a walk."

"Why don't you two make up?" Sebastian said.

"Why don't I get a direct answer from my children before the conversation veers off again?" she said. She turned to me. Everybody knew I was the easiest mark.

"We pretended, we—played pirates, and we buried the ten dollars in a box in the hole of a tree."

Joseph had not said we were pirates, and I thought I had been very clever.

My mother looked at me. "All right," she said. "I don't see why there had to be such a secret."

That night, in bed, Joseph didn't tell a story. Instead, we talked about how something had been wrong at dinner. Finally, proud of my invented story, I mentioned the buried money.

"She wasn't even mad," I said. "We can get the money tomorrow."

"She wasn't mad at you, but she was mad at me because I wouldn't answer."

"We can buy candy down at the store all month," I said.

There was a long silence. Then Joseph said, "The money's gone."

I didn't question it. He whispered, "The money's gone," and suddenly I knew that it was, that it was punishment for my having told the secret. Before we fell asleep he relented a little. "It might get put back somehow," he said. But when we whispered the next night it wasn't about the money, and we never dug for it or mentioned it again.

For years I forgot about it. I remembered it recently, riding the bus; I looked out the window and saw a squirrel run up a tree very much like the tree where we had buried the box. All at once I felt so sentimental I had to concentrate hard not to cry. I had remembered that there was something that was his and mine, that it was still there, and that I could go and get it. I got off the bus and walked to my room. It was a nice room with walls painted oyster-white, and the bare walls made me think of the rose-covered wallpaper all through the house in New Hampshire, and of what Sebastian had told me years before about the hospital he went to when he had his breakdown—how he would study the plain white walls and know that he had to get out of that place. The hairline cracks in them would appear in his dreams; imagined smudges would make him wake up, in a fit of anxiety. His obsession with the walls was only making him crazier.

In 1969 Joseph died in Vietnam. My mother received official notification, then a letter from a friend of his that was full of praise for his valor, his wonderful sense of humor, his skill with a rifle. It was an odd letter, one that the man probably would not have sent if he had thought it over. There was a paragraph near the end praising Joseph for having changed the man's taste in music, for Joseph's having explained what was really important musically. A list of several meaningful songs followed. The letter concluded mournfully, and he signed it "God bless." I read it over and over, all summer, and at the end, every time, I would hear Red Skelton's voice saying the "God bless." The man who had written the letter was obviously heartbroken, yet it just wasn't the kind of letter to send. He was alive and Joseph was not. He seemed to give equal weight to a sense of humor and rifle skills. What sort of person could he be?

Instead of going to the main beach, I went to the dock and sat at the end of it with my feet in the water and the letter beside me, carefully closed in a book so it wouldn't get wet.

He had a sense of humor, all right. He had such a fine sense of humor that he laughed when I told him to go to Canada.

Every day I sat on the dock, and when the sun went down I walked back to the house and had dinner.

For eight years my father has not lived in the house. He and my mother are not divorced, but the other day I saw an ad she had circled in the *Village Voice* about Haitian divorces. On and off, Curtis lives with her. Curtis is Phil Renshaw's younger brother, who works for Phil now that my father is gone.

One day at the end of the summer when my brother

was killed, my mother walked down to the dock. I was
smoking grass, as usual—staring out at the water.
When she came to the dock I was thinking about how
often my friends and I thought ironically, and how
irony had been absent from my childhood. The memory
of the conversation about how much my father liked
children began to come back to me. I was wondering
if children miss a lot of ironies, or whether that had
been a different world and everything in it really hadn't
been ironic.

My mother sat down. She didn't say anything about
what I was doing. Finally she said, "Your father is
totally irrational. He holds it against me. He thinks
that God did this to curse us, to even the score for that
abortion I had years and years ago." She took off her
sandals and put her feet in the water. It was wet where
she sat. She was sitting in a puddle on the dock. "Can
you imagine your father being religious?" she said.

"No," I said. "I can't imagine him living in Mexico
with a twenty-four-year-old girl either." I did not say
that I found it hard to believe that she lived with Curtis
Renshaw. He was plain-faced, less willing to work at
anything than even my father. And he was vain—he
always washed with a special soap. There was a plastic
soap dish in the tub with a bar of putty-colored soap
in it that was Curtis' soap.

"Your father loves you," she said. "He should pay
more attention to you. When Joseph died he lost all
perspective—he's forgotten what he's got."

I stared at our four feet, spooky and slender in the
water.

"He should have sent the money for the plane ticket.
He shouldn't have said he was going to and then not
done it." She brushed the hair out of her eyes. "Is that
part of why you're blue?"

"No," I said.

"I know," she said.

Then, being as deliberately cruel as my father had
been with his sarcasm and his silence, I said, "He didn't

send the money because she's going to have a baby and
he doesn't want me around now."

"Yes," she sighed. "There's that, too."

It didn't seem to have made her angry at me, though
I knew she could hardly stand to be reminded of it.

"She's twenty-four years old and a Catholic. I hope
he keeps her pregnant and that they have hundreds
of children for him to support, and no abortions."

The dock needed some boards replaced; that was why
there was the puddle next to me. She wouldn't repair
it, and Curtis wouldn't repair it, and I wouldn't. In
June I had finally repapered the living room because
the wallpaper was at once so faded and so garish. She
had always asked my father to do it, and now, years
later, I had done it with no prompting, wild for something to do with my hands. I suspect she didn't care
about the wallpaper anymore because she didn't care
any longer about the house. He had left it to her—his
parents' house (my grandmother had died five years
before; no longer even any reason to fix it up for her
summer visit)—as if to say: You care about material
things, here it is. Then he traveled and finally ended
up in Mexico City. What would have happened if she
had had the other baby? Would anything that simple
have kept them married?

"What's that you're reading?" she said.

I looked down at the book I held with the letter
closed inside it. The book was *Cooking with Wine.*

Sebastian comes to my apartment. "It's nice," he
says. "What? Don't you like it?" He sits on one of the
two Salvation Army chairs. "It's nice in here," he says.

He comes here often, and is always ill at ease. He
never knows what to say. After a dozen visits, today
is the first time he's passed comment on the apartment.
He used to call and invite himself over. After he had
called a few times I called him and began inviting him
because I knew that was what he wanted. He drinks
too much now. He knows I'm going to school and don't

have much money, so he brings his own bottle, and a bottle of white wine for me.

It's winter now, snowing. I was surprised he came, because you can't get a cab, and the streets are too bad to drive, so he had to take three buses to get here.

His shoes are on top of the newspaper in front of the door and he's sitting in the chair with his socks drying on the arm. His feet are so familiar. In the summer, in spite of rough floorboards and rocky beaches, nobody ever wore shoes.

He wants to take me out to lunch, but I don't want to go out into the snow. He looks a little relieved, and is happy when I bring him a plate of cheese and crackers to have with his Scotch.

"I got a letter from your father," he says, reaching into the breast pocket of his worn corduroy jacket.

I read it. It's a lot like the letter he sent to my mother, and the one he sent me. He has a nine-pound son, named Louis. Just like that.

"He wrote your mother, too." He says it so I know he thinks such letter sending is insane.

I go into the kitchen and get the rest of the brick of cheese. It is a one-room apartment and from where he sits, Sebastian can see me.

"It's nice of you to put up with me," he says.

"It was nice of you to bring me a present."

When he came, he brought with him six photographic postcards from the bookstore in the Square where he works. He knows that I like Walker Evans photographs; I won't mail any of them.

We sit, eat cheese, and fall silent.

I remember a night when my parents went dancing. It must have been the same year she had the abortion. Sebastian came to baby sit. He came upstairs, barefoot, and we didn't hear him. He found Joseph in my bed. "What are you two doing in bed together?" he said. He put the light on, and our eyes blinked—we couldn't help looking funny. That was the first time I knew there was something strange about it. Joseph must

have known, because somehow, long before, he had
gotten me to understand that I wasn't to talk about it.
When Sebastian spoke, I knew that what he was asking
about was something sexual. I thought about sex for
the first time, though I didn't know the word then, or
even what sex was.

Today, Sebastian isn't having much to drink. Usually by this time he's high, and the visit goes more
smoothly.

"I wish I had been your uncle," he says. "I always
liked children."

"You were *like* an uncle."

"Then I wish I had been a rich uncle. Then you really
would have liked me."

"When did we ever care about money?"

"You never had any. Your mother was always complaining because your father had quit his job in the
city and they were stuck in the country with no way
to do anything, or buy what she wanted."

The house, in those days, had broken-down furniture, and we sat on pillows on the floors instead of in
the old chairs with bulging springs, long before sitting
on floor cushions was fashionable. My mother inherited
money when Grandma died, and now there is new furniture, and a lot of the old pieces have been mended
and refinished by Curtis.

"This is a very nice place," Sebastian says. "It's not
easy to find a place this clean in the city."

The year I was nine Joseph and I stopped sharing
the huge upstairs room. It was nobody's idea but my
mother's that I have my own room. I got the small room
at the back of the house on the first floor. A bureau
was moved in, and a bed, and she hung white curtains
and put a straw mat on the floor that she had bought
that summer at an auction. I missed Joseph—though
long before, he had stopped telling me the stories. He
still told stories, but they were full of bravado, stories
that were about things that didn't amaze me; he had
hit a home run; he had carried Andrew's little sister

home when she broke her foot diving off the dock. In
the stories, he was always the hero. I didn't want my
own room, but I suspected that my mother would have
been angry if I had said so. Everybody else I knew had
her own room, or shared one with her sister. After I
moved into my room my mother would come in, once
or twice a month, and sleep in the bed with me instead
of with my father. I was a little embarrassed to have
my mother in bed with me because I thought sleeping
with your mother was childish, but something told me
not to say anything about that, either.

I remember when my father left—the summer before
Joseph left, to go to Vietnam. I remember that she was
angry at first, and then so sad that Sebastian seemed
always to be at the house.

"Your mother never really warmed up to me, in spite
of the fact that there was nothing I wanted more. But
you know that already," Sebastian says.

I reach out and put my hand around his hand, on
the glass. He was always there, so I could go off and
sulk and not worry about my mother. He was there the
next summer, too, working in the garden, the day we
got the news that Joseph had been shot.

It seemed that the winter would never end, and that
I would never be able to read all the books I was supposed to read for my courses, when suddenly, at the
end of March, there was a day as warm as summer.
Nick showed it to me first, having been awakened by
the children who had gone outside early to play. The
house in which I rented the apartment was across the
street from a playground. He shook me gently by the
shoulder and pointed out the window, at the bright
day. I got up and leaned on my elbow, and looked at
it: sunny, beautiful, the trees so still that there must
not have been the slightest breeze.

Nick and I had breakfast, and although he was in
his first year of law school and worked constantly,
didn't even question that we would leave the apart-

ment. We had coffee, then walked to his car. Our plan was to drive to the North Shore to climb the dunes and walk on the beach. But the plan got changed to going all the way to my mother's house. It was Friday, and we could spend the weekend. Nick loved the house. More amazing, Nick loved me. He had been living with a girl named Anita when I met him, but a few months before, he had called it off, come to my apartment one day and made it plain that the scene with Anita had been a bad one. He had come, but he wouldn't look at me for a long time. "You didn't come cheap," he said.

We stopped for more coffee, but even that plan changed. Inside the restaurant, with the windows open, coffee was too much a winter drink. We sat on stools at the counter and drank cold chocolate milkshakes.

When we got there, Sebastian's old white Buick convertible—top down—was in the drive. He was the first to see us, from where he was digging in the side yard. I gave him a hug and Nick shook his hand. "Great minds with a single thought," he said to me. Whenever he could take a day off, he would leave the city and go to New Hampshire. He was planting a little evergreen. Nick and I went around to the back of the house, where my mother and a woman who had moved into the LaPierre house next door and Curtis were talking. My mother stood and rushed across the lawn, happy to see us. She had on a sundress, and her hair pulled back in a ponytail, and looked young.

It started out as such a happy day that what happened seemed even worse than it might have, because no one expected anything. We had all gone down to the beach (Sebastian was talking to the new woman, who was a widow; I was hoping that she would like him), when Sebastian mentioned Joseph. For months it had been all right to talk about him, so there was no reason why it hit her wrong. I guess that it was such a perfect day that we had all been thinking of him: he thrived in the warm weather, bought tulip bulbs and planted them in the rocky side yard every spring, sailed from the dock that we were now walking past every day that it didn't rain.

"I might try to fix the boat," Sebastian said, as much to himself as to any of us. Except that he must not have said *the* boat, but *Joseph's* boat. And it *was* my brother's boat. He had bought it, and my mother and I had hardly ever rowed out in it alone.

"Why do you have to mention him?" my mother said, her mouth quivering. "What do you have to talk about *Joseph* for?"

Then she put her hands over her face and ran, without lowering her hands, like a person running from an explosion.

Sebastian's face was perfectly white. He looked like he might cry himself. The woman he had been walking with was the only one who stared after my mother. She had been living in the LaPierre house a week or so, and I don't know if she knew, then, who Joseph was.

"Oh hell," Nick said, putting his hand on Sebastian's shoulder. Then, though it was a dumb and obvious thing to say, he said, "She's just upset."

Sebastian didn't move. I went over to him and said, "Hey—it's okay. I was thinking about him too." I had been thinking that that night Nick would sleep alone in Joseph's room.

We continued the walk down the beach. Nick took my arm and we walked a little ahead, and Sebastian and Carolyn Little trailed behind. Nick chattered to me as nervously as he had when he had started to tell me how he loved the woman he lived with, but ended up, instead of telling me anything about his life with Anita, talking about how some noises that cars make can indicate serious trouble. I strained to hear what Sebastian was saying to Carolyn Little, but there was a hollow sound all around us—the whole beach was echoing like a conch shell. It was that constant, almost inaudible noise—background noise—that distracted me. I turned to look at Sebastian. He was holding Car-

olyn Little's arm, talking to her, and she was looking
at the sand.

I had been thinking about Joseph all day, long before
we got to New Hampshire. I had started to think of
him when Nick touched my shoulder. Joseph used to
do that when I was falling asleep and he still wanted
my attention. I could not stay awake long when I went
to bed, but once he began his storytelling he would be
energized. If I wouldn't listen to him, he at least wanted
me to be awake. "Look at the stars tonight," he'd say,
or he'd show me, in winter, sites for the snow fort we
could build in the morning. More than once I fell asleep
in the middle of one of his stories, and he nudged me
awake.

I don't know if it took him a long while to die, or if
he died suddenly. I don't know the name of the place
he died in, or if it had a name. Although there were
many random facts in the letter, the questions I really
wanted answered were not answered.

I went back to the house ahead of the others, leaving
Sebastian and Nick sitting on the dock after Carolyn
Little went home. As I had expected, my mother was
there, in the kitchen, drinking coffee. She was hanging
her head and I expected her—as she had done in the
past—to make me feel worse by apologizing for having
made a scene. She did not say anything for a minute,
and then she said, "You know what I hope? I hope that
when he was over there he spent all his money on dope
and laid every whore in Saigon."

She looked up. It was a challenging look, but she
didn't mean to challenge me. "I didn't even have the
courage to tell him, and you did. I heard you telling
him, and I should have told him too—'Go to Canada.'"
She said "Canada" with the reverence a minister would
use pronouncing the word "heaven."

"At least I hope he went crazy over there and did
whatever the hell he wanted." This time she just looked
at me sadly. We both knew he was not the kind to

storm through Vietnam. More likely, he would sit and
listen to the radio. When songs by any of the people on
the list his friend sent us came on the radio, my day
was ruined. All the lyrics took on horrible, ironic mean-
ings.

"And your father's great grief—all I get are 'remember when' letters from Mexico. They weren't even close.
Joseph and I weren't very close either. You two were."
She looked up again, no real expression on her face,
just a person stating facts. "It was mean of me to yell
at Sebastian," she said.

"Don't stay in here sulking," I said.

We sat there for a while, and then she pushed the
coffee cup away and went out. I imagine she went to
the dock. I got up and went to the bookcase and took
down the cookbook. The letter from Vietnam was still
in it. I already knew it by heart, so I just looked to
reassure myself that the letter was where I had put it.
It was strange that she had never asked where the
letter was. Strange, too, that she cursed when she got
a letter from my father (most of the letters, inevitably,
maudlin with memories of Joseph) but kept all of them
in a basket on her dresser.

When I went outside, Nick and Sebastian were gone,
and she was sitting on the dock where I had left them.
She was sitting there on the dock just where Joseph
and I had sat after our argument about his going to
Canada. As we sat there, I was already sure that if he
went, he would be killed. In the kitchen, he had argued
against going to Canada because it was dishonorable.
On the dock, I began to understand the real reason: it
wasn't a matter of principle, but simply that he thought
he wouldn't die; he thought he was indestructible. He
really thought that he would always be in control, that
he would always be the storyteller. I don't think I said
to him in so many words that I knew he was going to
die, or that he actually said he knew he was going to
live, but that's what our conversation was about. He
didn't understand how bad, and how pointless, things

were in Vietnam. No matter what I said, his attention didn't focus on it, and I couldn't make him understand.

I went out to the dock, where my mother was, and crouched there. A bird flew overhead. There was a nice mossy smell the breeze was blowing in off the water.

"Know where Nick and Sebastian went?" I said.

"Look at his poor boat," she said.

I looked down. The water was slopping against it, the breeze blowing ripples of water toward shore. The water made a slapping sound: put-put.

"I just can't snap out of it," she said.

I leaned over and kissed her cheek. Nick did that most mornings when it was time for me to wake up. Joseph had nudged me awake with his hand, squeezed my shoulder in the dark. It was nicer than any kiss.

I went to bed early and slept for a little while, then woke up. I put on an old lacy robe that belonged to my mother or grandmother, and went out of the room. The clock in the kitchen said one-thirty. Everyone had gone to bed. Going back to the bedroom, I saw the small lamp on and detoured to the living room. Sebastian hadn't gone home. He was stretched on the sofa, but not sleeping. There was a bottle and a glass on the table. "Howdy," he said quietly. My mother was asleep—or at least she was in her room in the dark. Her bedroom opened onto the living room. The door was cracked open a few inches. I waved to Sebastian and went back to my room. I looked at all the books that I couldn't remember having read, and at the pictures I no longer found attractive: a Picasso poster of a hand holding flowers, a drawing of lobstermen casting their nets, done by a boy who had had a crush on me in high school.

Joseph would have interrupted the silence with a story. I went out of the room and passed by Sebastian in the living room without looking in, and climbed the stairs to the attic.

It smelled the way it always smelled. The two beds

were still there. When I moved out, they left that bed in place. Nick was sleeping in the far bed. Without knowing who had slept where, he had chosen Joseph's bed. Nick had slept upstairs the other time he came to the house, but that time I hadn't gone upstairs to see where he slept. In fact, I hadn't been above the first floor in a long time. With the exposed beams and the low, triangle-shaped window, it still looked snug, like some room in a storybook.

"What are you doing here?" Nick whispered.

I went over to his bed. The room seemed to exist in a time warp; I could imagine stepping on one of Joseph's socks.

"She'll hear you," Nick said. He reached out his hand from under the covers. He had been asleep.

I sat there and held his hand. Then I lay on the bed. Finally, I got under the covers.

"We shouldn't upset her any more today," he said.

It was a rational, and even a nice thing to say, and I knew that I was wrong to hate him for saying it. He lay still in the bed and I lay beside him. My eyes were getting accustomed to the dark. I was looking around the room and thinking of how Joseph's shadow tiptoed to me, the pitch of his whispery child's voice. As I got older, if I told people about my brother, the stories would always be about my brother as a child—I got older, but Joseph was still frozen in childhood.

"What?" Nick said sleepily.

I had moved and thrown my arm over him, inadvertently. I wanted to say: Nick—my whole life just rushed by.

Nick fumbled for my hand and we held hands again. His hand was so warm. I could see in the dark now: his eyes closed, his mouth like the mouth of a Botticelli angel.

"There's a demon in the corner." I pointed. (Starlight on two metal coat hooks.)

He mumbled again: "What?"

He was trying to be kind, trying to stay awake. I

looked at the coat hooks. They did look like eyes glaring, and I had scared myself a little by calling them demons.

"A demon," I said again, and something in my voice told Nick he had to rouse himself, that the talk about demons was flippy.

"Okay," he said, struggling up, half sighing the second "Okay."

He smoothed my hair from my face and, kindly, kissed my neck, moved his hand up my ribs. It was not what I wanted at all, but I closed my eyes, not knowing now what to say.

# Tuesday Night

Henry was supposed to bring the child home at six o'clock, but they usually did not arrive until eight or eight-thirty, with Joanna overtired and complaining that she did not want to go to bed the minute she came through the door. Henry had taught her that phrase. "The minute she comes through the door" was something I had said once, and he mocked me with it in defending her. "Let the poor child have a minute before she goes to bed. She *did* just come through the door." The poor child is, of course, crazy about Henry. He allows her to call him that, instead of "Daddy." And now he takes her to dinner at a French restaurant that she adores, which doesn't open until five-thirty. That means that she gets home close to eight. I am a beast if I refuse to let her eat her escargots. And it would be cruel to tell her that her father's support payments fluctuate wildly, while the French dining remains a constant. Forget the money—Henry has been a good father. He visits every Tuesday night, carefully twirls her crayons in the pencil sharpener, and takes her every other weekend. The only bad thing he has done to her—and even Henry agreed about that—was to introduce her to the sleepie he had living with him right after the divorce: an obnoxious woman, who taught Joanna to sing "I'm a Woman." Fortunately, she did not remember many of the words, but I thought I'd lose my mind when she went around the house singing "Doubleyou oh oh em ay en" for two weeks. Sometimes the sleepie tucked a fresh flower in Joanna's hair—like Maria Muldaur, she explained. The child had the good sense to be embarrassed.

The men I know are very friendly with one another. When Henry was at the house last week, he helped Dan, who lives with me, carry a bookcase up the steep, narrow steps to the second floor. Henry and Dan talk about nutrition—Dan's current interest. My brother Bobby, the only person I know who is seriously interested in hallucinogens at the age of twenty-six, gladly makes a fool of himself in front of Henry by bringing out his green yo-yo, which glows by the miracle of two internal batteries. Dan tells Bobby that if he's going to take drugs, he should try dosing his body with vitamins before and after. The three of them Christmas-shop for me. Last year they had dinner at an Italian restaurant downtown. I asked Dan what they ordered, and he said, "Oh, we all had manicotti."

I have been subsisting on red zinger tea and watermelon, trying to lose weight. Dan and Henry and Bobby are all thin. Joanna takes after her father in her build. She is long and graceful, with chiseled features that would shame Marisa Berenson. She is ten years old. When I was at the laundry to pick up the clothes yesterday a woman mistook me, from the back, for her cousin Addie.

In Joanna's class at school they are having a discussion of problems with the environment. She wants to take our big avocado plant in to school. I have tried patiently to explain that the plant does not have anything to do with environmental problems. She says that they are discussing nature, too. "What's the harm?" Dan says. So he goes to work and leaves it to me to fit the towering avocado into the Audi. I also get roped into baking cookies so Joanna can take them to school and pass them around to celebrate her birthday. She tells me that it is the custom to put the cookies in a box wrapped in birthday paper. We select a paper with yellow bears standing in concentric circles. Dan dumps bran into the chocolate-chip-cookie dough. He forbids me to use a dot of red food coloring in the sugar-cookie hearts.

My best friend, Dianne, comes over in the mornings and turns her nose up at my red zinger. Sometimes she takes a shower here because she loves our shower head. "How come you're not in there all the time?" she says. My brother is sweet on her. He finds her extremely attractive. He asked me if I had noticed the little droplets of water from the shower on her forehead, just at the hairline. Bobby lends her money because her husband doesn't give her enough. I know for a fact that Dianne is thinking of having an affair with him.

Dan has to work late at his office on Tuesday nights, and a while ago I decided that I wanted that one night to myself each week—a night without any of them. Dianne said, "I know what you mean," but Bobby took great offense and didn't come to visit that night, or any other night, for two weeks. Joanna was delighted that she could be picked up after school by Dianne, in Dianne's 1966 Mustang convertible, and that the two of them could visit until Henry came by Dianne's to pick her up. Dan, who keeps saying that our relationship is going sour—although it isn't—pursed his lips and nodded when I told him about Tuesday nights, but he said nothing. The first night alone I read a dirty magazine that had been lying around the house for some time. Then I took off all my clothes and looked in the hall mirror and decided to go on a diet, so I skipped dinner. I made a long-distance call to a friend in California who had just had a baby. We talked about the spidery little veins in her thighs, and I swore to her over and over again that they would go away. Then I took one of each kind of vitamin pill we have in the house.

The next week I had prepared for my spare time better. I had bought whole-wheat flour and clover honey, and I made four loaves of whole-wheat bread. I made a piecrust, putting dough in the sink and rolling it out there, which made a lot of sense but which I would never let anybody see me doing. Then I read *Vogue*. Later on I took out the yoga book I had bought that afternoon and put it in my plastic cookbook-holder and put that down on the floor and stared at it as I tried to get into the postures. I overcooked the piecrust and it burned. I got depressed and drank a Drambuie. The week after that, I ventured out. I went to a movie and bought myself a chocolate milkshake afterward. I sat at the drugstore counter and drank it. I was going to get my birth-control-pill prescription refilled while I was there, but I decided that would be depressing.

Joanna sleeps at her father's apartment now on Tuesday nights. Since he considers her too old to be read a fairy tale before bed, Henry waltzes with her. She wears a long nightgown and a pair of high-heeled shoes that some woman left there. She says that he usually plays "The Blue Danube," but sometimes he kids around and puts on "Idiot Wind" or "Forever Young" and they dip and twirl to it. She has hinted that she would like to take dancing lessons. Last week she danced through the living room at our house on her pogo stick. Dan had given it to her, saying that now she had a partner, and it would save him money not having to pay for dancing lessons. He told her that if she had any questions, she could ask him. He said she could call him "Mr. Daniel." She was disgusted with him. If she were Dan's child, I am sure he would still be reading her fairy tales.

Another Tuesday night I went out and bought plants. I used my American Express card and got seventy dollars' worth of plants and some plant hangers. The woman in the store helped me carry the boxes out to the car. I went home and drove nails into the top of the window frames and hung the plants. They did not need to be watered yet, but I held the plastic plant waterer up to them, to see what it would be like to water them. I squeezed the plastic bottle and stared at the curved plastic tube coming out of it. Later I gave myself a facial with egg whites.

There is a mouse. I first saw it in the kitchen—a small gray mouse, moseying along, taking its time in getting from under the counter to the back of the stove. I had Dan seal off the little mouse hole in the back of the stove. Then I saw the mouse again, under the chest in the living room.

"It's a mouse. It's one little mouse," Dan said. "Let it be."

"Everybody knows that if there's one mouse, there are more," I said. "We've got to get rid of them."

Dan, the humanist, was secretly glad the mouse had resurfaced—that he hadn't done any damage in sealing off its home.

"It looked like the same mouse to me," Henry said.

"They all look that way," I said. "That doesn't mean—"

"Poor thing," Dan said.

"Are either of you going to set traps, or do I have to do it?"

"You have to do it," Dan said. "I can't stand it. I

don't want to kill a mouse."

"I think there's only one mouse," Henry said.

Glaring at them, I went into the kitchen and took the mousetraps out of their cellophane packages. I stared at them with tears in my eyes. I did not know how to set them. Dan and Henry had made me seem like a cold-blooded killer.

"Maybe it will just leave," Dan said.

"Don't be ridiculous, Dan," I said. "If you aren't going to help, at least don't sit around snickering with Henry."

"We're not snickering," Henry said.

"You two certainly are buddy-buddy."

"What's the matter now? You want us to hate each other?" Henry said.

"I don't know how to set a mousetrap," I said. "I can't do it myself."

"Poor Mommy," Joanna said. She was in the hallway outside the living room, listening. I almost turned on her to tell her not to be sarcastic, when I realized that she was serious. She felt sorry for me. With someone on my side, I felt new courage about going back into the kitchen and tackling the problem of the traps.

Dianne called and said she had asked her husband if he would go out one night a week so she could go out with friends or stay home by herself. He said no, but agreed to take stained-glass lessons with her.

One Tuesday it rained. I stayed home and day-dreamed, and remembered the past. I thought about the boy I dated my last year in high school who used to take me out to the country on weekends, to where some cousins of his lived. I wondered why he always went there, because we never got near the house. He would drive partway up their long driveway in the woods and then pull off onto a narrow little road that trucks sometimes used when they were logging the property. We parked on the little road and necked. Sometimes the boy would drive slowly along on the country roads looking for rabbits, and whenever he saw one, which was pretty often—sometimes even two or three rabbits at once—he floored it, trying to run the rabbit down. There was no radio in the car. He had a portable radio that got two stations (soul music and classical) and I held it on my lap. He liked the volume turned up very loud.

Joanna comes to my bedroom and announces that Uncle Bobby is on the phone.

"I got a dog," he says.

"What kind?"

"Aren't you surprised?"

"Yes. Where did you get the dog?"

"A guy I knew a little bit in college is going to jail, and he persuaded me to take the dog."

"What is he going to jail for?"

"Burglary."

"Joanna," I say, "don't stand there staring at me when I'm talking on the phone."

"He robbed a house," Bobby says.

"What kind of a dog is it?" I ask.

"Malamute and German shepherd. It's in heat."

"Well," I say, "you always wanted a dog."

"I call you all the time, and you never call me," Bobby says.

"I never have interesting news."

"You could call and tell me what you do on Tuesday nights."

"Nothing very interesting," I say.

"You could go to a bar and have rum drinks and weep," Bobby says. He chuckles.

"Are you stoned?" I ask.

"Sure I am. Been home from work for an hour and a half. Ate a Celeste pizza, had a little smoke."

"Do you really have a dog?" I ask.

"If you were a male dog, you wouldn't have any doubt of it."

"You're always much more clever than I am. It's

hard to talk to you on the phone, Bobby."

"It's hard to be me," Bobby says. A silence. "I'm not sure the dog likes me."

"Bring it over. Joanna will love it."

"I'll be around with it Tuesday night," he says.

"Why is it so interesting to you that I have one night a week to myself?"

"Whatever you do," Bobby says, "don't rob a house."

We hang up, and I go tell Joanna the news.

"You yelled at me," she says.

"I did not. I asked you not to stand there staring at me while I was on the phone."

"You raised your voice," she says.

Soon it will be Tuesday night.

Joanna asks me suspiciously what I do on Tuesday nights.

"What does your father say I do?" I ask.

"He says he doesn't know."

"Does he seem curious?"

"It's hard to tell with him," she says.

Having got my answer, I've forgotten about her question.

"So what things do you do?" she says.

"Sometimes you like to play in your tent," I say defensively. "Well, I like some time to just do what I want to do, too, Joanna."

"That's okay," she says. She sounds like an adult placating a child.

I have to face the fact that I don't do much of anything on Tuesdays, and that one night alone each week isn't making me any less edgy or more agreeable to live with. I tell Dan this, as if it's his fault.

"I don't think you ever wanted to divorce Henry," Dan says.

"Oh, Dan, I *did*."

"You two seem to get along fine."

"But we fought. We didn't get along."

He looks at me. "Oh," he says. He is being inordinately nice to me because of the scene I threw when a mouse got caught in one of the traps. The trap didn't kill it. It just got it by the paw, and Dan had to beat it to death with a screwdriver.

"Maybe you'd rather the two of us did something regularly on Tuesday nights," he says now. "Maybe I could get the night of my meetings changed."

"Thank you," I say. "Maybe I should give it a little longer."

"That's up to you," he says. "There hasn't been enough time to judge by, I guess."

Inordinately kind. Deferential. He has been saying for a long time that our relationship is turning sour, and now it must have turned so sour for him that he doesn't even want to fight. What does he want?

"Maybe you'd like a night—" I begin.

"The hell with that," he says. "If there has to be so much time alone, I can't see the point of living together."

I hate fights. The day after this one, I get weepy and go over to Dianne's. She ends up subtly suggesting that I take stained-glass lessons. We drink some sherry and I drive home. The last thing I want is to run into her husband, who calls me "the squirrel" behind my back. Dianne says that when I call and he answers, he lets her know it's me on the phone by puffing up his cheeks to make himself look like a squirrel.

Tonight Dan and I each sit on a side of Joanna's tester bed to say good night to her. The canopy above the bed is white nylon, with small puckered stars. She is ready for sleep. As soon as she goes to sleep, Dan will be ready to talk to me. Dan has clicked off the light next to Joanna's bed. Going out of the bedroom before him, I grope for the hall light. I remember Henry saying to me, as a way of leading up to talking about divorce, that going to work one morning he had driven over a hill and had been astonished when at the top he saw a huge yellow tree, and realized for the first time that it was autumn.

# Secrets and Surprises

Corinne and Lenny are sitting at the side of the driveway with their shoes off. Corinne is upset because Lenny sat in a patch of strawberries. "Get up, Lenny! Look what you've done!"

Lenny is one of my oldest friends. I went to high school with Lenny and Corinne and his first wife, Lucy, who was my best friend there. Lenny did not know Corinne then. He met her at a party many years later. Corinne remembered Lenny from high school; he did not remember her. The next year, after his divorce from Lucy became final, they married. Two years later their daughter was born, and I was a godmother. Lenny teases me by saying that his life would have been entirely different if only I had introduced him to Corinne years ago. I knew her because she was my boyfriend's sister. She was a couple of years ahead of us, and she would do things like picking us up if we got drunk at a party and buying us coffee before taking us home. Corinne once lied to my mother when she took me home that way, telling her that there was flu going around and that I had sneezed in her car all the way home.

I was ugly in high school. I wore braces, and everything seemed to me funny and inappropriate: the seasons, television personalities, the latest fashions—even music seemed silly. I played the piano, but for some reason I stopped playing Brahms or even listening to Brahms. I played only a few pieces of music myself, the same ones, over and over: a couple of Bach two-part inventions, a Chopin nocturne. I earnestly smoked cigarettes, and all one spring I harbored a secret love for Lenny. I once confessed my love for him in a note I pushed through the slats in his locker in school. Then I got scared and waited by his locker when school was over, talked to him for a while, and when he opened the locker door, grabbed the note back and ran. This was fifteen years ago.

I used to live in the city, but five years ago my husband and I moved up here to Woodbridge. My husband has gone, and now it is only my house. It is my driveway that Lenny and Corinne sit beside. The driveway badly needs to be graveled. There are holes in it that should be filled, and the drainpipe is cracked. A lot of things here need fixing. I don't like to talk to the landlord, Colonel Albright. Every month he loses the rent check I send him and then calls me from the nursing home where he lives, asking for another. The man is eighty-eight. I should consider him an amusing old character, a forgetful old man. I suspect he is persecuting me. He doesn't want a young person renting his house. Or anyone at all. When we moved in, I found some empty clothing bags hanging in the closets, with old dry-cleaning stubs stapled to the plastic: "Col. Albright,

9–8–54." I stared at the stub. I was eleven years old
the day Colonel Albright picked up his clothes at the
dry cleaners. I found one of his neckties wound around
the base of a lamp in an upstairs closet. "Do you want
these things?" I asked him on the phone. "Throw them
out, I don't care," he said, "but don't ask me about
them." I also do not tell him about things that need to
be fixed. I close off one bathroom in the winter because
the tiles are cracked and cold air comes through the
floor; the heat register in my bedroom can't be set above
sixty, so I set the living-room register at seventy-five
to compensate. Corinne and Lenny think this is funny.
Corinne says that I will not fight the landlord because
I did enough fighting with my husband about his girl
friend and now I enjoy peace; Lenny says that I am just
too kind. The truth is that Colonel Albright shouts at
me on the phone and I am afraid of him. He is also old
and sad, and I have displaced him in his own house.
Twice this summer, a friend has driven him from the
nursing home back to the house, and he walked around
the gardens in the front, tapping his cane through the
clusters of sweet peas that are strangling out the asters
and azaleas in the flower beds, and he dusted the pollen
off the sundial in the back with a white handkerchief.

Almost every weekend Corinne tries to get me to
leave Woodbridge and move back to New York. I am
afraid of the city. In the apartment on West End Avenue I lived in with my husband when we were first
married, I was always frightened. There was a bird in
the apartment next to ours which shrieked, "No, no,
go away!" I always mistook it for a human voice in the
night, and in my sleepy confusion I thought that I was
protesting an intruder in our apartment. Once a
woman at the laundromat who was about to pass out
from the heat took hold of my arm and pulled me to
the floor with her. This could have happened anywhere.
It happened in New York. I won't go back.

"Balducci's!" Corinne sometimes murmurs to me,
and moves her arm through the air to suggest counters

spread with delicacies. I imagine tins of anchovies, wheels of Brie, huge cashews, strange greens. But then I hear voices whispering outside my door plotting to break it down, and angry, wild music late at night that is the kind that disturbed, unhappy people listen to.

Now Corinne is holding Lenny's hand. I am lying on my side and peeking through the netting of the hammock, and they don't see me. She stoops to pick a strawberry. He scratches his crotch. They are bored here, I think. They pretend that they make the two-hour drive up here nearly every weekend because they are concerned for my well-being. Perhaps they actually think that living in the country is spookier than living in the city. "You sent your beagle to live in the country, Corinne," I said to her once. "How can you be upset that a human being wants to live where there's room to stretch?" "But what do you do here all alone?" she said.

I do plenty of things. I play Bach and Chopin on a grand piano my husband saved for a year to buy me. I grow vegetables, and I mow the lawn. When Lenny and Corinne come for the weekend, I spy on them. He's scratching his shoulder now. He calls Corinne to him. I think he is asking her to see if he just got a mosquito bite.

Last year when my husband went on vacation without me, I drove from Connecticut to D.C. to visit my parents. They live in the house where I grew up. The crocheted bedspreads have turned yellow now and the bedroom curtains are the same as ever. But in the living room there is a large black plastic chair for my father and a large brown plastic chair for my mother. My brother, Raleigh, who is retarded, lives with them. He has a friend, Ed, who is retarded, and who visits him once a week. And Raleigh visits Ed once a week. Sometimes my mother or Ed's mother takes them to the zoo. Raleigh's chatter often makes more sense than we at first suspected. For instance, he is very fond of Ling-Ling, the panda. He was not imitating the bell the Good Humor man rings when he drives around the neighborhood, as my father once insisted. My father has never been able to understand Raleigh very well. My mother laughs at him for his lack of understanding. She is a bitter woman. For the last ten years, she has made my father adhere to a diet when he is home, and he is not overweight.

When I visited, I drove Raleigh down to Hains Point, and we looked across the water at the lights. In spite of being retarded, he seems very moved by things. He rolled down the window and let the wind blow across his face. I slowed the car almost to a stop, and he put his hand on my hand, like a lover. He wanted me to stop the car entirely so he could look at the lights. I let him look for a long time. On the way home I drove across the bridge into Arlington and took him to Gifford's for ice cream. He had a banana split, and I pretended not to notice when he ate the toppings with his fingers. Then I washed his fingers with a napkin dipped in a glass of water.

One day I found him in the bathroom with Daisy, the dog, combing over her body for ticks. There were six or seven ticks in the toilet. He was concentrating so hard that he never looked up. Standing there, I realized that there was now a small bald spot at the top of his head, and that Daisy's fur was flecked with gray. I reached over him and got aspirin out of the medicine cabinet. Later, when I went back to the bathroom and found Raleigh and Daisy gone, I flushed the toilet so my parents would not be upset. Raleigh sometimes drops pieces of paper into the toilet instead of into the wastebaskets, and my mother goes wild. Sometimes socks are in the toilet. Coins. Pieces of candy.

I stayed for two weeks. On Mondays, before his friend Ed came, Raleigh left the living room until the door had been answered, and then acted surprised to see Ed and his mother. When I took him to Ed's house, Ed did the same thing. Ed held a newspaper in front of his face at first. "Oh—hello," Ed finally said. They have been friends for almost thirty years, and the visiting routine has remained the same all that time. I think that by pretending to be surprised, they are trying to enhance the quality of the experience. I play games like this with Corinne when I meet her in the city for lunch. If I get to our table first, I study the menu until she's right on me; sometimes, if I wait outside the restaurant, I deliberately look at the sidewalk, as if lost in thought, until she speaks.

I had Raleigh come live with my husband and me during the second year of our marriage. It didn't work out. My husband found his socks in the toilet; Raleigh missed my mother's constant nagging. When I took him home, he didn't seem sorry. There is something comforting about that house: the smell of camphor in the silver cabinet, my grandmother's woven rugs, Daisy's smell everywhere.

My husband wrote last week: "Do you miss wonderful me?" I wrote back saying yes. Nothing came of it.

Corinne and Lenny have always come to Woodbridge for visits. When my husband was here, they came once a month. Now they come almost every week. Sometimes we don't have much to say to each other, so we talk about the old days. Corinne teases Lenny for not noticing her back in high school. Our visits are often dull, but I still look forward to their coming because they are my surrogate family. As in all families, there are secrets. There is intrigue. Suspicion. Lenny often calls me, telling me to keep his call a secret, saying that I must call Corinne at once and arrange to have lunch because she is depressed. So I call, and then I go and sit at a table and pretend not to see her until she sits down. She has aged a lot since their daughter's death. Her name was Karen, and she died three years ago, of leukemia. After Karen died I began having lunch with Corinne, to let her talk about it away from Lenny. By the time she no longer needed to talk about it, my husband had left, and Corinne began having lunch with me to cheer me up. We have faced each other across a table for years. (Corinne, I know, tells Lenny to visit me even when she has to work on the weekend. He has come alone a few times. He gives me a few Godiva chocolates. I give him a bag of fresh peas. Sometimes he kisses me, but it goes no further than that. Corinne thinks that it does, and endures it.)

Once Corinne said that if we all lived to be fifty (she works for a state environmental-protection agency, and her expectations are modest), we should have an honesty session the way the girls did in college. Lenny asked why we had to wait until we were fifty. "Okay— what do you really think of me?" Corinne asked him. "Why, I love you. You're my wife," he said. She backed down; the game wasn't going to be much fun.

Lenny's first wife, Lucy, has twice taken the train to visit me. We sat on the grass and talked about the old days: teasing each other's hair to new heights; photo-album pictures of the two of us, each trying to look more grotesque than the other; the first time we puffed a cigarette on a double date. I like her less as time goes by, because things she remembers about that time are true but the tone of wonder in her voice makes the past seem like a lie. And then she works the conversation around to Corinne and Lenny's marriage. Is it unhappy? Both times she visited, she said she was going back to New York on the last train, and both times she got too drunk to go until the next day. She borrowed my nightgowns and drank my gin and played sad music on my piano. In our high school yearbook, Lucy was named best dancer.

I have a lover. He comes on Thursdays. He would come more frequently, but I won't allow it. Jonathan is twenty-one and I am thirty-three, and I know that eventually he will go away. He is a musician too. He comes in the morning and we sit side by side at the piano, humming and playing Bach's B-Flat-Minor Prelude, prolonging the time before we got to bed as long as possible. He drinks diet cola while I drink gin-and-tonic. He tells me about the young girls who are chasing him. He says he only wants me. He asks me each Thursday to marry him, and calls me on Friday to beg me to let him come again before the week is up. He sends me pears out of season and other things that he can't afford. He shows me letters from his parents that bother him; I am usually in sympathy with his parents. I urge him to spend more time sight-reading and playing scales and arpeggios. He allowed a rich woman who had been chasing him since Christmas to buy him a tape deck for his car, and he plays nothing but rock-'n'-roll. Sometimes I cry, but not in his presence. He is disturbed enough. He isn't sure what to do with his life, he can't communicate with his parents, too many people want things from him. One night he called and asked if he could come over to my house if he disguised himself. "No," I said. "How would you disguise yourself?" "Cut off my hair. Buy a suit. Put on an animal mask." I make few demands on him, but obviously the relationship is a strain.

After Corinne and Lenny leave, I write a second letter to my husband, pretending that there is a chance that he did not get the other one. In this letter I give him a detailed account of the weekend, and agree with what he said long ago about Corinne's talking too much and Lenny's being too humble. I tell my husband that the handle on the barbecue no longer makes the grill go up and down. I tell him that the neighbors' dog is in heat and that dogs howl all night, so I can't sleep. I reread the letter and tear it up because these things are all jumbled together in one paragraph. It looks as if a crazy person had written the letter. I try again. In one paragraph I describe Corinne and Lenny's visit. In another I tell him that his mother called to tell me that his sister has decided to major in anthropology. In the last paragraph I ask for advice about the car—whether it may not need a new carburetor. I read the letter and it still seems crazy. A letter like this will never make him come back. I throw it away and write him a short, funny postcard. I go outside to put the postcard in the mailbox. A large white dog whines and runs in front of me. I recognize the dog. It is the same one I saw last night, from my bedroom window; the dog was staring at my neighbors' house. The dog runs past me again, but won't come when I call it. I believe the neighbors once told me that the dog's name is Pierre, and that the dog does not live in Woodbridge.

When I was a child I was punished for brushing Raleigh with the dog's brush. He had asked me to do it. It was Easter, and he had on a blue suit, and he came into my bedroom with the dog's brush and got down on all fours and asked for a brushing. I brushed his back. My father saw us and banged his fist against the door. "Jesus Christ, are you *both* crazy?" he said. Now that my husband is gone, I should bring Raleigh here to live—but what if my husband came back? I remember Raleigh's trotting through the living room, punching his fist through the air, chanting, "Ling-Ling, Ling-Ling, Ling-Ling."

I play Scriabin's Étude in C Sharp Minor. I play it badly and stop to stare at the keys. As though on cue, a car comes into the driveway. The sound of a bad muffler—my lover's car, unmistakably. He has come a day early. I wince, and wish I had washed my hair. My husband used to wince also when that car pulled into the driveway. My lover (he was not at that time my lover) was nineteen when he first started coming, to take piano lessons. He was obviously more talented than I. For a long while I resented him. Now I resent him for his impetuousness, for showing up unexpectedly, breaking my routine, catching me when I look ugly.

"This is foolish," I say to him. "I'm going into the city to have lunch."

"My car is leaking oil," he says, looking over his shoulder.

"Why have you come?" I say.

"This once-a-week stuff is ridiculous. Once you have me around a little more often you'll get used to it."

"I won't have you around more often."

"I've got a surprise for you," he says. "Two, actually."

"What are they?"

"For later. I'll tell you when you get back. Can I stay here and wait for you?"

A maroon sweater that I gave him for his birthday is tied around his waist. He sits in front of the hearth and strikes a match on the bricks. He lights a cigarette.

"Well," he says, "one of the surprises is that I'm going to be gone for three months. Starting in November."

"Where are you going?"

"Europe. You know that band I've been playing with sometimes? One of the guys has hepatitis, and I'm going to fill in for him on synthesizer. Their agent got us a gig in Denmark."

"What about school?"

"Enough school," he says, sighing.

He pitches the cigarette into the fireplace and stands up and takes off his sweater.

I no longer want to go to lunch. I am no longer sorry he came unannounced. But he hasn't jumped up to embrace me.

"I'm going to investigate that oil leak," he says.

Later, driving into New York, trying to think of what the second surprise might be (taking a woman with him?), I think about the time when my husband surprised me with a six-layer cake he had baked for my birthday. It was the first cake he ever made, and the layers were not completely cool when he stacked and frosted them. One side of the cake was much higher than the other. He had gone out and bought a little plastic figure of a skier, for the top of the cake. The skier held a toothpick with a piece of paper glued to it that said "Happy Birthday." "We're going to Switzerland!" I said, clapping my hands. He knew I had always wanted to go there. No, he explained, the skier was just a coincidence. My reaction depressed both of us. It was a coincidence, too, that a year later I was walking down the same street he was walking down and I saw that he was with a girl, holding her hand.

I'm almost in New York. Cars whiz by me on the Hutchinson River Parkway. My husband has been gone for seven months.

While waiting for Corinne, I examine my hands. My gardening has cut and bruised them. In a picture my father took when I was young, my hands are in very sharp focus but the piano keys are a blur of white streaked with black. I knew by the time I was twelve that I was going to be a concert pianist. My father and I both have copies of this picture, and we probably both have the same thoughts about it: it is a shame I have almost entirely given up music. When I lived in New York I had to play softly, so as not to disturb the neighbors. The music itself stopped sounding right. A day would pass without my practicing. My father blamed my husband for my losing interest. My husband listened to my father. We moved to Connecticut, where I wouldn't be distracted. I began to practice again, but I knew that I'd lost ground—or that I would never make it as a concert pianist if I hadn't by this time. I had Raleigh come and live with us, and I spent my days with him. My father blamed my mother for complaining to me about what a burden Raleigh was, for hinting that I take him in. My father always found excuses. I am like him. I pretended that everything was fine in my marriage, that the only problem was the girl.

"I think it's insulting, I really do," Corinne says. "It's a refusal to admit my existence. I've been married to Lenny for years, and when Lucy calls him and I answer the phone, she hangs up."

"Don't let it get to you," I say. "You know by now that Lucy's not going to be civil to you."

"And it upsets Lenny. Every time she calls to say where she's flying off to, he gets upset. He doesn't care where she's going, but you know Lenny and how he is about planes—how he gets about anyone flying."

These lunches are all the same. I discipline myself during these lunches the way I used to discipline myself about my music. I try to calm Corinne, and Corinne gets more and more upset. She only likes expensive restaurants, and she won't eat the food.

Now Corinne eats a cherry tomato from her salad and pushes the salad plate away. "Do you think we should have another child? Am I too old now?"

"I don't know," I say.

"I think the best way to get children is the way you got yours. Just have them drive up. He's probably languishing in your bed right now."

"Twenty-one isn't exactly a child."

"I'm so jealous I could die," Corinne says.

"Of Jonathan?"

"Of everything. You're three years younger than me, and you look ten years younger. Look at those thin women over there. Look at you and your music. *You* don't have to kill the day by having lunch."

Corinne takes a little gold barrette out of her hair and puts it back in. "We don't come to your house almost every weekend to look after you," she says. "We do it to restore ourselves. Although Lenny probably goes so he can pine over you."

"What are you talking about?"

"You don't sense it? You don't think that's true?"

"No," I say.

"Lucy does. She told Lenny that the last time she called. He told me that she said he was making a fool of himself hanging around so much. When Lenny hung up, he said that Lucy never did understand the notion of friendship. Of course, he always tries to pretend that Lucy is entirely crazy."

She takes out the barrette and lets her hair fall free.

"And I'm jealous of her, going off on all her business trips, sending him postcards of sunsets on the West Coast," Corinne says. "She ran off with a dirty little furrier to Denver this time."

I look at my clean plate, and then at Corinne's plate. It looks as if a wind had blown the food around her plate, or as if a midget army had marched through it. I should not have had two drinks at lunch. I excuse myself and go to a phone and call my lover. I am relieved when he answers the phone, even though I have told him never to do that. "Come into the city," I say. "We can go to Central Park."

"Come home," he says. "You're going to get caught in the rush hour."

My husband sends me a geode. There is a brief note in the package. He says before he left for Europe he sat at a table next to John Ehrlichman in a restaurant in New Mexico. The note goes on about how fat John Ehrlichman has become. My husband says that he bets my squash are still going strong in the garden. There is no return address. I stand by the mailbox, crying. From the edge of the lawn, the big white dog watches me.

My lover sits beside me on the piano bench. We are both naked. It is late at night, but we have lit a fire in the fireplace—five logs, a lot of heat. The lead guitarist from the band Jonathan plays with now was here for dinner. I had to fix a meatless meal. Jonathan's friend was young and dumb—much younger, it seemed, than my lover. I don't know why he wanted me to invite him. Jonathan has been here for four days straight. I gave in to him and called Lenny and said for them not to visit this weekend. Later Corinne called to say how jealous she was, thinking of me in my house in the country with my curly-haired lover.

I am playing Ravel's "Valses Nobles et Sentimen-

tales." Suddenly my lover breaks in with "Chopsticks."
He is impossible, and as immature as his friend. Why
have I agreed to let him live in my house until he
leaves for Denmark?

"Don't," I plead. "Be sensible."

He is playing "Somewhere Over the Rainbow" and
singing.

"Stop it," I say. He kisses my throat.

Another note comes from my husband, written on
stationery from the Hotel Eliseo. He got drunk and was
hurt in a fight; his nose wouldn't stop bleeding, and in
the end he had to have it cauterized.

In a week, my lover will leave. I am frightened at
the thought that I will be here alone when he goes.
Now I have gotten used to having someone around.
When boards creak in the night I can ask "What is it?"
and be told. When I was little, I shared a bedroom with
Raleigh until I was seven. All night he'd question me
about noises. "It's the monster," I'd say in disgust. I
made him cry so many nights that my parents built on
an addition to the house so I could have my own bedroom.

In his passport photo, my lover is smiling.

Lenny calls. He is upset because Corinne wants to
have another child and he thinks they are too old. He
hints that he would like me to invite them to come on
Friday instead of Saturday this week. I explain that
they can't come at all—my lover leaves on Monday.

"I don't mean to pry," Lenny says, but he never says
what he wants to pry about.

I pick up my husband's note and take it into the
bathroom and reread it. It was a street fight. He de-
scribes a church window that he saw. There is one long
strand of brown hair in the bottom of the envelope.
That just can't be deliberate.

Lying on my back, alone in the bedroom, I stare at the ceiling in the dark, remembering my lover's second surprise: a jar full of lightning bugs. He let them loose in the bedroom. Tiny, blinking dots of green under the ceiling, above the bed. Giggling into his shoulder: how crazy; a room full of lightning bugs.

"They only live a day," he whispered.

"That's butterflies," I said.

I always felt uncomfortable correcting him, as if I were pointing out the difference in our ages. I was sure I was right about the lightning bugs, but in the morning I was relieved when I saw that they were still alive. I found them on the curtains, against the window. I tried to recapture all of them in a jar so I could take them outdoors and set them free. I tried to remember how many points of light there had been.

## ABOUT THE AUTHOR

A frequent contributor to *The New Yorker*, Ann Beattie is the author of two short story collections—*Distortions* and *Secrets and Surprises*. Her first novel, *Chilly Scenes of Winter*, has recently been made into a motion picture, *Head over Heels*. She has received an award in literature from the American Academy and Institute of Arts and Letters.

# CLASSIC BESTSELLERS
## from FAWCETT BOOKS

☐ THE WIND     04579   $2.25
    by Dorothy Scarborough

☐ THE FAMILY MOSKAT     24066   $2.95
    by Isaac Bashevis Singer

☐ THE GHOST WRITER     24322   $2.75
    by Philip Roth

☐ THE ICE AGE     04300   $2.25
    by Margaret Drabble

☐ ALL QUIET ON THE WESTERN FRONT     23808   $2.50
    by Erich Maria Remarque

☐ TO KILL A MOCKINGBIRD     08376   $2.50
    by Harper Lee

☐ SHOW BOAT     23191   $1.95
    by Edna Ferber

☐ THEM     23944   $2.50
    by Joyce Carol Oates

☐ THE FLOUNDER     24180   $2.95
    by Gunter Grass

☐ THE CHOSEN     24200   $2.25
    by Chaim Potok

☐ THE SOURCE     23859   $2.95
    by James A. Michener

Buy them at your local bookstore or use this handy coupon for ordering.

COLUMBIA BOOK SERVICE (a CBS Publications Co.)
32275 Mally Road, P.O. Box FB, Madison Heights, MI 48071

Please send me the books I have checked above. Orders for less than
5 books must include 75¢ for the first book and 25¢ for each addi-
tional book to cover postage and handling. Orders for 5 books or
more postage is FREE. Send check or money order only.

Cost $_____    Name _____

Sales tax*_____    Address_____

Postage_____    City _____

Total $_____    State _____ Zip _____

*The government requires us to collect sales tax in all states except
AK, DE, MT, NH and OR.*

**This offer expires 1 October 81**        8117

## NEW FROM POPULAR LIBRARY